ALL THINGS
NICE

About *Hunting Shadows*

'Marks the entrance of a major new talent.
Sheila Bugler delivers a chilling psychological twister of a novel, laced with
homespun horrors, a compelling central character in DI Ellen Kelly and a
strong contemporary resonance. Fans of Nicci French and
Sophie Hannah, prick up your ears.'

Cathi Unsworth

'Truly a *tour de force*.
Imagine a collaboration between Ann Tyler and AM Homes. Yes, the novel is
that good. Sheila Bugler might well have altered the way we view families and
the very essence of mandatory Happiness.
This is great writing.'

Ken Bruen

Sheila Bugler grew up in Ballinasloe, Co. Galway. After studying Psychology at University College Galway (now NUIG), she left Ireland and worked in Italy, Argentina, Spain, Germany and Holland. She lived in London for many years before finally settling in Eastbourne, East Sussex. She is married to Seán and has two children, Luke and Ruby.

ALL THINGS
NICE

NEVER FORGET. NEVER FORGIVE.

SHEILA BUGLER

AN IMPRINT OF O'BRIEN

First published 2016 by Brandon, an imprint of The O'Brien Press Ltd,
12 Terenure Road East, Rathgar, Dublin 6, D06 HD27, Ireland.
Tel: +353 1 4923333; Fax: +353 1 4922777
E-mail: books@obrien.ie
Website: www.obrien.ie

The O'Brien Press is a member of Publishing Ireland.

ISBN: 978-1-84717-735-3

1 3 5 7 9 10 8 6 4 2

16 18 20 19 17

Layout and design: The O'Brien Press Ltd.

Cover photograph: Shutterstock

Printed and bound by Nørhaven Paperback A/S, Denmark.

The paper in this book is produced using pulp from managed forests

Published in:

DEDICATION

For Luke and Ruby, always

ACKNOWLEDGEMENTS

First and foremost, a huge shout out to the wonderful,
talented, patient, funny and very wise Rachel Pierce. A great
editor and a very special person.

Thanks as always to the wonderful team at OBP: Ruth,
Nicola, Jamie, Emma (for the wonderful cover which I love!)
and everyone else.

Thank you to Michael for taking a gamble with me,
to Svetlana for putting up with me for so long.

Special mention to Gary Friel for being a true friend and
trawling through an earlier version of this when he had so much
else to do.

To all my fantastic friends – too many to name-check but I
hope you know that I love every single one of you.

Special mention also to:

my lovely godparents, Avice and Stewart;

my brilliant parents, who never fail to amaze and inspire me;

Seán, Luke and Ruby – you guys really do make
my heart sing.

FRIDAY

Face too close, his mouth shouting words she couldn't hear. Too many other sounds competing with his voice. A hand on her arm, pulling. She tripped, Merlot sloshed out of her glass, wetting the cuff of her black Donna Karan sweater. Outside. The night air cold after the intense warmth of the house. Smoking a fag with Ginny and some guy. Dermot. Big face and shouty voice.

'What are we celebrating?' he asked.

'Charlotte's birthday.' Ginny grabbed Charlotte and planted a wet kiss on her cold cheek.

Charlotte's glass was empty. Where had all the wine gone? She held it up, waved it in front of Dermot's face.

'We need more wine.'

He frowned. 'What was that?' Turned to Ginny, laughing.

'You've got your hands full with this one.'

Back in the house. Music. Loud. A woman she doesn't know shouts 'Happy Birthday'. Lots of people she doesn't know. What are they all doing here? Then a familiar face. Freya. She smiles, steps forward to say – what? Doesn't matter. By the time she reaches the other side of the room, Freya has gone.

Up on Blackheath now. How did she get here? She's with some guy. Can't remember his name. Declan, maybe. He's got his body pressed close to hers and she can feel his erection pushing against her leg.

She shoves him away, but he's not happy about it. Like she cares. Young enough to be her son. What is it about her and younger men? He's shouting at her but she's turned away from him, staggering towards home. A sudden twisting inside her gut and she's leaning over, puke pouring from her mouth.

When it's over, she stands and wipes the back of her hand across her mouth. The air is rich with the stink of what her body has expelled. No sign of Declan now. He's lucky she didn't puke all over him. She giggles, imagining his face if she'd done that.

She's cold. Shivering. Clasps her arms around her body and starts walking. It's lonely out here. The empty blackness of the heath stretches away from her on all sides, its edges lined with the twinkling lights from the windows of the tall Georgian houses.

She can see her own house in the background. Brighter than all the others, light pouring from every window in defiance of the dark night. She wonders if Freya is still there. Her mind flashes to her daughter's boyfriend. She doesn't want to think about him but his face is there, inside her head the whole time.

She tries to think if she's seen him this evening. Wouldn't be surprised if she went back inside the house and found him in there. For all his so-called principles, he's always been more than happy to eat her food and drink her alcohol.

Freya needs to leave him. The realisation hits her square in the stomach. She bends over, thinking she might be sick again. Retches, but nothing comes up. She staggers forward, moving faster now, knowing she has to hold onto this moment of clarity, find her daughter and tell her what a piece of shit her boyfriend really is.

A shape moves forward, appearing from nowhere out of the shadows. She lurches back, shouting out with fear. For one crazy moment she thinks it's him; he's come out here to find her.

'Charlotte! There you are. We've been looking for you everywhere.'

Ginny. The fear subsides. Ginny grabs her arms, starts pulling her towards the house, saying something about a cake and candles. Time to make a birthday wish. She remembers the noise and the heat and the people and she pulls her arm away. But Ginny is insistent and Charlotte's too tired and sick to fight.

The house is too bright and too warm and the people are too loud and too close. Bodies pressing against her, voices shouting at her. She pushes through it all, looking for her daughter.

Freya is in the kitchen. Standing by the sink, drinking a glass of water. A sour look on her face, like she's eaten a lemon. Or just seen her mother.

'He's a bastard.'

Freya frowns and Charlotte tries again.

'Kieran.' She's slurring, so she grabs Freya's arm and shouts because this is important.

'Kieran's a bastard.'

Freya pushes her. Hard. She staggers back, bangs into the kitchen table, hurting her hip bone.

'He doesn't deserve you,' Charlotte says. It's difficult getting the words out, but she forces them through her thick tongue. She thinks Freya's going to say something but she doesn't. She puts down the glass of water and goes to leave. Panic grips Charlotte's throat and chest.

'No!' She lunges. Grabs Freya and pushes her against the wall, pressing herself into her, determined now. One hundred percent focused on getting Freya to understand.

'He doesn't love you. Wouldn't say it if it wasn't true, but it is.'

She wanted to say more but Freya was screaming at her now, pushing her away. Charlotte's hands reach out to calm her down but her arms are all jerky and she hits Freya in the face by mistake.

She tried to say sorry, but Freya was still screaming and calling her a bitch. Charlotte tried to tell her that wasn't true but it was true, wasn't it?

'Come on, Lottie. Let's get you away from this.' Ginny's arm around her shoulders, steering her away from Freya. She looked back. Saw Freya still standing there but her face was blurred because Charlotte was crying. Couldn't stop.

'Is she okay?' someone asked.

'A bit too much to drink,' Ginny said. 'She'll be fine in a second, won't you, Lottie? We haven't done the cake yet. Come on.'

She couldn't face that now. She wants them all to go home and leave her alone. She's trying to tell this to Ginny, but Ginny isn't listening. Ginny is patting her back and telling her it's okay, it will all be okay.

Charlotte shakes her off, pushes her way out of the house and then – finally – she's free. Running up the hill and across the heath, running from the song she can hear. Except no matter how fast she runs, she can't get away from it because it's there, inside her head. The tinny pitch of the doll's voice rising the faster Charlotte runs.

'Sugar and spice and all things nice
Kisses sweeter than wine
Sugar and spice and all things nice
You know that little girl is mine.'

SATURDAY

ONE

An early morning jogger discovered the body. The killer had made no attempt to conceal the corpse. The victim – white, male, mid-twenties to early thirties – lay at the bottom of St Joseph's Vale, a quiet laneway off Belmont Hill in Blackheath. Beside the dead man, a congealed puddle of vomit from the unfortunate jogger.

'Lucky it's a Saturday,' Abby said. 'Otherwise it might have been a poor kid who found him on the way to school.'

'I'm not sure lucky's the word I'd use,' Ellen said.

She was kneeling down beside the dead man, examining the body. His eyes were open. Wide and empty and staring right at her. Light brown irises, turning black at the edges. Nothing like Billy Dunston's but reminded her of him all the same. Dirty-blonde hair, a short beard and strong features. The sort of guy you might look at twice if you saw him in a bar or passed him on the street and were in the mood to look twice at a good-looking fella young enough to be your son.

He was wearing jeans and a pale denim jacket. A grey tee-shirt underneath the jacket, stained black across the chest. The point of injury. A knife, Ellen guessed, although it was impossible to tell for sure without lifting the sweatshirt and looking at the wound. Something she couldn't do until the pathologist arrived.

She looked again at the dead man's eyes, imagined there was a question there. Knew it was her mind playing tricks with her and turned away from him before she did something stupid. Like talking to him.

She stood and stretched. She knew this road. Her brother Sean had gone to the Catholic boys' school that gave the road its name. St Joseph's Vale connected with Heath Lane, an affluent road in an area of affluent roads in and around Blackheath village south-east London. The body lay in the dip at the bottom of two hills, where both paths met.

'Looks like he's been here a while,' she said. 'Four hours or more.'

'It must have been a shock,' Abby said, nodding in the direction of the jogger, giving his statement to a uniformed WPC. 'No wonder the poor bloke chucked his guts.'

'I wish he'd thought to do it somewhere else,' Ellen said. 'God knows what it's doing to the crime scene.'

Abby tutted her disapproval at Ellen's lack of sympathy.

Ignoring her, Ellen looked again at the body. He was young. Too young for it all to be over. Another poor soul to add to the growing list of corpses that crowded her dreams and clustered in the shadows of her waking hours. They were here now, the names and faces and finished lives of all those dead people. A line of them that started with her sister and ended with this unknown man on a quiet back-road between Lewisham and Blackheath. Except it wouldn't end here. There would be more bodies after this. The knowledge depressed her beyond belief.

Questions crammed their way into her head, demanding details she didn't yet know about the dead man. Details that would make this harder than it already was when she knew about his life and his family and the people he'd left behind.

The immediate area was already sealed off and uniformed officers had been assigned to each end of the lane, ensuring no one came or went without Ellen's permission. For now, the only people inside the cordon were the five white-uniformed SOCOs scouring each centimetre of ground for evidence. Ellen and Abby wore the same protective clothing. In the muggy May sunshine, the additional layer felt heavy.

A trickle of sweat tickled down Ellen's spine. More sweat broke out across her forehead. She wiped it away, irritated.

'At least it's dry for once,' she said. 'Let's hope the SOCO crew can get through here before any more rain comes.'

'Forecast is dry for the rest of the weekend,' Abby said. 'Rain's due again on Monday, though.'

Ellen sighed. Another conversation about the weather was the last thing she felt like right now.

The constant rain of the last few weeks was all anyone seemed to speak about.

'Where the hell is Mark?' she asked.

As if on cue, the tall, gangly figure of Mark Pritchard, the pathologist, appeared at the top of St Joseph's Vale. Relieved, Ellen walked up the hill to greet him.

'Ellen, my love!' Mark grabbed her and planted a kiss on each cheek. 'Suspected stabbing?' He held her for a moment then released her, examined her face. 'You're looking good. Much better than the last time we met. Life treating you well, I assume?'

Ellen smiled. Mark's enthusiasm for life and all it offered was infectious. Being with him always made her feel better. Even during those grey, endless weeks following her husband's death, Mark had always managed to say or do something that made her smile. She realised she'd never told him how important that had been. Not just for her but for the children as well.

'Not too bad,' she said. 'Better now you're here.'

'Of course,' Mark said. 'That's always the case. Lead me to him, then. Haven't got all day, you know. Ah, DC Roberts. Wonderful. What a day this is turning out to be. And here's our poor victim. Any idea who's vomit this is?'

'A man found the body earlier,' Ellen said. 'Jogger. He'd obviously eaten before coming out for his morning run.'

'Who eats before they go jogging?' Mark asked. 'What time

was the body found?'

'Call came through at seven minutes past seven,' Ellen said. 'Looks like a stabbing.' She pointed to the stain across the dead man's chest. 'No sign of any knife, though. Not yet.'

'Okay,' Mark said. 'Let me take a closer look. If you two wouldn't mind stepping away? A bit further, that's it. Thank you.'

While Mark got to work, Ellen and Abby moved outside the cordoned-off crime scene. Once they'd ripped off their protective outer layer, they walked up Heath Lane, passing pairs of uniformed officers performing the standard door-to-door enquiries, gathering statements from the residents in the hope of uncovering some vital piece of information that would help them track down a killer.

'You could almost forget you lived in London in a place like this,' Abby said. 'It's beautiful.'

'Beautiful and way out of your league,' Ellen said. 'You'll have to change career if you harbour any ambitions of living somewhere like this one day.'

'Or find a rich man,' Abby said.

Ellen was saved from thinking up a suitable response by the appearance of a pair of uniforms coming out the gate of an elegant red-brick Queen Anne-style house.

'Anything so far?' Ellen asked.

'Couple at the top of the road had a party last night,' the male officer said. 'Noisy affair, by all accounts. Went on until the wee hours. Old dear in there,' he pointed his thumb in the direction of the house they'd just come from, 'says there was music blaring – her word, not mine – half the night.'

'Which house?' Ellen asked. 'A party means lots of people and the more people there were, the more chance we have that someone saw something.'

'The first one on the right as you come into this road,' the man said. So far, his female companion hadn't said a word. Ellen wondered if that was because she had nothing to say or if she was used to being talked over by her partner.

'PC McKeown, isn't it?' Ellen asked, turning her attention to the dumpy blonde.

'That's right, Ma'am,' McKeown said, blushing.

'I'd like you to head on up to the house where the party was. Find out who lives there, what was the reason for the party and see if you can get a list of names of everyone who was there. Okay?'

McKeown smiled. 'Of course, Ma'am. Absolutely.'

Ellen nodded. 'Good. You,' she pointed at the man, 'carry on with the rest of the houses. Think you can do that on your own or do you need someone else?'

'I'll be fine,' the man said. 'Ma'am.'

If he was pissed off he hid it well, and Ellen gave him credit for that. Maybe she'd misjudged him.

'Baxter, right?'

He nodded.

'Good work,' she said. 'Well done. Now on you go, both of you. Abby, let's get back and see how Mark's doing.'

Mark was already on his way to find them as Ellen and Abby made their way back down the hill.

'Single puncture wound on the left side of his body, underneath the heart,' he said. 'Knife wound, I'd guess. Another stabbing I'm afraid, detectives. No outer sign of any other injury. Although I won't know more until I examine him properly. I'll organise a tox test, too. But you won't get the results of that for at least a week.'

'How long has he been there?' Ellen asked.

'He was killed somewhere between midnight and one-thirty, I'd say. Although again …'

'I know,' Ellen said. 'You can't say for definite until you've done the post-mortem.'

'Mobile phone in his jacket pocket,' Mark said. 'And he had his wallet on him. Almost two hundred pounds cash inside. Which makes me think it might not be a robbery. There's something else too. I can tell you who he is.'

'You're joking,' Ellen said.

Mark shook his head. 'A student card in the inside pocket of his jacket. His name's Kieran Burton. Lives in Ennersdale Road, Hither Green. I'm assuming you'll want the full address?'

Kieran Burton. They had a name. Soon, they'd have a history. It had begun.

TWO

The first thing she saw when she opened her eyes was a slice of sunlight cutting through the hazy grey darkness of her bedroom. It was too bright and she closed her eyes. She was home. Safe in her own room.

Traces of the dream lingered. The song. Always the same song. Distant now but still here. Fading in and out. Scared, Charlotte sat up, scanned the room, checking every corner to make sure the song was all in her head and nowhere else.

Relieved to find the room empty, she sank back on the pillow. Scattered memories from last night skittered across her consciousness. She remembered a man, his body pressed close to hers. Another wave of panic hit her and she sat up. No one else there. Whoever he was, she'd dumped him before coming to bed. Good move. She searched the incomplete memory bank but couldn't find a single hint that she'd done anything too terrible.

So why the underlying sense that something bad had happened?

She did another quick check through the bits she could remember. Cocktails, sushi, wine, more cocktails. A lot more cocktails. Her stomach rolled. She wanted to lie down, go back to sleep until the worst of it had passed, but a raging thirst made that impossible. The promise of a large glass of cool, sparkling water was strong enough to drag her out of the bed and down the two flights of stairs, into the kitchen.

The house was empty and still as a corpse apart from the ghostly rhythm of last night's music beating inside her pounding head. The detritus from the party was all around her. She couldn't remember what time she'd booked the cleaners for.

The kitchen, a huge white and chrome affair, took up the entire lower floor of the house. By the time she'd reached the fridge and managed to retrieve a bottle of water from its chilly depths, her legs were shaking with the effort of walking so far.

Somehow, her fumbling fingers managed to unscrew the lid and get the bottle to her lips. Cold water trickled down her throat, across her chin and neck, soaking the top of the sweater she was still wearing. She drank until she could drink no more, until her insides were bloated from gas and liquid. When she was finished, she fell onto the cream sofa by the window, pushed a pile of paper plates off it and curled up in the corner. The sudden hit of water turned her body cold and she started shivering as she waited for the nausea to pass.

She picked up the remote control and flicked it at the flat-screen TV on the far wall. A pretty female presenter was interviewing Xavi Cheval, the celebrity chef who was all over the tabloids at the moment after leaving his wife and three children for a man twenty years younger than him. Charlotte watched with detached interest. She'd met Cheval several times and knew his sexuality was no secret to anyone in the restaurant business, least of all his wife.

The story made her think of Nick and she wondered where he was. She had no memory of seeing him at the party. She told herself she didn't care. Just like she'd told herself yesterday she didn't care that he'd forgotten her birthday. It wasn't like it was the first time.

The air inside the house stank of last night. A memory came to her. Bent over, vomit spraying from her mouth. Something else lurked in the shadows of that moment. Not something. Someone. A man. Her stomach clenched with fear. A name came to her. Declan. She relaxed. A stranger. She didn't care about that. She tried to picture Declan's face but nothing happened.

She stood up, unable to bear the claustrophobic smell and the mess and the general chaos of the place. Through the fog of her hangover, another sensation clawed its way to the surface of her consciousness. A craving. She moved around the room, rooting through the dirty napkins, discarded food and turned-over glasses. Her hand hovered for a moment over a half-empty bottle of Sauvignon Blanc before she changed her mind. She wasn't sure she'd be able to keep it down.

When she'd finished with the living room, she searched the kitchen. Still nothing. Not a single cigarette in the entire house. Unbelievable. She steeled herself for the effort required to go outside.

There was a small alcove off the inside porch where she kept her day shoes. She rooted around the neat rows of trainers and boots until she found her current favourites – the white YSL pair. They were dirty. Streaks of mud criss-crossed with splatters of red wine. Too often her clothes were the map that allowed her to find her way back to the things she'd done the night before. Vaguely, she remembered spilling wine. A red stain on her sleeve that looked like blood. She shook her head and the memory dispersed.

Trainers on, she got her purse and went outside to face the unexpected brightness of a perfect early summer morning. In a less desperate state, she might have noticed straight away that something was wrong. As it was, she'd reached the top of Heath Lane before she noticed the pair of uniformed policemen walking towards her. At the same time, she saw the lines of black and yellow police tape criss-crossed back and forth in front of her, preventing anyone from entering or leaving.

The first thing she felt was irritation. Followed closely by panic. If there was some sort of 'incident' – wasn't that the euphemistic phrase the police used for all sorts of human tragedies? – then she bloody well hoped it wouldn't stall her attempts to get to the shop for her Marlboro Lights.

'Sorry, Ma'am.'

The pair of plods positioned themselves in front of her, blocking the way.

'What is it?' Her voice sounded scratchy, like she'd done a lot of shouting the previous night. When she spoke, it felt like someone was grinding sandpaper against her vocal chords.

'You live here?'

They were both tall and dark and good-looking in the way that working-class young men sometimes are. All lean muscle, stubble-shadowed jaws and close-cut hair. The taller of the two – greeny-blue eyes that reminded her of a holiday in Morocco many years earlier – was doing all the speaking. He had a deep, rich voice and an accent that was pure south London.

'Of course I live here,' she snapped. 'What's it to you?'

'I'm afraid we'll have to ask you to go back home,' he said. 'We're not allowing anyone in or out at the moment.'

A stab of irrational, guilt-laced fear hit her. Again, she trawled through her damaged memories, trying to remember if there was anything she needed to worry about.

'What's happened?' she asked.

The greeny-blues flickered from her face to somewhere behind her. She turned around.

Heath Lane was a hill that curved up from the end of St

Joseph's Vale to the top, where Charlotte stood. The bend in the hill meant she was unable to see all the way down to the bottom. She could see enough, though, to know that whatever 'incident' the police were dealing with, it was serious. Men and women dressed in white were spread out along the lane, creeping their way slowly up the hill.

Charlotte turned back to the two policemen and asked them, again, what had happened. Instead of answering, the tall policeman took her gently – oh so gently – by her right arm and started guiding her back down the path, telling her that she'd better come inside, that there was something they needed to speak to her about.

Don't worry, he said, but how could she not worry? How could she not associate that moving force of white bodies with the noise and chaos and jumble of images that made up the incomplete picture of last night?

As they reached the front door – the policeman's arm still linked in hers, his voice still talking, telling her not to worry, that there was no reason for her to worry – she remembered something else. She remembered running across the heath away from her house and her party, running as fast as she could, her face wet with tears. No matter how hard she tried, though, she couldn't remember what it was she'd been running so fast to get away from.

Inside the house, she led the two men through the entrance hall into the large living room at the front of the house.

'I had a party last night,' she said, waving her hand at the mess.

She sat down on one of the pretty, floral-patterned sofas and motioned for the policemen to sit on the one opposite. They both perched on the edge of the sofa as if they were afraid of contamination. Neither man asked for a drink and she didn't offer, either. She didn't have the energy to play hostess.

'What's happened?' she asked.

'A body has been found,' Blue Eyes said.

Another clitter-clatter of panic across her chest.

'Who?'

'We don't have any details at the moment,' the other guy said. He had a soft Scottish accent that surprised her. Nothing London about him at all. Funny, she thought, how your first impressions could be so wrong.

'But you must know something.' She directed the comment at the Scottish one, wondering what it was about his accent she found so appealing. Until she realised it didn't matter. There was a dead person lying yards away from where she was sitting.

Her daughter's face flashed before her.

'Can you at least tell me if it's a man or a woman?'

The two men glanced at each other before the cute guy with the lovely eyes responded.

'A man,' he said. 'More than that, I can't say.'

'I had a party,' she said. 'Last night. My birthday. You'll want to know who was here, I suppose. I'm not sure I even know half the people who turned up. But maybe it's someone else. I mean, just because they were here doesn't mean … lots of people walk through this way, it's a short-cut between Lewisham and Blackheath. Well, parts of Lewisham.' She was babbling, needed to stop talking, but it was like her mind had lost the ability to control her mouth. 'What happened to him, anyway? You haven't told me that. I mean, did someone attack him or was it a heart attack or … no, not a car. Well, maybe. I mean, cars do come down this way, but …'

Her voice trailed off. She slumped back on the sofa, exhausted.

The Scottish guy stood up.

'How about I make us all a cup of tea?' he said. 'And then we can have a proper chat.'

They stayed for longer than she would have liked but after they left, part of her wished they were still here. The house felt too big, too lonely. She wanted to go back outside, to walk down the hill and see what was going on there. It would be all cordoned off, of course. The police wouldn't let her anywhere near the body.

They hadn't told her what had happened but she knew it wasn't good. Their presence and the probing questions they'd asked told her that. Oh they'd been kind enough. They just wanted to know so bloody much. Why had she had the party? Who had been here? Did she often throw parties like this? Were there any arguments? Why were there people here she didn't know? Was she in the habit of letting strangers into her house? And on and on and on.

She wished Nick was here. He might be a pain in the arse but at least he'd know what to do. Her weakness and indecision were two of the things Nick disliked most about her. Right now, Charlotte could understand why. She'd done nothing wrong, nothing at all, and here she was, hiding out in her own house like some sort of criminal. Whatever had happened at the bottom of her road, it had nothing to do with her.

She stood up and her resolve faltered as a wave of nausea washed over her. She waited for it to pass then went upstairs. The stink of stale booze in the bedroom made her gag. She ripped open the white silk curtains and pulled up the large sash window. Cool air on her warm skin. She stood by the window, looking out across the woods at the back of the house, waiting for her heart rate to slow down.

When she was able to move, she crossed over to the mahogany bedside table and picked up her phone. She'd been planning to call Ginny but when she switched her phone on, she saw that she had two missed calls and one voicemail.

The missed calls were from Freya. Why was her daughter trying to speak to her? It wasn't as if they had the sort of relationship that involved frequent phone calls to each other.

She dialled her voicemail, the clamouring in her chest getting worse as she listened to Freya's message.

'It's me. Kieran didn't come home last night and I'm just wondering ... It's not like him to stay out. Can you call me? Please?'

She told herself it didn't mean anything. Coincidence. Nothing more than that. Except Freya's voice ... she sounded so lost.

Vulnerable. Her little girl. A latent instinct kicked in and suddenly the need to see her daughter, to be with her and to make sure no harm came to her, was overwhelming.

Charlotte picked up her bag, stuffed her phone inside, and ran.

THREE

Ennersdale Road in Hither Green was a ten-minute drive from the crime scene in Blackheath. Victorian terraces lined the road, in various stages of disrepair and regeneration. Ellen guessed the properties were a mix of private owners and council housing stock.

Their victim's address was Flat 2, number 19 – a large, semi-detached property near the top of the road. Ellen parked outside the house and climbed out of the car. She was overdressed for the sudden sunshine and unzipped her jacket while she waited for Abby to join her.

'Patrol car will be here in a second,' Ellen said. 'We won't go in until that arrives.'

Like most streets around here, Ennersdale Road was quiet at

this time on a Saturday morning. Very little traffic and only a handful of people out and about. As Ellen walked towards the house, a couple approached, coming down the hill from Hither Green Lane. They had a small girl with them. She was riding a tricycle and giggling as she wheeled her way – dangerously fast, in Ellen's opinion – towards the spot where Ellen stood. At the last moment, the child swerved left, entering the garden of the house beside number 19. The couple came after her, smiling and nodding to Abby and Ellen before disappearing through the gate after the child.

'Are you sure you're okay to be here?' Abby asked.

'If you're going to ask me that every time we see any children,' Ellen said, 'it's going to be a long day. I'm fine. I've already told you, the kids are at their friends' house. When it's time to pick them up, I'll go. But in the meantime, you're stuck with me.'

Abby meant well, but the constant checking was getting on Ellen's nerves. Her new working arrangements meant she no longer worked weekends. Except with the children both on a playdate, what the hell else was she supposed to do with her time? She'd only popped into the office to pick up some files. Hadn't planned to stay. Sod's law – or a stroke of luck? – that the call about the dead man had come in at the same time. That's the way things happened sometimes. Nothing Ellen or anyone else could do about that. And she meant what she'd said. The moment it was time to collect her children, she'd be gone.

A marked patrol car appeared at the top of the hill and drove down the road. When it was parked, Ellen walked across and leaned down to speak to the two officers inside. She knew one of them.

'Okay, Maurice?'

Maurice Alter had been a uniformed officer longer than Ellen's entire time in the force. Reliable, consistent and unflappable, he was one of her favourite old-timers.

'Not so bad,' Maurice said. 'You want us to wait here?'

'To start with,' Ellen said, 'I don't want to go in mob-handed if we don't have to. If there's anyone in, chances are they're going to be very upset. No need to make things worse for them if we don't have to.'

'Fair enough,' Maurice said. 'Me and Jamie here, we'll be ready when you need us.'

Ellen patted the roof of the car and walked back to Abby. Together, they went into the garden of number 19. The house was one of the better maintained properties on the street. Painted a sunny yellow colour with a tidy front garden, it was obvious whoever lived here looked after the place.

Each of the two doorbells was neatly labelled – Flat 1, the lower one, and Flat 2, the upper one. Ellen rang the bell for Flat 2 and waited. Not for long. The sound of someone clattering down a flight of steps was followed by the creak of the front door as it opened. A plump, pasty-faced woman with mousy brown hair stood in the doorway.

'Yes?'

'Mrs Burton?' Ellen guessed.

The woman frowned. 'Sorry, I think you've made a mistake. It's Mr Burton you want. Kieran.'

'Ah. I thought you might be his wife,' Ellen said.

A flicker of something across the woman's face. Fear? It passed too quickly for Ellen to tell.

'Has something happened?' the woman asked. 'To Kieran, I mean?'

Ellen held up her warrant card and showed it to the woman.

'DI Kelly, Lewisham CID,' she said. 'This is my partner, DC Roberts. Could we come inside, do you think?'

The woman's eyes flashed from Ellen to Abby and back to Ellen again. She stood back and gestured for the two detectives to come past her into the house.

Inside, the woman closed the door, submerging the narrow space into sudden darkness. Ellen blinked, waited for her eyes to adjust. When they did, she saw she was standing in a well-maintained, communal entrance hall. The door to one flat on her left, a flight of stairs in front of her.

'Up here.' The woman pushed past them and started up the stairs, Ellen and Abby close behind. They followed her into a light and airy first-floor flat with large sash windows and views across Hither Green and Catford. The place was cheaply but tastefully furnished. Second-hand vintage pieces chosen over Ikea.

An original Victorian fireplace dominated one side of the room. A single, wooden-framed photo was the only decoration on the mantelpiece above it. There were two people in the photo: the woman who'd let them into the flat and a man. The woman's arms were wrapped around his neck. They were in the countryside somewhere. Both wearing sensible, outdoor jackets and both smiling at Ellen. The man looked different in life. People always did. But there was no mistaking who he was. The same pale brown eyes and tight-cropped blonde hair.

Ellen turned from his smiling face and back to the woman.

'Can we sit down?' she asked.

The woman lowered herself onto a low, overstuffed armchair beside the fireplace. Ellen chose the small two-seater sofa opposite, while Abby perched on a high-backed chair by the table near the window.

'Nice photo.' Ellen pointed to the photo on the mantelpiece.

'West Sussex,' the woman said. 'We spent two weeks there last September. Before you lot kicked us out. Is that what this is about?'

'Anti-fracking?' Ellen said. 'No, that's not why we're here. It's about Mr Burton. Kieran. You're his girlfriend, Miss …?'

'Lover,' the woman said. 'Kieran's my lover. I'm his. And it's Ms Gleeson. Freya Gleeson. Look, can you please tell me what this is about? I'm worried.'

'Any reason?' Ellen asked.

Freya snorted. 'Apart from you turning up unannounced, you mean? Wouldn't you be worried?'

'Kieran lives here with you,' Ellen said. 'Is that right?'

'Yes.'

'And he was here with you last night?'

Freya groaned. 'Please. Tell me what's happened.'

'We'll get to that in a minute,' Ellen said. 'Is that Mr Burton with you in the photo?'

Freya nodded. She looked scared now and Ellen dreaded having to tell her why they were here.

'When did you last see him?' she asked.

'Yesterday,' Freya whispered. 'We went to a party. Kieran left before me but he never came home. He wasn't here when I got back last night and I haven't seen him since. It's not like him and I've been worried. He's not answering his phone. Something's happened, hasn't it?'

'Where was the party?' Ellen said.

'Blackheath,' Freya said. 'It was my mother's birthday. She always throws these huge parties. It's not really my scene but she insists I come along. Even though she's usually too drunk to notice if I'm there or not.'

'A man's body was found in Blackheath early this morning,' Ellen said. 'We think he may be Kieran.'

Freya shook her head. Her mouth opened and closed like she was trying to speak but had forgotten how to. She leaned forward, arms clasped around her middle, gasping for air. Abby jumped up, ran to Freya's side and put her arms around her.

Freya shoved her away and started crying, loud, howling sobs that Ellen tried to block out. Like her colleagues, this was the bit of her job she hated the most. She'd learned early on that the only way to deal with moments like this was to shut herself down. Literally. She pictured her brain as a number of compartments. Each one responsible for different functions: breathing, moving, thinking, feeling. The feeling compartment – bigger than the others – was the one she closed off now. It was a skill she'd developed as a young child. A little girl's way of dealing with a trauma too impossible for a young mind to understand. Applying the same technique to her job was easy. The hard part came later. Finding the switch that got the compartment working again. Once she'd shut herself down, it was difficult to bring herself back sometimes. Difficult to open herself up once again to all the pain and the long line of dead people waiting to take up space inside her head once more.

Gradually, Freya's wailing diminished to a low, keening sound. Some long minutes later she wiped her face and looked up. Ellen saw raw grief and forced herself not to look away.

'Where is he?' Freya asked.

'He's been taken to the morgue,' Ellen said. 'The pathologist needs to examine him, see if we can find out exactly what happened. We can arrange to take you to him if you'd like. First, though, I'm afraid there's some questions we need to ask you.'

'Of course,' Freya said. 'Yes. What happened to him? You haven't told me that. Did … oh God, what was it? A hit-and-run or …?'

Ellen saw the dead man's face. The surprise she imagined in his wide-open brown eyes. The dark stain of blood spread across the front of his sweatshirt.

'We're not sure,' Abby said. 'Until the pathologist has had a chance to examine him, we can't confirm the cause of death.'

'But you must have some idea,' Freya said. 'I mean, you'd know if it was a heart attack or what-do-you-call-it, natural causes or …'

'Freya, please,' Ellen said. 'We shouldn't speculate. We need your help. Can you do that?'

Freya nodded.

'Good,' Ellen said. 'Can you start by telling us about yesterday evening? Talk us through it until when you left the party.'

'We had dinner here.' Freya's voice wobbled, but apart from that she'd done a good job of getting a grip on her emotions. She was either a very tough young woman, Ellen thought, or she'd had time to prepare. Ellen wasn't sure which.

'It was lovely,' Freya said. 'We've both been … oh God, I can't believe … we've been really busy. Kieran's studies take up so much time. He works … worked … so hard. We made the effort last night to spend some time together. Both of us wanted to stay in but we had to go out. My mother. She … well, she can be a bit needy. Oh God. Has anyone spoken to her yet?'

'We'll get to that,' Ellen said. 'Tell us what happened after dinner.'

'We went to her stupid party,' Freya said. 'Kieran met a friend for a quick drink and he joined me there later.'

'What friend?' Ellen asked.

Freya shrugged. 'Someone from his uni course, I think. He was at the party by nine. My mother was drunk already, of course. She can get a bit nasty when she's drunk and last night was no exception. She doesn't like Kieran. Didn't like him.'

Now they were getting somewhere.

'Where in Blackheath does she live?' Ellen asked.

'Heath Lane,' Freya said. 'Oh God, is that where you found him?'

She started wailing again. Ellen thought the sudden switch from control to hysteria seemed forced. She glanced at her watch. Three minutes to midday. She was due to collect her children at four o'clock. A while away yet. She considered calling Rosie and asking her to do it. Just as quickly, she changed her mind.

She stood up.

'Mind if I have a look around the flat?' she asked.

Freya wiped her face with the back of her sleeve and sniffed. 'You won't find anything.'

'It helps us get an idea of who Kieran was,' Abby said. 'DI Kelly won't mess anything up. And it won't take long. Why don't we let her get on with what she has to do? In the meantime, how about I make us both a nice cup of tea?'

'You think that will help?' Freya asked. 'You think *tea* is going to make this all right? When can I see him? That's all I want to do right now. Not sit here drinking fucking tea.'

Ellen caught Abby's eye and motioned for her to make the

tea, regardless. Quietly, she slipped out of the sitting room into the hall. From here, Ellen could see through open doors into the other three rooms in the flat – a small, galley-style kitchen, a blue-tiled bathroom and a bedroom.

She started in the bedroom. A small, dark room with a musty smell and a layer of dust across the window-sill and the second-hand wooden wardrobe. The double bed was unmade, with a faded-looking matching quilt and pillow set thrown on top. One pillow indented from where someone had slept on it. The other, fluffed up and untouched.

Ellen opened the wardrobe, flicked through the collection of jeans and shirts. It was difficult to tell which clothes belonged to Kieran and which were Freya's. A messy pile of posters sat by the side of the bed. Ellen picked one up. An advertisement for a Greenpeace demonstration that had taken place in London three months ago. The other posters were all Greenpeace as well. Otherwise, there were no personal touches in the room.

Beside the bed, there was a small cabinet with three drawers and another layer of dust across the top. Ellen opened each one of these. Neat piles of washed-out underwear in the top two drawers and a selection of cheap-looking tee-shirts in the bottom drawer. Nothing else.

The bathroom didn't offer anything, either. Cheap men's cleanser and moisturiser in the bathroom cabinet but no corresponding products for a woman. Ellen didn't think she was particularly vain, but sharing her partner's beauty products? That was a new one. Even if she had no money, she was pretty sure her bathroom cabinet would have female beauty products for sharing with a partner, not the other way around. Maybe Kieran was a bully who insisted his needs came first. Or Freya was a doormat who put his needs before her own? Ellen filed both thoughts away for later.

The galley kitchen was tiny. An old-looking oven and washing machine, a microwave oven. No dishwasher but no dirty plates in the sink and everything tidied away neatly. An unopened bottle of red wine from Aldi stood on the MDF worktop.

On her way back to the sitting room, the doorbell rang.

'I'll get it,' she said.

Whoever the caller was, they were determined to be let in. The bell rang repeatedly as Ellen ran to answer it. She noticed an empty coat-stand in the corner of the hall. Kieran Burton had been wearing a jacket when they found him. Ellen wondered if they'd shared that, as well.

Downstairs, she opened the door to a scrawny woman with skin that had spent too long under a sunbed and sticks of straw hair that protruded from her skull in random directions. When she spoke, the stink of stale booze nearly floored Ellen.

'Where is she?' the woman asked. 'What have you done with my daughter?'

The mother. First impressions – she was nothing like Freya. Ellen supposed last night's party might go some way to explaining the boozy breath and the dishevelled appearance. Although something about the woman made her suspect this was more than a one-off.

'Freya's mother?' she asked.

'That's right.'

'DI Kelly,' Ellen said. 'Lewisham CID. Freya's okay. So please don't worry about her. But I'm afraid I have got some bad news. You'd better come inside.'

FOUR

'I can't believe it.' Charlotte shook her head. 'No. I'm sorry. It just won't go in. Freya, darling, what on earth happened?'

Freya shrugged and edged her way along the sofa, away from her mother.

Charlotte looked at Abby. 'I don't know what I'm meant to do,' she said.

Ellen thought of her adopted parents, remembering what a strength they had been in the days and weeks and months after Vinny died. She doubted Freya would get anything like that from her own mother.

A strand of bleached blonde hair had fallen across Charlotte's face. The hand she used to brush it back was shaking. Shock or hangover or some combination of both.

'There's nothing you *can* do,' Freya said.

'How did it …?' Charlotte directed the question at Abby. She appeared to be doing her best to ignore Ellen. It was a reaction Ellen was used to. She knew she could come across as intimidating. Abby, on the other hand, exuded a warmth that made people – victims and suspects – instinctively trust her.

'We can't confirm that yet.'

Abby gave Charlotte her best sympathetic smile. Ellen didn't know how she managed it. Charlotte Gleeson was pathetic. All she'd done since she'd got here was cry and say how terrible it was and what were they going to do in the face of such a tragedy. Not once had she asked her daughter how any of this was affecting her, or how *she* was feeling.

Ellen remembered what Freya had said about her mother: *she can get a bit nasty when she's drunk and last night was no exception.*

'He was at your party last night?' Ellen said.

'Was he? I don't … I'm not sure, actually.' Charlotte frowned and looked at Freya as if she might have the answer.

'He didn't stay long,' Freya said. She looked at Ellen. 'Like I told you, it wasn't exactly his scene.'

Ellen looked at Charlotte. 'Did you have some sort of argument with Kieran? Is that why he left?'

Charlotte put a hand over her mouth and shook her head. 'Oh no. Definitely not.' She attempted a laugh but it sounded more like a sob. 'Freya, darling, why would she say something like that?'

'You were drunk.' The expression on Freya's face made up for the lack of emotion in her voice. Disgust mingled with hatred. Something that ran far deeper than whatever had happened between Charlotte and Kieran at the party last night.

'It was my birthday,' Charlotte said. 'Surely you don't begrudge me that?'

Freya looked like she begrudged it very much indeed but instead of saying that, she turned to Ellen.

'Can I see him?'

Ellen wanted to say no. You can't see him yet. Not until you tell me more about your mother and why you hate her so much and what she said that made your boyfriend leave the party early last night. But that would have to wait. Before she could get answers to any of those questions, she needed a formal ID that would confirm what she already knew. That the dead man was definitely Kieran Burton.

* * *

The tall, stern detective drove them across in a dark green Audi. The car was a surprise. Charlotte would have expected a Ford or a Vauxhall or something equally tasteless. She felt sick and would have sat in the front, but Freya got in there first. Clambering in beside the police woman without even checking if that was okay with everyone else. Not that Charlotte could really blame her. Poor Freya was probably still in shock. Charlotte certainly was.

The morgue was a red-brick Victorian building at the back of Lewisham Hospital. The detective pulled into a parking bay and got out without saying a word. Which was awkward really because it didn't give Charlotte a chance to ask what she was meant to do.

Beside her, the pretty one unstrapped her seatbelt and put her hand on Freya's shoulder.

'Ready?'

Freya twisted her head around and looked at Charlotte. 'Are you coming too?'

Oh God. Charlotte wanted to say no. She couldn't do it. Not like this. She licked her lips as she thought of a way out. There was a pub across the road. She'd spotted it on the way in. How bad would it look if she suggested they go there first? Just for one. She wasn't mental and she knew how important it was that they did this. But surely it would be easier with a bit of Dutch courage to help them along the way?

Freya shook her head and Charlotte recognised the familiar look of disgust in her daughter's eyes. Almost as if Freya knew what Charlotte was thinking. Which was stupid, she knew, but she couldn't help it. Her daughter always made her feel like this: stupid and pointless and nothing more than an irritation.

'What about Nick?' Charlotte managed. 'Shouldn't he be here?'

'Fine,' Freya said. 'Don't bother. I'd rather go in without you anyway.'

She opened her door and got out, the car shaking and swaying from the heavy movements.

'If you can't face it,' the pretty detective said, 'that's not a problem. I'll go with her, make sure she's okay.'

'No.' Charlotte got out before she could change her mind. Freya was right to be angry. This was the one time her daughter actually needed her. The one time she could do something that wouldn't make Freya angry or upset or any of the other things Charlotte made her feel, none of them good or positive or the sorts of emotions a mother should inspire in her daughter.

She leaned against the side of the car to stop herself swaying from the wave of nausea that ran through her body.

'I'm coming too.'

Freya was ahead of her, walking through the swinging glass doors behind the other detective. Charlotte tried to remember the woman's name as she hurried after them. Irish name. Kelly. Erin Kelly? Something like that. It didn't matter. All that mattered right now was getting herself through the glass doors and staying strong for Freya. It wasn't a lot to ask. She forced herself inside, into the cool, dark hallway. You can do this, she told herself. You can do this and you will do this and afterwards, when it's all over, Freya will see what you've done for her and she will be grateful for it. And that was something to hold onto.

If she'd known how bad it was going to be, she would have stayed outside. Nothing in the world could have prepared her. There was the smell, for starters. A pervasive, chemical stench that invaded her insides, growing stronger and more repulsive with every breath she breathed in and every step she took deeper and deeper into the heart of this terrible place.

The room where the bodies were kept burned under the white glare of strip-lighting that hurt Charlotte's eyes and made it impossible to focus on what was happening. Rows and rows of silver drawers. A body inside each one. She knew this because the man in the white medical jacket pulled one open and drew the drawer out to reveal the body they'd come to look at.

She saw a toe first. Sticking out from the pale green sheet. A single toe that could belong to anyone, but it was Kieran's toe. She knew it was Kieran because the man had pulled the body out completely now and it was there, lying in front of her.

His eyes were closed and he looked like a dead man and nothing like someone she'd ever known. But it was him. She knew the moment she saw him. Her head filled up with images and memories and smells and she remembered his hands on her body and his breath warm on her face and the way it had been with them, fast and desperate and wrong. So bloody wrong, and she'd hated him for it and hated herself more.

Freya screamed. The sound cut through Charlotte, hurting her. She closed her eyes and she could hear her daughter crying beside her, sobbing like a little girl. And Kieran, whispering in Charlotte's ear, telling her this was what she wanted and her own voice saying yes, yes, yes. And Freya crying and Charlotte's stomach twisting and vomit rising up her throat, burning and bitter.

She put her hand over her mouth but she knew she couldn't stop it. She swung around, away from the dead body and away from her daughter, still crying, doubled over as if the pain of it was too much. She ran towards the swinging glass doors and the light and the world outside without its dead bodies and its memories and her daughter, crying for a man she'd loved but who had never loved her back because he was only ever capable of loving one person and that was himself.

FIVE

After the morgue, the detectives said they needed to come to the station and make statements. Charlotte asked if that was really necessary but Kelly made it clear they didn't have a choice. There was something hard about her that made it difficult to like her. Charlotte preferred the other woman, Abby. She was pretty and kind and seemed to really understand how difficult this was for Charlotte. And for Freya, of course.

Charlotte assumed they'd be allowed to stay together to give their statements. Instead, Abby took Freya in one direction, while Charlotte found herself being led into a different room with Kelly. She wished it was the other way around and suspected Freya did, too. Abby's sweet, touchy-feely manner was bound to be an irritation.

'Take a seat,' Kelly said, as if she was welcoming Charlotte into her living room instead of into this horrible, grey room that smelled of bleach and sweat.

Charlotte tried to pull the chair from under the table but its legs were screwed to the ground. She slid herself onto it, trying to think clearly through the pounding in her head and the clawing, craving thirst.

Kieran was dead. Murdered. She knew this because if he'd died of a heart attack or something like that, she wouldn't be sitting here now. Images jerked through her head. All of them ending with a body on a gurney in a bleached bright room.

'Can I get you something?' Kelly asked. 'Tea or coffee?'

'Water,' Charlotte said. She wanted to ask Kelly what her first name was but she was afraid she'd look stupid. She knew the woman had told her already, but how were you meant to remember a detail like that when there was so much else to think about?

Kelly left to get the water and Charlotte forced herself to take deep, slow breaths, trying to calm the skitter-skatter heartbeat and the fear and panic that was making her chest tight and her head feel as if it was about to spin off her neck and away from her body.

Kieran was dead.

Someone killed him.

Noises and images inside her head. Noises, smells, people. A man's face. Rain on her face as she ran across the heath. Or was it tears? The burning taste of vomit in her throat. Her mother singing. No. Her mother hadn't been there. A reckless rage that burned until it hurt. And a knife. Kieran's hands on her body, his face looming over her. Replaced by her mother's face. A sudden, surprising spurt of blood splashing onto her arm and face. Warm and wet.

The door opened and Charlotte yelped with shock.

Kelly stood in the doorway looking at her. 'Are you okay?'

'Hungover,' Charlotte said. Teeth chattering, body shivering with the cold that crept through her body, ice in her veins.

'Drink this,' Kelly said. 'Not too fast, though.'

She took the paper cup in both hands, managed to lift it to her mouth without spilling too much. The water tasted good but it wasn't what her body craved. She waited for the spasm to pass then put the glass back down and looked at the detective.

'I'm Ellen,' the woman said. 'Detective Inspector Ellen Kelly. Is it okay if I call you Charlotte?'

She nodded.

'Your birthday yesterday?'

'Do I need a lawyer?'

'We can arrange a lawyer if that's what you want,' Ellen said. 'But you're not under arrest or anything. I just need to ask you a few questions about the party last night. Is that okay?'

'I suppose so.'

'Do you remember seeing Kieran there?' Ellen asked.

Lips and hands and the scratchy feeling of whiskers scraping her cheek.

'No,' she said. 'I don't remember. Freya was there. But she was on her own, I think. Kieran wasn't with her.'

Ellen glanced at the notes she'd brought in with her.

'So you don't remember having an argument with anyone?'

'Shouting,' she said. 'There was a man. He was shouting at me. I think. I'm sorry, I can't remember his name but I'm sure it wasn't Kieran.'

'How can you be so sure?'

Good question.

'I remember his face,' she said. Not completely true but there was no one to prove her wrong. 'And he wasn't Kieran.'

'Who was he then?'

'Some guy who gate-crashed my party,' Charlotte said. 'Why does it matter? It wasn't Kieran, right?'

'Okay.' Ellen shrugged like it was no big deal either way. Charlotte knew that was just an act but was glad she didn't have to explain herself any further.

'What can you tell me about Kieran?' Ellen asked.

Charlotte frowned. 'What do you mean?'

'What was he like?' Ellen said. 'What sort of person was he? Did you like him? Did he make your daughter happy?'

He was a bastard who didn't give a damn about Freya. She couldn't tell them that. If she did, they might get the wrong idea about Freya. Besides, it was none of their damn business.

'He was okay,' she said. '*They* were okay. I mean, they were living together. They wouldn't have done that, would they, if they didn't like each other?'

'Did you like him?' Ellen asked again.

Hands on her thighs. Hot, damp breath whispering to her.

'I don't know,' Charlotte said. 'I mean, well, I hardly knew him really. Freya and I, our lives are very different. We don't see each other very often. Oh, I know she only lives down the road – less than ten minutes in the car – but it's difficult. She's difficult, to tell you the truth.'

She stopped. What the hell was wrong with her? Babbling like an idiot, telling the police all sorts of things they didn't need to know about. Private things that were her family's business and no one else's.

'I didn't see Kieran last night,' she said. 'I wouldn't lie about something like that. He's dead and that's terrible, but it wasn't me. I had nothing to do with it.'

'Nothing to do with what?' Ellen said.

'Kieran's death,' Charlotte said.

'I never said you did,' Ellen said.

Charlotte wished she could work out if Ellen was messing with her head or being serious. Maybe there was nothing wrong. Maybe she wasn't a suspect. They didn't know about the text. She'd deleted it from her phone this morning and it was obvious they hadn't looked at his phone. Wasn't it?

Again, she saw the knife. Again, she felt the warm blood on her skin, sticky and meaty-smelling.

She closed her eyes, tried to focus on something else. But when she opened her eyes, Ellen Kelly was looking at her like she knew exactly what Charlotte was thinking. And the smell of blood seemed to linger in the room, mingling with the bleach and the sweat. When she looked at her hands lying flat on the table-top, she imagined she could see blood running down those too.

SIX

'Kieran Burton. Male Caucasian. Twenty-five years old. Mature student at Greenwich University. Doing a Master's degree in Sociology and Politics. In a relationship with Freya Gleeson. Victim's body found at the bottom of Heath Lane, where Freya's parents live. Single stab wound to the front of the body that penetrated the heart. Last night there was a party to celebrate Mrs Gleeson's birthday. It's possible the victim was on his way to or from the party when the attack happened.'

DCI Geraldine Cox stopped her pacing and looked around the room, pausing to make eye contact with each of the four detectives sitting in front of her. Ellen, Abby, Alastair and Malcolm.

'Right,' Ger said. 'What have I missed?'

'We think he was on his way home *from* the party,' Ellen said.

'According to his girlfriend, Kieran was there but he left early.'

'Is she telling the truth?' Ger asked.

'I think so,' Ellen said. 'She also says her mother and Kieran had some sort of disagreement. Charlotte admits she had an argument with someone but she swears it wasn't with Kieran. I think she was so drunk she can't actually remember.'

'Abby?' Ger said. 'You took Freya's statement. What do you think?'

'She was in shock,' Abby said. 'Obviously. It seemed genuine enough. She also says that her mother was rude to Kieran and that's why he left.'

'Rude how?' Ellen asked.

Abby shook her head. 'Freya claims not to know what was said. Just that Kieran was upset and he left.'

'Why didn't she go with him?' Ellen asked.

'She was angry,' Abby said. 'And she wanted to confront her mother, ask her what she'd said to Kieran. But she never got the chance. Says Charlotte started into her after Kieran left and she couldn't take it. So she left too.'

'Have we got a list of everyone who was at the party?'

'Charlotte has given a list of names,' Ellen said. 'People she invited to the party. But she says there were probably others there she didn't know. We've got six officers working through the list, getting statements from everyone.'

Ellen glanced at the clock on the wall behind Ger's head. Three forty-five. She had fifteen minutes.

'There's a backlog at the morgue,' she said. 'Mark's going to try to get the PM done quickly for us, though. Victim's parents are dead. He's got one sister living in Norfolk. We've already been in touch with the boys in Norwich. They'll let us know when they've notified her. With a bit of luck, should be some time today.'

'In the meantime,' Ger said, 'we're keeping the victim's identity out of the press. Not sure how long we can get away with that. You know the girl's father is Nick Gleeson?'

The name was familiar to Ellen but she couldn't place it.

'The restaurateur,' Ger explained. 'The guy behind the Totally Tapas chain.'

'Isn't he …?' Abby started.

'Going into business with Pete Cooper,' Ger confirmed. 'Yes. What some of you may not know is that Pete Cooper has recently come under scrutiny as part of Operation Rift. You're all familiar with that?'

Everyone nodded. Operation Rift was a Met-wide initiative to tackle organised crime in the city.

'Cooper's an influential businessman,' Ger continued. 'Like Nick Gleeson. Runs a chain of furniture stores across the southeast and is a property investor. On the surface, nothing dodgy about him, but there's a strong suspicion his business is being used to launder money from other, less salubrious workstreams. Probably also worth pointing out that Nick Gleeson is a good pal of our very own Detective Superintendent Nicholls. Both members of Royal Blackheath, apparently. And Pete Cooper's a member of the same club too.'

A mess, in other words. Ellen stood up. 'Sorry,' she said.

'It's fine,' Ger said. 'You shouldn't be in today, anyway. Go. I'll call you later.'

'Thanks,' Ellen said. 'What should we do about the press? Want me to pick things up with Jamala?'

Jamala Nnamani was the station's Communications Manager. She managed all dealings with the press. In a case like this, linked to a high-profile local businessman, the press would be all over the murder.

'Let me think about it,' Ger said. 'We can't release the victim's name until his sister's been notified. And I'm not sure how soon we'll want to reveal the connection with the Gleeson family.'

'So we need to make sure they don't get hold of the information before we're ready to share it,' Ellen said.

'That's right,' Ger said. 'But we can talk about that later. Right now I need to get down to the incident room and do the briefing. Malcolm's pulled together a team of officers. They're waiting to be told what to do next. I'll call you, Ellen. I promise.'

Knowing she'd been dismissed and feeling – irrationally – irritated, Ellen said goodbye to the rest of the room and left. She felt bad leaving at such a crucial stage in what promised to be a major investigation, but she had no choice. She'd promised her children – and herself – that work would come second from now on. It was a promise she had every intention of keeping.

* * *

Charlotte stood outside Freya's flat, finger pressed on the door-bell. She knew Freya was inside. She'd looked up at the window as she approached the house and had seen her daughter moving around up there.

She'd come straight from the police station. Almost. A brief detour to The Station pub for a quick restorative, just to get her back on an even keel. Heaven knows, she'd needed it.

When the interview was over, she'd expected to find Freya waiting for her but Ellen Kelly told her Freya had already left.

'She's probably gone home to tidy up,' Ellen said. 'We've finished searching the flat. I'm afraid our officers don't always do the best job of tidying up. I'm sure she could do with a hand?'

She said it as a question, but Charlotte understood the implication. You're Freya's mother. Surely it's a mother's job to help her daughter at a time like this. Well, yes, but Charlotte drew the line at putting on a pair of rubber gloves. She would offer to pay for professional cleaners if she thought Freya would accept that. Knowing her daughter, though, she'd do the whole martyr act and insist on tidying the place herself.

In fact, when Freya finally came to the door and let her inside, Charlotte saw the place wasn't too bad at all.

'I'm glad they didn't make too much mess,' she said, doing her best to sound bright and optimistic because how else were you meant to sound in a situation like this?

'I've spent the last two hours tidying up,' Freya said. 'That's why it's not looking too bad now. I could have done with a hand, to tell you the truth.'

Two hours? Charlotte looked through to the microwave in the kitchen. Green digits on the clock told her it was three minutes to seven. How was that possible? She'd hardly spent any time in the pub.

'The police kept me for ages,' Charlotte said. 'I came over as soon as I could, darling.'

Freya's face closed. A look Charlotte knew too well. Freya was shutting her out. Like she always did.

'Maybe I shouldn't have come,' Charlotte said.

'No,' Freya said. 'You should have stayed in the pub instead.'

The injustice of the comment made Charlotte angry. Before she realised that poor Freya couldn't be thinking straight.

'I'm sorry,' Charlotte said. 'You must be exhausted. I know I am. Why don't you sit down, darling? I'll make some tea.'

She thought Freya was going to object but to her surprise, she nodded.

'Tea sounds good,' she said. 'I should probably eat too. I just can't face it.'

A day without food wouldn't do Freya any harm, although Charlotte was clever enough not to say that. There was a bottle of wine on the worktop in the kitchen. She considered suggesting they open it but was clever enough not to do that, either. Besides, it was red wine and Charlotte didn't think she could face that so soon after last night.

After the tea was made, they sat in the horrible second-hand armchairs Freya claimed were 'full of character'. In fact, they looked cheap and dirty. Freya had got them in a charity shop and every time she sat in one of them, Charlotte couldn't help imagining an old person's corpse slowly rotting in it.

'Did they take much?' Charlotte asked.

'The police?' Freya said. 'They took the laptop. Some of Kieran's college notes. Although what on earth they need with them, I have no idea.'

'Should you have waited until they got a warrant to search the flat, do you think?' Charlotte said.

Freya sighed. 'It's a murder investigation, Mother. As far as they're concerned, everyone's a suspect right now. I'd rather they do things properly. That way, I know there's more of a chance they'll find out what happened to him.'

For the second time today, Charlotte wished Nick was here. He'd always been good with Freya, even when she was at her most challenging. Which, in Charlotte's opinion, was most of the time.

'I've tried calling your father,' she said. 'But his phone is switched off. As usual.'

'You didn't tell him in a message?' Freya said.

'Of course not.' Charlotte frowned. 'I'm not completely stupid, you know.'

'Good,' Freya said.

'You should call him too,' Charlotte said. There was every chance Nick would come running if he knew Freya was trying to speak to him. It was only messages from his wife he seemed to ignore.

'Don't you think I've done that?' Freya said. 'I left a message asking him to call me as soon as he can. I'm sure he will.'

Charlotte was sure he would too. Nothing was ever too much for Nick's precious daughter. In Freya's entire life, Charlotte had never heard Nick say no to Freya. Whatever Freya wanted, Freya got. Which was why, when Freya said she wanted to move out, Nick had bought her this place. Charlotte understood it made sense to help Freya out, get her started on the property ladder. But in Hither Green? Charlotte didn't even pretend to understand the logic behind that decision.

'It happened at the bottom of my road,' Charlotte said, changing the subject to the first thing that came into her head. 'The place was crawling with police and the bottom of the road was all cordoned off with that tape, you know. Like something you see on the TV.'

The look on her daughter's face told Charlotte she'd said the wrong thing.

'This is nothing like TV,' Freya said. 'He's bloody dead, Mother. Christ almighty. He was stabbed.'

Charlotte's heart jumped. She remembered a knife and blood. The shock on her mother's face. She shook her head and Mother disappeared.

'How do you know?' she asked.

Freya looked at her as if she was stupid. 'The police told me. Imagine that. Imagine sticking a knife into someone. Who would do a thing like that?'

The gin and tonics she'd had earlier swilled around Charlotte's stomach. She didn't want to think about it, but her mind refused to let it go. A knife plunging into the skin and up inside his body, puncturing his heart. The burst of blood and the screams. Because he would have screamed, wouldn't he, if someone did that to him? She imagined him staggering back, in agony, his hands over his chest, blood pumping through his fingers.

'It's so horrible,' Freya said. 'Beyond anything anyone could ever imagine.'

Freya's eyes filled with tears and Charlotte wished she could find the courage to wrap her arms around her daughter's shoulders.

'Is there anything I can do?' she asked.

Freya used her sleeve to wipe her face. Charlotte thought about offering a tissue but wasn't sure it was the right thing to do. She thought tissues might be another middle-class affectation her daughter despised.

'Sorry,' Freya said. 'I just … it's so hard, you know?'

And worse with a hangover, Charlotte thought. A part of her wondered at the fact the hangover could keep its hold on her, even in the face of something like this. She'd have thought the shock would obliterate everything else. Seemingly, that wasn't the case. The short-term effect of the earlier drinks was starting to wear off and she felt like death. Again.

Freya's flat was so tiny, Charlotte was able to see into the kitchen from where she sat. She looked longingly at the bottle of wine. Surely at this stage it was okay to suggest a drink? But if she did, Freya would say something cruel, so she kept her mouth shut. She could always drop into The Station again on her way home. If she could last that long.

'Will you tell me about it?' Freya asked. 'I won't mind, I promise. I'd never even ask normally, it's just, now he's gone, I sort of need to know.'

Charlotte wondered what she'd missed. She'd been distracted, thinking about a drink when she should be concentrating on Freya. Self-loathing mingled with a vague panic threatened to turn into something worse. Her breath caught in her throat and she closed her eyes, forcing herself to concentrate. The last thing Freya needed was having to deal with one of Charlotte's panic attacks. Breathe. Focus on the breathing. In, out, in, out. If only the room wasn't so bloody hot.

She stood up, took off her jacket and gave what she hoped was a reassuring smile. Freya stared at her, like she was waiting for her to say something. Charlotte scrabbled through her thoughts, trying to find something she could say that would sound like she was in control of the situation.

'What is it you want to know, darling?'

'You and Kieran,' Freya said.

The clatter started up again in her chest and the roaring in her head blocked out everything else. She could see her daughter's mouth moving but the words, so difficult to grab hold of the words and make sense of them. Something about being angry with Kieran and saying there was something Freya needed to know. Dear God.

'It was nothing.' She'd spoken too loudly. Shouted. Freya shrunk back in her chair. The way she used to when she was very little. Before she'd learned to shout back.

'Sorry,' Charlotte managed. 'I really wasn't angry about anything. Why would I be?'

A look of sneering contempt crept across Freya's face. Something else Charlotte was only too familiar with.

'Maybe you don't remember,' Freya said. 'You were pretty bad last night, even by your standards.'

'It was my birthday,' Charlotte said. Pathetic, she knew. No matter how much Freya hated her, it wasn't as much as Charlotte hated herself. She wished Freya understood that. If she did, maybe she could find it in her heart to … what?

'I'm forty-four,' Charlotte said. 'I hate growing older. You know that. But you're right. I shouldn't have got so drunk. I'm sorry.'

She would have added a promise about it not happening again, but they both knew the promise would never be kept.

'You were angry,' Freya said. 'Told me he didn't deserve me and begged me to leave him. You said all sorts of crazy stuff.'

'Like what?'

'It doesn't matter,' Freya said. 'I'm sure you didn't mean half of it.'

Another wave of self-loathing sucked her down. If only she could remember. She wanted to ask Freya what – exactly – she'd said. But she wasn't sure she wanted to hear the answer. Surely, no matter how drunk she'd been, she wouldn't have told Freya. Would she? She didn't think so. On the other hand, she'd obviously come close.

It hit her all over again. He was dead. For minutes at a time, it seemed so unreal, like someone had made it all up. Then the brutal fact of it slammed into her, shocking her as bad as the first time she'd heard it. And if it was like this for her, what must poor Freya be feeling?

'It's terrible,' she said. 'I'm so sorry, darling. So very sorry.'

'What for?' Freya asked. 'It's not your fault. I mean, it's not like you killed him, is it?'

Charlotte couldn't work out if Freya was joking. Or not. She tried to think of something to say but before anything came to mind the doorbell rang, making them both jump.

'I'll get it.'

Relieved for an excuse to get out of the room, Charlotte ran down the narrow staircase to the front door. She knew who it was before she opened the door. Recognised his outline – tall and broad-shouldered – through the opaque glass.

Fixing her face into a smile, she pulled the door open.

He saw her, took a step back like she was the last person in the world he wanted to see right now. Well tough, she thought. She's my daughter too and if I want to be here with her, that's what I'll do.

'Hello, Nick.'

SEVEN

'I want to sleep on my own tonight.'

Ellen was in the kitchen, tidying up after dinner. She had her back to Pat, hadn't even heard him come into the room. Resisting the urge to turn around, she stayed where she was.

'Okay,' she said, keeping her voice as neutral as she could. 'Good idea. I'll only be next door, anyway, if you need me.'

'And can we watch a film together first? After Eilish goes to bed. Please, Mum?'

She closed her eyes and counted to three. She really needed him in bed early tonight. So much work to catch up on.

'I'm not sure we'll have time for a film,' she said. 'But how about a double episode of *The Simpsons*?'

She risked turning around then, weak with relief when she

saw he was smiling.

'Great,' Pat said. 'Will I go and get it ready?'

'Not so fast,' Ellen said. 'I need to get Eilish up to bed first. Give me half an hour, okay?'

Two hours later and feeling like she'd spent too much time in the company of Homer and his family, Ellen finally got Pat into bed. In his own room. After kissing him goodnight, she stood outside his bedroom for a moment, savouring the rare feeling of jubilation.

Pat's counsellor had assured her – again and again – that Pat was improving. Ellen had noticed changes herself but had been too scared to hope. Tonight, though, she was willing to let her guard down, just for a moment. She was desperate for things to get back to normal before he started secondary school in September. Four more months. Tonight, for the first time, she thought maybe everything was going to be okay.

* * *

'Where's Freya?' Nick stayed on the doorstep, looking at Charlotte as if she'd done something wrong.

'I've been trying to get hold of you all day,' Charlotte said. 'Where on earth have you been?'

His strawberry blonde hair had flopped down over one eye. He flicked his head and the hair swung back. Strange to think she'd once found that move attractive. Until she actually saw him practice in the mirror once when he thought she wasn't looking.

She'd never known a man could be so vain.

He went to push past her but she stood firm. For once they would do things her way.

'Freya!' He shouted over her shoulder, his voice loud, hurting her ear.

'Calm down,' Charlotte said, smile still fixed in place, despite her irritation.

Typical of him to come here before calling her first. It had been like that for as long as she could remember. The two of them against her. She was the outsider and neither of them had ever done a single thing to make her feel included. Acting like they didn't care about her when she was the one doing all the cooking and caring and being the wife and mother she was meant to be.

'Something's happened,' she said.

Again, he tried to go past her. Again, she stood her ground.

'Tell me,' he said. 'Please. It's Freya, isn't it? I've been going out of my mind the whole way over here. I came as quickly as I could.'

'From where?' The question was out before she could stop it.

Something crossed his face, a look she'd seen before. Disdain or disgust – both, maybe – mixed with weariness.

'Does it matter?'

Of course it matters, she wanted to scream. *I'm your wife! Your place is here with me.*

She knew where he'd been. Not the details, of course. It was a different woman every time. She'd hired a private detective once, back when she'd still cared enough. These days, he didn't even bother being discreet about it.

'It's Freya,' she said. 'You're right.'

His mouth fell open and he wobbled, actually wobbled, as if he might fall. Face full of horror giving her a sharp sense of satisfaction. *Gotcha, you bastard.*

He fell against the doorframe, head in his hands.

She put a hand on his shoulder.

'Kieran's dead,' she said. 'We think he's been murdered.'

An electric shock might have elicited a similar reaction. He grabbed her wrists and stared at her with an intensity she had forgotten.

'He's dead?' he said, voice rasping and unnatural. 'You'd better not be fucking with me, Charlotte. If this is your idea of a sick joke, I swear to you ...'

Suddenly, inexplicably, Charlotte felt scared. She tried to pull her arms free but he was holding her too tight. She started talking. Words tumbling over each other as she rushed through it all, not the way she'd planned it but not even caring about that, just wishing he'd stop holding her wrists so tight and stop looking at her like he'd lost his mind.

When she'd finished speaking, he pushed her away and ran into the house, taking the stairs two at a time, shouting for his daughter. Charlotte went after him, got upstairs in time to see Freya falling into his arms, crying and saying thank God he was here, over and over.

Charlotte slid past them and picked up her bag. At least with Nick here, she could leave for the pub without feeling guilty. Besides, it wasn't like she was needed. The last thing she wanted was to sit and watch Nick play the superhero parent while she sat on the sidelines, unnoticed and unwanted.

Outside, the night air was cool and crisp and it felt so good after the stuffy warmth of Freya's flat. Charlotte lifted her face and let the breeze cool her hot cheeks. The lights were on in Freya's flat but the curtains were still open. She could see the shadows of her husband and daughter, moving around inside.

She was better out of it. Freya's grief was suffocating and Charlotte didn't have the skills to deal with it. And with Nick there, it wasn't like anyone would miss her. But even though she told herself this as she hurried down the hill, away from Freya's flat to The Station pub, Charlotte couldn't quite shake off the feeling that – given the choice – she would rather be back there with her daughter, helping her through this, whether it was what Freya wanted or not.

EIGHT

Ellen knew Pat might not want to sleep alone tomorrow night, knew there was every chance a nightmare would wake him later. Even so ... it felt like they'd turned a corner. As she went back downstairs, her spirits were lighter than they'd been at any time over the last five months.

In the sitting room, she put on some music, pulled out her laptop and started going through her work files. She had barely started when her phone rang. Ger, calling for an update.

'I've got Abby looking into Burton,' Ger said. 'The tech guys are trawling through his computer and phone records. Nothing so far.'

'What about his mobile?' Ellen asked.

'The handset and SIM are password-protected,' Ger said.

'Abby's already asked Freya if she knows the code, but she claims she has no idea.'

'Odd,' Ellen said. 'I wonder what was on his phone that he didn't want her to see.'

'We should find out soon enough,' Ger said. 'Abby's managed to get hold of Kieran's sister, Emer Dawson. She's on holiday in the Canaries. She's sorting her flight back and hopes to be in London by Monday at the latest.'

'What about Nick Gleeson?' Ellen asked.

'He's with Freya,' Ger said. 'I got Abby to drop by on her way home. She spoke to both of them. Charlotte wasn't there. I'm not sure what that tells us. Nothing, maybe.'

'Freya and her mother don't get on,' Ellen said. 'I wonder what her relationship with her father is like.'

'Can you look into the family?' Ger said. 'Nick, Charlotte, Freya. Speak to Raj. See what he can tell us about Pete Cooper, Gleeson's business partner.'

'You think there's a link between Cooper and the murder?' Ellen asked.

'It's possible,' Ger said. 'See what you can find out. Think you can handle that?'

The question wasn't meant to be patronising but Ellen felt patronised, nonetheless. Which made her more determined than ever to show Ger Cox what she was capable of. She ended the conversation and got down to work.

She started by building a profile of Nick Gleeson. A self-made businessman, he was best-known for his phenomenally success-ful chain of Spanish restaurants, Totally Tapas. Family-friendly, reasonably priced tapas restaurants, Ellen was familiar with the chain; the local Greenwich branch was a favourite with her and the children.

Gleeson himself had a reputation as a straight-talking, straight-up guy. A family man who gave the impression of being cleaner than clean. No rumours of dodgy business dealings or extra-marital affairs. Nothing. He was also adored by the local media. Ellen found several nauseating interviews with Gleeson, several of them picturing his 'glamorous and supportive wife, Charlotte'. No photos of Freya, Ellen noted.

A search on Freya came back empty. Unlike her mother. Two drunk-driving charges and an alleged assault on a taxi driver. Kieran Burton, too, had been in trouble more than once. In his teens he'd been done for shoplifting, D&D and possession of cannabis. Over the last few years, Burton seemed to have got his act together. A degree in Politics was followed by an MA in Sociology and Politics, which he would never finish.

Ellen thought back to earlier that day. When she'd broken the news about Burton's murder to Charlotte Gleeson. The woman had seemed genuinely upset. Would she have reacted that way if she'd disapproved of her daughter's boyfriend? Probably, Ellen concluded. Death was death, after all. Always tragic, no matter who the victim was.

Too many questions and she was too tired to concentrate.

She shut down the lid of the laptop and stood up. The music had stopped ages ago and the room felt too quiet. Even quieter without Rosie. Ellen wondered why the au pair wasn't back yet. Then she remembered. Rosie was staying over with a friend tonight.

Ellen sent Rosie a text, asking if she was okay. It was unnecessary, Ellen knew that. But she missed Rosie's cheerful, noisy presence. A few minutes later, her phone rang. When she saw Rosie's number on the screen, Ellen answered.

'Hi Ellen, how're things?'

Ellen smiled. Vinny's niece had that effect on her. Her sunny nature was such a tonic. And such a constant reminder of Vinny, too. Although Rosie looked nothing like Ellen's dead husband, the family resemblance was still strong. Rosie had the same irrepressible personality, the same long limbs and the same soft west of Ireland accent that Ellen loved.

'Good,' Ellen said. 'How's your night going?'

'Oh Ellen, it's amazing! I'm at this artists' studio place in Deptford. It's this big old building and all the rooms have been converted into studios. It's some sort of open evening so you can go and see all the artwork and meet the artists.'

'Who are you with?' Ellen asked.

Rosie's talent for digging out interesting people and making friends with them had been a constant source of surprise since the girl arrived in London two months earlier.

'Well,' Rosie said. 'I met Karen earlier and we bumped into

this group of people she knows from Spain. She works with one of them in the market.'

Rosie's best friend Karen had come to London with her. Karen was living with an English family, working as an au pair during the week and helping out at a stall in Greenwich market at the weekends.

'They're awesome,' Rosie said. 'Anyway, one of them, this guy Carlos, he's an artist and he invited us over.'

'What time are you heading back to Karen's?' Ellen asked. 'Don't leave it too late or you'll miss the last train.'

'I'll be grand,' Rosie said, laughing. 'You're some worrier, you know that?'

'Yes,' Ellen said. 'I know that. Listen, go back to your mates and have a great night. Just remember to stay safe and send me a text when you're back at Karen's, okay?'

Hanging up, Ellen's thoughts drifted from Rosie to her children, Pat especially. The elation returned. She wanted to jump up and down, wrap her arms around someone and dance. She wanted to tell someone about tonight's milestone.

She picked up the phone to call her parents. Put it down again. They were on holiday, meant to be having a break from all this. Besides, it wasn't as if Pat was the only one affected by the events that afternoon five months ago. Part of the reason for her parents' holiday was to give Ellen's mother a break. Like Ellen and Pat, she'd been caught up in the whole mess that had resulted in Ellen's house being burnt to the ground. Which was why Ellen and her children were now renting this house beside the park.

Ellen felt the tug of wanting something else. Her hands twitched with the desire to dial another number. She looked at the phone. Such a harmless thing, really. She reached out, touched it. Pulled her hand back as if she'd been burnt.

Five months ago, she'd finally found the courage to call her birth mother. It hadn't gone well and rejection had fuelled the hungry ache that drove her to sit like this, night after endless night, trying to build up the courage to do it again.

Briony, her counsellor, used to say Ellen was looking for closure. Ellen didn't like the word but knew Briony was partly right. She hated the unfinished feel of it. But there was more to it than that. The lack of control, the fact that she couldn't bend things the way she wanted, couldn't make Noreen – her birth mother – speak to her. That was what really got to her.

Like she'd done so many times before, she went back over the night she'd made the call. It hadn't been easy. Heart racing, blood pounding inside her head as she waited. A woman answered. Not Noreen. Ellen knew that straight off. Her mother was Irish. This woman, with her rich, musical Newcastle voice, definitely wasn't Irish.

'I'm looking for Noreen McGrath.'

'Noreen? Of course. I'll just get her for you. Can I tell her who's calling?'

How to answer that?

'I'm an old friend.'

Pause.

'And your name?'

'Ellen.'

'Okay, Ellen,' the woman said. She had a kind voice. 'Let me go and get her. One moment, please.'

An interminable wait and then, here it came. The moment she'd been building up to ever since she lost her mother on a cold and wet night in a high-rise flat in Peckham all those years ago. Down the line, all the way from Newcastle, the sound of someone picking up the phone, breathing down the line.

The rapid build-up of excitement, replaced instantly by confusion. And something else she didn't understand straightaway. In the months that followed, she realised what it was. Anger.

'Ellen?' The same woman who'd answered the phone. Soft, northern, sympathetic. 'I'm sorry. I made a mistake. Noreen's not around right now. Do you want to call back later, maybe?'

She said yes, of course, that would be fine. She would call another time. But she never did.

Her mother had been there that night and had refused to come to the phone. The truth was staring Ellen in the face. Had been staring her in the face all this time. Their mother had left them because she wanted to. Because she didn't love them and probably never had loved them. Because if she had loved her children, she would never, ever have killed one of them.

* * *

Ellen woke, sweating, traces of a dream whispering around the edges of her brain. It took a moment to shake the dream away and work out where she was. Even then, his face stayed with her. Billy Dunston. The man who'd killed her husband, causing a crack in Ellen's perfectly ordered world and changing everything forever.

She'd refused to let it go. Refused to accept a world in which Billy Dunston could carry on living and breathing while Vinny – her beautiful, perfect Vinny – was no longer here.

Moments like this, alone in the dark, lazy silence of the night, she wondered if Dunston's ghost was haunting her. He seemed to be always with her and sometimes she felt she remembered his face, the moment before she shot him, better than she did her own husband's.

Two women walked past the house. The click-clack of their heels and their whispery, giggling voices filling the empty night, drifting into Ellen's bedroom. She pictured them outside, young and pretty and bursting with life.

Billy Dunston's face was still there. Behind her eyes, inside her head. Dead. Ellen lay back on the pillow, closed her eyes. Watched Dunston's face disappear as she held the gun against his head and pulled the trigger. She fell asleep, smiling.

* * *

'What are little girls made of, Charlotte?'

She was playing with her Bella doll and hadn't heard Mother come into the room. Charlotte's tummy started to hurt. She held on tight to Bella and looked down at her dress, searching for stains. She didn't see anything, but that didn't mean much. Often she thought there was nothing wrong but Mother managed to zone in on something Charlotte hadn't even seen.

'Charlotte, dear. I'm waiting.'

'Sugar and spice and all things nice,' Charlotte said.

Mother smiled and Charlotte felt better straightaway. Better again when Mother carefully pulled up the bottom of her tight skirt and crouched down until her face was level with Charlotte's. Mother looked so pretty when she smiled. Charlotte wished that she looked like Mother. Instead of taking after dull old Daddy with his too long legs and his nose that was too big and hair that was dark and nothing like Mother's shiny, blonde, wavy hair that reminded Charlotte of golden candyfloss.

Mother asked Charlotte if she wanted a treat for being such a good girl, and Charlotte nodded and said yes please without even thinking about it. A mistake. The moment she said it, Mother stopped smiling.

Charlotte's tummy rumbled. She tried as hard as she could to make it stop, but it was no good. Even Mother's face wasn't enough to stop it making that horrible noise. Her tummy was trying to tell Charlotte that she was hungry, but she knew she couldn't be. She'd had a bowl of cereal this morning and though that felt like ages ago, Mother told her again and again that she just needed to 'exert some self-control' and if she did that, she'd be fine.

'Maybe we could paint our nails together?' Charlotte asked. Her voice sounded little and far away, which was weird because it wasn't like her body had moved or anything.

But it didn't matter what her voice sounded like. The important thing was that she'd done the right thing. She hadn't asked for a sweetie treat. Painting nails was a good thing to do. Mother was happy now because she knew Charlotte was focussing on what was right instead of being weak like so many women who stuffed their faces and treated their bodies as dumping grounds instead of their single greatest asset.

Mother lifted Charlotte's hand and examined her fingernails.

'Have you been biting these again?'

Charlotte shook her head.

Mother sighed. 'Well, they're horrible. We've got some serious work to do before we can even think about putting varnish anywhere near these. Come with me.'

Mother grabbed Charlotte's arm and dragged her across the room and towards the bathroom. Charlotte remembered the last time Mother had taken her in there to sort her nails out. She started to cry, wishing she was brave enough to tell Mother this wasn't what she wanted. But that would only make Mother worse. 'I'm sorry.' She was crying properly now. Bawling like a baby. Tears mingling with snot, making her look even uglier than she normally did. Bella slipped from her hand. Charlotte managed to grab the string that came out of Bella's back. As she pulled it, Bella started singing the song Charlotte knew off by heart.

Mother didn't hear Bella. She was too busy concentrating on Charlotte's hands. Pulling them together before she wrapped the white tape around them again and again.

And Charlotte was still crying only now no one could hear her because Bella was singing, Mother humming along with Bella's high-pitched doll voice, smiling to herself as Bella reached the chorus:

'Sugar and spice and all things nice.

You know that little girl is mine.'

SUNDAY

ONE

Abby woke early. Streams of sunlight streaked through the gap where she hadn't closed the curtains properly. Sunday morning. A time of rest and relaxation. For others. She checked the time and jumped out of bed, keen to get into work. Keen to get as much done as she could before Ellen showed up.

After a quick shower, she got dressed to a soundtrack of Melt Yourself Down. Sam, the guy she'd got talking to on Friday night, had told her about this band. She'd downloaded the album yesterday and hadn't stopped listening to it since. Much the same way she'd thought of little else except Sam. Which was silly and unprofessional. She was in the middle of a murder investigation. A real chance to prove herself. Especially now Ellen was taking a bit of a back seat. It wasn't that she didn't like Ellen. She adored her. When Ellen wasn't driving her mad. Which was approximately fifty percent of the time. More, maybe. It's just that she was really enjoying the extra responsibility she'd had these past few months.

Of course, Ellen was still the boss. Abby wouldn't want it any other way. Nor would she wish what had happened to Ellen's family on anyone. But there was no harm – surely – in also admitting that she was enjoying the new challenges presented by having to do more work alone, without Ellen's guiding hand always there, checking up on her.

Abby's favourite track, 'Kingdom of Kush', came on and she turned up the volume, losing herself in the funky jumble of blaring horns, pounding drums and tribal beats. Sam said he'd like to meet her again. She'd given him her number, told him to call if he meant what he said. Playing it cool, thinking that was the best approach. Except that was Friday night and it was Sunday already. She'd expected a text, at least, by now. She was starting to think she'd got him wrong. He'd seemed sincere enough but maybe that was just an act. She supposed it wasn't the end of the world if he didn't get in touch. Pride a bit bruised but she'd survive.

She finished applying her make-up and stood back, surveying herself in the mirror. Shiny dark hair, perfectly straightened, framed a face she knew men found attractive. She liked the way she looked. Liked the effect her appearance had on those around her. She didn't think it was big-headed to acknowledge this. Just honest. To pretend anything else was plain stupid.

If Sam didn't call, that was his loss.

In the kitchen, she tidied up and made a cup of coffee, drank it sitting on the balcony, enjoying the brief moment of peace before her day proper began. She ran through the case, planning the day ahead, prioritising what needed to be done. She had some reports to finish off first thing. Including a summary of her telephone conversation with Kieran's sister, Emer. Living in Norwich, currently on holiday in the Canaries, married with two children, working as HR advisor for a large chain of supermarkets.

It had been a difficult conversation. Emer cried through most of it and Abby had struggled to get any sense from her. In fact, Emer seemed more upset than Freya. Although Abby knew as well as anyone that a person's outward reaction was no indication of how they were really feeling.

In front of her, and all around, the Docklands' glass and concrete shimmered and glimmered in the warm morning sunshine. Abby had lived in this apartment for a year now and adored it. Hated knowing she had to leave soon. She tried her best not to think about it, but she couldn't avoid it forever. Lucy raised the topic again yesterday, wondering how Abby's flat-hunting was going and whether there was anything Lucy could do to help. Subtext: when the hell are you going to move out so I can have this place to myself?

Used to getting her own way, Abby felt irrationally annoyed every time Lucy mentioned it. Even though, in fairness to Lucy,

Abby was bang out of order. They'd agreed everything three months earlier, when Lucy first announced that Crispin was moving in.

And now he was here. Abby didn't like Crispin and living with a pair of loved-up lovebirds was far from perfect. But so was moving out. She'd done a bit of searching, realised what sort of place she could afford on her crappy police salary, and gave up almost immediately. As soon as this case was over, she'd concentrate on finding somewhere new to live. First, she had work to do. A killer to find and a new boss to impress. No time to lose.

The DLR journey from Canary Wharf to Lewisham passed quickly. Abby adored the electric train and never grew tired of travelling to work this way. She always experienced a vague sense of disappointment when they arrived in Lewisham and her journey was over.

Off the train, she was almost at the station when she heard someone calling her name. Turning, she saw Malcolm McDonald running towards her, big stomach out in front, wobbling. It looked like a balloon that someone had tied to his body.

'Was about to call you,' Malcolm said. 'Left a message for Ellen, but she hasn't replied yet. You don't know where I can find her, do you?'

'She won't be in until later,' Abby said. 'If she's in at all. You know she's not working weekends anymore?'

Malcolm's white face was shiny with sweat and he wiped it dry with a crumpled navy handkerchief.

'I forgot,' he said. 'I got something on the CCTV this morning, thought Ellen would want to see it straightaway. You think she'll be in later?'

'We don't need to wait for Ellen,' Abby said. 'What is it?'

Malcolm had been allocated the task of trawling through CCTV footage from a camera on Belmont Hill, near the entrance to St Joseph's Vale.

'I'm not sure I should tell you,' he said. 'Wouldn't she want to see it first?'

'Don't be ridiculous,' Abby said. 'Ellen's the last person who'd want us delaying things just because she's not here. Come on, McDonald. Spit it out. What have you got?'

There was a separate viewing room on the ground floor of the station for watching CCTV recordings. When Abby followed Malcolm into the room, she found Alastair already in there. Abby wondered if he ever went home or had any sort of life outside of work.

'Been here all night?' Abby said.

'I've been going through the witness statements,' Alastair said.

'Anything interesting?' Abby asked.

'Maybe,' Alastair said. 'Take a look at this first.'

'There's ten hours of recording here,' Malcolm said as Abby sat down. 'Most of it's useless. I was nearly giving up when we found this. Look, here's the top of St Joseph's Vale. It's dark so it's not easy to see anything, but keep your eyes on the lane when I hit Play. Tell me what you see.'

The screen was frozen. At first, it was difficult to make out anything at all. As she kept looking, Abby was gradually able to distinguish some detail amongst the shadows on the screen. The lighter grey line running horizontally across the screen was Belmont Road. Midway across that, a darker patch indicated the entrance to St Joseph's Vale. A digital clock on the bottom right-hand side of the screen told Abby this scene had been recorded at three minutes past midnight.

When Malcolm hit the Play button, the digits on the clock flickered forward second by second. Apart from that, nothing else happened. At first. A sudden flash of light lit up the screen, head-lights from a passing car as it swept along Belmont Hill. And then, just as the car passed St Joseph's Vale, Abby saw something else.

'Rewind,' she said. 'And move it forward slowly. As slow as you can get it to go.'

The scene replayed again. This time, as the lights lit up the road, Abby kept her eyes on the entrance to the lane. Even in slow motion, it was difficult to know for sure. The hint of a shadow moving across the screen. Looked like it might be a person but could just as easily turn out to be something else. A trick of the light, a shadow cast by the passing headlights.

'Right there,' she said.

The screen froze. Abby stared at the shadow. Too dark to know for sure but ...

'It's a person,' she said. 'But it's odd, they just seem to be standing there.'

'Like they're waiting for someone,' Alastair said.

The figure was almost completely hidden. Impossible to make out any distinguishing features. Almost impossible.

'Rewind a tiny bit,' Abby said.

The headlights reversed back across the screen.

'And now forward again.'

The lights came back. Briefly, so briefly she almost missed it, Abby caught the faintest flash of colour on the upper half of the shadow.

'Look.' She grabbed Alastair's arm as she pointed at the screen. 'Right there, see? What is it?'

'I thought maybe a weapon?' Malcolm asked.

Abby shook her head. 'I think it's a logo.'

The blank expressions on the two men's faces told her they had no idea what she was talking about.

'I'd have thought you Orkney boys would be familiar with that sort of outdoorsy gear,' she said. 'The thing is, I'm sure I know the brand.'

A memory tugged at the edge of her consciousness. She tried to focus on it but it kept slipping out of reach.

'Can we get Rui to take a look?' she said. 'Focus on that image, see what he can do with it. Maybe if I see it more clearly, I'll remember.'

She stood up. At the same time, the door opened and Ellen appeared in the small room. Abby wanted to point out that it was a Sunday and Ellen wasn't meant to be here, but she knew better than to say anything.

'Heard you were here,' Ellen said. 'Would someone like to tell me what you're all looking so happy about?'

TWO

Warm morning sunshine poured through the glass wall and ceiling, drowning the kitchen in white light. It was early enough and the heat from the sun was still mild. At this time of year, the kitchen was bearable. It was only later, in the thick heat of summer, that the room turned into a furnace. Charlotte sat at the island in the middle of the vast space, drinking cups of black coffee and waiting for her husband to come home.

She'd had a late night. Unable to sleep. Going over her interview with Ellen Kelly, replaying each question and the answers she'd given. Trying to convince herself she had nothing to worry about. But as the night grew longer, the details of the interview blurred with other things. Ellen Kelly's rich south London voice turned into her mother's. All high-pitched and Hyacinth

Bouquet. Not asking questions like Ellen Kelly had done. Shouting accusations instead.

Why hadn't Nick come home? She'd left messages for him all through the night. Each one getting angrier in direct proportion to the amount of wine she'd drunk. Nothing she'd said had made the slightest bit of difference. He didn't call her back and he didn't come home. He might have stayed at Freya's, she supposed. But even if he had, he should have told her that.

He told her his time was taken up with his new restaurants. The first one was due to open in a few weeks. But the last time she'd dropped in unannounced at Tipico Totale, there was no sign of him.

Finally this morning, a text.

Home by 10.00.

It was 10.37 now and still no sign of him.

They'd been happy once. But those days seemed so far away, she wasn't sure she could trust her memories of them. This, the miserable nothingness they now shared, had been the reality for so long, it was difficult to imagine she'd ever lived any other way.

She heard his car pulling into the front drive. The low growl of the Beemer's engine as he braked in front of the house. He was a careless driver. Careless about so many things. She'd found that attractive once. Now, it was just another thing that made the sheer fact of his existence a source of rage.

When the front door opened, she tensed, anticipating the row they hadn't yet had.

'Charlotte?'

He'd called her Charlie. At first. Until one day, early in their marriage, she'd told him she didn't like it. Why had she ever said that?

'In here,' she called.

By the time he reached the kitchen she was already preparing a fresh pot of coffee. He favoured Brazilian beans these days. Charlotte poured the beans into the grinder and switched it on, letting the noise drown out everything else. When the beans were ready, she scooped the grains into the cafetière and poured hot water – hot but not boiling because it burns the coffee – over them. She stirred the water and carefully placed the lid on the cafetiere.

Only then did she turn to her husband, standing in the doorway, glowering.

'Coffee?' she held up the cafetiere and gave him her brightest smile. 'Extra strong, just the way you like it.'

He took a few steps into the room but stopped well short of the island where she'd laid out a white cup and saucer, a silver spoon and an exquisite silver pot of sugar. All for him. She was glad she'd managed to get the cleaners in yesterday. He hated coming home to a messy house.

'Place is crawling with press,' he said. 'All huddled together where it happened like a pack of wolves. Christ knows what it will get like for us when they realise he was Freya's bloke. Have you heard anything else?'

Nice to see you too, she thought.

'Not so far,' she said. 'How was last night?'

'How do you think?' He shook his head, sighed. 'I couldn't leave her, Charlotte. Surely you can understand that?'

'Of course.'

She hated him. The way he twisted everything, made it seem like all the problems between them were her fault. All he'd had to do was tell her he was staying at Freya's. If she'd known, then she wouldn't have sat here half the night imagining all sorts of things. And she wouldn't have called him so many times. But she had and he was angry about it and he couldn't see it was his fault, not hers.

'I was worried,' she said. 'That's all. I'm sorry.'

She was always the one who apologised, doing all she could to keep this crumbling marriage together. Knowing it was up to her because if she left it to him, they'd have been divorced years ago.

She lifted the cafetière and carried it across to the island. Her sleeve rode up her arm, revealing the purple marks from where he'd squeezed too tight last night. There were similar marks on the other wrist. Her fair skin bruised so easily. She made a note to get a photo before the bruises faded. Just in case.

'A policewoman came to the flat last night,' Nick said. 'She was pleasant enough but it was obvious she was checking up on us.'

'They won't tell us anything.' Charlotte poured the coffee and watched him move forward and lift the cup without bothering to thank her.

'Why were they here, anyway?' Nick said. 'Surely one of your parties is the last thing Freya would be interested in. She said you and he argued. What was that about? Or have you forgotten?'

He stressed the 'forgotten' and she hated him for it. He was the liar in this relationship, not her.

'Could have been a mugging gone wrong,' Nick said before she had a chance to answer. 'Yeah, that makes sense. I mean, down there at the bottom of the lane. It's quiet at night-time. Taking your life in your hands if you walk through there after dark. So, he comes to the party. Stuffs himself on the free food and booze, bloody parasite. And once he's done that, he pisses off. Too tight to get a taxi, of course, so he walks. Some nutter tries to mug him and it all goes wrong. That sounds about right, doesn't it? I mean, what else could it have been?'

'Why do you care so much who killed him?' Charlotte said. 'I thought you hated him.'

She wanted him to say it was because of Freya. That Freya was his only child and he knew how heartbroken she must be. And that even if Charlotte and Nick hadn't liked Kieran very much, that was irrelevant because Kieran was dead and the only thing that mattered right now was Freya.

Of course, he didn't say any of that. He stuck to the habit of a lifetime by disappointing her and saying exactly what she knew he would.

'It's business. My new restaurant's about to open. I can't afford any scandal. Don't you get that?'

'Of course.'

He drained his cup, leaned across the counter for the cafetière. Charlotte looked past him, to the window with its view over the back garden. A mist of grey clouds moved across the sky, preparing to hide the sun. As the sky darkened, the shadows that had stretched across the green lawn stretched out until the shades of light and dark disappeared completely, as if the very life had been sucked out of the garden, leaving nothing behind.

THREE

Ellen was annoyed and didn't mind who knew it. Abby's explanation, that she hadn't realised Ellen was in the office, was a poor excuse. This was the problem with not working fulltime. Everyone seemed to give up on you.

'It's a bloody murder investigation,' Ellen said. 'Why the hell wouldn't I be at work?'

'Because it's a Sunday.' Abby sounded every bit as pissed off as Ellen felt. 'You don't work Sundays. Remember?'

'I don't work Sundays *normally*,' Ellen said. 'But this isn't a normal Sunday, is it? We have a high-profile murder on our hands. What did you expect? That I'd sit at home playing happy families while you ...'

She stopped just in time. Was about to say: *while you solve the case yourself and claim all the credit.*

'You should have called me,' she said.

She would have said more but Abby's phone beeped with a text message. Whatever the message said, the mood lightened instantly.

Abby smiled. 'Sorry, what was that?'

Ellen nodded at the phone. 'What was that more like? Something you'd like to share with me?'

'A guy I met the other night,' Abby said. 'It's nothing important.'

'Course not,' Ellen said. 'That's why you're grinning like a bloody fool. Well put him out of your head for now.' She undocked her laptop and picked it up. 'I'm going to set up downstairs. Are you coming?'

Abby shook her head. 'Kieran's phone is with the tech guys. I'm going to see if they've got through the password yet. If that's okay with you?'

'Of course,' Ellen said. She should have thought of that herself. Unfairly, she blamed Abby for that too. 'Just make sure you come to me as soon as you find anything.'

The second floor was made up of a series of incident rooms. The largest of these had been set up for the murder enquiry. Ellen found a spare desk where she was able to plug in her laptop. As she waited for it to charge up, she looked around the room. A large whiteboard on the wall at the front; photos of the dead man sat alongside a single headshot of Kieran before he was killed.

Smiling across the room at Ellen, no idea what fate had in store for him. She recognised the image. It had been taken from the photo on the mantelpiece at Ennersdale Road. Freya had been cut out of the photo. Much as Kieran had been cut out of her life.

She turned away from the board and scanned the room. Recognised WPC McKeown in amongst the rows of uniformed officers sitting at desks near the back. Seeming to sense Ellen's eyes on her, McKeown looked up, blushed when she saw who was looking at her.

'How's it going?' Ellen asked, walking over.

'Okay, I think,' McKeown said. 'Just typing up the last batch of witness statements.'

'Anything interesting?' Ellen asked.

'I haven't found anyone yet who remembers seeing Kieran at the party,' McKeown said. 'Freya's the only person who can confirm he was there.'

Maybe Freya was lying, Ellen thought. Or maybe everyone else was too drunk to notice a scruffy student hanging around the edges of the party.

'Good,' she said. 'What else?'

'I spoke to a Dermot Hogan,' McKeown said. 'He was at the party, too. Says Mrs Gleeson was really upset about something. Hogan said he tried to comfort her but it did no good. When I asked Virginia Rau about it – that's Mrs Gleeson's friend – she said Hogan was lying. Her story is that Hogan made a pass at Mrs Gleeson and that's what upset her.'

'But you don't believe her?' Ellen asked.

McKeown frowned. 'I'm not sure. The thing is, Virginia Rau didn't say anything about Mrs Gleeson being upset until I asked her about it.'

'Good point,' Ellen said. 'If this Hogan bloke upset Mrs Gleeson like you say, then it would seem sensible for Virginia Rau to tell you about it straightaway. Good work, McKeown. When you're finished here, why don't you speak to Rau and Hogan again? See if you can find out which one of them's telling the truth. And why one of them would want to lie to us.'

McKeown blushed and smiled simultaneously. It made her look suddenly pretty.

'That's great,' she said. 'Thanks, Ma'am.'

'Ellen!' Abby called. 'Come take a look at this.'

She was holding a mobile phone in her hand. An expensive Nokia model. Ellen recognised it because Sean had the same one. He'd chosen it because you could take high-quality photos with it and he fancied himself as something of an amateur photographer.

'Kieran's mobile,' Abby said. 'Look.'

'Strange,' Ellen said, taking the phone. It jarred with the image she was starting to form of Kieran Burton. Everything she'd seen yesterday told her Kieran and Freya didn't have much money. The phone told a different story.

'What's strange?' Abby asked.

Ellen shook her head, deciding not to share until she knew what the phone meant.

'Doesn't matter.'

She scrolled through the phone, checking texts and call records and scanning the extensive photo album. Landscapes mainly, lots of atmospheric shots of the Thames. Only one photo of Freya. Something else to think about.

'Look at the texts,' Abby said.

A lot of texts from Freya of the practical, rather than romantic, variety. Asking Kieran what he wanted for dinner, giving him a list of things to pick up on his way home, or making arrangements to meet.

And a single text message received at 9.30pm on Friday night. Sent from a number that wasn't in Kieran's list of contacts. Ellen read the message, smiled and handed the phone back to Abby.

'Now we're getting somewhere,' she said. 'Get onto the telephone company. Find out whose mobile number the text was sent from. Good work, Abby.'

Beaming like a giddy kid, Abby took the phone and skipped across the office to her desk. Ellen waited while Abby made the phone call. An interminable wait later, Abby was back, looking – if it was possible – even more pleased with herself.

'You're not going to believe this,' she said.

* * *

They took a pool car. Ellen drove, not trusting Abby to get there quickly enough. At Blackheath, she turned into Heath Lane and drove through the open gates into the gravelled driveway of the Gleesons' house. In front of her, a dark blue BMW was parked carelessly across the driveway. Ellen pulled up behind this and switched off the engine.

The house – three storeys, double-fronted, Georgian – stood in its own half-acre of grounds. Ellen estimated it was worth at least five million. Possibly more.

Together, the two detectives walked up to the impressive porch. Ellen rang the doorbell and seconds later a tall, good-looking man opened the door.

'Can I help you?'

'Mr Gleeson?' Ellen guessed. She showed him her warrant card and introduced herself. She nodded at Abby. 'You've already met DC Roberts, I think. May we come inside?'

'Is this about Kieran?' the man said. 'Terrible business. Terrible. Please. Come inside. What can I do for you, detectives?'

They'd wanted to see Charlotte Gleeson, but having her husband here was a bonus. He stepped to one side, making space for Ellen and Abby to pass.

His hair had flopped forward over one eye. He flicked it back with a throw of his head and flashed a row of white teeth at Ellen. She resisted the urge to cringe.

'Nick,' he said, holding out a hand. 'And you are ...? Sorry, I've forgotten your name already. Terrible with names.'

'DI Kelly,' Ellen said, ignoring the outstretched hand. 'I'd like to ask you a few questions if that's all right.'

'Kelly,' he said. 'My family's from county Kildare originally. How about yourself?'

'Cork,' Ellen said, repelled by his obvious desire to ingratiate himself. 'We'll need to speak to your wife, too. Is she around?'

'I'll call her,' Gleeson said. 'This won't take too long, I hope? I was just on my way out. I was with my daughter all last night. I'm very concerned for her. As you can imagine.'

'Of course,' Ellen said. 'We'll be as quick as we can.'

Gleeson called for his wife and led Ellen and Abby into a large, airy sitting room decorated in various shades of white. The three of them sat on matching floral-patterned armchairs and listened in silence as Charlotte Gleeson's footsteps tottered across the parquet flooring towards the sitting room.

She looked different from the last time Ellen had seen her. Yesterday, her appearance had been dishevelled. Today, she was sleek and elegant in a white trouser suit and patent nude court shoes with a heel that added several inches to her height. Her carefully applied make-up hid the broken veins scattered across her too-thin cheeks and her blonde hair was slicked back and tidy. As she moved across the room, a waft of light, flowery perfume followed.

Ellen and Abby were sitting on a sofa by the fireplace. Nick sat opposite on an identical sofa. Ellen expected Charlotte to sit beside him but she chose a high-backed chair further away, closer to the large bay window that looked out over the well-tended garden. Charlotte crossed her legs carefully and gave

Ellen a nervous smile.

'Have you got some news for us?' she asked.

'Mrs Gleeson,' Ellen said, 'can you sit over here beside your husband, please? We've got several questions to go through. It would be easier if you're both together.'

She hesitated and Ellen thought she was going to protest. But then she smiled and went over to sit by her husband. Ellen noted the way she edged away from him until she was pressed against the side of the sofa.

Ellen looked at Nick. 'Where were you on Friday night?'

'Working.' He gave Ellen another flash of those teeth and she realised she didn't like Nick Gleeson one bit. 'You've probably read that I'm about to open a new chain of restaurants.'

'With Pete Cooper,' Ellen said. 'Yes, I'm aware of that. Is that where you were, then? With Mr Cooper?'

The flop of hair fell forward again. Ellen wondered why he didn't bloody cut it off. Surely everyone else found it as irritating as she did.

'For some of the time, certainly,' he said.

'And the rest?' Ellen asked.

'Well, I had an early dinner with an old college friend,' Nick said. 'Then after that I went back to the office to carry on working. I spent the night there. It's something I do quite often at the moment. When I'm working late I don't like to come home and disturb Charlotte. It's not fair on her, you see.'

'You don't have an office here?' Ellen asked. 'I'd have thought this place is plenty big enough for a home office. It's just the two of you, right?'

'I, well, yes. But I prefer to work at the restaurant,' Nick said. 'Don't like bringing work home. Prefer keeping it separate. Helps maintain that all important work-life balance we're always being told about, you know?'

Ellen glanced at Abby, who nodded. She'd noticed it too. The man was a rubbish liar.

'Setting up a new business,' Nick said. 'It takes a lot of time and hard work. Not many people realise that. People think, you know, that all this,' he spread his arms out, 'that it comes easily. It doesn't, let me tell you. It's the product of years of hard graft. One percent inspiration, ninety-nine percent perspiration.' He smiled. 'A quote from the great poet himself. Do you like poetry, Detective?'

'And you didn't mind that your husband was too busy to find the time to come to your birthday party?' Abby cut in.

Charlotte gave a smile that was as false as it was bright.

'Of course not. Well, naturally I'd have liked him to be here. But it's like Nick says, his business is very important. It takes up all his time. I understand that. Of course I do.'

Ellen was hit by a sudden, unexpected anger. A man had been killed. Their daughter's boyfriend. And here the two of them sat in their tailored clothes and protective blanket of wealth, thinking they could lie their way out of whatever mess they were in. She hated both of them.

'Is that why you were so desperate to see Kieran?' Ellen asked. 'Maybe with your husband not there you decided to turn to your daughter's boyfriend instead?'

The shock on Nick Gleeson's face was genuine, Charlotte went for shock as well except in her case it didn't work. Mainly because the shock was mingled with something else. Fear.

'I'd like you both to come with us to the station,' Ellen said. 'We'll need formal statements from each of you. I hope you haven't any other plans for today but if you have, I'm afraid I've just cancelled them.'

Nick jumped up and started blustering, telling Ellen she was out of order and demanding to speak to her superior. She held a hand up, silencing him.

'Mr Gleeson, I'm asking you – politely – to accompany us to the station. We're dealing with a murder investigation and you'd be wise to remember that. Now, you have a choice. You can come voluntarily, and we'll be very grateful if you do, or I can arrest you and your wife on suspicion of murder and take you with us whether you like it or not. Which is it to be?'

'I can't see you're giving me much choice,' he said.

Ellen smiled, giving him a decent flash of her own teeth.

'Let's go then, shall we?'

FOUR

Ellen knocked on the door of Ger's office and walked in without waiting for an answer. Ger was working on her laptop, the only item on her faultlessly tidy desk.

'A welcome distraction from reporting,' Ger said. 'What can I do for you, Ellen? And don't worry, I'm not even going to ask why you're in on a Sunday. I'm too happy for something to talk about that's not data, data, data. Take a seat.'

'I've got Nick Gleeson and his wife here,' Ellen said, sitting down opposite Ger. 'We're about to question both of them. Do you want to sit in on either interview?'

Ger drew breath in through pursed lips. 'Was that necessary?'

'Was what necessary?'

'Nick Gleeson plays an important role in the local business

community, Ellen. A community we've spent a long time building good relationships with. All I'm asking is if you have a good
reason for questioning them both here. Surely you could have
asked what you wanted at their house?'

'This is because he's a mate of Nicholls,' Ellen said. 'Isn't it?'

'It's got nothing to do with that,' Ger said. 'Tell me why you
brought them in.'

'Gleeson doesn't have an alibi for the night of the murder,'
Ellen said. 'Plus, he's lying about where he was.'

'You sure about that?'

'Positive,' Ellen lied.

Ger frowned. Ellen looked around the office, remembering
the countless times she'd sat here discussing cases with Ed Baxter,
her previous boss. She hadn't realised how much she missed him
until she got the news, two months ago, that he'd passed away.
Finally defeated by the cancer that had forced him into an early
retirement.

'Have you heard from Andrea recently?' she asked, referring to
the widow of her ex-boss.

'Spoke to her last week,' Ger said. If she was surprised by the
sudden change of topic, she didn't show it. 'She's doing okay,
considering. Still misses Ed, of course. Says she can't imagine that
will ever change. But you'd know how that feels, I imagine.'

Ellen nodded.

'She asked after you,' Ger said. 'You should go and see her.'

'I will,' Ellen said, meaning it.

'Good.' Ger pushed her chair back and stood up. 'Let's go and see Nick Gleeson then. If nothing else, I can make sure you don't antagonise him any further than you have to. What about his wife? Any reason to drag her in as well or was it just more convenient?'

'Far from it,' Ellen said. 'In fact, when I tell you, I think even you'll agree I've done the right thing.'

* * *

Charlotte's stomach growled, startling her, the rumbling too loud in this silent room. A burst of acid burned its way up her gut, pain so bad she doubled over. When it had passed, she sat up, leaning against the hard back of the wooden chair, waiting for her breathing to slow down. The room felt too hot but it was difficult to tell if that was her own body, over-heating as it tended to do, or if the temperature was actually too high.

A polystyrene cup stood on the plain wooden table in front of her. It contained something they'd told her was coffee. One sip was enough to convince her not to touch it again.

Abby, the pretty police woman – detective, rather; wasn't that what she was meant to call them? – had brought her here, fetched the coffee and left her alone. Charlotte called after her, asking how long she'd have to wait, but Abby had closed the door without answering.

The rumbling in her stomach stopped, replaced by a nagging nausea. She tried to remember the last time she'd eaten. A sandwich after she'd left Freya's house yesterday; nothing since then.

Is that why you were so desperate to see Kieran?

On the drive over, sitting in the back of that horrible little car, squashed up beside Nick, she tried to convince herself it was nothing. A stupid text. That's all. She couldn't even remember sending it. She'd only seen it when she'd checked her phone yesterday.

Random images from Friday night battered the inside of her head. A mix of noises and smells. A man's face. Rain on her cheeks as she ran across the heath. Or was it tears? The burning taste of vomit in her throat. Through all of it, she searched for Kieran but he wasn't there.

The door swung open and two women came in. Ellen Kelly and another one she hadn't seen before. This new woman was tall too, but blonde. And stunning. Dressed in a beautifully cut black trouser suit that screamed Jasper Conran. When she sat down, she crossed her legs, revealing a pair of smart leopard-print court shoes with a thin heel. Charlotte recognised the shoes because she had the same pair herself. Kurt Geiger, from the spring collection.

She felt something close to relief. Here was someone she could relate to. She smiled, focussing her attention on her ally.

'I was starting to worry you'd forgotten me. This won't take too long, will it? I'm hoping to get across to my daughter later this morning.'

The blonde introduced herself, not bothering to return Charlotte's smile.

'I'm Detective Superintendent Ger Cox, Mrs Gleeson. I understand you've already met my colleague, DI Kelly. Thank you for coming in this morning.'

'I didn't have much choice about it.' Charlotte made sure to smile when she said it, not wanting to provoke them.

'We're very grateful you did,' the blonde woman said. What did she say her name was? Something unusual. 'I'll get straight to the point. Can you tell us, please, about your relationship with Kieran Burton?'

Is that why you were so desperate to see Kieran?

'He was my daughter's boyfriend,' Charlotte said. She gave a little laugh. 'Or *partner*, as Freya insisted on calling him. Apparently "boyfriend" is an out-dated term that implies, oh I don't know what it implies. Something that's offensive to women, I think. Freya has all sorts of odd ideas about things like that.'

'Things like what?' Ellen asked.

Charlotte would have thought that was obvious and wasn't surprised it was Ellen who asked the question not her colleague who, Charlotte guessed, understood exactly.

'Oh you know, relationships and her *role* as a woman and being an equal partner in the relationship. All nonsense, of course, but it's no use telling her that. I've tried, believe me. She won't listen. Thinks she knows best. Always has done. I mean, what on earth is wrong with finding yourself a decent man and marrying him?

Why do young women today think that's such a terrible idea?'

'Charlotte,' Ellen said, 'when we spoke yesterday, you told me you didn't remember seeing Kieran at the party.'

'I don't,' Charlotte said. 'I'm not making that up. I'd had a lot to drink. It was my birthday, you see.'

'You also told me you had an argument with someone at the party,' Ellen said.

Charlotte's mind darted back to yesterday. Sitting in a room like this, Ellen firing questions at her. The hangover making everything else impossible. Her mouth was too dry. She picked up the cup, remembered what the coffee tasted like and put it down. Licked her lips twice before she spoke.

'I can't recall the details,' she said.

A man's face.

'But it wasn't Kieran. I'm sure of that.'

'How can you be so sure?' the blonde one asked. 'When you seem to remember so little else.'

Her hands on his chest, pushing him away.

Because I wouldn't have pushed Kieran away.

'I just am,' she said. 'He was some guy who tagged along after the bar. Dermot or Declan or ... Look, I've already told you.'

'I know,' the blonde woman said. Charlotte tried to remember her name. Jerry? No, not a man's name. 'It was your birthday.'

Rude of her, Charlotte thought. Still, maybe she had gone on a bit too long. They were probably as keen as she was to get this over with.

'Anything else?' the blonde asked.

Ger! That was her name. Charlotte smiled, relieved. It was okay. Going to be fine. Ger Cox, with her lovely suit and shoes, didn't know. No one knew. Charlotte's smile widened as her body started to relax.

'Why did you want to speak to Kieran?' Ellen asked.

They'd checked his mobile, of course. They hadn't told her that's what they'd done but she'd worked it out herself. Wasn't that what they did when something like this happened? They went through the victim's phone records to see who he'd been in contact with in the days before he died. Funny to think of a scumbag like Kieran as a victim. Funny if it wasn't so terrible.

I need to see you.

She groaned before she could stop herself. Stopped when she saw both women staring at her.

'I was drunk,' she said. 'And I'd got it into my head that I wanted him to propose to Freya. Call me old-fashioned, but it made me uncomfortable the way she'd shacked up with him so easily. I didn't want her to make things that easy for him. I thought, you see, she deserved better. I wanted to tell him that.'

She tilted her head and lowered her gaze, smiling slightly. The Princess Di thing that usually worked on people who didn't know her very well.

She looked up again, still smiling, eyes connecting with Cox's startling blue ones.

'It was silly of me,' she said. 'But what can I say? Too much wine made me emotional. I decided my little girl should have someone with her who could take care of her.'

She supposed, if she ever had to go to court, she'd have to swear that what she was saying was the truth, the whole truth and nothing but the truth. It wasn't, of course, but under the circumstances, this was as close as anyone was ever going to get to nothing but the truth.

Because the truth would break Freya's heart and no matter how difficult her daughter was, Charlotte would not let that happen. She might not be the best mother in the world but she could do that, at least.

They asked her some more questions, going around the same things over and over again. Trying to trip her up. But she was prepared today and she gave the same answers each time. No, she didn't see Kieran at the party. No, she had no reason to argue with him. Yes, she had sent a text but only because she had her own daughter's interests at heart. What mother wouldn't want the best for her child?

By the time they let her go, she was tired but jubilant. She had performed well. Hadn't said anything stupid or told them something she shouldn't have. She stood outside the station, wondering if she should wait for Nick. Told herself there was no point. She had no idea how long he would be.

It was Sunday afternoon and the sun was shining. She deserved a drink after all that. She looked around for a black cab, doubtful of finding one easily here in Lewisham. But her luck was in.

There, driving slowly down the street like he was looking for his next fare. Like he was looking for her.

Charlotte ran down the steps that led from the front door of the station to the street below, her hand already out. The cab slowed down, pulled into the side of the road, waiting. Charlotte jumped in the back, smiling at the driver's face in the rear-view mirror.

'The Princess Louise,' she said.

Within ten minutes, she was standing at the bar ordering a glass of Sauvignon Blanc.

'Large, medium or small?' the girl serving asked.

'Large,' Charlotte said.

The girl poured the wine, slid the glass across the bar and took the ten pound note from Charlotte's outstretched hand. Sunlight streamed through the front windows of the pub, catching the colours in the wine, green and gold shot through with silver.

When she lifted the glass, the colours shimmered and shifted and Charlotte thought she'd never seen anything so beautiful.

FIVE

So far, the interview with Nick Gleeson had told Ellen nothing she didn't know already. Like his wife, he'd had plenty of time to get his story worked out.

'So let me get this straight,' Ellen said, giving it one last try. 'On Friday night, instead of going to your wife's party you stayed at work?'

'Correct,' Gleeson said. 'I've already explained all this to you.' He looked at Ger and smiled. 'As I'm sure you understand, Detective Superintendent, I'm a busy man. I'm afraid there are times in my life when work has to come first. Friday night was one of those times.'

'You have a very understanding wife,' Ger said, returning the smile.

Nick sighed. 'Something like that. The truth is.' He leaned

across the table like he was about to reveal a big secret. 'Charlotte and I, we've grown apart over the last few years.'

Ellen rolled her eyes. She was getting bored with this.

'You sleep at the office?' she asked, putting emphasis on the word office to express her disbelief.

'Ah,' Gleeson said. 'I actually have a small apartment that I use from time to time. I don't like to come home late and disturb Charlotte. Especially given that things are a bit tense between us. She can be somewhat unpredictable, you see.'

Ellen interpreted 'small apartment' to mean shag pad. Nick Gleeson had a mistress. She saw the pink tinge in Ger's face and knew Ger had picked it up as well.

'You'd be happy to give us the address of your apartment?' Ger said.

Gleeson nodded. 'Of course. Um, the only thing is, Charlotte doesn't know. She wouldn't like it, you see. She already thinks – well, she suspects I'm seeing other women.'

'I wonder why she'd think that,' Ellen murmured.

Gleeson's face coloured. 'You can be as snide as you want, Detective Kelly. You don't know what it's like, living with an alcoholic.'

Freya had implied something similar about Charlotte and even though she didn't like Nick Gleeson at all, Ellen felt a twinge of sympathy for the slimey git.

'I get the impression Charlotte and Freya don't see eye to eye,' she said.

'Freya hates her mother,' Gleeson said. 'And frankly I don't blame her. She's grown up watching Charlotte drink herself to death.'

'If things are that bad,' Ger said, 'why don't you leave?'

Gleeson's hair flopped down in front of his eyes. Again. He shook his head, flicking the hair away from his face. Again.

'She's unpredictable,' Gleeson said. 'I worry what she might do if I wasn't there to take care of her.'

'Except from what you've told us, you're not there very much anyway, are you?' Ger said.

Nick sighed. 'I do my best.'

They asked him some more questions but didn't get anything interesting from him. Ger told him he was free to go.

'I hope I've been some help,' he said, shaking Ger's hand and gazing into her eyes with a look of such fake sincerity it was all Ellen could do not to drag him back into the interview room and give him a further grilling. 'And that you find whoever did this before too long.'

'I'm sure we will.' Ger gave him her best smile. 'We'll be in touch shortly.'

'Of course,' Gleeson said. He let go of her hand and reached inside his coat pocket, pulling out a silver business card-holder.

'My details.' He handed a card to Ger. 'Office and mobile numbers are both there. Call whenever you need to.'

Ellen, standing behind Gleeson, pretended to stick her fingers down the back of her throat. Ger ignored her as she ushered

Gleeson down the corridor.

'What a creep,' Ellen said, when Ger returned.

'Couldn't agree more,' Ger said. 'I don't like him. Or trust him. So, now we've seen both of them, what do you think?'

'I think she's lying about why she sent that text,' Ellen said. 'And I think he's having an affair.'

'Why not give us a name?' Ger said. 'If he was with someone on Friday night, then that's his alibi sorted.'

'Maybe he meant what he said about Charlotte,' Ellen said. 'If she's as unpredictable as he says, who knows what she might do if she found out he was seeing someone else?'

'She already knows he's screwing around,' Ger said. 'I'd put money on it. It could even be the reason she started drinking. And we still don't know why she sent that text. I wonder if there was something going on between her and Kieran?'

'Her daughter's boyfriend?' Ellen said.

Ger shrugged. 'Why not? She must get lonely sitting in that big old house waiting for a husband who never comes home to her.'

'Okay,' Ellen said. 'So let's say there was something going on between Charlotte and Kieran. That would explain the text. If Nick found out, it would explain why he didn't turn up at her birthday party. And if he thought Burton – his daughter's boy-friend – was shagging his wife, there's our motive.'

'It's a motive for Freya, too,' Ger said. 'If she knew about it. But that's all we've got. If, if, if. We need more. Call Pritchard. Get an update on the PM. The tech team are going through

Burton's computer and online profile. He didn't seem to be big on social media, but he had a cloud storage account which he used for college stuff and photos. Lots of photos, apparently.'

'I saw some of them on his phone,' Ellen said. 'Landscapes, I think.'

'River scenes,' Ger said. 'I was going to ask you to look through them all. Pritchard first, though.'

Ger had obviously forgotten Ellen wasn't meant to be here. Which was good. Ellen would much rather be here, in the thick of things, than spending time alone with her own thoughts.

Mark answered the phone straightaway.

'Ellen. I was just about to call you. I finished the PM on your bloke this morning. Bloody starving now. I don't suppose you're free to meet for lunch? I can go through the PM with you then.'

Ellen was 'bloody starving' herself. The thought of lunch with Mark was tempting, but she had so much to do.

'I'd love to,' she said. 'But I can't. Not if I want to get out of here in time to see my kids before they go to bed.'

'Ah well,' Mark said. 'Another time, maybe?'

'Sure,' Ellen said. 'So, what have you got for me?'

'The killer got it right first time,' Mark said. 'Single knife stroke through the lower thoracic wall, puncturing the lower right ventricle. He would have died pretty quickly.'

'Would the killer have known what they were doing?' Ellen asked.

'Difficult to say,' Mark said. 'A few centimetres either side and there's a chance the knife would have hit bone, preventing it from going too far in. On the other hand, he'd still have died unless he got medical treatment pretty quickly. Even if our killer completely missed the heart, no one found him until the next morning. He'd still have been dead by then.'

'If I was trying to kill someone,' Ellen said, 'I'm not sure I'd know how to make sure I hit the heart first time.'

'That's reassuring,' Mark said. 'The killer used a knife with a thick blade. Similar to many of those you've seen in other knife killings recently. Apart from one thing.'

'What's that?'

'With most of the stabbings across Lewisham,' Mark said, 'the killer has used a hunting knife. It's the most common knife used in gang killings, for example. Sorry, you know that already. With Kieran Burton, the knife had a smooth blade. You can tell from the wound.'

A moment ago she'd been starving. Now, Ellen felt as if she would never want to eat again.

Mark had nothing else useful to tell her and Ellen finished the conversation and went to find Abby. She wanted to make it perfectly clear that she would be here all day. This was Ellen's case and she wasn't about to sit back and let Abby try to take it from her.

SIX

There were too many people crowded into the flat. Freya couldn't move, could barely breathe. Stevie and Anna were in the kitchen making some sort of vegetarian curry that was stinking the flat out and she knew would taste of nothing except cauliflower and curry powder. Alex and Paula hovered around the sitting room, treating her like she was some sort of mad woman in an attic about to crack up. Slash and Johnno and Mac were all sitting on the floor, backs against the wall, passing a joint back and forth between them, stoned and talking several shades of shit.

Freya wanted to scream at them all to go away and leave her in peace.

'I've made some more tea.'

Alex was back, carrying a tray and putting it on the ground at

Freya's feet. Like an offering, Freya thought sourly.

Alex folded herself onto the floor beside the tray, crossing her long, skinny legs. She wasn't wearing a bra, she never wore a bra, and Freya could see her skinny breasts hanging down as Alex leaned in to pour the tea. Freya looked away quickly, repulsed.

'None for me,' she said.

'You sure?'

The sympathy and kindness in Alex's face was unbearable. Freya stood up and went into the bedroom, the only room in the house that didn't have anyone else in it. She sat on the bed and closed her eyes. Impossible to imagine this was her life from now on. Alone in this flat that she'd never wanted in the first place. Getting onto the property ladder was Kieran's idea. He'd convinced her, somehow, that owning their own home didn't make them capitalists.

'It gives us freedom to make some important choices,' he'd said. She hadn't agreed but, as always, she'd let him talk her around. And all for nothing, as it turned out. Because he wasn't here anymore and it was up to her to make all the choices on her own.

A knock on the bedroom door and Alex's head appeared.

'Okay if I come in?' Without waiting for Freya to answer, Alex came and sat on the bed and put her arm around Freya's shoulders. It took everything Freya had not to shake her off.

'I'll go if you want,' Alex said.

Freya shook her head. 'It's okay.'

It wasn't okay but she didn't know how to say that without

revealing what she knew. She'd promised Kieran she wouldn't say anything. But then Alex squeezed her shoulders and it triggered such a surge of anger she couldn't keep quiet.

'Please,' she said. 'Don't start pretending now that you care about me.'

The look of hurt on Alex's face almost made Freya want to laugh. And slap Alex's pale, pretty face at the same time.

'I know,' Freya said.

Alex shook her head, frowning like she had no idea what Freya was talking about.

'You and Kieran,' Freya said. 'What? You think he wouldn't tell me something like that? Jesus, Alex. You're meant to be my friend.'

'I *am* your friend,' Alex said. 'That's why I … look, Freya. I don't know what Kieran told you, but nothing happened between us. I swear to you.'

'Only because he wouldn't let it,' Freya said.

'Oh Freya,' Alex said, voice dripping with a sickening pity that made Freya hate her more than any betrayal. 'Is that what he told you? My poor love.'

'Shut up!' Freya jumped up and opened the door. 'Shut up and get out. I don't want to hear it.'

Alex stood up but she didn't leave the room.

'Freya, don't do this. You're my friend. I love you very much.'

Freya put her hands over her ears, refusing to listen to another word. Love. Alex threw the word around like loving someone was an easy, effortless thing. Like it didn't require hard work and commitment and having your heart broken so many times it was like you could stop feeling things altogether.

Alex, with her long legs and her perfect face and her little pert breasts, what could someone like that know about love?

'He didn't deserve you, Freya,' Alex said. 'I hate saying it but it's the truth.'

'Get out!'

Freya was vaguely aware of the others coming to see what was going on. Faces peering at her, pitying her. She knew what they were thinking, what they'd always thought, but they'd been too cowardly to say it to her face when he was alive. Now he was dead it would all start. The secrets and the lies they'd hidden from her. All of them finding a quiet moment to tell her what he was really like.

Swarming around her, murmuring their meaningless words of sympathy, pretending they were sorry for her loss when all of them – every single one of them – really believed she was better off without him.

Closing in on her, with their stinking smell of weed and patchouli and dirty hair. She lashed out, wanting so badly to hurt someone. To thrash her way through the glazed eyes and the swinging dreadlocks and the baffled pity on their unknowing faces. All of it spinning around her, faces and voices and smells and she was falling, spinning down and away and she could hear her own voice, shouting at them, but she sounded so far away and she didn't know how she could stop this.

'Freya.'

And just like that, she wasn't falling anymore. Her father was here, and his arms were around her, holding her tight, keeping her safe. Just like he always did.

SEVEN

The flat stank of curry and dope. Nick had opened the windows but it didn't seem to make much difference. He had succeeded in kicking Freya's friends out, but their smell remained. He should probably speak to her about the dope but now wasn't the time. The poor kid was a mess. Nick tried to put himself in her position and knew he would be just as bad.

'I wish there was something I could do,' he said.

They were sitting together on her small sofa, Freya curled up against him the way she used to when she was a little girl.

'You're here,' she said.

'I'm always here for you, princess. You know that.'

His arm was around her shoulders and he twisted his wrist so he could see his watch without her noticing. Two twenty. He had to be at the apartment by three but that wasn't a problem. He'd been here two hours already. When he told her he had to go, she would understand.

The book he'd brought sat beside him on the arm of the sofa. A collection of poems about loss and death. One of his father's old favourites. He wanted to read her something but when he'd suggested it she'd frowned and said a stupid poem was the last thing she needed right now. He'd been disappointed by her reaction but did his best to hide how he felt. Told himself she couldn't know what she was thinking or saying. Maybe he'd give it another go before he left.

After his mother died, poetry was the thing that held him and his father together. Every night, the old man would sit by little Nick's bed and read to him. Their favourite poem was 'When You are Old'. Dad would recite the lines, tears pouring down his face as he thought of his dead wife who would never grow old and grey.

'None of it feels real,' Freya said. 'I mean, it's like this sort of stuff only happens to other people. Do you know what I mean? Paula said I should do something. Like a memorial, you know? She says it's important. What do you think?'

Nick was thinking about later. Thinking he could be a few minutes late and it wouldn't make any difference. Might even be better that way. Let her arrive first and get ready for him. He would text her along the way. Tell her to get undressed and start thinking about what he was going to do to her.

'Dad!'

'Sorry, love. What was that?'

That was the problem with being in love. It distracted you, made it difficult to focus on the things that really mattered. Like Freya. And the fact that he'd spent his morning being interrogated by the police.

His throat constricted at the memory. The two women – supercilious and smug – treating him like a common or garden criminal. Acting like they knew something even though he was certain they couldn't because if they did, wouldn't they have said?

No.

He had to stop this. Had to stay calm.

The police didn't know. This morning was nothing more than a fishing exercise. He was no more of a suspect than anyone else at this stage. Less of a suspect than Charlotte, in fact. What the hell had she been thinking? When the police told him about the text she'd sent, he'd thought at first that she knew. And in that moment, his overwhelming reaction had been relief. Because if Charlotte knew, then it was all out in the open and he could stop pretending. But no. It seemed she had no idea. So what was she playing at?

'Freya, love.'

'Yeah?'

He hated doing this, knowing it might make things worse than they already were for her, but he didn't see that he had a choice. He had to know what Charlotte was up to.

He cleared his throat, trying to find the best way to ask her.

'The police,' he said. 'Well, the thing is, they told me that your mother sent a text to Kieran on Friday night.'

She didn't say anything but he could feel her body stiffening. He wished he could see her face so he would have some idea what she was thinking. But curled into his side like this, all he could see was the top of her head.

'Freya?'

She sighed. 'Oh Dad, you know what she's like. She was out of her head on Friday night. Really bad. She … well, she had this fixation about Kieran. She even said … no. It doesn't matter.'

'Of course it matters,' Nick said, forcing himself to sound calm even though he didn't feel it. Bloody Charlotte. What the hell had she said?

'Freya.' He shook her gently. 'You've got to tell me.'

'Why?'

'It could be important. And even if it's not, I'm your dad. I want to know so I can help you.'

'Okay.' She sniffed. 'But I warn you, it sounds crazy.'

'Crazy?' he said. 'Charlotte? No way.'

At least that got a laugh.

'Well there was a bit of the usual stuff,' Freya said. 'You know, he's not good enough for me and I could do so much better and blah, blah, blah. But then it all got a bit weird, to be honest. She started saying he was evil and someone needed to stop him.'

The fear again. Like fingers of ice squeezing the life from his body.

'What did she mean?' he asked.

Freya shrugged.

'Fucked if I know.'

He winced, hating to hear her swear.

'Sorry,' she said. 'Anyway, who cares? She was drunk and ranting. Pretty much her normal state, wouldn't you say?'

Drunk and ranting and violent. Grabbing a knife and lashing out at the person she wanted to hurt. The more he thought about it, the more he could see how easy it was to imagine she'd done it.

A memory of a long ago night. A full moon, huge and yellow. Highlighting the streaks of blood on Charlotte's arms and reflecting off the silver blade of the knife she was holding. Tears running down her face, telling him over and over again that she was sorry, she didn't mean it, sorry.

The fear receded. Replaced by a timid, flickering ray of hope. If the police thought Charlotte had killed Kieran, they would lock her up. She'd be out of his life once and for all.

He shook his head, told himself he was being stupid, fanciful. Maybe. But with good reason. She'd done it before. Who was to say she wouldn't do it again?

EIGHT

'It's such a mess,' Charlotte said. 'And you know the worst of it? I can't help thinking it's all my fault, somehow.'

'That's silly,' Ginny said.

The wine bottle was empty. Ginny waved at Jacques, the bartender, indicating they wanted a replacement.

Charlotte wasn't even sure she felt like another drink. But what else was there to do? The thought of going home to that big, empty house alone was too depressing for words.

'I wish I knew she was okay,' she said.

'Freya?' Ginny asked. 'It can't be easy for her. Especially if things between her and Kieran haven't been so great recently.'

A flutter of fear in Charlotte's stomach. She hadn't said anything to Ginny. Had she?

'What do you mean?'

Ginny shrugged, trying to pretend it was no big deal. But Charlotte knew her too well. Knew there was something her friend wasn't telling her.

'Ginny?'

'It's nothing,' Ginny said. 'It's just, when I asked her at the party how he was, she seemed ... angry, I think. But maybe it was something else. She wasn't herself at all on Friday night. I thought it was because ... oh, never mind. Listen to me, going on about nothing. What about you? Was it terrible today with the police? They're pretty relentless, aren't they?' Ginny shuddered. 'I've already been interviewed twice by some jumped-up little tart in a uniform.'

Jacques appeared with another bottle of the Sauvignon Blanc. The basement wine bar had been Ginny's idea. She'd got a thing for Jacques, the owner, and these days it was difficult to get her to go anywhere else.

Not that Charlotte was complaining. The place had a decent wine list and never got too packed. Plus, the last few times she'd been here it had stayed open late enough to sate even her appetite for wine.

A mellow, jazz soundtrack played in the background – Miles Davies, one of Nick's favourites. Thinking of her husband, some of her earlier rage returned.

'The police were horrible,' she said. 'Nick was worse, though. I swear, Ginny, he's acting like he thinks I actually killed Kieran myself. And part of me can't blame him for that. Because he knows what I'm capable of.'

Ginny put her hand over Charlotte's.

'Listen to me,' she said. 'That's all in the past, Lottie. The only people who know what happened that night are you, your mother, me and Nick. Your mother's dead and there is no way in the world I'll ever speak about it. Nick won't either. He cares too much about his precious reputation. And that leaves you. You can't bring that up now. You do understand, don't you?'

Charlotte nodded. She knew Ginny was right. It was just so hard. She'd thought about little else ever since she'd heard how Kieran had died.

'Maybe if he'd been killed some other way,' she said. 'It would be easier to separate the two things.'

Ginny refilled both their glasses and replaced the bottle in the wine cooler.

'You'd better find a way of doing it,' she said.

'It doesn't help that I can't talk to Nick about it,' Charlotte said. 'He acts like he hates me.' She sniffed, letting herself be consumed by self-pity. 'It's silly, isn't it? I thought in times of crisis, couples were meant to pull together. But it's like this has had the opposite effect. However bad things were before, they're a million times worse now. You know what he told me? He said if I hadn't been such a drama queen and insisted on having a party that no one wanted, then there was every chance Kieran would still be alive. How callous is that?'

Ginny held Charlotte's hand tighter. 'Darling, I know we've had this conversation before, but don't you honestly think your life would be so much better if you left him? The man's a total bastard and he treats you so badly. Has he told you where he was on Friday and Saturday night yet?'

Charlotte pulled her hand away, resisting the urge to cover her ears. Why did Ginny have to start on about all that, now of all times?

'Don't,' Charlotte said. 'I can't talk about it. You know that.'

It was so easy for Ginny, who ditched husbands at the drop of a hat. Charlotte wasn't like that. She'd been brought up to believe in marriage and, by God, if it was the last thing she did, she would make her own one work. Because without her marriage, what was she? Nothing.

'Okay,' Ginny said. 'Sorry. Let's talk about Kieran instead. Do the police have any suspects yet?'

'Apart from me, you mean?'

'They don't really suspect you,' Ginny said. 'You know that. They're just going through the motions. It's something they have to do, I expect.'

She wished she could tell Ginny that it wasn't that simple. That she'd done something so stupid she would regret it for the rest of her life. And then she'd compounded it by sending him a bloody text saying she needed to see him. She tried – again – to trawl through her memories of Friday night, wondering at what point she'd got so desperate that she'd sent the text. Nothing came to her, though. Again. All she could remember was the sudden, blinding clarity that came with her decision to tell Freya to leave Kieran. She'd been so certain it was the right thing to do.

'We had a row,' Charlotte said. 'Kieran and I. Do you remember that?'

Ginny frowned. 'I don't remember seeing Kieran at the party at all. Are you sure about that?'

'Maybe I rowed with him outside somewhere,' Charlotte said. 'I'm not sure.'

'If you're not sure,' Ginny said, 'then how do you know it's what you did?'

'Freya told me,' Charlotte said. 'She said I was really angry with him about something.'

Ginny opened her mouth to speak, then seemed to change her mind at the last moment.

'What?' Charlotte asked. 'What's the problem?'

'Nothing,' Ginny said. 'I'm just thinking, if you did have some sort of argument, chances are the police will hear about it sooner or later. If I was you, I'd speak to Freya as soon as possible and find out what the hell she's talking about.'

'You think it's important?'

Ginny grabbed her hand and squeezed it tight. 'He's been murdered, Lottie. Of course it's important. Believe me, you'll want to be ready with a story by the time the police come knocking on your door, asking why the hell you argued and did it make you so angry you decided to kill him?'

Charlotte took a slug of wine as she tried to think of something funny to say that would lighten the mood. Nothing came to her. Instead, all she could think of was the one thing she couldn't say, not to Ginny, not to anyone. That she had loathed Kieran Burton more than any other human being and that the absence of his painful presence in her life was a thing to be celebrated, not mourned.

NINE

At eight o'clock, Abby saved the file she was working on and switched off her PC. She pushed her chair away from the desk and stood up, rolling her shoulders, stiff from hours hunched over the computer keyboard.

The office was quiet at this time in the evening. Apart from Abby, the only other person still here was Alastair. Nothing unusual about that; Alastair was always here. Abby walked to the door and glanced down the corridor. The door to Ger's office was open, meaning the boss was still here too.

Abby walked along the corridor towards the toilets, slowing down as she passed Ger's office, hoping to be noticed. It worked.

'Still hard at it?' Ger called.

'I really want to be on top of things,' Abby said. 'Ellen's always said the first two days of a murder investigation are the most important.'

Ger smiled as if Abby had said something funny. 'Why's that?'

'Everything's still fresh,' Abby said, feeling defensive even though she was pretty sure there was no need. 'Not just for those affected by the crime. For us too, the people doing the investigation. As a case drags on, we get tired and it becomes harder to believe you'll ever find the person you're after. In the beginning, you believe – really believe – that you can solve the case. And something about that feeling makes you see things more clearly. You're less constrained somehow.'

She trailed off, uncertain again. But Ger nodded like she understood. Abby was glad she hadn't sounded completely stupid.

'Makes sense to me,' Ger said. 'So, where does that leave us with this investigation? What insights can you share with me?'

'There's something off between Freya and her mother,' Abby said.

'Lots of mothers and daughters don't get along,' Ger said. 'Come in, Abby. You make me feel like a headmistress standing in the doorway like that.'

Abby did as she was told.

'It might not matter,' she said, sitting down when Ger pointed to the empty chair. 'But it's what I was talking about, the different way of seeing things. I think it might matter but I'm not sure why. Not yet.'

'You think Charlotte could have killed him?' Ger asked.

'I think either of them could have,' Abby said. 'Or neither. Charlotte seemed almost unhinged yesterday. And I don't think it was just shock. There's something hysterical about her. Freya's nothing like her. She's some sort of lefty activist and I can't imagine her mother shares any of her political views. Sorry, I'm rambling. It's difficult to get a feel for what they're really like. The only real thing I picked up was the tension between them.'

'Well I don't need to tell you that you shouldn't focus solely on that,' Ger said. 'But you shouldn't ignore it, either. If you've got that feeling, Abby, it's there for a reason. Don't ignore it. Anything else?'

Abby shook her head. 'I was thinking I might pop by the Meridian. The wine bar in Hither Green? It's near The Station pub. Do you know it?'

Ger smiled. 'You asking me out for a drink?'

'No,' Abby said. 'I mean, if you'd like that, then sure, of course. The Meridian is where Freya works. I thought if I go over there this evening, I might be able to chat to some of the locals, see if I can dig up anything on Freya.'

'Good idea,' Ger said. 'I'd offer to come with you but I'm about to head home. My husband's been sending texts, asking if I remember I still have a family. Cheeky bugger. Is Alastair around?'

Abby nodded, confused by the sudden change of subject.

'Take him with you,' Ger said. 'He needs to get out more.

Thanks for the update, Abby. I'll see you in the morning.'

Abby knew when she was being dismissed. She stood up, said goodnight and left. The prospect of dragging Alastair to the pub with her didn't appeal but she knew better than to disobey a direct order.

She went back into the open-plan office half-hoping he'd be gone home. No such luck. There he was, long body hunched over his PC, lost in his own world of whatever it was he did.

'Al?'

He looked up, blinked at her and seemed to take a moment to recognise her.

'You okay?' he asked.

She told him where she was going and repeated Ger's instructions that he was to go with her. She'd expected him to protest and was surprised when his frown lifted and he smiled instead.

'A pint on a Sunday night?' he said. 'With you? I'd love to. Thanks so much for asking.'

'It's not a date,' she said quickly. 'I only asked you because the boss thinks it would be good for you. She thinks you don't get out enough.'

'She's right,' Alastair said. 'And don't worry, Roberts. I know it's not a date. If I thought that for a second, I'd have said no. You're so not my type.'

* * *

The phone was ringing. Ellen barely heard it through the din her children were making, shouting over each other as they attempted to tell her about their day. She slid past them, their voices following her out of the sitting room and into the hall.

She'd been expecting the phone call. Her parents had phoned at the same time every evening since they'd been away. They were back in Ireland, their first trip together since Ellen's wedding in Westport fourteen years earlier.

'You're not missing us too much, I hope?' her father said when she answered the phone.

Guilt gnawed her insides. Truth was, she wasn't missing them half as much as she'd expected. Work, kids and her unhealthy obsession with Noreen all taking up her time and emotional energy.

'We're coping,' Ellen said. The gnawing turned into a savaging. 'Don't worry about us. Tell me about Cormac.'

Cormac Flanagan, her father's older brother, was losing what was left of his life to Alzheimer's. Cormac was the reason for this holiday. When his wife called Ellen's parents with the news, Ellen insisted on paying for them to go back and see their families. If she'd hoped the gesture might make her feel better about herself, it hadn't worked.

'We had a good day today,' Ellen's father said. 'One of the few, I'm afraid. Anyway, who wants to talk about that? Put me on to one of the children, would you?'

The phone was passed around from Pat to Eilish to Sean to Terry. When everyone had had a turn, Ellen got the phone back, told her parents there was no need to call every night – as if it made any difference – and hung up before they'd spent their entire holiday money on a single phone call.

'We should have done this years ago,' Sean said. 'Paid for them to go back, I mean.'

'We tried,' Ellen said. 'Don't you remember? Dad always refused to consider it. And Mum would never go back on her own.'

'Why's that?' Terry asked.

They were seated around the country farmhouse-style table in the homely kitchen at the back of the house Ellen was renting while her own house was being rebuilt.

'I think he finds it too difficult,' Ellen said. 'In his heart, he's never really left Ireland. Going back is a reminder that he's an outsider now. He's lived more of his life out of the country than in it. So each time he goes there he's more and more of a stranger.'

She thought of her own life. How, apart from those early, difficult years, she'd never lived anywhere but Greenwich. Never wanted to, either.

'We're lucky,' she said. 'We've never had to leave a place we love to start a new life somewhere else.'

'It's hardly like they moved to the other side of the world,' Pat said. 'It's not that different, is it? Ireland, I mean.'

Before Ellen could answer, the front door banged open followed by the clatter of someone in the hallway.

'Ellen? Hiya! Are you there?'

Ellen caught Sean's eye and smiled.

'In the kitchen,' she called to Rosie.

Heels click-clacked loudly on the parquet flooring and a vision in fuchsia and blue burst into the kitchen. Rosie was home.

'Here you all are! Sean and Terry, too. Cool. What do you think of my hair, lads? Isn't it brilliant?'

'It's blue,' Ellen said, when she could get her mouth to work.

'Like Katy Perry!' Eilish squealed. 'Mummy, can I get my hair like that too? Please?'

Rosie pirouetted around the kitchen while the children gathered around her, reaching up to touch her cropped blue spikes. When she'd left yesterday morning, the same hair had been shoulder-length, brown and glossy.

'Your parents will kill me,' Ellen said.

'What's wrong with you?' Sean asked. 'She's young and beautiful and her hair looks amazing. Leave the kid alone, Ellen.'

'I'm meant to be looking after her,' Ellen said. 'And you know what Caroline and Martin are like.'

'Mum and Dad will love it,' Rosie said. 'Okay, maybe not. But they won't have to see it. I've no intention of going home any time soon and I sure as hell don't want them coming over here. I bet you don't either, right? So it's grand. By the time they get to see me again it'll be back to the way it was.'

Ellen laughed. It was impossible not to love her. Something Rosie knew only too well and used to her full advantage.

'Rosemary Kelly,' she said. 'You have no intention of growing out that blue hair now or anytime soon. Besides, aren't you due to Skype them later this evening?'

Rosemary winked at Sean. He winked back.

'Should never have taken a job working for a detective. Impossible to pull the wool over this one's eyes. You're right, Ellen. I am due to Skype them. In fact, I'm going to head upstairs and do it now. Get it over and done with. Wish me luck!'

As Ellen listened to Rosie's footsteps banging up the stairs, through the house and to the loft room at the top, she felt a sudden, sharp loss, like something terrible had just happened. She knew what it was. More than either of her children, more than any other member of the Kelly clan, Rosie reminded Ellen of her dead husband. Being with Rosie, Ellen was reminded – again and again – of what she'd lost.

TEN

The Meridian was a small wine bar outside Hither Green station, standing alongside a flower shop and a café. The place was busy when Abby and Alastair turned up. Squeezing their way through the Sunday night drinkers, they found a clear corner near the bar.

'So,' Abby said as they waited to get the barman's attention. 'Who exactly is your type?'

'I'll need a few pints inside me before you'll get that sort of information out of me,' Alastair said, tapping the side of his nose. 'This place is mobbed, hey? Not my idea of a quiet pint. The Dacre. Now there's a proper pub. No TV, no loud music and no bloody crowds.'

'I don't like pubs,' Abby said. 'Prefer wine bars.'

'Why doesn't that surprise me?' Alastair said. 'Ah, here we go.'

The barman – tall, good-looking, early twenties – smiled as he approached. Stopped smiling pretty quickly when Abby produced her warrant card and asked to speak to whoever was in charge.

'Is this about Freya's fella?' he said. His accent was pure Liverpool and reminded Abby of Sam.

'Is there somewhere we could go that's a bit quieter?' Alastair asked.

He pointed to a door behind the bar. 'Office is in there. Come on through and I'll get Alan, the manager. He's around somewhere. I'll find him and tell him you're here.'

Thanking him, Abby and Alastair walked around the bar. The door opened into a surprisingly large office with two ugly black leather sofas and a TV screen hooked up to a camera that gave a good view of the busy bar.

'Take a seat,' the guy said. 'Ben won't be long.'

'I remember when this place was a real dump,' Alastair said once they were seated, side by side, on one of the sofas.

'The bar or the area?' Abby said.

'Both,' Alastair said. 'Ach, Hither Green's always been all right but it's changed a lot in the last few years.'

'Everywhere in London has changed,' Abby said.

'Five years ago,' Alastair said, 'an area like this, you'd find teachers and key workers living here. They're all being pushed out by the bankers and the doctors and the lawyers who like the area because it's close to central London and the houses are affordable – by their standards – for Zone 3. It's a crying shame, Abby, I tell you. You live in Docklands, right? How do you find that? Can't see the appeal myself.'

'I love it,' Abby said. 'But I won't be there for much longer. My flatmate's bloke is moving in so I have to move out.'

'Ah,' Alastair said. 'Sorry I asked.'

Through the open door, Abby could see the Liverpool barman talking to another, older man with dyed blonde hair and a tan. She hoped he was the manager. She didn't know how much longer she could carry on with this stilted conversation. It had always been this way between them. Everyone else in the team she had a great relationship with. Alastair, of course, was adored by her colleagues. She just couldn't feel it and suspected that was because he didn't like her. He hid it well enough and had never been anything but civil to her. But when he was with her, he held back in a way he didn't seem to with anyone else.

'What about you?' she asked. 'Where do you live?'

'Wapping,' Alastair said. 'I love it. If I couldn't live there, I don't think I'd live in London at all.'

Abby glanced at him, wondering if he was taking the piss. His face looked serious but even still ... Wapping had to be one of the coolest, most expensive places to live in the city. Nothing about Alastair said cool or money.

'Wapping?'

He smiled. 'No need to sound so surprised.'

She would have said more but the blonde man was here now,

face fixed into one of the fakest smiles Abby had ever seen.

'Ben Lowe, pleased to meet you both.'

Abby and Alastair introduced themselves and waited while Ben sat down opposite them.

'Fergus is sorting out some drinks,' Ben said. 'Sorry you've had to wait so long. We're very busy, as you can see. And with no Freya tonight we're a person down. Terrible news about poor Kieran. How can I help?'

'Did you know Kieran?' Abby asked.

'Of course,' Ben said, looking very sombre. 'He was a regular here. Often came when Freya was working. Lots of people in here tonight would have known him. We've had people asking about it all evening.'

'What was he like?' Abby said.

'Like?' Ben frowned. 'He was fine. Yeah. I mean, I only knew him from the bar, you know. But he seemed pleasant enough. I'm sorry there's not more I can tell you.'

'Were they happy together?' Abby said. 'Kieran and Freya.'

'I suppose so,' Ben said. 'I mean, they're both into all that demonstrating and stuff. Not my thing but whatever rings your bell. Know what I mean?'

'How did he seem on Friday night?' Alastair asked.

Ben frowned. 'Friday? Sorry, I don't understand. He wasn't in here then.'

'But you met him,' Alastair said. 'You were with him in The Dacre Arms from 9pm till a little after ten, isn't that correct?'

Alan's jaw dropped. Abby knew exactly how he felt.

'How did you know that?' Ben asked. 'Sorry, that sounded wrong. I mean, yes, we met, but only for a quick drink. He was on his way to a party. His mother-in-law's. She's a bit of a party animal, by all accounts.'

'You had a row,' Alastair said. 'Care to tell us what about?'

Ben rubbed a hand across his face.

'I think I need a solicitor,' he said. 'Before I answer any more questions. Can I call someone?'

'We can arrange that at the station,' Alastair said. 'If you come with us quietly, we won't make a fuss. No need for handcuffs or anything like that.' Alastair smiled. It was a kind, sweet smile. Like he was offering Ben Lowe a piece of friendly advice. 'After all, Mr Lowe, the last thing we'd want to do is embarrass you. Ready?'

Abby watched as Ben Lowe stood up and meekly followed Alastair through the crowded pub. She hurried after them, wondering how the evening had changed so suddenly and how – without warning – Alastair had taken control of the investigation.

* * *

Charlotte got out of the taxi and paid the driver. He'd been miserable company and she didn't bother with a tip. She could see he wasn't happy about it but she didn't care. After he drove off, she turned to face the dark, empty house.

Times like this, she hated the place. Too big, too lacking

in anything resembling homely warmth. It was meant to be a family home. When they'd first moved here, with Nick, she'd been so excited. They had a big family planned. Four children – two boys, two girls. The place was big enough, for God's sake. Six bedrooms meant each child could have their own room and there'd still be room for guests to stay over. Except then she had Freya and everything changed.

She stepped forward, wobbling as she tried to navigate the gravelled driveway. Told herself it was her heels, not the wine, that made her unsteady. Wasn't as if she'd drunk that much, anyway. Bottle, bottle and a half at the most. Which, by her standards, was pretty damn good.

Inside, she didn't bother switching on the lights. The curtains weren't closed and she could see as much as she needed to. A huge chandelier hung in the hall – French, antique – and it flooded the room with a brightness she didn't think she could face right now. Far better this grey, shadowy half-light.

She kicked her heels off, luxuriating in the sudden release of pressure on the balls of her feet. If only she were brave enough, or tall enough, not to have to bother with shoes like that.

She moved towards the stairs, stopping at the bottom step when she heard something overhead.

'Nick?'

No answer. She waited, listening for other sounds, but she heard nothing. She breathed a sigh of relief. Another confrontation was the last thing she needed. He was being such a bastard right now. It had been bad for a while but this business with Kieran made everything a whole lot worse. As if she didn't have enough to deal with.

Charlotte wondered who his latest piece was. Some little bitch Freya's age or younger, wearing perfume that smelled of flowers in spring. She picked it up from his clothes sometimes.

Some day she'd tell Freya, let her know exactly the sort of man her dear daddy really was. She'd thought about it before, many times, but always backed out at the last minute. Told herself she couldn't face the argument that would follow, although that wasn't why. The real reason she'd never found the courage to tell Freya about Nick's numerous affairs was that she knew Freya would find a way of blaming her. That was how things were between them. No matter what Charlotte did, no matter how hard she tried to build some sort of relationship with her daughter, Freya always found a way of twisting it, making it look as if Charlotte was the one who'd done something wrong. It wasn't fair.

The staircase wound its way up through the centre of the house. At one stage, when she'd cared about things like that, this had been her favourite feature in a house full of beauty. Now, as she pulled herself up, step by step, she only wished it was shorter.

Alone and exhausted, her mind wandered past the defences she'd built up so carefully. She pretended – just for a moment – that she was living a different life. She paused, closed her eyes and imagined it. A loving husband waiting for her in the bed they shared. The bedrooms full of children, each one asleep, safe in his or her own little world of dreams. She pictured herself moving from room to room, straightening bed clothes, bending down to kiss flushed cheeks and search for the soft, reassuring sound of each child's slow, even, sleepy breathing.

The thump-thump of footsteps jolted her back to reality. Someone was up there.

Charlotte froze, heart pounding, making it difficult to hear anything else.

'Who's there?'

The alarm. She couldn't remember switching it off when she'd come inside. Usually, it beeped when she opened the front door, reminding her she needed to enter the code that switched it off. Shit. She had forgotten to turn it on before she went out. Again. Which made it easy for someone to break in.

'I'm calling the police!'

Her voice sounded pathetic. Weak and shaky, exposing the fear she felt. She pictured several of them – dirty, rough-speaking men – getting ready to hurt her.

A shadow loomed above her. Someone was standing at the top of the stairs. Moving towards her. Fast. She turned to run, tripped and nearly fell forward. Managed to grab the banister just in time.

The footsteps got closer. She couldn't see in front of her and she was terrified of falling.

A hand shoved into her back, propelled her forward. Suddenly there was nothing underneath her feet. Her legs pedalled wildly, trying to find something solid. Hands reached out for the banister but too late. She was falling forward, into the darkness, and there was nothing she could do to stop it happening.

ELEVEN

It felt like the longest day. Midnight had been and gone hours earlier and she was still awake. She'd opened a bottle of wine when she'd got in earlier and had sat here ever since. Drinking red wine and listening to music, trying to calm the clamouring mess inside her head. The memories of the last few days kept rearing up, like a pack of wolves threatening to devour her. The pressure of it was unbearable. She didn't know how much more she could take without cracking up completely. She tried to tell herself it would be okay. All she had to do was stay calm and everything would come good. It wasn't easy.

From the CD player, Elvis' rich voice crooned out to her. This album was one of her favourites. One of several Elvis CDs her dad had given her over the years. Elvis and Yeats. His two great passions, passed on to him from his own father and down the generations. If Freya ever had children she would teach them to love music and poetry, just like Dad had done with her.

The opening chords of 'Love me Tender' poured over her. Freya closed her eyes, let herself imagine Kieran was here, sitting beside her. The song was so beautiful. A perfect summation of the love she'd felt for him. The love they'd shared. She sang along softly, her voice barely a whisper and no match for the mighty king.

Kieran used to pretend he didn't really like Elvis. It didn't stop him listening, though. Especially after a few drinks. Most of the time, Freya went along with it, smiling as he made his jokes about cheesy music. Even though, deep down, she knew there was nothing cheesy about how this voice made her feel.

So much time wasted pretending. Not just Elvis. Everything. Acting like they'd fallen into this living together arrangement. As if it was something that had happened without any planning or forethought. Pretending they were the sort of laidback people for whom the day-to-day mundanity of life was something they could take or leave. Always busy, too preoccupied with the bigger issues: global warming, third world poverty, child slavery and living in a world where 1% of the population owned 99% of the wealth.

Yes, she knew all of that mattered and of course she still cared about it. But right now, the only thing she really gave a shit about was how empty everything suddenly was. This time last week, her life was perfect. Living here, in this flat, with a man no one had ever thought would settle for someone like her. A life with meaning and passion and purpose. Different in every way from the vacuous path her mother had chosen.

Freya wasn't stupid. She knew Kieran wasn't perfect, but she didn't get why that had to be such a big deal. So what? No one else in the world was supposed to be perfect, were they? Besides, whatever faults he had, the important thing was this: out of all the women in the world, he had chosen her. And there was nothing her mother or Alex or anyone else could do about that. He had chosen Freya and now he was gone.

She poured herself more wine from the bottle at her feet. The taste of it soured her mouth and burned her stomach and reminded her too much of her mother. She drank it anyway, needing to do something to stop the churning swell of images and noises and smells that seemed to be not only inside her head but all around her, closing in until it felt like she would suffocate from it all.

She would not end up like her mother. A miserable alcoholic clinging onto an empty, meaningless life with a man who didn't love her. Freya shook her head. No. She was better than that.

Her dead boyfriend looked down on her from the photo on the mantelpiece. She'd lit candles earlier, preferring the warm glow they gave to the harsh brightness of the overhead light. Kieran's face – and her own – flickered in and out of focus in the shimmering, shifting light colours.

His arm was draped carelessly over her shoulders. He wasn't smiling. Strange how she'd never noticed that before. Sometimes, it was only possible to see things clearly when you stepped away from them. Or when you knew the full facts of a situation and were able to see it for what it really was.

Her eyes slid from Kieran's face to her own, shiny with happiness. They'd had sex that morning. In the small tent they were sharing. She remembered being worried about the others hearing them but not letting that stop her. Not for a second. Back then, they were having sex all the time. No bloody wonder she looked so happy.

She forced down another mouthful of wine, but it triggered memories of her mother, wallowing in wine and self-pity, and she put the glass down, disgusted. She wished Dad was here. He'd promised he would drop by later but so far there was no sign of him. It wasn't his fault. She knew he would be here if he could. But he was so busy and she couldn't expect him just to drop everything and spend the next few days sitting here watching her mope around the place feeling sorry for herself. Just like her mother. She shuddered.

Her mobile phone buzzed with a text. She pulled it from the pocket of her fleece, hoping it was her father. But it was only Emer. Again.

I need to speak to you. Please call.

Freya deleted the message without responding. Kieran's older sister hadn't given a damn about him when he was alive. Too late to start pretending now he was dead.

The song ended sorrowfully, the last chord drifting away until it was nothing more than an echo in the silence. A new song, faster beat this time. *Suspicious Minds*. Unsurprisingly, Freya's thoughts turned to her mother once more. Stupid cow crying and acting like she gave a shit when everyone knew the only person her mother ever cared about was herself.

Anger replaced grief. She picked up the remote and cut the music.

Enough Elvis and enough self-pity.

She'd felt so sick earlier. Sick with worry and fear and the pure, vertiginous shock of his death. Part of her still couldn't accept it was true. Kept hoping – with a fervour that was dangerous but inevitable, she supposed – that it was all some big mistake and any second now the door would open and in he'd come as if nothing at all had happened.

He's never coming back.

She looked back at the photo, hating it for the lie it promised. Her smiling face, his arm around her, their matching jackets that screamed to the world that they were a couple. A happy pair of deluded fools with a lifetime of happiness stretched out in front of them.

He's never coming back.

The grief was physical, a hard lump of pain that spread out from her chest and clogged her throat and made it difficult to see or hear or breathe. She stood up, lifted the photo from the mantelpiece and flung it across the room. It hit the wall, glass shattering into tiny pieces that scattered across the stripped floorboards, sharp shards that reflected the light from the candles, so that the whole floor seemed to move and dance in the twinkling light.

MONDAY

ONE

Alastair was already at his desk when Abby got into work on Monday morning. She was damp and cold. It had started raining while she was on the DLR. Optimistically, she'd let the early morning blue sky fool her into thinking it would be dry today, and left her umbrella behind. By the time she got to work, she was soaked.

Alastair grinned as he watched her shake out her coat before carefully hanging it on the coat-rack. She thought he looked unbearably smug. Which was unfair of her, she knew. He had every reason to look smug. Until last night, Abby hadn't understood why Ellen and everyone else rated him so highly. Now she totally got it. His work identifying Ben Lowe was nothing short of genius. She had to hand it to him, even if – at the same time

– she couldn't stop the sharp stab of jealousy that pinched her ribs. Maybe that was why she made a show of praising him to Malcolm when he came in a few minutes later.

'Did you hear about this one last night?' she asked.

'The guy from the pub?' Malcolm said. 'Aye, Al told me you'd brought him in for questioning. Not happy about being held overnight, apparently. Duty Sergeant said he kicked up a right stink during the night.'

'Hang on,' Abby said. 'Are you saying genius boy here hasn't told you how he knew Ben Lowe was our man?'

'He didn't really say much,' Malcolm said. 'You know what he's like, right? Muttered something about a happy coincidence then spent the rest of his time on the phone to someone.'

She'd been too dismissive of Alastair. She could see that now. Had mistaken his quiet shyness and lack of ego for a lack of something else. A personality, maybe. She'd been stupid. The jealousy disappeared. Replaced by respect.

'He'd already been through the case notes in minute detail,' Abby said, speaking to Malcolm but watching Alastair the whole time. Willing him to take credit for a great piece of work.

'There's a note in there from one of the uniforms who did the door-to-doors. As well as speaking to the neighbours, they checked the local pubs. Freya had told them Kieran met someone for a drink before the party. There was a good chance he went to a pub near Charlotte's house. Turned out that's exactly what he did. The landlady of The Dacre Arms remembered him. Said he was in there with another bloke. Didn't stay long. Midway through the second drink, the men had some sort of argument. Landlady didn't know the details, but she said Burton stormed out of the pub. Left almost a full pint behind him. The other bloke followed him about half an hour later.'

'And that was Ben Lowe?' Malcolm said.

Abby nodded. 'Yep. Landlady didn't know who he was but she gave a description to our officer who dutifully noted it all down. Alastair read the description and remembered it when we were in the pub.'

'It was just a guess,' Alastair said. 'A shot in the dark, that's all. There was every chance I could have been wrong.'

'But you weren't,' Abby said. 'That's what counts. And because of that, we have our first real lead. All thanks to you.'

Alastair waved away the compliment and motioned for Abby to sit down.

'And now we've got something else,' he said. 'If you'd ever stop talking, I can tell you what it is.'

Abby pulled out the chair beside him and sat down.

'It's about Charlotte Gleeson,' Alastair said.

* * *

The postman caught Ellen as she was rushing out the door with the children on Monday morning.

'Just the one letter,' he said, handing her a white envelope with a logo on the front. She registered the logo as she shoved the envelope, unopened, into her bag to read later. It was from the secondary school Pat was starting at in September.

She got the kids to school just as the morning bell was ringing and raced across to Lewisham. She bumped into Raj as she was going inside and persuaded him to come across the road to Danilo's.

'I'll buy you a coffee,' she said. 'And in return, you can tell me everything you know about Pete Cooper and Operation Rift.'

'Not much to tell,' Raj said, once they'd settled at a Formica table by the window, hot drinks steaming the air between them – cappuccino for Raj, double espresso for her.

'Well, nothing you probably don't know already. The focus of Operation Rift is money-laundering. We think it's our best chance of getting to some seriously bad people. Cooper wasn't on our radar at first. On the surface, he's respectable enough. One of these guys with a portfolio – as well as the furniture shops, he's part-owner of two hotels in Greenwich, has a string of high-end properties he rents out across the south-east, and he's one of the main investors in Tramp.'

'Ah,' Ellen said. 'So that's why you're interested in him?'

Tramp was an 'exclusive' gentlemen's club recently opened in a new development on the riverfront, near Greenwich Yacht Club. The owner of Tramp, Rob Brinton, was a leading figure in south-east London's organised crime scene.

'Cooper and Brinton go way back,' Raj said. 'Went to school together. We think Brinton's been using Cooper's business to syphon off money from his less salubrious income streams. Brinton's into everything. Prostitution, dealing, probably trafficking too. Hard to tell Cooper's involvement at this stage, but he's definitely someone we're interested in.'

Ellen blew on her coffee and took a sip. It was good. It always was in Danilo's.

She was familiar with investigations like Operation Rift. They were part of a nationwide initiative. If you can't get the criminals for one crime, get them for something else. End result is still the same. They're locked up. They'd tried something similar with another south London bad boy a few years back. William – Billy Boy – Dunston. In Dunston's case, the investigation never got as far as a conviction. Ellen had killed him first. Although not for money-laundering. Her motive had been purer than that. Revenge.

A series of memories fast-forwarded through her head. Ending with the stench of burnt flesh and the image of Dunston's ruined face after she'd pulled the trigger a second time.

'You think Gleeson's involved too?' she asked.

'No.' Raj shook his head. 'He's just an idiot who's let Cooper talk him into investing in this new chain of restaurants he's starting up. My guess is that he's been wanting to start this new venture for a while. It's ambitious. He's taken over the building beside his existing restaurant in Greenwich. It's meant to be the first of a chain. The tapas chain has been a success and this is basically the same concept only the food's Italian, not Spanish.

Maybe he feels safer going into it with someone else. Cooper can be charming enough when he wants and, on the surface, he comes across as pretty respectable. He's the money behind the enterprise, Gleeson's the brains. From Gleeson's point of view, he probably thinks he's got himself a pretty good deal.'

Ellen thought of the smug, conceited man she'd dragged in for questioning the day before. Nick Gleeson oozed comfortable, well-off respectability.

'Wouldn't he know it's potentially harming his reputation going into business with someone like Cooper?' she asked.

'He probably has no idea,' Raj said. 'Like I told you, Cooper puts up a good front. Gleeson's a businessman, Ellen. Even the best of them don't really care who they do business with once it brings in the money. Don't tell me you've never watched *The Apprentice*?'

'Never,' Ellen confirmed. 'And I hope I never will, either.'

Raj grinned. 'Should have guessed. Anything else?'

'Is it possible Cooper is using Nick Gleeson's new business as a channel for his mate's dodgy money?' Ellen asked.

'Very possible,' Raj said. 'That's one of several things we're looking into. Tell me, Ellen, what do you know about Pete Cooper?'

'I know he plays golf with Nicholls,' Ellen said. 'And I know he's probably involved in all sorts of dodgy stuff but proving it is the difficult thing. Why?'

'This isn't the first time he's been the focus of an investigation,'

Raj said. 'I'm not sure if you're aware of that?'

Ellen shook her head.

'Fifteen years ago,' Raj said, 'Cooper's wife disappeared. Annalise. Her body was found a few days later at the bottom of Beachy Head.'

Two images side by side in Ellen's head. Vinny's body. Lying on the road after the car drove over him. Billy Dunston's face disappearing a split-second after Ellen pulled the trigger.

'Cooper was a suspect?' she said.

'The inquest gave an open verdict,' Raj said. 'But no one was ever charged with the death. And, of course, it's possible she did kill herself.'

Ellen thought of other suicides she'd investigated. She knew an open verdict wasn't unusual in those cases. She knew, too, there was usually a reason why the coroner chose not to confirm the death as suicide.

'You don't think so?' she asked.

Raj shrugged. 'I wasn't part of the investigation but I spoke to a retired detective who was. He said they all knew Cooper had killed her. Proving it was the problem. He had a cast-iron alibi for the night she went missing. And the investigation was never able to prove he'd got someone else to do it.'

'Why was everyone so sure?' Ellen asked.

'Annalise was having an affair,' Raj said. 'With a guy who did some occasional work for Cooper. Dan McNulty. The thing is, McNulty disappeared the same night as Annalise. His body was never found. The case is still officially open. Sitting with a pile of other cold cases, waiting for the day someone has time to revisit them.'

'Did he ever remarry?' Ellen asked.

'Never,' Raj said. 'There's a kid, too. A daughter. Cooper's brought her up alone since Annalise died. From everything I've heard, he's a devoted father. The girl is twenty-two now. Still lives at home. Post-grad student at Greenwich University.'

'Where Kieran Burton was doing his MA,' Ellen said. 'I wonder if they knew each other.'

Raj pushed his chair back and stood up. 'Let me know what you find out. I've got a briefing in five minutes. Need to get back.'

Through the steamed-up window, Ellen saw the blurred outline of Abby crossing the road towards the coffee shop.

'I need to be getting off as well,' she said. 'Thanks for your help, Raj.'

'No problem,' he said. 'Take care, Ellen.'

He touched her shoulder and then he was gone. Ellen watched him chat to Abby on the pavement before he ran across the road and disappeared inside the white, concrete hulk of the building that housed Lewisham police station.

She drained the last bit of coffee and stood up, just as Abby came inside, brushing rain off her face.

'Charlotte Gleeson's in hospital,' Abby said. 'Claims she was attacked in her house last night.'

'Claims?' Ellen asked.

'She'd had a few too many,' Abby said. 'Fell down the stairs. She says someone pushed her. Two of our boys answered the emergency call. They seem to think it's more likely she fell. I've spoken to the hospital. We can go over any time this morning.'

'Tell you what,' Ellen said, 'you scoot across to the hospital, see what Charlotte's got to say. I'll go back to the station and deal with Ben Lowe, okay?'

They walked out into the wet morning. A gust of wind cut down the street, gathering up bits of rubbish as it went. A blue plastic bag rose from the ground, floated high above Ellen's head, then drifted down again, landing at her feet like a present.

She pulled up her hood, stepped over the bag and motioned for Abby to follow her. By the time she reached the station, the lingering image of Billy Dunston's face was gone.

TWO

They'd kept Ben Lowe in overnight. Deliberately delaying the interview until the following morning. The longer they drew things out, the harder it was for the suspect. A night in the cells sent stress levels rocketing. Made suspects say things they shouldn't. Sometimes.

After giving disclosure to Lowe's solicitor, Ellen went into the interview room. Ellen didn't recognise the solicitor, a striking black woman who introduced herself as Janet Azikwe.

It had been Abby's idea to ask Alastair to be part of this. Ellen would never have thought of it. She'd always assumed Alastair preferred the other side of the job: the research, trawling through mounds of evidence, looking for things other people missed. But when she suggested this to him, he jumped at the chance. She'd have to try to remember, in future, to let him try new things. Alastair wasn't the only person in her team who needed more development opportunities. When she compared her own management skills to some people she'd been lucky enough to work with over the years, she didn't feel good about herself. Somehow, along with juggling the other demands of the job and being a semi-decent mother, she would have to find the time to be a better manager.

Straightaway, Ben Lowe started mouthing off. Banging on about his rights and how he had a business to run and blah-de-blah-de-blah-de-blah. When he finally shut up, Ellen pressed the button on the CD-recorder and started the interview. She noted the time and the names of everyone in the room, then sat back in her chair and stared at Lowe.

He was a man who clearly cared about the way he looked. Blonde highlights through his thinning hair, a tan that definitely didn't come from any natural source, and clothes that looked good even after he'd slept in them. It was a pity, Ellen reflected, he didn't dedicate as much time to his personality as he did to his appearance.

'You met Kieran Burton for a drink on Friday night,' she said. 'Why?'

'Hang on a second,' Lowe said. 'Haven't you heard a word I just said? I asked you why the hell you've kept me locked up all night and when you're going to let me out of here? I haven't done anything wrong and you're treating me like a bloody criminal. It's not right and I'm not having it. You hear?'

'Friday night,' Ellen repeated.

He started to protest – again – but Janet Azikwe put a hand on his arm. With an expression of weary patience that reminded Ellen of her mother, Janet suggested to Ben that answering questions was the fastest way out of here.

He shrugged off Janet's hand and scowled at Ellen.

'Yeah, I met him,' he said. 'He's a pal. Wanted a bit of advice so we went for a drink. Chose the Dacre because there was less chance of bumping into someone we knew.' He snorted. 'Not that it seems to have made much difference. Someone obviously saw us. Who was it? Not Freya, I know that much. She had no idea Kieran was meeting me.'

'How do you know that?' Ellen asked.

'Because he didn't tell her,' Ben said. 'She can be a bit much, you know? It was easier for him to do his own thing from time to time.'

'And what was his *own thing*?' Ellen asked.

Ben shrugged. 'The guy just needed a bit of space sometimes, you know? Listen, I work with Freya, yeah? So I know what she's like. Full of her own importance. She didn't treat him like he was her boyfriend. It was weird. She acted more like she was his mother. I mean, don't get me wrong. She looked after him all right. But that came with a price, you know?'

'No, I don't know,' Ellen said. 'What sort of price?'

'She wanted to control him,' Ben said. 'Everything he did, she had to know about it. Which is why he went AWOL from time to time.'

'What about uni?' Ellen said. 'Freya couldn't keep tabs on him there, surely?'

Ben smirked. 'She didn't know the half of it. Ironic, if you think about it. She spent all that time and effort and money trying to turn him into her personal lapdog and all the while he was off at college everyday getting up to all sorts.'

'All sorts of what?' Alastair asked.

'Let's just say,' Ben said, 'Kieran was the sort of bloke who didn't put much importance on monogamy. Far as I know, he had several girls on the go. Some of them real lookers as well. In a different league to poor old Freya.'

'You don't know any of this for sure, though,' Ellen said. 'This is only what Kieran told you?'

'He was seeing other women,' Ben said. 'I'm telling you. I even met one of them. Bloody gorgeous she was.'

'Sounds like you and Kieran were good mates,' Alastair said.

'We were,' Ben said. 'I still can't believe it, if I'm honest. I mean, for all I know I was one of the last people to see him before it happened.'

'Or the last,' Ellen said.

'I didn't kill him,' Ben said. 'We met for a drink, that's all. Well, okay, maybe it was more than one. We had a few drinks and then he went on to the party and I headed back to the bar. You can ask anyone who was at the Meridian that night. I was back by ten at the latest.'

'If you were such good pals,' Alastair said, 'what was the fight about?'

'Nothing,' Ben said. 'Like I said, we'd had a few. Said some stuff we shouldn't have. But that's what happens with drink sometimes, you know?'

Ellen nearly laughed. Ben Lowe had had all night to come up with a story about why he and Kieran had argued. She couldn't believe this was the best he could think of. From the look of barely concealed contempt on his solicitor's face, neither could Janet Azikwe.

Ellen leaned forward in her chair and stared at Alan. He stared back at first then dropped eye contact and fidgeted in his seat. His right hand was on the table in front of him, fingers tapping a discordant rhythm on the stained Formica.

'Alan.'

The tapping stopped and he looked up. His face was blank, but Ellen saw the first flicker of real fear in his blue eyes.

'We have several witnesses who can confirm they saw you and Kieran rowing on Friday night. You were overheard threatening to kill him at one point. A few hours later, Kieran was killed. At this point in the investigation, you are our number one murder suspect. Believe me when I tell you it isn't helping your case in any way by deliberately lying to me. If you really want me to believe you didn't kill Kieran, you'd better start telling me the truth. And if you think for one second that I'm going to believe you can't even remember why you argued, you can think again. So let me ask you for the final time. What was your argument about?'

Kieran glanced at Azikwe, who rolled her eyes.

'DI Kelly,' she said. 'Could you give us a moment, please?'

Ellen located the Pause button on the CD-recorder and stood up.

'We'll take a break,' she said.

She left the room with Alastair. They got coffees from the machine and Ellen asked Alastair what he thought so far.

'He's a nasty bastard,' Alastair said. 'But I don't think he killed Burton.'

'Why not?' Ellen asked.

'He's not scared enough,' Alastair said. 'I agree he's lying and I'm intrigued to find out why. From what he's said so far, it wouldn't surprise me if the row was about a woman. Just not poor Freya. Maybe they were both sleeping with the same girl, something tawdry like that.'

Ellen agreed. Ben Lowe wasn't their killer. Which left them right back where they'd started. The task ahead suddenly seemed impossible. A huge, impassable mountain she didn't have the strength for. She didn't think she could continue to do this, over and over and over.

'You okay?' Alastair asked.

'Fine,' she said, giving the same lie she always gave. 'Come on. Let's go back and finish this.'

She pushed open the door and walked back into the interview room. The expression on Ben Lowe's face was defiant, like he was preparing for a fight. Resisting the urge to punch him, Ellen sat down, pressed the button to start the CD recording again.

* * *

Whatever advice Lowe's solicitor gave him, it worked. When Ellen and Alastair went back in, he was ready to talk.

'We did row,' he said. 'You're right.'

'So what was it about?' Ellen asked.

Lowe glanced at his solicitor, who nodded.

'Kieran was meant to be getting me a bit of speed,' Lowe said.

'You're telling me Kieran was dealing drugs?' Ellen said.

Lowe shrugged. 'I wouldn't call it dealing. He got me some speed from time to time. But only because he knew some bloke at the uni who could get some easily.'

'And the row was about the drugs?' Ellen asked.

'Just speed,' Lowe said. 'Not *drugs* like I was getting all sorts. Kieran stole my money. I gave him fifty quid and never saw a thing for it. He told me his usual guy had taken the money then refused to give him the speed. Said there was nothing he could do about it. He was a lying bastard. He kept the money for himself. When I challenged him, he laughed and said if I didn't believe him, I could always go to you lot.'

Ellen's spirits deflated. A petty row over a petty drug deal. Ben Lowe was a piece of shit but Ellen was pretty sure he hadn't killed Kieran over fifty quid. In a pointless attempt to make herself feel better, she charged Ben Lowe for conspiracy to supply drugs under the Illegal Drugs Act. After that, all she could do was have him released on bail pending an appearance before the Magistrate in a fortnight's time. He would get a fine and a record. Which was something, she supposed.

When she'd finished with Lowe, she went back to her office and found a note on her laptop: *Gone to hospital. Ger wants to see us both for a coffee and catch-up when I'm back. A*

Ellen rolled her eyes. The prospect of a decent coffee was poor compensation for being dragged away from her work just because Ger Cox felt like it. What the boss wanted, the boss got. Ellen knew that was the way things worked. But knowing it didn't mean she had to like it.

THREE

Nothing was broken. The doctor – tall and thin with an over-long nose – told Charlotte she was lucky. She didn't feel very lucky. She had concussion and her right arm was badly bruised. It hurt like hell, despite the painkillers they'd given her. She'd made the mistake of asking the doctor if she could drink on them.

'I'd have thought alcohol would be the last thing on your mind right now,' he said.

Supercilious bastard. No point telling him – again – that someone had done this to her. She'd seen from his face what he thought of her.

She was in a public ward. Eight beds in the room. Each one occupied. She was wearing a pale blue, nylon nightgown that they'd put her into when she arrived. One of the nurses, the fat blonde one, said that her clothes were in the small bedside locker. Which meant they'd be horribly creased when she put them back on.

She closed her eyes. The doctor would be back soon. If he was happy with everything, they would discharge her. She didn't want that. Couldn't face going back there. Not yet.

'Hey.'

Charlotte opened her eyes. Saw Ginny's lovable face staring at her. She wasn't wearing any make-up and her face, usually so vibrant, looked grey and tired. Charlotte couldn't remember the last time she'd seen her friend's face make-up free.

'I came as soon as I got your text,' Ginny said. She sat on the side of the bed and took Charlotte's hand in hers. Instantly, the fear and anxiety became bearable.

'You gave me a fright, Lottie, you know that? I saw the word hospital and ... well, you know how much I hate these places.'

'Sorry,' Charlotte said. 'I didn't know who else to call.'

'Oh don't be silly.' Ginny's hand squeezed hers. 'I didn't mean it like that. Of course I want to be here with you. Look at you, darling.' Very gently, she touched Charlotte's right cheekbone, which hurt like hell. 'You've got a real shiner coming up. What on earth happened?'

Charlotte relayed the story again, stumbling and stuttering as she tried to convey the terror of it. The dreadful certainty that she was about to die.

'They think I'm lying,' she said.

'Who does?'

Charlotte shrugged, then wished she hadn't as pain shot down her bruised arm. At least it was her left arm. She supposed she was meant to feel lucky about that too.

'The police, the doctor looking after me. Everyone.'

'Mrs Gleeson?'

Charlotte groaned. Abby, the pretty detective, had come into the ward and was standing at the end of the bed.

Abby. Pretty name for a pretty girl. She looked around the same age as Freya. Totally different in every other way, of course. It pained Charlotte to compare Abby's glossy hair, manicured nails and perfect skin with her own daughter. If only Freya made the effort once in a while. It wouldn't kill her. And at that age, it really didn't take much to keep yourself looking good. Of course, Freya would need to work on her weight too, but that was perfectly doable.

Maybe that's what she needed. Now she'd got herself free of Kieran, maybe it was the right time to reinvent herself. They could do it together. A mother-daughter project. Charlotte tried to picture herself and Freya going shopping together, getting their hair and nails done. The image refused to come. She sighed. Of course not. Freya wasn't going to change. Charlotte would just have to accept that, no matter how unpalatable it was.

'Shall we close the curtains?' Abby asked, already drawing them around the rail. She smiled at Ginny. 'Maybe you could give us a few minutes?'

'No.' Charlotte clung onto Ginny's hand. 'I want Ginny to stay.'

'Of course,' Ginny said. 'I'm not going anywhere. Don't worry.'

Abby moved in until she was practically pressed against the side of the bed. It made Charlotte feel vulnerable, lying down like this while the detective towered over her. She tried to shift her body so she was sitting up, but it was difficult. Everything was difficult when your whole body hurt.

'Can I help?' Abby leaned forward and helped Ginny to move her until she was comfortable.

'Thank you,' Charlotte said.

'How are you feeling?' Abby asked.

'How do you think she's feeling?' Ginny asked. 'Someone tried to bloody kill her.'

'Please, Mrs Rau,' Abby said. 'I need to hear Charlotte's version of what happened.'

Ginny frowned. 'I assume you know who I am because I've already given a statement to your colleagues. Good. Can we get on with this, please? Lottie needs her rest.'

'Her doctor said she's well enough to answer some questions,' Abby said. She turned away from Ginny, focusing her attention on Charlotte. Charlotte tried to smile to show she wasn't intimidated.

'Tell me about the accident,' Abby said.

Again, Ginny cut in before Charlotte had a chance to answer for herself.

'It wasn't an accident. Someone did this to her. Pushed her down the stairs in her own house. Isn't it possible that whoever did it is the same person who killed Kieran? I've been thinking about it, you see. And Lottie, well she'd had a bit to drink on Friday night so she mightn't remember everything.' She squeezed Charlotte's hand tighter, letting her know she wasn't being critical, just getting her point across. 'But I think she saw something she shouldn't have. I think she saw the killer and whoever that is, they came back last night to … to make sure she'd never be able to tell anyone if she did remember.'

Charlotte wanted to pull her hand away but Ginny was holding on too tight. She didn't like this. Didn't want to think it was anything more than a burglary gone wrong.

'Do I have to go through it again?' she asked.

'I'm here to help,' Abby said. 'The best way I can do that is understanding exactly what happened. I'm your ally, Charlotte, not your enemy.'

She smiled when she said this and the kindness made Charlotte want to cry.

'Thank you,' she whispered.

Abby patted the hand that Ginny wasn't holding. 'Take your time. There's no rush.'

'I was on my way to bed,' Charlotte said. 'I'd been out. I was tired and wanted to go straight to bed.'

'Where had you been?' Abby asked.

'A wine bar in Greenwich,' Ginny said. 'Nothing wrong with

that, is there? And why does it matter where we were. Shouldn't you be concentrating on who did this? Not where she was or who she was with before it happened. Lottie, listen to me. Think. You were okay last night when I left you. There must be something you remember, something that will help us find who did this to you.'

There was something off about Ginny this morning. Charlotte got that her friend was worried but her certainty that someone had done this deliberately felt wrong. Why would Ginny, of all people, think that anyone would want to hurt her? She wanted to ask Ginny about it but she couldn't do that with Abby watching her. Again, Charlotte scrabbled through her memories of Friday night, trying to find something that would explain what Ginny was thinking. Again, she hit a blank. Huge gaping holes where memories should be. A random patchwork of scattered images. Nothing that made any sense.

'What do you mean, she was okay last night?' Abby asked.

'I'd had a drink,' Charlotte said. 'But I wasn't drunk. That's what she meant. Anyway, even if I was, so what?'

'No reason at all,' Abby said. 'After what's happened with Kieran, I can't say I blame you. You're probably still in shock.'

At last. Someone who understood what she was going through.

'I am,' Charlotte said. 'I mean, I'm totally devastated over poor Kieran. Freya is all I can think about at the moment. I want to help her but she won't let me.'

'I'm sure she'll come round,' Abby said. 'So, last night. You came home. What happened next?'

'I was on my way upstairs,' Charlotte said. 'When I heard a noise. I think I called out, asked who was up there. The next thing I know …'

She stopped speaking as it rushed back at her. The dark, the fear and the hand shoving into her back. The sudden, shocking certainty that she might die.

'It must have been terrifying,' Abby said. 'Do you have any idea who it was? I only ask because two officers responded to your 999 call last night. They searched the house. There was no sign of any break-in.'

As if those useless lumps would be able to tell. They hadn't believed her, either. Speaking to her in slow, loud voices, like she was some sort of bloody retard. They only bothered looking for an intruder when she started screaming at them.

'They didn't believe me,' Charlotte said. 'I could tell from their faces they thought I was lying. Why would I lie about something like that?'

'I'm sure you wouldn't,' Abby said. She smiled again and Charlotte smiled back, waiting.

'Just one more question,' Abby said in the same kind voice. 'In October last year …'

Charlotte stopped smiling, knowing what was coming.

'… you accused a taxi driver of trying to assault you. That wasn't quite true, was it?'

Trust the police to bring that up again. Use it to twist things around, make it look as if she was the sort of person who went around accusing people of doing things they hadn't.

Ginny started to say something but Charlotte spoke over her.

'That was different.'

Abby raised her eyebrows.

'I *was* drunk that night,' Charlotte said. 'But I assume you know that already.'

'You accused the taxi driver of assaulting you,' Abby said. 'When in actual fact, it was you who hit him. You threw up inside his taxi and then assaulted him when he tried to get you to sit up so you weren't lying in your own puke.'

Uptight cow. Might do her good to let go occasionally. Charlotte knew it was no good. Whatever she said, the police wouldn't believe her. She closed her eyes, willing Abby to piss off back to her shitty, self-important little life and leave her alone. She felt Ginny's hand and she held on tight, as if Ginny was the only thing stopping her from falling.

She heard Abby say goodbye and say she'd be in touch over the next few days. Then there was the whoosh of air across her face as the curtain was pulled back, followed by the click-clack of heels gradually fading as the detective walked down the ward, away from her.

When she couldn't hear the footsteps any longer, she opened her eyes. Saw Ginny's pale, pixie face frowning.

'What is it?' Charlotte asked.

Ginny shook her head, gave a smile that was false and bright and had none of the warmth of her real smiles.

'She didn't mention Freya or Nick,' Ginny said. 'Don't you think that's odd?'

Charlotte remembered how she'd thought it was Nick. Moving around upstairs in the dark. She wondered if she'd been right about that and if it was worth calling the detective back to tell her.

She decided not to bother. It wasn't as if Abby would believe her, even if she did.

FOUR

Nick sat in his car, watching the grey river sludge past him on its way east out of the city. He was parked on a stretch of riverside concrete in Woolwich, a spot he knew from his childhood. He'd grown up in one of the tall council buildings around the corner. He hated Woolwich but loved this unlovely stretch of river. It reminded him of his old man. They used to walk out here on Sunday mornings, father and son, talking about everything and nothing. Dead twenty-five years and it still hurt.

He'd tried hard to make his father proud. But his father hadn't lived long enough to see Nick's progress from Woolwich tower-block to Blackheath mansion. The only real regret in his life. There was other stuff, things he wasn't proud of, but he could live with those. His marriage, for example. A right bloody disaster zone, but at least it had produced Freya. She mightn't be every father's ideal of a perfect daughter but by Christ he loved his little princess.

Which made all of this worse. He hit the steering wheel, pounded it with both hands, rage and fear and frustration ripping through him, until his hands hurt. He couldn't bear to see her suffer. He'd called around first thing this morning and her pain had been almost too much. She'd done her best to hide it, but he could see how deep it went. It cut him up. Especially when the piece of shit she was grieving for wasn't worthy of such emotion.

Nick stayed with her for as long as he could but after a while he'd had to get out of there. He needed to clear his head, work out what he was going to do. Impossible to do that when he was with Freya.

He was scared. A difficult thing for a man like him to admit but there you had it. All the years of bloody slog and here he was, in danger of losing it all. He got out of the car and walked to the railings overlooking the river. A sharp wind cut across the water and sliced through his body. He opened his jacket, welcoming the cold. It helped him focus.

Kieran fucking Burton. He should never have let things get as far as they did. It was obvious from the first time he met Freya's boyfriend that the bloke was a lazy tosser who was only with Freya for what he could get from her. Why the hell hadn't Nick done something back then? What sort of a father did it make him, knowing his daughter was shacked up with a lowlife piece of scum like that and not doing a single thing about it? Sitting back and watching that sleazy little shit worm his way into the seams of his family and rip apart the last few threads that held them together.

He started walking, feet pounding the hard concrete, face turned towards the easterly wind, forcing his mind to go back over every angle, making sure he hadn't missed anything.

He kept his phone tidy so no problems there. There was always a risk that Kieran had kept the photos on his phone but Nick didn't think so. The coppers would have checked that by now. If the photo was there, they'd have found it.

There was Loretta, of course. She might be tricky. Especially with their history. Maybe he could have handled that one better but how was he to know this would happen? He'd have to have a word all the same. Make sure she knew what would happen if she didn't keep her mouth shut. She was a clever woman so he wasn't too worried. If he gave her the choice between a decent bonus or the chance to lash out, she'd take the money.

He walked until he'd gone through every possibility, every single way he could be caught out. He examined each one in turn, made sure his arse was covered, then moved on to the next. At the end of it, the fear was gone. He felt in control again. The coppers didn't have anything on him. He was in the clear.

The knowledge restored him. Restored something else as well. He closed his eyes, remembering how good last night had been.

He took his phone from his pocket and dialled her number. Held his breath until she answered.

'Are you free?' he said. 'I really need to see you.'

'I was hoping you'd call,' she said. 'I was just thinking of you.'

The sound of her voice sent a shiver of lust through his body. He pictured her face, her body, her lips. Remembered what those lips felt like. He moaned. She laughed. He told her where to meet and hung up. Walked quickly to the car and drove off.

Moments earlier he'd been asking himself if she was worth all this. Now, he couldn't even remember why he'd ever thought that. He'd do anything to keep her and make her his own. He'd known it the first time he'd met her. Nothing had changed. If anything, the longer he was with her, the more determined he was to keep her. No matter what the consequences.

FIVE

'How did you get on with Ben Lowe?' Ger asked.

The three women were sitting around Ger's desk, drinking freshly made coffee and discussing the case. Ellen was trying – and failing – not to feel patronised. This wasn't how she'd worked with Ed, her previous boss. Her irritation was made worse because she didn't have much time. She'd finally got around to reading the letter from Pat's new school. As soon as she'd finished it, she'd picked up the phone and called his counsellor. She had an appointment to see him in an hour.

'Disappointing.' Ellen forced herself to stop thinking about Pat and focus on work. 'He's not a pleasant person, but I don't think he's a killer. Kieran stole some money from him.'

'Surely that's a motive?' Ger said.

Ellen shrugged. 'Fifty pounds. It was money for speed which Kieran never provided. Lowe was pissed off but not enough to kill. I don't think so, anyway. Even if he was, he'd have had to rush out straight after the row, find a knife from somewhere, find Kieran and know – somehow – that he was on St Joseph's Vale so that he could kill him. The landlady at the Dacre has already confirmed that Kieran left the pub first. Ben stayed and had another pint after that. The timings would only work if Ben had planned it all in advance. And I don't think that's true.'

'Well let's keep him on our list of suspects for now,' Ger said. 'What about Charlotte? Any luck there?'

'She certainly believes someone was in the house,' Abby said. 'But she'd been drinking. She doesn't deny that. She claims she hadn't much to drink but the manager of the wine bar says Charlotte and her pal consumed two bottles of wine that evening.'

'So this was an accident,' Ger said. 'Is that what you're saying?'

'I'm not sure.' Abby looked embarrassed at having to admit she didn't have a definite answer. 'Going by the facts alone, I'd say yes. She drank too much, came home pissed and fell down the stairs.'

'But?' Ger said.

'I think I believe her,' Abby said. 'She seemed so … I don't know, vulnerable somehow. She had a friend with her. Virginia Rau. She's on our witness list and she also happens to be who Charlotte went drinking with on Sunday night. She seems convinced that Charlotte saw something on Friday night that's connected with the murder.'

'One of the PCs interviewed her,' Ellen said, remembering her conversation with WPC McKeown. 'She thought Mrs Rau was hiding something.'

'What?' Ger said.

'I'm not sure,' Ellen said. 'Charlotte was upset the night of the party, apparently. Mrs Rau claims some guy at the party upset her. I got all this from WPC Laura McKeown. She didn't believe Rau's story and even interviewed her a second time. Didn't get any fresh information but came away with the same feeling.'

'But it's so stupid,' Abby said. 'I know she wanted me to think it was the killer who pushed Charlotte. But pushing someone down the stairs? It's not exactly a foolproof way to kill someone, is it? As demonstrated by the fact Charlotte's still alive.'

Ger smiled and nodded her head in agreement.

'We know it wasn't a burglar,' Ellen said. 'There's no sign that anything was taken. Why would a burglar break in and not steal anything? I'm definitely going to speak to Virginia Rau again. Even if you don't want to.'

'I didn't say I didn't want to,' Abby said. 'I'm just trying to work it out in my head, that's all.'

'Who knows the code for the alarm?' Ger asked. 'It had been switched off, right?'

'Or Charlotte forgot to turn it on before she went out,' Abby said.

'According to the statement she gave last night,' Ellen said, 'the only people who know the code are Charlotte herself, Nick and their Polish cleaner who comes every day. Nick and the cleaner both have alibis. He was at the restaurant till late. Plenty of witnesses. The cleaner was at a Polish club until midnight.'

'What about Freya?' Ger asked.

'Good point,' Abby said. 'Why don't we ask her? Ellen and I are going over there later.'

'Why later?' Ger said. 'Can't you go now?'

'Emer Dawson's on her way to the station,' Abby said. 'Kieran's sister, remember? She flew in from her holiday early this morning. She's due here in half an hour.'

'I've got an appointment with Pat's counsellor,' Ellen said. 'So I was wondering, would you mind meeting Emer without me? I won't be long with the counsellor and we can go across to Freya's together after that?'

Abby's face flushed a pretty shade of pink.

'Of course I wouldn't mind. Thanks, Ellen.'

Ger pushed her chair back and stood up.

'What say we finish this conversation across the road? I could kill one of Danilo's extra strong coffees. Jamala's organised a press conference for later today. I'm going to need some severe caffeine inside me to get through that.'

'Mind if I don't come?' Ellen said. 'I've got this appointment. Don't want to be late.'

Ger nodded. 'Of course. Give me a call later. Abby?'

The three women left the office together. Ellen watched Ger

and Abby walk together along the corridor to the lift at the end. Ger leaned towards Abby and said something that made Abby laugh. Something uncomfortable settled in Ellen's stomach, heavy like a stone.

The lift doors slid open and Ger stepped back, motioning for Abby to go first. Inside the lift, the two women stood side by side, facing Ellen. Abby waved before the doors closed and she disappeared. Ellen could hear her, still laughing, the sound echoing back along the empty corridor to where she stood. Until eventually the laughter was gone too.

When she could no longer hear Abby, Ellen turned and walked the other way, trying not to think about why she suddenly felt so lonely.

SIX

Larry Paxman, Pat's counsellor, worked from the ground floor of a converted warehouse building in a narrow street behind the river in Rotherhithe. Ellen found a parking space near the underground station and walked from there. She had an umbrella with her but as she approached Larry's office she barely needed it. The tall buildings either side seemed to lean across the street towards each other, leaving only the narrowest strip of sky above. Ellen had first come here on a sunny day in early winter. The white light had cast long shadows that zigzagged across the street, giving it character and atmosphere. Today, it just felt miserable.

Inside, she was greeted by Larry's receptionist who brought her straight into his office.

'Ellen.' Larry shook her hand and sat down on a low, comfy-looking armchair. 'Take a seat.'

She sat opposite him and waited.

The room was painted daffodil yellow. Walls covered in children's paintings. Two red plastic boxes in the corner, both overflowing with toys. It was a welcome contrast to the rest of the world.

'Pat's doing well,' Larry said. 'It took a while, but I think we're really making progress. He's a bright kid, but you already know that, right?'

'It's difficult to be objective when it's your own child,' Ellen said.

Larry smiled. 'I know that. But he really is. He's not just academically bright, either. There's a real emotional intelligence there, too. Of course, this means he's very sensitive to everything that's happened, which can sometimes have a negative effect. But it also means he's very good at articulating how he feels about things. And that's one of the things that's helping right now.'

'He feels everything so deeply,' she said. 'It makes him vulnerable. I'm so worried, you see, that he won't be able to get past this. That it will stop him getting on with his life and doing all the amazing things I know he's capable of doing.'

She was talking too much. Like she used to in the counselling sessions she'd had after the Billy Dunston incident. What was it about these people that made her do that? It was their silence, she decided. She looked at Larry, looking at her. He had a kind face. Watery blue eyes and a white beard. A completely bald head. So bald that she guessed he must shave it to get it so smooth.

Like he knew what she was thinking, Larry rubbed his hand along the top of his shiny head. Embarrassed, Ellen looked away quickly.

'Is that what you wanted to see me about?' Larry asked.

'Sort of,' Ellen said, still not looking at him. Staring instead at a picture on the wall. A child's drawing of a face. Impossible to know if it was a man or a woman. Just a circle with two dots for eyes and a curved line for a smiling mouth. Either side of the face, the imprint from a child's hands that had been dipped in green paint.

'Is that supposed to mean something?' She pointed at the picture.

'Do you want it to mean anything?' Larry asked.

She glared at him, only realising it was a joke when she saw he was smiling.

'Lots of the younger kids I see draw pictures for me,' he said. 'I like to put them up so I can see them. It reminds me why I do this.'

'How much longer will you need to see him?' she asked.

'It's hard to tell,' Larry said. 'Like I said, he's making really good progress. Listen, Ellen, am I missing something? Until today, I got the impression you were pretty happy with how we were doing. If there's a reason you want the sessions to end, then please tell me. If you're not satisfied, that's okay. It happens sometimes. I can help you find another counsellor if that's what you want.'

'No,' Ellen said. 'It's not that. Sorry, Larry. I got a letter from his new school this morning. You know he's starting secondary school in September?'

Larry nodded.

'There's a parents' evening coming up,' Ellen continued. 'I have to go along in a month's time to find out all about the school and what his curriculum will be like and what sports he'll be playing and God knows what else. And I can't stop wondering, what if he's not ready?'

'For what?' Larry asked.

'Secondary school,' Ellen said. 'It's only a few months away. I know it's a good school and everything. And of course I'm going to tell them that he'll need special attention and they'll need to take extra care of him but even still, he's so little and he's been through so much already. Maybe I should keep him back a year. It wouldn't do him any harm to have another year in primary school, would it? I mean, he loves it there and it's a safe environment and ...'

'Ellen.'

She stopped speaking. Realised – too late – that she'd been babbling like a fool again.

'He'll be fine.'

'You can't know that.'

'I do know that keeping him back would be a huge mistake,' Larry said. 'He needs to carry on living his life as normal. Yes, he had a terrible experience. But he's dealing with it. He's a clever, resilient boy and he's doing fine. Terrible things happen in life. We can't avoid that. What we can do is give ourselves the tools, the mental strength, to deal with the bad stuff when it happens. That's what we're doing with Pat right now. Okay?'

She nodded, not trusting herself to speak straightaway. Larry was right. You couldn't protect anyone from the shit life threw at you. No matter how much you wanted to.

She left soon after that, thanking Larry and promising she'd try harder not to worry so much. Outside, the rain had stopped and shafts of sunlight cut down through the gaps in the tall buildings, creating pools of light in the narrow street.

Ellen didn't go straight back to the car. Instead, she turned right and walked to the river. The tide was in and the water was high. A cold wind blew across the water, rippling the surface and creating small waves that caught hold of the sunshine so that the river seemed to sparkle and dance with every gust of wind.

* * *

Charlotte sat on the sofa, legs tucked underneath her, watching Nick pace around the place like a deranged caged beast.

'I wish you'd sit down,' she said. 'You're making it impossible for me to relax. And you know what the doctor said. I need complete rest for the next forty-eight hours.'

'Sorry.' He sat on the sofa opposite. 'It's difficult, that's all. So much has happened over the last few days, I can't get my head around it. Jesus, Charlie, when the police came to the restaurant earlier, I thought, Christ ... first Kieran, now this. Tell me again what happened?'

So she went through it all again. And waited for him to accuse her of being drunk and falling by herself. But he didn't do that. Hadn't done it once, in fact, since he'd arrived at the hospital to bring her home. She wondered why he was being so nice. Not that she was complaining. She only wished she'd worked out earlier what she needed to do to get him to pay her a bit of attention.

She shifted on the sofa, wincing more than she needed to when the movement caused pain. Immediately, he was on his feet and rushing across to help her.

'I'm fine.' She smiled, following it up with a grimace, as if the pain was too much for her. 'I'm so glad you're here now. I don't think I'd feel safe, being here on my own. Not after what happened.'

He looked away and a surge of pure hatred rose up inside her. The bastard. She wondered whether he'd say it now or wait until later.

'I was so scared,' she said, before he had a chance to speak. 'I thought I was going to die, Nick. All I could think of was Kieran and what had happened to him. I was certain the killer had come back.'

She turned her head away, as if she couldn't bear for him to see her crying. He crouched down beside her, took her face with his hand and used his thumb to rub her tears away. No need for him to know they were tears of rage, not fear.

'It must have been awful,' he said. 'I'm so sorry I wasn't here. I worked late and didn't want to wake you. If I'd known what had happened, I'd have been here in an instant.'

'You're here now, darling,' she said. 'That's all that matters.'

A hesitation. He was so bloody transparent. She watched him pretending to grapple with his conscience, waited for him to come to the inevitable conclusion.

'Darling,' he began, 'I'm so very sorry.'

'Don't,' she said.

'It's just, we're at such a crucial stage with the new restaurant,' he continued, determined to have his say whether it was what she wanted or not. 'I can't afford to let up, not even for an afternoon.'

'Not even for me, you mean.'

She wanted him gone. His betrayal was worse because he'd been acting so kind. Like he really cared about her. When all the time he was thinking about how he could get away. She wanted to ask him if it was the restaurant or his latest little tart that he couldn't keep away from, but there was no point. Besides, if she stayed dignified, maybe she could make him feel bad at least.

'I know how important it is,' she said. 'It's your work and I respect that. But I'm so scared, Nick. Surely you wouldn't leave me alone after what's happened. Would you?'

He was up again, pacing the room worse than ever. Speaking fast, the way he always did when he wanted to get his own way.

'I've already spoken with the police,' he gabbled. 'They've got someone keeping an eye on the house. I'll get onto Pete, too. Ask him if we could borrow one of his boys for the night.'

'I will not share my house with one of Pete Cooper's thugs,' Charlotte said.

'They won't have to come inside,' Nick said. 'I'll arrange for them to park out front. Stay in the car. That should do the trick. And I won't be long. I've got a few bits and pieces to finish off but I should be back home by ten, at the very latest.'

When he said ten, he meant closer to midnight, of course.

'What about Ginny?' he asked. 'Why don't you ask her to come over? I'll go and pick her up. How about that?'

He looked so pleased with himself, like he'd just given her a bunch of flowers or told her he was taking her away for the weekend.

'Ginny's not answering her phone,' Charlotte said. 'I've tried calling her a few times but she's not picking up.'

Again, that feeling that something wasn't right. Ginny's phone was like an extra part of her body. Even if she couldn't take a call, for whatever reason, she almost always called back within a few minutes. But Charlotte had called three times over the last hour and still nothing.

'Freya?'

Charlotte rolled her eyes. 'Oh please. You think she'd want to spend an evening here, just me and her? She'd rather stick pins in her eyes. Besides, I don't want her to know about what happened.

She's got enough to worry about at the moment.'

Nick nodded. 'Of course. Sorry, I wasn't thinking.'

He never did. The only person he ever thought of was himself.

'It's like someone's out to get us,' he said. 'Do you know what I mean? I can't help wondering if this is some sort of jealousy thing. You know, someone who resents how successful I am?'

'Why does it have to be about you?' Charlotte asked. 'Think about it, Nick. If someone wanted to get at you, why would they kill Kieran of all people? It can't have been a secret that you two didn't like each other.'

'It wasn't that we didn't like each other,' Nick said. 'I just didn't think he was the right guy for Freya. I did try to be civil, you know.'

'Well you didn't try very hard,' Charlotte said. 'Anyone could see you disapproved of him.'

'Hope you haven't said that to the police,' Nick said.

'What do you mean?'

He ran a hand through his hair. 'Christ almighty, Charlotte. Think about it. If you go spouting on about Kieran and I not liking each other, don't you think that gives them a motive? The last thing I want is the police digging around into my business. Especially at the moment. We can't afford any negative publicity. Not now, not ever. My whole business is built on my reputation as a decent, hard-working family man. Nothing – and I mean nothing – can happen to damage that.'

She wondered then if he was capable of murder. And decided

yes, he probably was. But under the right circumstances, wasn't everyone?

She didn't think Nick had killed Kieran, though. Not because it was beyond him to do something like that. No. Her reasons for believing her husband's innocence were more practical than that. He'd said it himself. He was about to open a new chain of restaurants. Their success depended on his unsullied reputation as a man of the people. One of the good guys. He wouldn't do anything to mess that up. He cared too much about his precious restaurants for that.

If only, Charlotte thought, he could find it in himself to care that much about his marriage. Maybe then, there would be some hope for them.

SEVEN

The front desk called, told Abby that Emer Dawson had arrived. Finally.

'That lady sitting over there,' Ron Felix, the officer on the front desk, told her.

Abby looked over, saw a tall, thin woman with bobbed blonde hair sitting on the bench, an oversized handbag placed carefully on her lap.

'Mrs Dawson?' Abby asked, walking over.

'Emer.' The woman stood up and shook Abby's hand, attempting a smile without much success.

'Thank you so much for coming,' Abby said.

'I'm sorry it took me so long,' Emer said. 'It wasn't easy, arranging all the flights at the last moment. Steve – my husband – he thought we should wait. We only had another four days left of our holiday and he said it was a waste of money booking new flights. But I had to come.'

'Of course,' Abby said. 'I'm very sorry about your brother.'

Emer's face crumpled as if she was about to cry.

'There's a café across the road,' Abby said. 'Serves really good coffee. Why don't we go over there and we can have a proper chat?'

In Danilo's, Abby ordered the drinks and the two women sat across from each other at a table by the window.

'You're right,' Emer said, taking a sip from her cup. 'This is good.'

'Much better than the muck served in our staff canteen,' Abby said.

'It's all so surreal,' Emer said. 'Sitting here with you like this. I can't get my head around it.'

'Were you close?' Abby asked. 'You and Kieran?'

Emer shook her head. 'Not really. There's a fifteen-year age gap. Kieran was only a little kid when I left home to go to university. We got on fine. It's just we never had that much in common really. Our parents are dead. Mum first, then Dad two years later. I thought maybe that would bring us closer together but if anything, we drifted further apart from each other.'

Abby thought of her own, dead brother and how close they'd been. Thought how lucky she was to have had the special bond.

'I'm sorry,' she said.

Emer shrugged. 'Nothing to be sorry about. The truth is,

Kieran and Freya didn't really approve of me. I work for a super-market chain, I married a banker and I send my kids to private school. All things they don't agree with.'

'Have you spoken to Freya yet?' Abby asked.

'I've tried,' Emer said. 'But she's not answering my calls or replying to my texts. I'd like to go over there but I'm not sure I can bear a confrontation. What do you think?'

'I'm going to see her later,' Abby said. 'Why don't I ask her?'

'You'd do that?'

'Of course,' Abby said. 'When was the last time you saw Kieran?'

'Six months ago,' Emer said. 'We had a row. I don't know if you need to know that or not. He was a scrounger, my brother. Always asking for loans of money which he never paid back. It used to drive Steve mad. Steve's my husband, by the way. Normally I was a bit of a soft touch. Kieran knew that.

'I was in London, I called to see if he was free for lunch. I was sort of surprised when he said yes, to tell you the truth. Usually when I wanted to meet he had some excuse or other.

'Anyway, we met. I took him to a really nice restaurant. He spent the time criticising my lifestyle while also managing to eat all the food I'd ordered and drink the best part of the bottle of wine. At the end of the meal he let me pay, then had the cheek to ask me for a loan. I said no. First time I'd ever said no to him.'

'He didn't like that?' Abby said.

'Not one bit,' Emer said. 'Called me a stuck-up selfish bitch and stormed out on me. I didn't hear from him again. I tried phoning but he never answered my calls. I got through to Freya once and she … well, she wasn't very pleasant. She blamed me for not giving him the money he asked for. She said he needed it to pay his fees. And now he's …'

She started to cry, sobbing quietly.

'Sorry,' she whispered. 'I don't even know why I'm so upset. Steve says it's stupid of me.'

Steve sounded like a piece of work, Abby thought.

'It's perfectly natural,' she said. 'He was your brother.'

Emer wiped her face with the back of her hand and sniffed.

'We were a whole family,' she said. 'Me, Mum and Dad, Kieran. And now all that's gone and there's only me left. I don't know what to do.'

Abby knew she had to ask more questions. Like where Emer was on Friday night and whether she could think of anyone who might want to kill her brother. Anyone like Steve, her husband, for example. But that could wait a few minutes.

She reached across the table, patted Emer's hand and told her to take as long as she needed. Emer held on to Abby's hand, squeezed it tight while she cried, clinging on as if her life depended on it.

* * *

There were no parking spaces and Ellen had to drive around the block twice until she found a gap she was able to squeeze her car into. As she walked briskly up Ennersdale Road, she collided with a woman coming down the hill, walking just as fast.

'Ouch!' The woman jumped back, rubbing her shoulder. 'Watch where you're going, would you?'

She was small and exquisitely turned out in a pea-green collarless woollen jacket, tight black leather jeans and patent red, knee-high, calf-hugging boots.

'Sorry,' Ellen said automatically, before she realised it hadn't even been her fault. At least, she was pretty sure it hadn't.

The woman shook her head.

'No, I'm sorry. I was distracted.'

Ellen shrugged. 'We'll both survive.'

'For now, at least.' The woman grinned, exposing a set of perfectly white, perfectly symmetrical teeth. 'Bye then.' She winked at Ellen as she tottered past. A silver Porsche was parked near the end of the road. The woman pointed her keys at this, unlocked it and climbed inside. Ellen watched until she drove away then walked up to number 19. She saw Abby, walking towards the house, coming from the opposite direction.

'I've just finished with Kieran's sister,' Abby said. 'Poor woman's really upset.'

'Is she coming to see Freya?' Ellen asked.

'Freya's refusing to talk to her,' Abby said. 'Seems to blame Emer for not helping Kieran out when he had problems paying his college fees a few months ago.'

'Is she a suspect?' Ellen asked.

Abby shook her head. 'She and her husband were in the Canaries on Friday night. She said she rarely saw her brother and I believe her. How was the counsellor?'

'Fine,' Ellen said. Not wanting to talk about that, she rang the doorbell, hoping Abby would get the hint.

Freya answered quickly, almost like she'd been expecting their visit.

'I told you ...,' she began, then stopped and shook her head, face turning red. 'Sorry. I thought you were someone else.'

'Who?' Ellen asked.

'It doesn't matter,' Freya said. 'I suppose you want to come in?' She stepped inside and went upstairs, not bothering to see whether the detectives were following or not.

Freya went into the sitting room and sat down. Ellen sat down, motioned for Abby to do the same, thinking if they waited for an invitation it might never come.

'I've just seen Emer Dawson,' Abby said.

Freya snorted. 'Suppose the stuck-up cow pretended to be upset?'

'She is upset,' Abby said. 'She wants to see you.'

'Well I don't want to see her,' Freya said. 'You can tell her that. Save me the trouble of having to speak to her myself.'

'We were hoping to speak to you about your mother,' Ellen said.

A flush spread across Freya's cheeks and there was a flash of something in her eyes. Ellen thought it might be anger but she couldn't be sure.

'What about her?' Freya asked.

'I assume you've heard what happened,' Ellen said.

Freya leaned forward in her chair, eyes drilling into Ellen.

'I haven't heard anything,' she said. 'But that's hardly a surprise, is it? You lot like to keep everything to yourself until you've got no choice about it. What's happened? What's she done?'

'She hasn't done anything,' Ellen said. 'I'm sorry.' There she went again. 'I just assumed ...' Stupid, stupid. Why should she have assumed anything? Wasn't it totally possible that Charlotte Gleeson had deliberately concealed her accident to avoid causing her daughter any further distress?

'Your mother had a slight accident,' Abby said. 'She's fine, so please don't worry. A bit bruised, that's all.'

Rather than being distressed, the news seemed to relax Freya. She sat back in her chair and crossed her legs.

'I assume she was drunk? Oh, come on. You must have worked it out by now. My mother's a pisshead. A raving, raging, pathetic alcoholic.'

Ellen managed not to wince as a slew of memories came into sharp focus. Night after lonely night with nothing but wine for company. Using alcohol as a way of ignoring the things she was meant to be dealing with.

'What?' Freya asked. 'You think I'm making it up? If you don't believe me, speak to my father. Her drinking is the reason their marriage is so fucked up. It's the reason ... No. That's not fair. I promised.'

'Promised what?'

Freya wouldn't look at her. Kept her head turned to one side, staring at the bare mantelpiece.

'She ... look, it was only once and she was really wasted. It didn't mean anything. I mean, she's my mother for crying out loud.'

'What did she do?'

Freya waved a hand in the air, like she was already dismissing what she was about to say.

'She made a pass at Kieran,' she said. 'But it's not as bad as it sounds, I swear. She made a fool of herself, that's all. Kieran was mortified, of course. We all were.'

Ellen tried – and failed – to picture herself ever getting that drunk. Never. She thought of Jim O'Dwyer. How foolish she'd been, mistaking lust for something deeper.

'Your mother must have been the most embarrassed,' Ellen said.

Freya smirked. 'I don't think she remembers. She's never mentioned it and neither have I.'

'What about Kieran?'

'God, no,' Freya said. 'He certainly didn't say anything to her. He just wanted to forget the whole thing had ever happened. I mean, it's disgusting.'

'It can't have been easy for you,' Ellen said. 'Has she always had a problem?'

'Always,' Freya said. 'It's my fault. That's what she used to tell me. They were happy – supposedly – until I came along and ruined everything.'

Ellen hated this. The secrets she uncovered as part of her job. People's lives were so messy and horrible. She didn't want to know about Charlotte Gleeson's drink problem. She certainly didn't want to know about a little girl who'd been brought up believing she was the cause of all the unhappiness in her family.

She cleared her throat. 'You don't believe that, do you?'

'I did,' Freya said. 'For the longest time, of course that's what I believed. What child wouldn't? Then I grew up and realised she was the fuck-up, not me. It was one of the most liberating moments of my life the day I worked that out.'

'We need to ask you about last night,' Ellen said, steering the conversation back to the reason she was here.

'What about it?' Freya asked.

'Were you here all night?'

Freya reared back, as if Ellen had tried to smack her.

'Why?'

'We need to know,' Ellen said. 'That's why.'

'Is this to do with my mother? I thought you said it was an accident.'

'She fell down a flight of stairs,' Ellen said. 'She claims some-one pushed her.'

Freya smirked.

'Claims? Of course she does. Well you can rule me out. I was here all night. Drinking wine, listening to music and generally feeling sorry for myself.'

'Anyone able to prove that?' Abby asked.

When Freya shook her head, Ellen felt a pang of sympathy. She'd been there herself, using wine and music to deal with the impossible grief.

'My dad was meant to come over,' Freya said. 'But he was caught up in work. You could ask him, I guess. I was here when he phoned me. Sorry. Stupid. He wouldn't know I was here, right?'

'Where was he?' Ellen said.

'Work,' Freya said. 'And he really was. I mean, I could hear the restaurant. You know, the noise and that. I know what it sounds like and I swear to you, that's where he was.'

Ellen asked what time they'd spoken on the phone but Freya claimed she didn't remember, blaming the wine. Certain they'd got as much as they could for now, Ellen motioned to Abby that they should go.

'One more question,' Ellen said, on the way out. 'We'll be going through Kieran's bank statements later. Is there anything in particular we should look out for? He hasn't come into any money recently or anything like that?'

Two blotches of colour appeared on each of Freya's cheeks but when she spoke her voice was calm, uninterested almost.

'We don't have any money,' she said. 'It wasn't important to us. My parents kept trying to force me to take handouts but that was the last thing I was going to do, believe me.'

'And yet you were angry with Emer for not helping Kieran out when he asked for money?' Abby said.

'That was different,' Freya said. 'Kieran was asking for a loan, not a handout. He would have paid her back. We're not the sort of people to take something for nothing.'

She sounded so earnest when she said this, Ellen didn't think she was lying. Or rather, she didn't think Freya was the sort of person to take something for nothing. The problem was, she didn't think she could say the same thing about Kieran.

EIGHT

Ger stood on the raised platform at the front of the room. Behind her, a projector screen displayed an image of Kieran Burton's dead body. The shot had been taken at the crime scene and Burton's lifeless eyes stared at Ellen.

The briefing was for the benefit of every officer involved in the case, from the PCSOs and uniforms to the Special Investigations Unit detectives sitting alongside Ellen at the front. Ger had just finished going over everything they knew so far about the victim and their potential witnesses. Ellen, already familiar with every detail, only half-listened, more focussed instead on avoiding the question she still saw in Kieran's eyes.

When Ger finally finished, she invited Harry Grahame to come up. Harry was one of the station's senior SOCOs and, like

Ellen, a Lewisham old-timer. She liked Harry. More than that, she respected him.

He stood at the front, waiting patiently for everyone in the room to quieten down and let him speak. His eyes scanned the room, making eye contact with those he knew. When he saw Ellen, he smiled. By the time she returned his smile, he had moved on and was already looking at someone else.

Harry started by giving a summary of the different pieces of evidence they'd found at the crime scene. He spoke in detail about soil samples, tyre treads and footprints.

'Then there's the victim's clothes,' he said. 'As you know, it's standard procedure in a case like this for the clothes to be handed to us so we can examine them properly. I could go on for some time about the origins of the cotton used to make Kieran's denim jacket and the brand of jeans he wore.' He paused and everyone in the room smiled obediently. 'But I'm sure you don't want that so I'll focus on the one particular piece of evidence we found. Take a look at this.'

He lifted the remote control for the projector and Kieran's face was replaced by a long strand of hair lying on its own on a white background.

'This piece of hair was found on Kieran's tee-shirt,' Harry said. 'You've all seen a picture of the victim and you'll know he had short blonde hair. The chances of a long piece of hair like this drifting through the air and sticking to his tee-shirt are slim. It's far more likely he was in physical contact with the person whose head this came from. And it's likely – but not definite – that the physical contact happened close to the time of the murder. If it had happened earlier in the day, the hair would probably have fallen away. We have no way of knowing at this point if the hair came from a man or a woman. However, it has been sent off for testing. When the test results are back, we will know whether it was a male or female and we should also be able to see if its DNA matches any of our suspects.'

Harry stopped speaking and a murmur spread across the room as people started to work out the implications from this single piece of evidence.

'How long before we know the test results?' a voice from the back of the room asked.

'It could take up to a week,' Harry said. 'Maybe longer. We use a lab in Dartford for all our Forensic testing. They're really good but because of that they're also very busy. I promise you I'll get any results back as quickly as we possibly can.'

Ger thanked Harry and invited Jamala Nnamani, the team's communications manager, to step forward.

'We held a press conference earlier,' Jamala said. 'Lots of interest, as you'd imagine. Especially when we told them who the victim's girlfriend was.'

'We could have left the Gleesons out of it,' Ger said. 'But we figured someone would make the connection sooner or later. Jamala and I decided it was best to get in there first.'

'Correct.' Jamala nodded. 'That way, we can control how they run with it. I imagine there'll be something in today's *Evening Standard*. We can expect the main news programmes will do a piece this evening. And then we've got the broadsheets tomorrow.'

Jamala looked at Abby.

'You may want to warn the family. They're going to find themselves getting a lot of unwanted attention over the next few days.'

Jamala went on to brief everyone on what they could – and couldn't – say if they were approached directly by a journalist. Ellen let her mind drift, as she formed a picture of Kieran's last few minutes alive. Had he gone to the laneway to meet someone? The hair on his tee-shirt could belong to Freya. A DNA test would confirm that one way or the other. But if it came back negative, did that mean Kieran met someone else in the laneway? Another woman?

At some point during the question-and-answer session with Ger and Jamala, the projector screen went into standby mode, leaving the screen blank. But when Ellen looked at it, she imagined Kieran's face was still there, trying to work out who had killed him, and why. She remembered the question she'd seen in his dead eyes and imagined it would remain there, following her around, boring inside her head, until she knew who killed him. And why they'd done it.

* * *

On Monday, Ellen and the children had supper at Sean and Terry's apartment in Limehouse. They ate homemade pizza and garlic bread. Like everything she'd ever eaten at the apartment, the food was delicious. Afterwards, Eilish persuaded Terry to put on some Katy Perry music and dance with her while Ellen and Sean tidied up.

'Doesn't look like he needed much persuading,' Ellen said, watching Terry take Eilish's arms and twirl her around the room. He danced well, unlike Eilish who had inherited her father's utter lack of rhythm. Like Vinny, it didn't stop her throwing herself into the dancing with an enthusiasm that bordered on manic.

'Why don't you join them?' Ellen suggested. 'Doesn't take two of us to clear this up.'

'I don't mind,' Sean said. 'Besides, it means we can chat. I bumped into Jim the other day. He was asking about you.'

'I don't know why,' Ellen said. 'He sees me often enough. If he wants to know how I am, he can ask me himself.'

Sean touched her arm. 'Don't be like that, El.'

She shook his hand off.

'Leave it, Sean. Please?'

She turned away from him before he could interrogate her any further and watched her daughter instead. Freckles and strawberry blonde hair. Limbs too long and out of proportion for a body that hadn't caught up with them yet. The sunniest personality in the entire world. Often, Ellen wondered if any of her genes had made it in there at all. Eilish was like Vinny. Most times, this constant reminder of her husband was a blessing. Occasionally, like right now, the similarities brought their own kind of pain.

At the beginning, the grief had felt like a huge animal devouring Ellen from the inside. Gobbling away at every part of her, hollowing her out, until there was nothing left. Gradually, moment by moment then day by day, the beast lost its strength. It never left her but it went into a sort of hibernation, still there but bearable. Just.

And then, with no warning, the beast woke up and wham! The attack every bit as powerful as those awful early days. It hit her now. The way Eilish moved, the song that was playing, all of it got mixed up in her head with memories of Vinny until she couldn't breathe. The wrongness of it, the unjust, unfair bloody fucking wrongness. It was unbearable.

She pushed past Sean, out of the open-plan living room and onto the balcony. Breathing in big mouthfuls of cold, grimy London air, vaguely aware of a barge drifting past on the river below as she clutched her hollowed-out stomach and howled silent howls to an uncaring world.

'Mum?'

Pat. Her very own mini-me. As much Ellen as Eilish was Vinny. Standing beside her, a worried frown creasing his perfect little face. Her beautiful, complex, perfect boy. She nearly told him she was okay. Nearly told him to go back inside and not to worry about her, that she was fine and she'd be back inside in a moment. Something stopped her.

'Sorry, darling. I was thinking about your dad and I needed a moment, that's all.'

The frown cleared and Pat nodded.

'That happens to me sometimes as well. Like, I'll be in the park watching a dad playing football with his kids and I remember Dad doing that with me. He wasn't very good, was he?'

And just like that, the beast drew back, defeated by the compassion of an eleven-year-old boy and the power of a mother's love.

'He was rubbish,' she said. 'But it never stopped him trying. And you know what, Pat? I loved him for that.'

'I wish he didn't die,' Pat said. 'It's not fair, is it?'

'It's not fair,' Ellen said. 'And I hate it too. But we have each other. And Sean and Terry and Eilish and Gran and Granddad. We're lucky.'

'Yeah,' Pat said. 'I know.'

But he didn't sound like he knew it. Didn't look it either, scowling his anger at her. Ellen opened her arms and he let her hug him. She kissed the top of his head.

'Your hair needs washing,' she said. 'Again. Hormones. Happens when you get to your age.'

'Mu-u-um!' He squirmed his way out of her arms. 'Will you stop going on about that? Please?'

But he was smiling, mock-anger replacing the real thing. Ellen smiled back and suddenly they were both laughing.

On the river below, the barge stopped right beneath their balcony, almost as if it couldn't bear to pass without pausing and sharing this perfect moment.

TUESDAY

ONE

The main campus of the University of Greenwich was based in three baroque buildings designed by Christopher Wren and situated on the south bank of the River Thames.

Ellen had arranged to meet Abby by the entrance, across the road from the Trafalgar pub. She arrived early but Abby was there already, standing by the wrought-iron gate, ignoring the looks from several male students as they passed her.

'Beautiful morning,' she called as Ellen approached. 'Spring is certainly in the air. I can feel it.'

'What's got you so cheery?' Ellen asked. The sky was grey and overcast and the best that could be said about the weather was that it wasn't raining. Yet.

'This way,' Abby said, leading Ellen across the courtyard to the building closest to the river. 'Sociology Department is in here. I've already checked.'

As Abby bounced ahead, Ellen realised why the FLO was so chipper this morning.

'Your date,' she said, catching up. 'Went well, then?'

Abby tapped the side of her nose and grinned. 'I'm saying nothing. Oh okay then, if you insist. He was amazing, Ellen. We really hit it off. I expected him to be really dull. I mean, a City lawyer. I thought he'd be an arse.'

'But he wasn't?'

Abby beamed. 'He's adorable. His name is Sam and I'm seeing him again this evening. He's taking me to the Shard. There's a champagne bar at the top, did you know that?'

Ellen remembered a night in the same bar six months ago. She hoped Abby would have more luck after a date there than she had.

'I know it,' she said. 'I'm sure you'll have a great time. Ah, here we are.'

She stopped at a door marked Sociology.

'Sorry for going on about Sam,' Abby said. 'I won't do it again. Promise.'

Ellen smiled. 'Don't be silly. Come on. Let's go find this Professor Holmes.'

Wrongly, Ellen had assumed Professor Holmes would be a man. She had formed a vague picture in her head of a middle-aged, stuffy academic with frizzy grey hair and glasses. When they finally tracked the professor down to a large office on the second floor, Professor Holmes turned out to be a petite bombshell with long, luscious red hair and a cartoonishly curvaceous body.

Her office was an airy, tidy room with a huge window that looked out across the river.

'Thanks for seeing us,' Ellen said, eyes flickering past the professor's fiery hair to the amazing view behind her desk.

'Wonderful, isn't it?' Professor Holmes said. 'I'm sure I'd have left Greenwich long ago if it wasn't for this office. Please, sit down.'

Two chairs had been placed side by side opposite the professor's big wooden desk.

'I'm afraid I left my glasses behind this morning and I can't see a bloody thing without them,' she said. 'Would you mind pulling the chairs closer so I can see your faces? That's better. Thanks.' She looked from Abby to Ellen. 'I assume you're here about Kieran?'

'We're trying to build a picture of the sort of person he was,' Ellen said. 'We've spoken to his girlfriend, of course. And our colleagues have been busy interviewing students on campus. As you were Kieran's course tutor, you must have formed a pretty good impression of him. We want to know what he was like and if you can think of any reason at all that someone would want to hurt him.'

All the while Ellen spoke, Professor Holmes stared at her

intently, eyes squinting as if she was looking for something she couldn't find on Ellen's face. Ellen knew it was the lack of glasses but she found it disconcerting nonetheless. It was a relief when the professor sat back in her chair and relaxed her face as she considered Ellen's question.

'I didn't like Kieran very much,' Professor Holmes said. 'Sorry, I'm sure it's bad manners to speak ill of the dead but I'd rather be truthful with you. I can't see the point in this conversation other-wise. He thought he was terribly charming and I suspect a lot of the younger students, especially the women, fell for his act. I'm a bit too long in the tooth. He made my skin crawl quite frankly.

'He was popular enough, I suppose. I never understood why. He was the sort of fellow to switch the charm on for someone he was interested in – the pretty young girls, especially. But if you weren't important to him, he didn't care how he behaved. He could be quite nasty to people when he wanted to.'

'Nasty how?' Ellen asked.

'So there's a girl called Marina in his tutor group,' Professor Holmes said. 'She's overweight and painfully shy. Whenever she built up the courage to ask a question during a lecture, Kieran would start sniggering and whispering about her. I've had to pull him up on it more than once. And I've watched him in the can-teen too. He's the sort who sat there with his mates for hours, making snide remarks about anyone unlucky enough to pass their little group. Horrible.'

She stopped talking and smiled at Ellen – a wide, inviting

smile that hid absolutely nothing. Ellen decided she liked this woman.

'Maybe you think I'm cruel, Detective. I promise you I can be quite lovely when the situation requires. But you did ask.'

'I did indeed.' Ellen returned the smile. 'What about Kieran's girlfriend? Did you ever meet her?'

The professor frowned. 'Girlfriend? I didn't know he had one. Well, there's Cosima, of course, but I don't think there was anything going on there. If you ask me, Cosima couldn't stand Kieran any more than I could. Besides, she is way out of his league. No. I can't see a girl like that falling for someone like him.'

'Cosima?' Abby asked.

'Cosima Cooper,' Professor Holmes said. 'She's a Psychology student here at the university. Kieran was taking Psychology as one of his options. They were in the same class. He was forever sniffing around her but, like I said, she never seemed the least bit interested.'

The name rang a bell somewhere in the furthest reaches of Ellen's mind. She tried to focus on the connection but Abby was speaking again and she had to concentrate on that instead.

'Kieran's girlfriend is called Freya,' Abby said. 'They shared a flat together in Hither Green.'

Professor Holmes shook her head.

'I had no idea. Well, if that's true, all I can say is that he didn't act like someone who was in a relationship. Poor woman. She may be better off without him.'

Ellen thought of Freya – dumpy and unattractive – and agreed with the professor. Which left Ellen with two questions. One: what the hell was a Lothario like Kieran doing hooking up with someone like Freya Gleeson? And two:

'This Cosima Cooper,' she said. 'Can you tell us where we might be able to find her?'

The professor smiled again. 'That's easy. She'll either be at the Psychology Department. I can give you directions. Or else she's still at home. She lives in Blackheath. In one of those whopping great Georgian houses right on the heath. Cosima lives in her father's house. He's Pete Cooper. Maybe you've heard of him?'

TWO

Professor Holmes offered to gather Kieran's tutor group together so Abby and Ellen could speak to them. Ellen wanted to go directly to Cosima's house so she left Abby to deal with the tutor group.

Being on campus was a strange experience. Abby was part of the new generation of police officers who'd gone to university first. Something she was careful not to brag about in front of her colleagues. Raj was the only other person in their team with a degree. She'd spent three very happy, uncomplicated years at Sussex University, not learning very much about English Literature but an awful lot about relationships, particularly with the opposite sex. She'd had a steady string of boyfriends, none of whom she'd felt more than a passing affection for. Apart from a handful of female friends, she had lost contact with most of her uni pals.

Coming here today brought a rush of memories. For the first time since leaving Brighton she felt a flicker of nostalgia for that brief time when life seemed infinite and full of possibility. It was only six years ago but it felt like longer.

The students milled around her as she crossed the open courtyard with Professor Holmes. In one corner, a group of girls had gathered, giggling over something on a mobile phone. There were four of them in total. Each one, tall and slim with shiny hair and an air of confidence Abby remembered working hard to replicate, copying the other girls around her.

She'd never planned on joining the police. It was towards the end of her degree, when the future loomed ahead exciting and uncertain, that she considered it. They had a careers day. People from different businesses came and talked to the students, told them about the different opportunities open to them if they joined this bank or that public sector body or ... Every single one had bored Abby beyond belief. Until the final speaker stood up. A tall, distinguished-looking man with silver-grey hair and a look of George Clooney about him. He was a senior detective in the Met. He spoke about the police, his job and, as she listened, Abby felt something she hadn't felt throughout the rest of that long day. A glimmer of excitement. The sense that maybe, just maybe, this might be for her.

Then two months later, her brother was killed. After that,

joining the police became her only option. Six years on, she didn't know any more if she'd made the right choice. The problem was, the longer she stayed, the more difficult it became to consider doing anything else.

'They've just finished a lecture,' Professor Holmes explained as they walked. 'I called my colleague, Richard Blakely, and I've asked him to keep behind the eight students you need to speak to. These are the ones who knew Kieran the best, I think.'

The lecture hall was in an old part of the building that was once part of the naval college. Following the professor along endless winding corridors, Abby knew she had no hope of finding her way out again without help.

Nine people were waiting for her inside the lecture hall, seated in a semicircle, chatting quietly to each other. Nine faces looked curiously at Abby as she entered the room behind Professor Holmes. Eight of them were young. The other one, an older man, walked over and held out his hand.

'Richard Blakely,' he said. 'Senior lecturer in Social Psychology. I'll introduce you to the students and leave you to it, okay?'

His smile was as fake as his teeth where white and he held Abby's hand for too long after shaking it. Late forties, Abby guessed, with pale skin, shoulder-length dark hair and ice-blue eyes that stared intently at her.

Abby withdrew her hand, resisting the urge to wipe it on her trousers, and didn't bother to return his smile.

'Thank you,' she said. 'Professor Holmes, I wonder if you'd

mind waiting with me while I interview the students? I'd be more comfortable having someone from the university staff sitting with me.'

'No need, Harriet,' Blakely said smoothly. 'I can stay.'

He took Abby by the elbow and started to steer her across to the group of waiting students.

'Come and let me introduce you.'

For the second time in under a minute, Abby pulled a part of her limb out of his grasp and turned back to Professor Holmes, who was looking at Blakely with undisguised disgust.

'I'll stay if you'd like me to,' she said.

'Yes, please.' Abby looked at Blakely. 'That will be all. Thank you.'

He frowned. 'You don't need me?'

She wished Ellen was here. Abby wasn't able to express her dislike for people quite as obviously or as vocally as her boss.

'Really,' Abby said. 'It's fine.'

She turned her back on him before he made another attempt to engage and smiled encouragingly at the students.

'My name is Abby Roberts,' she said. 'I'm a detective with Lewisham CID. You all know why I'm here. I'm investigating the death of Kieran Burton. None of you are under suspicion or anything like that. And I know most of you have already spoken with some of the uniformed officers who've been on campus since yesterday. I'm here to get a better insight into what Kieran was like – the sort of person he was, who his friends were, the sort of things he was into; anything at all that will bring me closer to finding out how he died.'

She looked along the semicircle, making eye contact with each student, hoping to show she was being sincere. One of them – a slender brunette with huge, soulful eyes and an elfin haircut – looked past Abby to Blakely, still standing where Abby had left him.

'Mr Blakely,' Abby said. 'I'd like you to leave now.'

He started to say something but she spoke over him, channelling her inner Ellen.

'Go,' she said. 'If you've got something to tell me, then I'll come and find you afterwards. I can arrange to take you to the station where you can give a full statement.'

One of the students sniggered and Blakely's face flushed red. It wasn't like Abby to deliberately antagonise people and she wondered what it was about this man she found so irritating.

'Don't let yourselves be intimidated,' Blakely said, speaking over Abby to the students. 'Remember, you're not obliged to say anything if you don't want to. If you feel uncomfortable ...'

'Richard!' Professor Holmes' voice was sharp. Several people in the room, Abby included, jumped.

'We'll be fine,' the professor said. 'Just go. Now.'

After he left, Abby and Professor Holmes sat down facing the students, who stared silently at them.

'Maybe we could start with a difficult question,' Abby said. 'Could you tell me your names?'

That got a few smiles. It was a start, at least.

'Bethan,' one girl volunteered.

'Hi Bethan.' Abby smiled and the girl smiled back. She was a sturdy, attractive kid with a freckled face and shiny dark hair cut in a tidy bob. She looked the sort of no-nonsense girl who, Abby hoped, might give her an objective view of Kieran.

'How about the rest of you?' Abby said. She nodded to a long, lanky boy with long, lanky hair and a scruffy beard, who sat at one end of the row. 'What's your name?'

'Jed.'

She said hi to Jed and moved along the row, one by one, getting each person's name. An overweight girl with short hair and thick glasses introduced herself as Marina; the girl Professor Holmes had mentioned earlier.

'Thanks for that,' Abby said when they'd all given their names. She smiled at Marina. 'I know this isn't easy for any of you. You've lost a friend in horrible circumstances and I'm sure sitting here speaking with me is the last thing you feel like doing right now. But it's really important.'

This was met with silence and Abby was starting to wonder if she'd ever find a way of getting some conversation going. Finally, Bethan said something.

'It's just so horrible. How are we meant to, like, process something like this?' She looked at Professor Holmes. 'I know you said yesterday we should think about setting up sessions with the college counsellor but you know what? I don't see how that helps.

I'm sorry, it's just … I mean he was *here* with us, just like this, a few days ago. And now he's, like, dead?'

'It's totally unreal,' the boy called Jed said. 'I keep expecting him to walk in, you know?'

He looked along the row and several of them nodded in agreement. Even Marina looked sad, Abby thought.

'I do understand,' Abby said. 'I lost my brother a few years ago. It's not something you ever get over, I don't think.'

'I heard he was stabbed,' Bethan said quietly. 'Is that right?'

These poor kids, Abby thought. What a thing to have to deal with so early in their lives.

'That's right,' she said.

Bethan blinked and turned her face sideways, like she didn't want anyone to see her. A girl called Cazzie – tall and pretty – started to cry.

'I don't know why you're pretending to be so upset, Bethan,' she said. 'You couldn't stand him when he was alive. You have no right to pretend to be so upset.'

Bethan wiped her face.

'We weren't friends,' she told Abby. 'Cazzie's right about that. But that's not why I'm upset. I *knew* him, you know? I sat beside him in lectures and argued with him about stuff and even though I didn't like him, he was alive, you know? And to think of someone killing him, it's just so horrible. I can't stop thinking about it. Imagining how awful it must have been for him.' She sniffed. 'No matter what he was like, he didn't deserve that.'

'Well maybe you should have been a bit nicer to him then,' Cazzie said.

'Was there any reason you didn't like him?' Abby asked Bethan.

'We're just … we *were* very different people,' she said. 'Kieran thought I was some posh airhead, just because I'm from Reading and my dad's a surgeon. He … well, it doesn't matter.'

'Everything matters,' Abby said.

Bethan sighed. 'He had a bit of a funny thing about people with money. You know, like a class thing?'

Cazzie, who had stopped crying, rolled her eyes.

'That is *so* not true! Kieran was a *complete* sweetie. And he was really funny too, yeah? Really perceptive about other people and stuff like that.'

Abby remembered what the professor had said about Kieran earlier and she guessed 'perceptive' could possibly mean 'bitchy'.

'He liked Cazzie coz she's pretty,' Marina said. 'He was a bit, he only hung out with the cool, pretty kids?'

Cazzie shook her head, her mouth set in a sulky pout.

'Did any of you ever meet Freya?' Abby asked.

The only response she got was eight blank stares.

'His girlfriend?' Abby tried.

'No way!' Bethan put her hand over her mouth, eyes wide with shock.

'He wasn't like that,' Cazzie said.

'What do you mean?' Abby asked.

'You know, boyfriend and girlfriend and monogamy and all

that. It so wasn't Kieran's thing. He was *freer* than that, yeah? This so-called girlfriend? She's probably someone he slept with a few times? I mean, it's not like there's anything wrong with that. If you're upfront about it, then everyone knows where they stand and no one gets hurt, yeah?'

Abby guessed Cazzie was reciting Kieran's words. She was getting a sense of the sort of person Kieran was. Not someone she would have liked.

A petite oriental girl called Hisako put her hand up.

'Please?' she whispered.

Abby smiled encouragingly. 'Yes, Hisako?'

'I met them together,' she said. 'She works in a wine bar, I think?'

'Just because they were together,' Cazzie said, 'it doesn't mean they were *together*, Hissy.'

Hisako frowned.

'She said she was his girlfriend. That is what she told me.'

Cazzie sighed and shook her head. Obviously thinking no one understood her lovely Kieran like she did.

'If he was properly with someone, don't you think I'd have known about her? He was my friend, Hissy.'

'She not a friendly person,' Hisako said. 'I was in wine bar with my friends and I go to say hello to Kieran when I see him but it is like she doesn't want me to be there.'

'Maybe she'll turn up tomorrow,' Bethan said.

'Why tomorrow?' Abby asked.

Bethan flushed and looked to Jed.

'Apparently his friends have organised some kind of, like, memorial thing. Jed told me about it.'

'Yeah.' Jed nodded. 'It's on Kieran's Facebook page. It's this guy Mac? He's one of Kieran's mates. Him and a group of others are doing some sort of service by the river tomorrow morning.'

Abby got the details and asked the students if there was anything else she should know.

'Have you spoken to Cosima?' one of the boys said. A sweet kid with long dark hair and a cute smile. 'He had a bit of a thing for her, I think.'

'That was nothing,' Cazzie said quickly.

The boy shrugged. 'Maybe not. But it's like she said.' He nodded at Abby. 'Everything is important, right?'

'Absolutely.' Abby beamed at him. 'Cosima is Cosima Cooper?'

'Yeah.' The boy nodded. 'I'm not saying it was serious or anything. It's like Cazzie said, he wasn't really into all that serious stuff. But he liked her for a bit.'

'It was *nothing*,' Cazzie said. 'He thought she was pretty. Big deal. He thought lots of people were pretty.'

'If it was nothing,' the boy said, 'why did she get her dad to scare him off, then?'

Connections coming together, Abby could feel it. That sizzle in your brain, like lighting a trail of gun powder.

'What happened?'

'I only ever got Kieran's side of the story,' the boy said.

'According to him, Cosima's old man threatened him. Pushed him around a bit and said there'd be more of that if Kieran ever went near his daughter. I think her dad's a bit of a nutter.'

Abby asked a few more questions but when she got nothing else, she finished the session. Before she left, she handed out her card and asked each of them to contact her if there was anything else they could think of.

Back outside, a shy sun was trying to push its way through a cloak of clouds. Abby stood in the central courtyard, watching the students meander around her, moving slowly in groups, time and youth on their side. She pulled out her phone, punched in Ellen's number, held the phone to her ear and willed Ellen to answer.

THREE

Pete Cooper lived in a three-storey, detached house on the south side of the heath. Ellen walked up the wide, well-kept path to the house, passing a baby-blue Mercedes convertible and a rudely large 4x4, both parked in front of the house.

The house had a big porch, with a daffodil-yellow front door framed on either side with plates of antique stained glass. Ellen couldn't see a doorbell so she lifted the polished bronze, claw-shaped door knocker and banged it twice against the door.

A short, blonde woman answered the door.

'Yes?'

'Cosima?' Ellen said.

The woman shook her head.

'Who wants to see her, please?'

Ellen showed her warrant card, watched the woman's eyes widen as she looked at it.

'One moment.'

Ellen didn't have to wait long before the woman was back, inviting Ellen to step inside. Ellen followed her through a cathedral-sized entrance hall into a large room with a bay window that overlooked the heath. Something about the room reminded Ellen of the living room in Nick Gleeson's house. Similar elegant, expensive furniture, muted colours and discreet artwork on the off-white walls.

There was a giant, overly ornate white marble fireplace that Ellen thought was ugly. A portrait of a young woman hung on the wall above it. Slender, with dark hair and a serene smile, the woman was very beautiful. Ellen wanted to walk across and take a closer look but the same woman in the painting was already here in the room, watching her.

'Cosima Cooper.' The girl walked over to Ellen and held her hand out. Ellen shook it, noted the damp palm but didn't see anything in the girl's face that indicated she was scared or nervous. In fact, there was nothing at all in the girl's face. It was as expressionless as a mask.

'Please.' Cosima waved her arm around in a vague gesture. 'Take a seat.'

She waited until Ellen had settled on one of the larger sofas then chose a chair opposite. She sat very carefully, back straight and legs neatly together, her hands resting in her lap.

'Nice portrait,' Ellen said.

'It's my mum,' Cosima said.

'Oh.' Ellen frowned. 'Sorry.'

'No big deal.' Cosima shrugged. 'Everyone makes that mistake. I guess I look just like her.'

'It's beautiful,' Ellen said.

Ellen remembered Raj telling her how Cosima's mother had died. She looked at the portrait again, searching for some sign of distress that would drive the poor woman to throw herself off Beachy Head. The woman smiled down at her, serenely. Nothing to show she was depressed. Or scared. She looked happy, Ellen thought. And a lot more animated than her daughter did right now.

'Are you here to ask me about Kieran?' Cosima asked.

Ellen nodded. 'Is that okay?'

'Sure. I've kind of been waiting for someone to come and speak to me about him.'

'Why is that?'

Cosima sighed. 'He kind of had this thing for me. When I heard he'd died, I kind of figured you'd hear about it.'

'We're trying to speak to everyone who knew him,' Ellen said. 'It's standard procedure, that's all.'

'Sure,' Cosima said. 'I get that. Oh God, where are my manners? Do you want something to drink? Like a coffee or something?'

'Coffee would be good,' Ellen said. 'Thanks.'

Cosima lifted the receiver of a black telephone on a table beside the cream sofa and spoke softly, requesting a pot of coffee and a selection of biscuits.

She hung up and smiled.

'Won't be long.'

Her smile was extraordinary. It lit up her whole face, enhancing her beauty. Ellen wondered how often she used that smile to get what she wanted from life.

'I didn't know Kieran very well,' Cosima said. 'I mean, I know he was into me for a bit but that was a while ago now. We didn't hang around together or anything like that.'

She had a soft, well-modulated voice with no trace of a south London accent. Like her posture, Ellen guessed a lot of money had gone into getting that voice.

'How did you know he was into you?' Ellen asked.

Cosima frowned, like that was a stupid question.

'He made it obvious, I guess? You know, if we were in the same lecture he'd make a point of sitting beside me. And he started calling by the house in the mornings so we could walk in together. He made out like he was just passing but it was more than that. He flirted. Really badly too.' She shuddered. 'Like I'd fall for that sort of "ooh there's such a connection between us and I think our souls met in a previous life". Seriously? Like I'm some stupid teenager with nothing going on up here.'

She stabbed a finger into the side of her head. Her face flushed from the sudden emotion and Ellen was glad to see there was a real person underneath that cool façade.

'You didn't like him,' Ellen said.

Cosima was saved from answering by the well-timed appearance of the short, blonde woman pushing a trolley into the room. On top of the trolley sat a silver coffee pot and various other accoutrements, including a large white plate of chocolate biscuits.

'Thank you, Miriam.' Cosima dismissed the blonde with a wave of her hand and started dispensing coffee, playing the role of genial hostess to perfection.

'I didn't *not* like him,' she said, when she'd finished serving the drinks. 'I just thought he was a bit immature.'

'And nothing happened between you?'

'God, no,' Cosima said. 'Never. Besides, I knew he was living with Freya.'

'Of course,' Ellen said. 'Is she a friend of yours?'

Cosima shrugged. 'Not really. But I know her, yeah. Poor Freya. God. I can't imagine what it would be like to be in her position right now. It's awful. Is she okay?'

'She's coping,' Ellen said. 'It's what you do. I'm guessing you had to learn that pretty early on yourself.'

'Maybe.'

'How did Kieran get on with the other students?' Ellen asked.

Cosima took a sip of coffee and seemed to consider this.

'Fine, I think. I mean, he was a bit brash. And he seriously fancied himself. A lot of girls were into him so he obviously had something. I never saw it but I don't think I'm like most people.'

She placed her cup and saucer carefully on the table beside the black phone. The slight tremor in her hand caused her to almost knock her cup over but she righted it just in time. Ellen wondered if the tremor was caused by too much caffeine or nerves. Except what did this poised young woman have to be nervous about?

Ellen's phone started to ring. Apologising, she took it out of her bag, saw Abby's name on the display and answered it.

'Ellen?' Abby sounded excited. 'Are you still at Cooper's place? There's something you should know.'

Ellen listened as Abby updated her on what she'd learned at the university. When she ended the call, Ellen turned her attention back to Cosima.

'You didn't tell me what you did,' she said.

'What do you mean?'

'To stop Kieran pestering you,' Ellen said.

Cosima's face burned a dark shade of puce.

'I didn't do anything,' she said. 'I didn't have to. He got the hint in the end. And that was that.'

'Only after you got your father to warn him off,' Ellen said.

'No.' Cosima shook her head. 'That's not true. I never … look, I didn't say a word to Daddy. I wouldn't do that.'

'Why not?'

'I just wouldn't.'

'Because you would be scared of what he might do?'

A flash of something in Cosima's dark eyes. Fear, Ellen thought.

'It's not that.' She smiled, a real beamer this time. 'Daddy's a bit old school,' she said. 'I'm his little princess. He loves me to pieces and he worries about me. I didn't tell him about Kieran because I didn't want him to worry about me.'

She kept smiling, as if she believed the smile could hide the fact she was clearly lying.

'You're a very attractive woman,' Ellen said. 'You must have a lot of men who are interested in you. What about boyfriends? Do you tell him about them or is that another thing you keep secret from him?'

Cosima lifted her coffee cup then put it down again without drinking from it.

'I don't have boyfriends,' she said. 'I'm not saying I never will, but I'm not interested in any of that for now. All I want to do is focus on my studies, get the best grades I can and do something with my life.'

She sounded so sincere, reminding Ellen of her own drive and determination when she first joined the force. She had been driven by a desire for truth and justice. A desire that seemed naive and overly simple to her older self. She looked around the huge room, at the painting of Cosima's dead mother, and wondered what made the young woman in front of her so focussed on 'doing something' with her life.

'Is there anything else you can tell me about Kieran?' she asked instead.

When Cosima shook her head, Ellen stood up and handed her a business card.

'If you think of anything,' she said, 'give me a call.'

Cosima put it on the mantelpiece without looking at it. There was a photo on the mantelpiece, beneath the portrait. Cosima – or her mother, it was impossible to tell – standing on a snowy hill beside a middle-aged man who had his arm wrapped around her shoulders. The man was smiling but the woman looked serious. Expressionless.

'Your mother again?' Ellen asked.

'That's me,' Cosima said. 'With Daddy. We go to Courchevel every year, in February.'

'Courchevel?'

'A ski resort,' Cosima said. 'In France. Very lovely. You should go there sometime. Do you ski?'

'No.'

Ellen looked again at the portrait and the photo, noting the similarities in the two women's faces. She wondered if the circumstances of her mother's death might explain the strange emptiness in her daughter's identical eyes. Or if there was another reason.

'One final thing,' Ellen said at the front door. 'Can you tell me about your relationship with the Gleeson family?'

It was a shot in the dark. Ellen knew there was every chance the question would provoke no response. To her surprise, the shot in the dark seemed to hit its target. Cosima's jaw dropped open and she stared at Ellen for a full three seconds without speaking, as another flush crawled across her neck and up those pretty cheeks.

'What do you mean?' she asked.

'Just that,' Ellen said. 'How well do you know the family? I mean, you've already told me you didn't know Freya too well but I didn't ask you about Nick and Charlotte.'

'There's nothing to tell you,' Cosima said. 'He's nice. I don't know her.'

'I heard she's a bit of a drinker,' Ellen said.

'I wouldn't know,' Cosima said. She smiled again but it seemed forced. 'You'll have to excuse me, Detective. I'm late for uni.'

Ellen thanked the girl for her time and handed her a card with her contact details, telling her to call if she remembered anything else.

She waited until Cosima closed the door and then she pulled out her phone and called Abby.

* * *

'She claims her father had no idea Kieran was chasing her,' Ellen said.

'Is she telling the truth?' Abby asked.

'I don't know,' Ellen said. 'She's a strange one. I'd like you to speak to her at some point. See what you think.'

'I'm intrigued,' Abby said.

'She's got dark hair,' Ellen said. 'But so has Freya. We'll wait till we get the forensics back on the hair sample. If it's female, we'll get DNA samples from both of them. What are you up to now?'

'There's a message from Rui,' Abby said. 'He's got something from those CCTV images. I'd like to go and take a look right away.'

'Good idea,' Ellen said. 'I'm heading back to the station too. Call me after your meeting with Rui.'

'You sure you trust me to speak to him on my own?' Abby asked.

Ellen smiled. 'Positive. Now get going before I change my mind.'

Ellen cut the call and put her phone into her bag. A light sprinkling of rain started to fall. Ellen lifted her face and let the water cool her cheeks as she left the elegant affluence of Blackheath and walked down Lewisham Hill into the belly of southeast London.

FOUR

Rui didn't move like any person Abby had ever met before. He bounced. Like there were invisible springs on the soles of his high-top, red-and-white Converse trainers. She wondered if the constant movement explained his extreme thinness or whether that was down to a super-fast metabolism. Or maybe he just plain didn't bother with food.

'Here.' He flung a long arm out, pointing at a chair covered in sheets of paper. 'Sit down.' In a single, fluid movement, the arm swept the paper to the floor and he pushed the chair towards Abby. It rolled towards her at a ferocious pace and she thrust out her hands to stop it crashing into her.

Rui grinned. 'Sorry about that.' He grabbed a handful of his thick curly hair and shoved it back from his eyes. 'Don't know my own strength. Come over here. See what I've done so you can tell me what a genius I am. Take a look at these.'

Rui's office was a small, square room with a wooden work surface running along three walls. Every inch of the work-top was covered. Abby counted three laptops amongst the mess of paper, files, pens and God only knew what else.

Ignoring the chaos, she took the bundle of photos he had put onto her lap. Rui shoved some more papers onto the floor to clear some space in front of Abby.

She laid the photos out in front of her, sitting back as Rui leaned in to arrange them the way he wanted.

'See here.' He pointed at the photo furthest to the left. 'That's the original image from the camera.'

Abby remembered it. The flash of colour, like someone had been moving fast, the camera barely capturing the movement.

'Then look along the others,' Rui said. 'You see the way I've focussed on the orange, like you asked me to. Here, on this one, I enlarged it but you don't get any definition. So then I used a different piece of software that works in a different way – it manipulates ... oh never mind. Here's what I got.'

He lifted the final photo in the array, holding it so Abby could see.

'Is that definitely it?' she asked.

Rui frowned. 'I don't understand.'

'I mean,' Abby said, 'if you play around with the image, is this an enlarged version of the original image or a *possible* version of the original?'

'Ah.' Rui nodded, a manic movement that caused his hair to bob wildly like it was an animated animal sitting on top of his head. 'Gotcha. It's impossible to give you one hundred per cent certainty. But this is as close as you'll get. I played around with it for a while, tried a few different approaches. Always ended up with the same thing. Pretty good, huh?'

Abby nodded. Pretty good indeed. Her original hunch had been right. The flash of orange was a logo. A tiger leaping forward, with a word written underneath.

'Taylor's.' She read the word out loud.

'Brand of sports and outdoor clothing,' Rui said. 'I've already checked. Low-end product. The sort of stuff worn by amateurs or people who don't care about what they look like. Cheap and nasty. Wouldn't catch me wearing shit like that. It's seriously naff.'

'So what does that tell us about our killer?' Abby wondered.

'If that is your killer,' Rui said.

'It's the best lead we've got so far,' Abby said. 'I know that.'

'*If* that's your killer,' Rui repeated, 'then you're not looking at some random mugging. Not by any local Lewisham boy, that's for sure.'

'What makes you say that?'

'Abs, just look at that jacket and think for a second. The local bad boys, say what you want about them but they have a sense of style. You wouldn't catch any of them wearing shit like that.'

Abby thought about the lowlife drug dealers and petty

criminals who were the bread-and-butter of her job. Rui had a point. Most of them were seriously into their designer kit. Most, but not all.

'What about the Eastern Europeans?' she asked.

Rui shrugged. 'Maybe. It's not really their scene though, is it?'

'Who knows?' Abby said. 'This is great, Rui. I'll get one of the guys to get me some facts on Taylor's. Stats on where their clothes are sold, who their main customer base is, that sort of thing. I'll also see if Ger thinks it's worth going to the press with this. You're a genius, Rui. You know that?'

He winked at her. 'Yeah. I know.'

'Oh,' she said. 'I nearly forgot. Kieran's laptop. Find anything yet?'

Rui shook his head. 'We've gone through everything. He was on Facebook, but no other social media profiles that we can find. Seemed to mainly use the laptop for emails and writing college assignments. He has a One Drive as well.'

'What's that?' Abby asked.

'Cloud storage,' Rui said. 'Guy had a decent phone. Took a lot of photos on it. Stored the images up there.' He waved his hand around wildly. 'In the cloud. You don't do that?'

Abby shook her head.

'Yeah, well.' Rui shrugged. 'Maybe you should. Means if you lose your phone, all the photos you've taken, you don't lose them.'

'So where can I see the photos?' Abby asked.

'I've given Malcolm two memory sticks,' Rui said. 'One's got copies of all his college stuff, emails, etc. He's taken some pretty cool photos. I've stored those on a separate stick. Malc's got that too.'

With Rui's help, Abby gathered the photos into a plain manila folder which she took with her. The tiger logo was familiar. As she walked back to her office, she tried to remember where she'd seen it before. Nothing came to her. Eventually, she gave up. She could have seen it anywhere.

FIVE

Charlotte poured herself a small glass of wine, taking care not to put too much into the glass, saving it for later. Ginny was coming over and Charlotte was determined not to drink too much. She took the glass into the den and settled on a sofa.

She was tense and jittery, jumping every time she heard an unexpected noise. This house was full of noises – creaking floorboards, branches rattling against the windows as the wind grew stronger, the low hum of the fridge when she was in the kitchen, the distant rumble of traffic moving around the perimeter of the heath. Worst of all, the screeching, keening, squealing of the foxes that lived in the small wood at the end of the garden.

She didn't think she'd noticed any of those noises before. Tonight, they were deafening. She lifted the remote and switched on the TV. The volume was up high and she jumped as sound blasted through the room. She'd just turned the sound down when her mobile started ringing. Again she jumped, wine sloshing out of the glass onto her wrist. She watched the wine soaking into the cuff of her sleeve. It reminded her of something but she couldn't think what.

She put her glass down and looked at the phone. Saw Freya's number was flashing on the screen. Quickly, she calculated how much she'd drunk. A glass, two at the most. Nothing that would be heard in her voice.

She grabbed the phone.

'Darling, what a lovely surprise. How are you?'

She winced as she said it. Stupid, stupid question.

'Sorry,' she said. 'I didn't mean ...'

'I heard you had an accident,' Freya said. It was impossible to know from her voice whether she was accusing Charlotte or expressing concern.

'It wasn't an accident,' Charlotte said. Too late she remembered she was meant to be protecting her daughter from more worry. 'Oh I'm sorry, darling. Maybe it was. I can't remember, you see. Not because of that. I hadn't been drinking, I swear to you. It's just, well, when I fell I knocked myself out. Silly of me, I know. And my arm is badly bruised. Bloody uncomfortable. Nothing broken though, so I suppose I'm lucky really.'

She laughed but there was no corresponding laugh on the other end. Just silence.

'Can I come and see you tomorrow?' she said. 'I am thinking about you, you know.'

'Where's dad?' Freya asked.

'Out.'

'You're alone then?'

She hoped Freya wasn't about to suggest coming over. She didn't think she was up to that.

'Ginny's on her way,' she said. 'Well, not on her way exactly. I'm expecting her about nine.'

'You're not serious? A drinking session's the last thing you need right now.'

'That's not why she's coming,' Charlotte said. 'If you must know, she's got something important to tell me.'

'What?' Freya asked.

'I don't know.'

Charlotte shifted on the sofa, trying to get comfortable. No matter what position she sat in, her arm still hurt.

She stopped. She didn't owe Freya any explanation. Whatever she and Ginny chose to do, it really was none of Freya's business.

'She's probably bought a new pair of shoes,' Freya said dismissively.

Charlotte chose not to reply.

'Sorry,' Freya said into the silence. 'It's good of her, I suppose. What time did you say you're seeing her?'

'About nine,' Charlotte said. 'She's walking across. She's got this new app on her phone. It counts how many steps she does each day, apparently.'

She ended the phone call as soon as she could. The last thing she needed now was a self-righteous lecture from her daughter. She might have known Freya would think the accident was Charlotte's fault. The child had taken against her from the moment she was born.

It was strange now to remember how excited she'd been. Pregnancy had been easy. She'd enjoyed it. Ate well, exercised and looked after herself throughout the entire nine months. She'd put on just over half a stone in weight and was confident she'd lose it right after the birth.

The birth. That's when it started. The slow break-down of everything she'd worked so hard for. Nothing had prepared her for it. They'd attended anti-natal classes. Nick hadn't missed one session, despite the pressures of work. NCT sessions in a big old Victorian house in West Greenwich. The classes, like everything else back then, had been fun. Weekly sessions with other young, affluent couples. Charlotte let herself believe it was the start of something. The amazing life she'd always hoped for.

The NCT woman – overweight and overbearing – advocated a drug-free labour. Charlotte and the other expecting mothers giggled their way through a series of exercises aimed at 'relaxing their bodies' in preparation for 'the birth'. *A loose jaw means a loose vagina*, was the only line Charlotte remembered now. She suspected she'd deliberately made herself forget the rest in the days following Freya's birth. The single most traumatic event in her life. Two days of horror, pain and unbearable indignities.

Nick stayed with her the whole time, for all the good he did. His ineffectual attempts to ease her suffering were the first hint of the loathing she would feel for him in the months and years that followed.

And then, as if all of that wasn't enough, there was the child. A screaming bundle of fury that Charlotte was meant to ... what, exactly? It was impossible to love something that made such a racket the entire time. Even the nurses admitted, smiling like it was a fucking joke, that she was 'a screamer'.

She didn't want to think of all that. She wondered what Ginny wanted to speak to her about. She'd sounded strange when she'd called earlier, like something was worrying her. But when Charlotte asked for more information, Ginny said it would have to wait until this evening. Charlotte hoped it had nothing to do with Friday night. The underlying anxiety was still with her. Anxiety based on fear. And the knowledge that she had lied to the police.

Had she said something to Ginny? Possibly. But if she had, what was Ginny going to do about it? Unless Ginny had suddenly developed some sort of social conscience – any sort of conscience – then Charlotte was probably safe enough.

She shook her head and a ziz-zag of random images exploded like a firework through her brain. Things she couldn't bear to think about. She drained her glass and stood up. Sitting here waiting for something to happen was unbearable.

She checked the time. Seven-thirty. The time between now and nine o'clock seemed infinite. Moments like this, when she felt cooped up inside the madness of her own head, she liked to go for a drive. She loved night driving. Cruising the quiet, suburban streets, imagining the happy family lives going on behind the curtained windows of the houses she passed.

Blackheath, down to Lee, through the sleepy streets of Hither Green and across to Ladywell. Up the hilly roads around Brockley, then curving back home via Deptford and Greenwich, keeping as close to the river as she could for as long as she could.

She touched her bruised arm. She shouldn't do it. But the car was an automatic. If she was careful and drove slowly, she thought she could probably manage it. She decided to have one more – small – glass of wine while she considered it. If nothing else, the wine would help pass another twenty minutes or so.

SIX

Shivery and shaky with nerves. A new feeling. Not exactly pleas-ant but tinged with an excitement that made it special, somehow. They'd arranged to meet at the entrance to London Bridge Sta-tion. Abby was early. Or he was late? She checked her watch. She was definitely early. She pulled her jacket tighter around her body, looking around, hoping he'd be here soon.

Someone brushed past her. Big and burly, he was moving fast, nearly knocked her over as he banged into her. A hand on her elbow, steadying her.

'Are you okay?' Sam's voice, his breath warm against her cold skin.

She barely heard him. Her attention focussed on the man who'd bumped into her. The man wearing the black jacket with the orange logo. She ran after him, grabbed his arm, forcing him to stop.

'Hey!' He swung around, angry at the interruption. A man on a mission. People to see, places to go.

'Sorry.' She gave him her best smile. Saw the way it softened him, ever so slightly. 'It's your jacket,' she said. 'I wondered where you bought it. I want to buy one for my boyfriend.'

The man looked surprised, then flattered.

'Present from my wife,' he said. 'Truth be told, I don't like it very much. I only wear it to keep her happy. But you're telling me you like it?'

'Oh yes,' she said. 'I adore it. Thanks so much.'

'What was that about?' Sam asked. He had flowers with him. A huge bouquet of red roses. They were beautiful. He looked awkward, like he wasn't sure what to do with them.

'I wanted to ask about his jacket,' Abby said.

Sam frowned, not understanding. She looked at his expensive, woollen trench coat and laughed. He smiled, then seconds later he was laughing along with her, even though she was sure he had no idea why. She wasn't sure she did, either. Just knew that it felt good, being here with him and laughing for no reason. She tried to remember the last time she'd laughed like this but it was so long ago, she had no memory of it.

When they finally managed to control the giggles, Sam leaned forward and kissed her softly on the lips.

'You have the loveliest smile,' he said. He might have said

something else but his words got lost as she kissed him back. All around them, people passed by, moving in and out of the station, getting on with their busy lives. There was something she needed to work out. Something to do with the black jacket and the orange logo. Except she couldn't focus. Her mind was too full of Sam. No room for anything else. And whatever she was meant to understand, it would have to wait.

SEVEN

After she got the children to bed, Ellen spent the evening sorting through paperwork, updating her notes. The picture of Kieran Burton was becoming clearer. The more she learned about him, the less she liked.

According to Freya, her relationship with Kieran was rock solid. She was either deluded or lying. Ellen made a note to find out who paid the rent and the bills for the flat. She guessed the answer would be Freya, working to support herself and Kieran while he finished his studies. Ellen wondered how Freya might have reacted if she'd discovered what her boyfriend was really up to at university everyday.

In the corner of the room, the TV was on with the sound turned down. When the news came on, Ellen turned up the volume. Kieran's murder was the third item, after the growing refugee crisis in Europe and a new story about an MP accused of having an affair with his son's wife.

The piece on Kieran's murder was pretty comprehensive. Lots of shots of the murder scene before the cameras shifted to Nick Gleeson's Totally Tapas restaurant in Greenwich. A pretty news reporter stood outside the restaurant talking to camera, giving a summary of Gleeson's background and career to date. Going over the same, familiar story of the local boy who'd made a fortune with his chain of family-friendly, affordable restaurants. Nothing, Ellen noted, about his alcoholic wife, his affairs or his dodgy business partner.

Bored, Ellen switched off the TV and went into the kitchen to make another cup of tea. She was trying not to drink wine during the week. She wasn't doing too badly, although it was difficult at times like this. With the children in bed and Rosie out, the house felt too quiet. There was a pile of ironing to do but the thought of facing that right now depressed her even further. Quashing down the old feelings of self-pity, she took her tea into the sitting room and put some music on.

The iPod and speakers were a present from Sean. After the fire, he'd set up an iTunes account for her and downloaded a huge selection of her favourite music. He'd given it to her on Christmas Day. She hadn't understood, at first, the significance of the present. It was only when Sean explained how it all worked, scrolling through the music library, showing her album after album of old familiar titles that she got it. And promptly burst into tears.

She scrolled through her playlists and selected a collection of schmaltzy love songs, each one triggering a slew of memories. All of them good. The collection kicked off with Frank Sinatra and the Count Basie orchestra singing 'Fly Me to the Moon'. After that, the Count's music was replaced by the other count, John Count McCormack. His pure, pure voice filling the space around her, wrapping her in memories.

The song was 'Macushla'. A soaring, heartbreaking song of love and loss. Ellen remembered Brendan, Vinny's father, rocking Pat to sleep in his arms, singing this song to him with a voice that, although not a patch on McCormack's, wasn't half bad. Unlike Vinny, who couldn't sing to save his life but sang all the time anyway, not caring how bad he sounded.

She listened to a few more songs then went back to her notes, tried to concentrate on work. It wasn't easy. The brief moment of relaxation had opened the floodgates. Memory after happy memory assailed her. A lifetime's worth of happiness in such a short time.

Enough. She had work to do and it was getting late.

She opened the file she'd borrowed from the archives on the death of Annalise Cooper. There was a photo of the dead woman in the file. In the picture, Annalise was sitting on an armchair, wearing a white sleeveless dress. A chubby baby girl on her lap. Even at that age, the resemblance between mother and child was striking. The same dark hair, sallow skin and huge dark eyes. A beautiful young woman with a gorgeous, healthy child and her whole life ahead of her. No wonder she was smiling.

Ellen flicked through the rest of the witness statements and detective notes. She read fast, skimming the pages so quickly that when a familiar name appeared, she almost missed it. It was a witness statement from Annalise's cousin. The statement itself didn't contain any new information. It claimed that Annalise and McNulty were definitely an item and there was no way the dead woman would have killed herself. There were several other signed statements in the file that said more or less the same thing. What interested Ellen, however, was the name of the witness. Virginia Rau. Charlotte Gleeson's friend.

On a sheet of paper, Ellen started to note down the different connections she was uncovering. Kieran Burton and Cosima Cooper were at university together. Pete Cooper and Nick Gleeson were in business together. Virginia Rau and Charlotte Gleeson were best friends. And now this. A direct link between Charlotte's friend and Cooper's dead wife.

The answer to Kieran's murder was here. Hidden in the connections that linked these people together. Ellen added another name to the list. Freya Gleeson.

Freya and Cosima. What was Ellen missing?

She opened her laptop and did a Google search on Cosima Cooper. No links to the usual places like Facebook, Instagram or Twitter. Nothing on Goodreads or LinkedIn, either. Cosima Cooper must be one of the few women of her generation living in the UK who didn't use social media.

Ellen heard the front door open and the scuffle of someone taking their jacket off. A moment later, Rosie's blue head popped around the door.

'Hey, Ellen. How's it going?'

Ellen smiled, her spirits instantly lifted. When she wasn't loving every moment of Vinny's niece living with them, she was dreading the day Rosie announced she would be leaving them.

Ellen patted the space beside her on the sofa. 'Come in. Tell me what you've been up to. I'm desperate for a bit of company.'

Obediently, Rosie bounced across the sitting room and plonked herself on the sofa beside Ellen.

'I've been out with my Spanish mates,' Rosie said. 'They're great.'

'Where did you go?' Ellen asked.

'A new bar in Deptford,' Rosie said. 'Real arty crowd. It was fun.'

Rosie pointed at the photo of Annalise with baby Cosima on her lap.

'A friend of yours?'

'The child's involved in a case I'm working on,' Ellen said. 'She's an adult now. Actually, she's doing a degree at Greenwich. Maybe you've seen her around? She's the image of her mother.'

Rosie grinned. 'What? You think I know her because all us young folk hang out in the same places, is that it? No, I don't recognise her. I mean, you're not likely to forget a face like that, are you? She's beautiful. Well, the mother is. If the daughter looks just like her, then I think I'd remember her. What's she studying? Rafael's girlfriend goes to Greenwich, I think. I could ask her about the girl if you'd like?'

'No,' Ellen said. 'I don't want you doing anything of the sort, thank you very much.'

'Annalise Cooper,' Rosie said, reading the name under the photo.

'That's the mother,' Ellen said. 'The daughter's called Cosima.'

'Nope,' Rosie said. 'Never heard of her.'

'Best to keep it that way,' Ellen said.

Rosie grinned. 'Don't worry. I won't do anything silly. Okay, I'm wrecked. I'm going to make myself a cup of tea. Do you want anything?'

'No thanks,' Ellen said. She picked up her phone. 'I need to call someone.'

'Grand,' Rosie said. 'I'll see you in the morning. Night.'

Ellen didn't reply. She'd already dialled Abby's number.

'Ellen!' Abby's voice was light and happy.

'Sorry for calling so late,' Ellen said. 'You never got back to me about your meeting with Rui.'

Abby giggled. 'I didn't forget. I called but your phone was engaged and then I meant to try again later but by then I was running late and I didn't want to leave Sam waiting for me. God, Ellen, I've had the best evening.

'We went to the Shard first and then afterwards he took me

to this amazing French restaurant in Bermondsey. And now he's back here at mine and I'm not going to let him go home anytime soon.'

Ellen couldn't help smiling. The girl sounded so darn happy.

'He bought me flowers,' Abby said. 'They're so beautiful. I'll ... hang on. How can I send a photo? Do you know how to do that? I'm useless with stuff like that. Maybe Sam will know. Sam, darling? Can you come here a sec?'

'Forget about the flowers,' Ellen said. 'How did you get on with Rui?'

'Rui's worked out the image on the jacket,' Abby said. 'It's the logo for a brand called Taylor's. Heard of them?'

'No.'

'I'm not surprised. Couldn't see you in something like that. They're outdoor clothing. Jackets and stuff. Cheap, mass-produced. I saw someone wearing one of the jackets tonight.'

'So?' Ellen said. 'There must be thousands of people in London with a jacket like that.'

'Yeah but I've seen it somewhere else too,' Abby said. 'Seeing it on that guy earlier, it reminded me.'

'Of course you've seen it before,' Ellen said. She was tired and grumpy and wanted to go to bed. It didn't help that Abby was loved-up and tipsy. 'I thought we'd just established the fact that people all over London are wearing them.'

'I wish I could remember where I'd seen it,' Abby said. 'I think it might be important.'

'Sleep on it,' Ellen said. 'Maybe you'll remember in the morning.'

'I'm not planning on much sleep tonight,' Abby said.

Ellen smiled. 'Too much information. Just make sure you're up bright and early tomorrow.'

Abby groaned. 'Oh God, Kieran's memorial thing. I'd forgotten all about that. What time does it kick off again?'

'Five am,' Ellen said. 'They wanted to do it as the sun rises over the river, apparently. Symbolic or some such crap.'

'I called Emer Dawson earlier,' Abby said. 'Told her about it. That's okay, isn't it?'

'I guess so,' Ellen said. 'He was her brother, after all.'

In the background, Ellen heard a man speaking. She didn't catch the words but they were enough to set Abby off on another round of giggles. Ellen said goodnight and hung up.

She was old enough and wise enough to know when she was in the way.

EIGHT

'What if I'm wrong?'

The question hung in the air, long after she'd asked it. Possibly because there was no one here to answer it.

It stayed with her as she pulled on her heavy Giuseppe Zanotti biker boots, wrapped herself inside her new Marc Jacobs cashmere coat – so soft, so warm – and walked out into the cool London night.

She lived in a pretty, double-fronted Georgian cottage on Point Hill in West Greenwich. The house was around the corner from her old home on Diamond Terrace, where she'd lived until her last divorce. Her ex had kept the house, and most of everything else too. She hadn't fought him for any of it. The divorce was her fault and she knew most of his vindictive behaviour throughout the drawn-out separation was caused by heartbreak rather than innate nastiness.

She should never have married him. Foolishly, for a short period of time, she'd allowed herself to believe in a happy ending. He was crazy about her and she thought that might be enough. The fact she didn't feel the same way about him barely came into it. She was incapable of loving any man. It wasn't his fault, but it wasn't hers either. And she'd done her best, God knows. Until the day she realised she'd rather die alone than spend another day watching him slurping Alpen into his greedy mouth morning after endless morning. Or spend another night blocking him out as he lay on top of her, pretending that what he was doing was an act of love.

She'd had an affair. With the chauffeur. An Italian Adonis, more in love with himself than anyone else. She'd ditched him the day her *decree nisi* came through and hadn't looked back since.

There were still men, occasionally. When she'd drunk enough not to care or had fooled herself, for a short while, into thinking this one might be different. They never were, and it was always a relief when the morning came and she could leave whatever bed she'd ended up in and come back home to her own, private place.

She hadn't always been like this. Once, a long time ago, there'd been a man she loved beyond reason. A man she would have done anything for. But he had hurt her in ways she hadn't known possible. After him, she'd never been able to be close to anyone else. With one exception. Which was what made all of this so difficult. This *thing* she knew, it would destroy that person if the truth ever got out. She wanted to be wrong. More than anything, she wanted that. She'd done everything she could to convince herself she hadn't seen what she had seen. But each time, her mind reared back from the denial.

Her teeth ground together as she walked. Frustration making her jaw tight. She needed to think about what she would say.

She went through the chronicle of things that had happened on Friday night. She'd been drinking, but not so much that she couldn't remember. It took a lot of drink before her memory went. Many times in the past she'd wished that wasn't so.

She was nearly there. Past Blackheath Hill and making quick progress along Hare and Billet Road. She walked faster, keen to get it over with. Knowing she had to do it; didn't really have a choice.

At the corner of Hare and Billet Road and Mounts Pond Road, she paused, peering left and right into the dark, checking for cars before she stepped onto the road. At the same time, she heard the roar of an engine screeching into life. The sound came from her left. She swung her head around, just in time to see the glare of headlights as the car roared towards her.

Confusion made her slow. Certain the car couldn't be driving right at her, she paused. When she realised what was actually happening she threw herself sideways. Not fast enough or far enough. The noise of the engine was all around her now. The low, monotone roar of a sports car.

She tried to get up. The car swerved, slammed against the side of her body. She flew back, crashed to the ground, head smashing against the kerb. Still conscious, she rolled onto her front and scrabbled forward, off the road onto the narrow pavement and the heath beyond.

She heard the screech of brakes. Saw the car swing around. The driver's face appeared in profile, then was gone again. Bright lights. Racing towards her. She stood up and ran forward. Right leg wasn't working, wouldn't hold her weight. She fell over. Tried to keep going, dragging herself forward on her stomach.

If she could just make it onto the grass, maybe she'd be okay. She inched forward, screaming in pain and fear. The noise from the engine drowned out her voice.

As the weight of the car rode over her, a single thought came to her in a flash of certainty. She had her answer. She hadn't been wrong. She knew who had killed Kieran Burton and why. The weight of the car pushed down on her and the knowledge of what she knew disappeared. And with it, everything else as well.

WEDNESDAY

ONE

The memorial for Kieran took place on the edge of the Thames early Wednesday morning. It was another dull day, the rising sun hidden behind a grey blanket of sullen clouds. The whole affair was miserable enough to make Ellen almost feel sorry for Kieran. When it was her turn, she sincerely hoped her nearest and dearest found a more jolly way to send her off.

A young guy with a thick black beard gave a speech. Ellen tried her best to focus on what he said but it wasn't easy. He spoke about Kieran in a rambling, roundabout way, bringing everything back to the environment and the damage mankind was wreaking on their world.

There were about twenty people in total, including Ellen, Abby, Nick Gleeson and Emer Dawson, who arrived late and stood at the back as if she didn't want to draw attention to herself.

Some journalists had also turned up, doing their best to maintain a discreet distance, although Ellen thought their very presence was an intrusion. She recognised one of them. A local hack called Martine Reynolds. Ellen hated Martine Reynolds and was pretty sure the feeling was mutual.

'See that Reynolds woman?' she whispered to Abby. 'I've a good mind to go over there and tell her to get lost. Those people have no right to be here.'

'They come with the territory,' Abby said. 'Unfortunately. There's no sign of Charlotte. I wonder why she's not here. Maybe Freya didn't want her. Although, if you ask me, that's a crap excuse. I mean, Emer's here, right? And Freya didn't want her to come either. You'd think the least Charlotte could have done is to show her face.'

'Maybe Freya didn't tell her about it,' Ellen said.

'Nick's here so she must know.' Abby said something else but Ellen zoned out. Abby had barely stopped for breath all morning. Her mood was unbearably upbeat and Ellen was exhausted by it. She hadn't dared ask about Sam, dreading the increase in chatter and smiles if she did. Besides, there was no need to ask. Abby's mood was proof enough that the night had gone well.

Abby was still talking when Freya walked to the front. Ellen nudged Abby in the ribs, hard, and put a finger on her lips.

'Shhh.'

'Sorry,' Abby said. 'Oh God, she's going to do a reading, isn't she? I wonder what she'll do. Hardly something from the Bible. They're all a bit too new agey for that.'

'Abby!'

'Oh, right. Sorry.'

At the front of the crowd, with the river behind her and the rays from the pink sun sneaking through the clouds, Freya cleared her throat and began speaking.

'Thanks,' she said. 'It means a lot to see you all here today. Some people I don't even know.' She nodded at the group of students huddled together. 'Um, thanks to Mac as well.' Another nod, this time to the bloke with the black beard. 'We decided to have the service here by the river because this was one of his favourite places. I guess most of you know that, right? Kieran really cared, you know? About everything. He was passionate, in life and in his love of politics. I have no doubt he would have gone on to do great things if ...' She broke off in a sob and Ellen had to look away.

'Sorry,' Freya said after a moment. 'It's not easy, you know? I wanted to read something. A poem.' She looked across the crowd to her father, who smiled at her.

'Thanks to my dad who found this for me. It's by a man called James Mary Plunkett. Sorry. Joseph. Joseph Mary Plunkett. Um, I chose this because Plunkett was a warrior, just like Kieran. Both men fought for what they believed in. For Plunkett, the fight was for Irish freedom.'

Freya paused, looked across the people gathered in front of

her, making eye contact with several of them, Ellen included.

'For Kieran, the fight was bigger than that. His fight, friends, is our fight. And even though he's not with us any longer, the fight must go on.'

She stopped again and a few people clapped. One bloke, short hair and an acne-scarred face, gave a whoop.

'The fight is for the world we live in,' Freya said. 'We can't give up, friends. This land, this beautiful, wonderful land we live in, is in danger of being destroyed. Kieran knew that, and he dedicated his life to saving it. Today, I make him a promise. That I will continue his good work, I will continue the fight. Together, we will save this world of ours!'

More applause and a few more whoops from acne face and then Freya was off, reading a poem Ellen had never heard before, and didn't care if she never heard again. It was all about seeing someone everywhere after they had died. Ellen didn't need a poem to remind her what that felt like.

Ellen was interested in the different side of Freya she'd seen this morning. Freya's little speech had impressed her. Once she'd got over her initial nerves, Freya was a passionate, convincing speaker. For the first time, Ellen thought she understood why Kieran might have been attracted to her. He may have been a shit, but he was a shit who cared about the impression he made. In certain circles, a partner like Freya could be an asset.

When the poem finished, Freya invited everyone to light one of the candles they had been given at the beginning. The lighted candles were then placed in a row along the edge of the river, where the wind kept blowing them out.

Then the bloke called Mac thanked everyone for coming and that appeared to be it. As people started to disperse, Ellen went across to introduce herself to Emer Dawson. But Freya got there first, lunging past Ellen, screaming.

'You! Who said you could be here today? How dare you show up like this? It's meant to be a private event. For the people who loved him. Not for people like you who didn't care one bit about him.'

'Please,' Emer said. 'Don't be like this.'

'Like what?' Freya said. 'You want to pretend we're friends, is that it? You didn't want anything to do with us when Kieran was alive. It's too late to pretend you care now.'

'That's not fair,' Emer said. 'I tried my best, Freya.'

'Bullshit.'

'It's not bullshit!' Emer's voice rose to match Freya's. 'I would have loved to see more of him, to see more of both of you. But Kieran only wanted to see me when he needed something. For someone who claimed not to care about material things, he certainly wasn't afraid of asking for money when he wanted it.'

'You liar.' Two little pink circles had appeared on Freya's cheeks. 'He only ever asked you for something once. And that was a loan. We would have paid it back to you as soon as we could. What sort of sister were you?'

'Oh Freya.' Emer shook her head. 'If that's what he told you, then he lied. I'm sorry. The truth is, I lost count of the money I gave him over the last few years. Every time we met, he wanted more. I never minded at first. He was my baby brother and I thought it was my responsibility to make sure he was okay. But I couldn't go on like that. It got so bad that I started to dread meeting him, wondering what he'd want from me this time.'

'Freya?' Nick Gleeson appeared at Freya's side. 'Freya, love. What is it?'

'Can you take me home?' Freya turned away from Emer and leaned her head against her father's chest. 'Please, Dad.'

Emer went to say something else but Abby put a hand on her arm, stopping her.

'Best leave her for now,' she said, as Nick led Freya away.

'I don't know what to do,' Emer said. 'I thought … I wanted to support her but she's so angry. Do you think she's right?'

'About what?' Abby asked.

'About me being a rubbish sister,' Emer said.

'Emer?' Ellen stepped forward. 'DI Ellen Kelly. Abby's boss. I'm leading the investigation into your brother's death.'

'Hi.' Emer shook Ellen's outstretched hand. 'Sorry. Can we … can we go somewhere else? I don't think I can bear to be here a second longer.'

She told them she was staying in the Novotel in Greenwich. She'd got a taxi across this morning and was planning to walk back, but when Ellen offered her a lift she accepted gratefully.

'I'm heading home today,' she said, as Ellen pulled up outside the hotel ten minutes later. 'Steve's been off work looking after the kids but he can't take any more time off. I don't want to go. I mean, I miss Steve and the kids. Of course I do. But how can I go without knowing what happened to Kieran?'

'We'll keep in touch,' Abby said. 'You have my phone number. And my email address. You can contact me any time and I'll keep you updated. I promise.'

'He didn't tell her,' Emer said. 'Did he?'

'Tell her what?' Abby said.

'Kieran never told Freya about all the money I gave him,' Emer said. 'He wanted to keep it for himself. He always was selfish. Poor Freya. I feel sorry for her, really.'

She thanked Abby and Ellen for the lift and the three women got out of the car. Emer asked Abby if it was okay to call her later.

'Of course,' Abby said. 'Anytime, like I said.'

'I don't think Freya was right,' Ellen said. 'About you not being a good sister. It sounds to me as if you did a great job. He just didn't appreciate it.'

'And now he never will.' Tears ran down Emer's face. She didn't bother to brush them away.

'You've both been very kind,' she said. 'Thank you.'

'It's weird,' Abby said, as Emer walked away. 'Freya acts like money is the worst thing in the world and yet she's so angry with Emer for not giving Kieran some when he asked for it. What's that about?'

'I think Emer's telling the truth,' Ellen said. 'I think she probably gave him money lots of times. But he never told Freya about it. And then the one time Emer said no to him, he probably turned it into a really big deal and got Freya all upset by going on about it all the time. Makes him sound like a spoilt little boy, doesn't it?'

'Spoiled by his parents, his sister and then his girlfriend.' Abby stretched her arms over her head, yawning. 'Fancy a coffee?'

Ellen looked at her watch. Six thirty-five.

'Definitely,' she said. 'And after that, how do you feel about paying an early morning visit to Pete Cooper?'

'Can't think of anything I'd like more,' Abby said. 'But coffee first. Come on.'

She jumped into the car and beeped the horn, making Ellen jump. Abby laughed and Ellen groaned. She would have to find a way of escaping later. A whole day in the company of loved-up Abby was too much for any sane person to endure.

TWO

'Mounts Pond Road is still closed,' Abby said. 'We'll have to go around this way and park further along. Hit and run, wasn't it? Female victim. No ID on her so we don't know who she is yet. Happened just after nine. Bloke out walking his dog saw the whole thing. Says the car ran into her on purpose. So sad.'

She didn't sound sad but before Ellen could point that out, Abby was off again.

'Do you really think Cooper could be our killer? Makes sense, I guess. He's got form. If he found out Kieran was sniffing around his daughter, who knows what he might have done? He must have been stupid. Surely he would have realised the risk he was taking, upsetting someone like Pete Cooper? Ooh look. Parking space right here. How perfect is that?'

The grey day had got greyer, the impression of winter made worse by a cold wind blowing in from the east, whipping bits of discarded litter into a frenzied dance.

Abby manoeuvred the Mazda into a small space between two bigger cars. Ellen was out of the car before the engine was switched off, wrapping her coat tight around herself in a pointless attempt to stop the wind cutting through her.

'House is this way.' She marched ahead, then slowed and waited for Abby. Just because her own love life was nothing to shout about, she could, at the very least, show a bit of interest and pleasure in someone else's.

'I take it things with Sam went well?' she said.

Abby beamed. 'Sorry. I know I'm a bit hyper this morning. Yeah, it went really well. He's different to anyone I've ever met before.'

An image flashed through Ellen's head. Abby with their previous boss, Ed Baxter. Or Teddy, as Abby called him. Sam had to be an improvement on that relationship. Ellen was about to say she hoped this time round Abby had picked someone who wasn't married. She stopped herself just in time.

'I hope it works out for you,' she said, meaning it. 'Here's the house. Time to put Sam to one side for now. Think you can manage that?'

Abby sighed, fake melodramatic. 'If I really have to.'

The 4x4 was still here, mud-splattered as if someone had driven it cross-country. The blue convertible was there, too. Ellen guessed the car belonged to Cosima. It was a pretty snazzy car for a student.

Ellen used the bronze claw to knock on the door. They didn't have long to wait. The blonde woman Ellen had met yesterday opened the door.

'Cosima is not here,' the woman said before Ellen had a chance to speak.

'That's fine,' Ellen said, pushing past her into the hall. 'We'll speak to Mr Cooper. Where is he?'

'Here.'

A tall, broad man came down the stairs and stood in front of her.

'Who the hell are you?'

Ellen recognised Pete Cooper from the photo on the mantelpiece yesterday. Dressed in perfectly pressed navy corduroys and a pale pink sweater, the image Cooper portrayed was a country gent at leisure. The voice told a different story. Low, gravelly and pure south London, it reminded anyone who heard it where Pete Cooper's real roots were.

'Detective Inspector Ellen Kelly.' Ellen showed him her warrant card, watched the way Cooper's face shut down when he heard she was police. It reminded Ellen of his daughter the day before.

'Lewisham CID,' she said. 'I'd like a word, please.'

Cooper's mouth turned up in an imitation of a smile. Nothing else on his face changed.

'I thought my daughter answered all your questions yesterday,' he said. 'Of course, I'm happy to help in any way. The Gleesons are family friends. It's a terrible business. But I barely knew the poor bloke. I'm afraid there's nothing I can tell you, Sergeant Kelly.'

'Detective Inspector,' she said. 'And I think you're wrong. A witness has come forward. Claims you and Burton had a run-in.'

Cooper's face displayed no emotion apart from the red flush that spread from his neck and across his cheeks.

'Someone's been telling you porky pies. Listen, love, my heart goes out to poor Freya. It really does. But I can't help you.'

'How far would you go to protect your daughter?' Ellen asked.

'Cosima?' Cooper said. 'I'd do anything for my kid. Course I would. What parent wouldn't? But that doesn't make me a killer. My Cosima had nothing to do with that bloke who got killed. And neither did I.'

'We heard that she was dating Kieran,' Abby said.

Cooper's gaze slid from Ellen to her partner.

'Cosima's got better things to think about than a fella like that.'

'So who is her boyfriend?' Abby asked.

'No one,' Cooper said.

'Your daughter's very beautiful,' Abby said. 'Girls like that, they're never short of men wanting to go out with them.'

'Sure,' Cooper said. 'Lots of blokes interested. You can see it in their faces wherever she goes. Like her mother that way. But she's smart, Cosima. She knows better than to start dating someone behind her old man's back. We're like this.' He held up his right hand, fingers crossed.

'You remind me of my dad,' Abby said. 'He thinks the same about me. Truth is, he hasn't a clue what I get up to most of the time.'

Cooper's hands clench into fists.

'Not my Cosima,' he said. 'She wouldn't do something like that.'

'You mean she's scared of you?' Abby asked.

Cooper looked like he wanted to kill her. His arm twitched.

'There's nothing more I can tell you,' he said. 'I never met the bloke and I had nothing to do with his death. If you lot show up again without a proper warrant, I'll sue you for harassment. Got that?'

'Daddy?'

Cosima came towards them from the back of the house.

'It's all right,' Cooper said. 'I'm dealing with this.'

Ignoring him, Cosima kept walking. When she was close enough, her father put his arm around her shoulders, pulling her close to him. Ellen thought she saw the girl stiffen but it was impossible to know for sure and, as always, her face gave nothing away.

'They think that fella who died was your boyfriend,' Cooper said.

'I already told you,' Cosima said to Ellen. 'Kieran had a girl-friend and it wasn't me.'

'We need to ask you some more questions,' Ellen said. 'Can you spare us another few minutes?'

Cosima glanced at her father like she was asking his permission.

'She can't tell you anything you don't already know,' Cooper said.

'We'll be the judge of that,' Ellen said. 'We can speak to you here or take you with us to the station. What's it to be?'

Cooper started to protest but Cosima put her hand on his arm, silencing him.

'It's all right, Dad. Let me speak to them.'

Ellen prepared for more bluster and protest. Instead, Cooper nodded and said fine but only if he was present while Ellen asked her questions.

'I'm afraid that's not possible,' Ellen said. 'Your daughter is over sixteen. She doesn't need an adult present when we speak to her.'

'She's my daughter,' Cooper said. 'I'll sit with her if I want.'

That decided it.

'Right,' Ellen said. 'We'll do this down at the station.' She looked at Cosima. 'You're coming with us.'

With a curt goodbye to Cooper, Ellen and Abby led Cosima outside.

Cooper trailed after them like a devoted dog, following them all the way to the car. He hovered uncertainly, watching them. Despite her instinctive dislike of the man, Ellen admired his determination to protect his daughter.

As they drove off, Ellen looked in the rear-view mirror and

saw Cooper, still standing where they'd left him, his body gradually growing smaller and less distinct.

THREE

At the station, there was a message waiting for Ellen. Leaving Abby to deal with Cosima, Ellen went downstairs. She found Charlotte standing outside, chainsmoking her way through a packet of Marlboro Lights. Despite the weather, she was wearing a short skirt and a pale pink cotton jacket. She was shivering and her lips and cheeks were tinged blue. She looked dreadful.

'Come inside,' Ellen said. 'You look half-frozen. Is this about this morning?'

'This morning?' Charlotte looked confused. 'Oh, you mean Freya's thing. No, it's not about that. She didn't want me there so I didn't go. I'm here about something else. There was an accident last night. At the top of my road. They said it was a woman. On the news. They said it was a woman and she'd been killed. She can't be dead, though. Not Ginny. Can I see her? Please. You've got to let me see her.'

'And you've got to calm down,' Ellen said, keeping her voice gentle. The woman was so brittle she was on the verge of breaking.

'How can I be calm?' Charlotte shouted. 'She's my best friend. My only friend. We've known each other forever. I won't be able to *live* without Ginny.'

'Charlotte, we don't know who the victim is yet,' Ellen said. 'We've got no ID yet. She could be anyone. Chances are she's not your friend at all.'

'You don't understand,' Charlotte said. 'She was coming to see me last night but she didn't turn up. And she's not answering her phone. I've tried calling her loads of times. She wouldn't do that. She's never let me down. Not once. That's the sort of person she is. If she says she's going to do something, she'll do it. She's one hundred percent reliable and the fact that she didn't turn up last night is proof that something's happened to her. She's not even answering her phone. Have I told you that? I mean, why wouldn't she answer her phone?'

A small crowd had gathered, waiting to see what the hysterical woman would do next.

'Come into the station,' Ellen said softly. 'Maybe you can give me a description of what your friend looks like and I'll see what I can find out for you?'

Charlotte wiped her nose with her sleeve.

'You'd do that?' she asked.

'Of course,' Ellen said. 'I can see you're upset and I'd like to help.'

Charlotte nodded. 'Okay. I've got a photo of her here on my phone. Look.' She rummaged around inside her oversized handbag and produced a small, pink, expensive-looking mobile phone.

She played around with the buttons for a moment then shoved the phone at Ellen, who saw a pretty woman smiling on the screen.

'That's her,' Charlotte said. 'That's Ginny.'

Ellen didn't reply. She was too busy trying to remember where she'd seen this woman before. When she'd worked it out, she looked at Charlotte and nodded.

'Let's go and see what I can find out. I'll need some more information. Ginny's full name and address, next-of-kin. Just in case.'

Back at her desk, Ellen found the name of the detective leading the hit-and-run investigation. DI John Cope, based over at Greenwich. When she called him, Cope told her the dead woman was in the morgue awaiting a PM which would confirm what they already knew, that someone had run her over and killed her.

'If we're lucky,' he said, 'we might get some detail about the car that hit her. We've got one witness who claims she was hit on purpose. An appeal's going out on the local news tonight. Maybe that'll give us something.'

'Any ID?' Ellen asked.

'Not yet,' Cope said. 'Unless you've got something you'd like to share with me?'

She told him about Charlotte and Cope sighed and said it was worth a try, he supposed.

'Get the image off her phone,' he said. 'And email it across to me. I'm going over to the morgue now. I'll call you back within half an hour.'

Ellen had left Charlotte in the care of a young WPC. Both women looked exceedingly pleased to see Ellen when she came into the room and asked for Charlotte's phone. Getting the image from the phone was an easy task. All Charlotte had to do was email it to Ellen's work email. A moment later, her Blackberry beeped with the incoming email and she forwarded it straightaway to the email address DI John Cope had given her.

'What do we do now?' Charlotte asked.

'We wait,' Ellen said. 'But don't worry. It won't take long. I'm going to ask WPC Harris here to go and get us both some coffees. While we wait, you can tell me a little bit about you and Ginny.'

Charlotte frowned. 'What do you want to know?'

'Everything,' Ellen said. 'How you met, how long you've known her, how does she get on with your family? Freya, for example.'

'Freya?' Charlotte said. 'Oh they don't. Get on, I mean. Freya and Ginny hate each other. Why do you ask, anyway? Is it important?'

Ellen's mind travelled back to the last time she'd visited Freya at her flat. The pretty, petite woman she'd bumped into on the street. The woman had seemed angry, as if something – or someone – had upset her. What was she doing at Freya's flat if the two women hated each other?

Charlotte was looking at her, waiting for an answer. Ellen reached out and patted her hand.

'I'm sure it's nothing,' she said. 'Try not to worry.'

FOUR

It started in the pit of her stomach. A tight, twisting sensation that pulled at her insides until it felt like that was all she was – this twisted-up knot of terror that consumed her and made it impossible to focus on anything else.

She swallowed, but there was no saliva in her mouth and the action hurt her throat. She tried to breathe but the clitter-clatter of her heart set the pace for the rest of her body, an over-fast metronome that speeded everything up so that she felt as if she was hurtling towards the thing she was most scared of and there was nothing in the whole world she could do about it.

'Can I get you anything else?'

Charlotte jumped. She hadn't expected the young police woman to say anything. Had forgotten she was even there.

She shook her head.

'How long will it take?' she asked.

'As long as it takes, Ma'am.'

Whatever the hell that meant. She had her phone. The last time she'd been here they'd taken her phone. This time, Ellen said she could keep it. She tried Ginny's number again, knowing it was pointless. The call went straight to voicemail. Again. Charlotte hung up without leaving a message.

She tried to imagine what she'd do if Ellen came back and said Charlotte was right. That the dead woman was Ginny. She couldn't do it. Each time she got as far as Ellen coming into the room, Charlotte's mind shut down. Unable to face the single worst thing she could imagine happening.

Maybe this was her punishment. She'd always known it would come. Foolishly, she'd believed her failure to keep her husband or love her child had been punishment enough.

Sugar and spice and all things nice.

Her mother's face pushed up close to Charlotte's. The dirty stink of cigarettes and red wine on her breath. That stupid doll singing in the background.

No!

Charlotte banished the face and the voice, focussed on Ginny instead. Remembered how Ginny had saved her that night. Turning up in her new Citroën, taking charge of everything and not even minding when blood stained the leather seats.

Ginny couldn't be dead. Charlotte wouldn't let it be true. What had she been thinking? Of all the people living in this huge city, why had she believed for one moment that the dead woman might be Ginny?

She stood up.

'I need to go.'

The police woman frowned and shook her head. 'DI Kelly said you were to wait here, Ma'am.'

She was a dumpy little thing. Short and chubby with dirty blonde hair tied back in a messy ponytail. Charlotte felt sorry for her.

'I don't have to,' Charlotte said. 'Do I?'

'She won't be long,' the police woman said. 'If it was me, I'd stay. I'd want to know.'

'Know what?'

'If it was my friend,' the woman said. 'You've waited here this long already. You might as well stick it out now.'

She was right. Charlotte checked the time. Ellen had been gone for over fifteen minutes. She'd got a message on her Blackberry and left the room, telling Charlotte she wouldn't be long. Made Charlotte wonder what Ellen's definition of 'long' was.

She needed a cigarette. She was meant to be giving up but who cared about that? The urge for nicotine triggered a memory. So sharp and perfect, every detail so clear, it was like she was right back there. The first time she'd ever smoked.

A hazy autumn evening. In the woods behind the school. A bottle of cider to keep them warm. A packet of cigarettes. The pale sun had set and the night was creeping in, catching them quicker here under the tangled branches of old trees, making Charlotte shiver.

'Nervous?' Ginny asked.

Charlotte shook her head, teeth chattering so loud she was certain Ginny could hear.

'Just cold,' she said. 'I never thought I'd say this, but I can't wait to get back inside.'

Inside was the school building where she'd been boarding for the past four years. Ever since her tenth birthday. She hated the place but Mother had made it perfectly clear that Charlotte had no choice in the matter.

Ginny grinned, her teeth white and perfect in her small mouth. Charlotte wished she had teeth like that. Hers were big and uneven, like donkey teeth. She'd been wearing a brace for nearly three months, but so far she couldn't see any difference. And even if it did straighten her teeth, they'd still be big and ugly. No brace could fix that.

She unscrewed the lid on the bottle and drank some cider. It hit her stomach too fast. Too much gas. She burped twice. Took another swig and passed the bottle to Ginny.

Charlotte was frightened about smoking but pretended to be excited, telling Ginny to hurry up with the box of matches. She wasn't sure what you were meant to do. Said Ginny should go first because they were Ginny's cigarettes.

Ginny put a cigarette into her mouth, struck a match and used it to light the tip. Charlotte watched, mesmerised, as the orange tip burned brighter the harder Ginny sucked. Eventually, Ginny stopped sucking, held her breath and then – casually – turned her face to the inky-blue sky and blew out a single streak of pale grey smoke.

Both girls watched the smoke as it drifted up in lazy, rotating swirls. When they could no longer see it, Ginny passed the box of matches to Charlotte.

'Your turn.'

Charlotte grabbed the bottle, took another swallow of the sweet cider and looked at the cigarette. Ready.

'What's it like?'

Excited now, not scared now. Ginny looked so cool. All she needed was a long cigarette-holder and her hair tied up in a bun and she'd be a dead-ringer for Audrey Hepburn in Breakfast at Tiffany's, their favourite film. Along with Pretty in Pink with Molly Ringwald.

'It's great,' Ginny said. 'Light up and see for yourself.'

She did it exactly the same way Ginny did. Cigarette, match, suck, suck, suck. The smoke rushed into her mouth and down her throat, burning. The cigarette fell from her mouth as great, hacking coughs exploded from her lungs. Head spinning, stomach churning like a washing machine, eyes watering so bad she couldn't see. And coughing like she was going to die.

She wiped her eyes and saw Ginny grinning at her.

'It's easier the second time,' Ginny said.

'You sure about that?'

'Trust me,' Ginny said. 'You'll be fine.'

It took a few more attempts but Ginny was right. She got there in *the end. They smoked one more each. When they'd finished, Charlotte felt like she'd been smoking her entire life.*

'It's brilliant,' she said.

Ginny laughed, even though Charlotte wasn't trying to be funny. For a moment she felt unsure, wondering if she'd sounded stupid.

'I told you,' Ginny said, managing to get the words out in between the laughing. And Charlotte realised Ginny wasn't laughing because Charlotte had done something stupid. Ginny was laughing because she was happy.

Still laughing, Ginny threw her arms around Charlotte's neck and kissed her cheek.

'It's all brilliant,' Ginny whispered. 'Everything in the whole world. It's ours, Charlotte. Do you understand that?'

Maybe it was the combination of cider and nicotine, but Charlotte felt dizzy, like she'd been lifted up on a giant cloud and was spinning around, up and up through the sky like the perfect streams of smoke she'd watched earlier.

A wind whipped through the woods, lifting dead leaves and making the branches over her head sway and dance, like the wind carried a song that only they could hear.

Charlotte lifted her head, watched the branches doing their crazy dance under the spotlight of a fat, white moon and wondered if she'd ever again be as happy as she was right here, right now.

Charlotte realised – wondered why she never had before – that Ginny must already have been smoking by then. She'd already gone through the coughing and nausea that comes with those first, nasty drags that are the start of nicotine addiction.

Charlotte would have liked to ask Ginny about it. She wanted to know when Ginny started to smoke and why Charlotte hadn't known about it. Suddenly, this seemed like the most important thing in the world.

She wanted to tell Ellen, who had come back into the room and was sitting down beside Charlotte, taking her hand and speaking to her. Charlotte pulled her hand away, refusing to listen. If she didn't listen, if she couldn't hear what Ellen was trying to tell her, then it wouldn't be real.

Ellen was looking at her but it wasn't Ellen's face Charlotte could see. It was Ginny's. Memory after memory tumbling through Charlotte's head. And through all the memories, her own voice, screaming at Ellen Kelly, telling her to shut up.

But Ellen wouldn't shut up. She kept on talking. And when Charlotte put her hands over her ears, it made no difference, she could still hear Ellen, telling her what she didn't want to hear.

Charlotte couldn't bear it. She lashed out, desperate to stop it. Ellen's arms wrapped around her, Ellen's voice speaking to her. Soft and gentle, whispering that she was sorry, so sorry. Over and over and over.

Kelly held her like that, until she had no fight left and all she could do was lean against this tall, strong woman and cry.

* * *

Pete Cooper sat in the car, staring out the window, waiting for his daughter to walk out of Lewisham police station. The glass doors swung open and Pete's insides flipped over. He straightened his back and cleared his throat. But it wasn't her. Instead of his daughter, he saw a skinny woman, greasy hair pulled back from a pointed face in a tight ponytail. She moved quickly, eyes darting this way and that, like she was looking for someone. Some pathetic bloody crackhead.

Thinking of his girl in there with scum like that was unbearable. The pain of it sat in his stomach, heavy like a rock. She would need a shower when she came home to wash off the stink and dirt of it all.

He was scared. Scared of losing his little girl. Scared that his carefully built world was about to come crashing down around him. Again.

This wasn't right.

He closed his eyes, pictured Cosima in a police cell, a shining bright light, white and pure, surrounded by the darkness and the filth.

He didn't mind Ellen Kelly so much. Women like that he could cope with. There was no pretence to Ellen Kelly. What you saw was what you got. Pete respected that. Abby Roberts was a different proposition altogether.

Abby. Annalise.

Pretty women with pretty smiles so sweet it would break your heart. A man could be easily fooled by a woman like that. A woman whose whole appearance told the world she was one thing when all the time she was something else entirely.

Abby. Annalise.

Bitches.

In the corner of his eye, something shifted and when he looked again, suddenly there she was. Standing at the top of the steps, staring at the car. Spirits soaring, Pete pressed the button and the window rolled smoothly down.

'Cosima!'

She didn't move at first and for one horrible moment he thought she wasn't pleased to see him. But then she was walking down the steps and coming towards him and he was jumping out of the car to hug her and lead her inside and take her home, where she belonged. With him.

And just like that, his world was whole again.

FIVE

A heavy rain was falling as Ellen pulled up outside Freya's house. She got out of the car and ran to the house, pressing repeatedly on the doorbell until Freya appeared.

'What is it?' Freya pulled open the door and peered out at Ellen, cowering under the inadequate porch.

'Can I come in?' Ellen didn't wait for an answer as she pushed past Freya into the dark hallway.

'You can't just barge in here uninvited,' Freya said. 'I've got rights, you know.'

'Where were you at approximately nine o'clock last night?' Ellen asked.

'Why?' Freya asked. 'Has something happened?'

'Answer the question,' Ellen said.

'I was here,' Freya said. 'No, hang on. I went down to the Meridian. I can't ... I find it difficult being here on my own. Every corner of the flat reminds me of Kieran. I can't stand it.'

Ellen's anger abated. She understood exactly how Freya felt. She wanted to say it got easier but she wasn't sure that was true. She took a deep breath and when she spoke again, her voice was calmer.

'I assume someone can confirm you were there?' she said.

Freya nodded. 'Of course.'

'Any chance we could go upstairs?' Ellen asked. 'There's something I need to tell you.'

Upstairs, the flat had a stale, unpleasant smell and the sitting room was stiflingly hot. She pictured Freya, sitting here day after day, trying to adjust to life alone.

'Nice service earlier,' Ellen said. 'You spoke very well.'

'Thanks,' Freya said. 'It was important to do something, you know?'

'Kieran obviously had a lot of friends,' Ellen said.

'He was a good man.' Freya frowned. 'But that's not why you're here, is it?'

'Your mother came to see me earlier,' Ellen said. 'She was worried about her friend, Ginny.'

'What's that got to do with me?' Freya asked.

'I wondered if you'd seen her recently,' Ellen asked.

'We don't get on,' Freya said.

'That wasn't what I asked,' Ellen replied.

'What's happened?' Freya asked. 'I know something's happened or you wouldn't be here asking about Ginny. You said my mother's worried about her. Why? Oh God. You think she had something to do with what happened to Kieran?'

'You think she's capable of something like that?' Ellen asked.

Freya snorted. 'That woman's capable of anything.'

'What makes you say that?'

'She's a nutter,' Freya said. 'Her and my mother, they're like a psychotic version of those women in *Ab Fab*. And don't think I'm making it up. Ginny drinks like a fish, smokes like a chimney and shags anyone who'll look at her. She's loaded, of course. Married some poor sap with tonnes of cash. He left her when he found out she was shagging the chauffeur. Since then, she's lived on her own as far as I know and all she seems to do is go out to wine bars with my mother and get shitfaced.'

'They live this shallow, *nothing* life. I mean, they've got all this money and what do they do with it? Buy designer clothes and go to expensive restaurants where they hardly touch the food because they're so worried about putting on a single pound in case – God forbid – they can't fit into those size six skinny jeans they bought the day before which were designed for someone twenty years younger. It's pathetic.'

She stopped talking, panting slightly, as if the effort of speaking so much at one time had tired her out.

'And you've rebelled against that by trying to make the world a better place?' Ellen said.

'It's not a rebellion,' Freya said. 'That would imply I care enough about my mother to want to rebel. I don't give one shit about her. I choose to live my life this way because I want to. If you don't do anything, if you don't try, at least, to make this world a better place, what's the point of it all? But you didn't come here for that. And you didn't come here just because my mother told you she's worried about Ginny. What the hell is going on? Please. Just tell me.'

'Ginny was killed last night.'

'Sorry?'

'Virginia Rau is dead.'

'What happened?' Freya's voice wobbled. Ellen thought she might cry but she didn't.

'Hit and run,' Ellen said. 'We think she'd been on her way to visit your mother when it happened. There's not much else I can tell you, I'm afraid. Hopefully the post-mortem results might give us something.'

'I don't understand,' Freya said. 'I mean, I know she was a pain in the backside but why would someone want to kill her? Surely it was an accident?'

'Maybe.' Ellen stood up. 'I must get going. I'm sorry to be the bearer of bad news a second time. Will you be okay or do you want me to call someone?'

'I'll be fine,' Freya said. 'I already told you how I felt about Ginny. I'm shocked, but not upset. Sorry if that sounds cold but it's just how it is. God, what about my mother? Does she know?'

'Yes,' Ellen said. 'She's very upset. Obviously. You should give her a call.'

'Yeah,' Freya said. 'Maybe I will.'

The rain had stopped, replaced by a cold, bright sun that flooded the room with pale light, illuminating Freya's already white face. She looked exhausted and made no effort to stand as Ellen prepared to leave.

Ellen said goodbye and promised to be in touch.

'One more thing,' she said. 'You still haven't told me when you last saw Ginny.'

'Ah,' Freya said. 'That's easy. She was here yesterday.'

'And?'

'And nothing,' Freya said. 'She came to ask me to visit my mother. Said she was worried about her.'

'What did you say to that?' Ellen asked.

'I told her to go to hell,' Freya said. 'And she left.' The corners of her mouth twitched, like she was about to smile. 'I didn't realise it would be the last time I'd ever see her.'

Outside, before she got into her car, Ellen turned and looked back up at the flat. The sun's reflection glared off the glass in the sitting-room window, making it difficult to see inside the room. She thought she saw someone standing at the window but she couldn't be sure. She stayed where she was for a moment, staring up at where she thought Freya was standing. The shadow moved. Ellen couldn't tell if it was Freya or the reflection of a cloud passing overhead.

SIX

Eight o'clock and Ellen was still at work. Both children would be in bed by the time she got out of here. This was the part of her job she hated the most. The long hours that meant she never seemed to spend as much time with her children as she felt she should. She could have left earlier. Ger had done her best to push her out the door, but Ellen had stood her ground. There were times – and this was one of them – when work had to come first.

She was in an interview room with Ger, Pete Cooper and Cooper's lawyer, an overweight Scot with a completely bald head called James Wilson. The interview was Ellen's idea. Virginia Rau was a cousin of Cooper's dead wife. The connection had to be more than just coincidence.

'My client's already told you,' Wilson said. 'He was at a Rotary

Club dinner last night. There are plenty of witnesses who can attest to that fact. He couldn't have killed Virginia Rau. It's not possible.'

They'd already checked out the dinner and had confirmation that Cooper was there. Which meant they'd have to let him go soon unless they got something else.

'Mr Cooper.' Ellen straightened in her chair and tried one final time. 'After your wife died, Virginia Rau was one of the people who gave a statement at the time, implying you had something to do with your wife's death.'

'She was lying,' Cooper said.

'She also said your wife was having an affair,' Ger said.

The now-familiar flush crept up Cooper's cheeks.

'She lied about that too.'

'Kieran Burton,' Ger said. 'Now Virginia Rau. Two people you are directly connected to and they're both killed within a few days of each other.'

'Both connections are tenuous at most,' James Wilson said. 'Mr Burton was the boyfriend of the daughter of one of Mr Cooper's associates. The two men didn't know each other.'

'We have witnesses who say otherwise,' Ger said.

'More liars,' Cooper said.

'What about Virginia?' Ellen asked. 'She accused Mr Cooper of killing his wife.'

'Ginny wasn't right in the head,' Cooper said. 'If you did your job properly, you'd know that already.'

Ellen felt a twinge of uncertainty. Their investigations into the dead woman were in the early stages. All they knew so far could be summarised in a few short sentences. Three times divorced, no children, only child of Alberto and Sandra Rau of Esher, Surrey. Both parents deceased. Her father five years ago and her mother a year later. Her last husband, Sylvester, was on holiday in Dubai. Local police had informed him of his ex-wife's death and he was flying home tomorrow for questioning. So far, they hadn't uncovered any hint of mental illness.

'Would you care to elaborate?' Ger asked.

Cooper smiled. 'Not really my place, is it?'

'What about your daughter?' Ellen said, going for Cooper's only weakness. 'Was she close to Ms Rau?'

'They got on okay,' Cooper said.

'Cosima must be very upset' Ellen said.

Cooper shrugged. 'She'll get over it. Not like losing her mum, is it?'

They let him go soon after that, Ellen and Ger both frustrated by the lack of information they'd got from him.

'Cooper's wife,' Ellen said. 'Kieran Burton and now the Rau woman. There's only one thing that connects all three deaths. And that's Cooper.'

'Or his daughter,' Ger said.

Ellen considered that. 'Yeah. Except she was only a kid herself when her mother died.'

'Find out how close she really was to Rau,' Ger said.

'I'll get Abby to speak to her,' Ellen said. 'I'll ask her to go to the college and see if she can get to her without Daddy there to protect her.'

'Good idea.' Ger yawned and looked at her watch. 'I'm knackered. You must be too. Let's both go home, get a decent night's kip and see how things look in the morning.'

It was almost nine o'clock. If Ellen left now, there was a tiny chance Pat might still be awake and she'd get to say goodnight to him. A tiny chance, but it was enough to put a spring in her step as she left the office and walked along the corridor to the lift.

SEVEN

She was empty. A shell. She'd thought the morgue would be the worst bit but she was wrong. The worst bit was now and all the endless days and weeks and months and years ahead. All that time wasted just existing – because it wasn't living when you felt like this – in a world without Ginny in it.

It hit her in waves, like a bad hangover. In the lulls, the sense of it remained, gnawing at her insides. She could endure that. Just. Existing in a numb bubble of anxiety, pain and emptiness. Then, out of the blue, with no warning, the grief hit again – a tidal wave that crashed into her and consumed her for minutes, maybe hours, at a time.

A bottle of wine and an empty glass sat on the coffee table in front of her. At some point, she must have opened the bottle and drank some wine. She didn't remember that. She was sitting in the conservatory. Didn't remember how she'd ended up in here, either.

A table over by the wall with photos on it. Lots of her and Nick. Most from their first few years together, including a selection of wedding snaps. A song started in her head. The Human League, 'Don't You Want Me'. Playing in the club the first night she met him. Phil Oakey's voice echoing her own devotion to Nick when they'd started dating. Before she realised the sort of man he really was.

A horrible photo of Freya and Kieran. A copy of the one that sat on the mantelpiece in Freya's flat. Kieran with his arm around Charlotte's daughter. Freya looking like she'd just won the bloody lottery. Beside it, an older photo of Charlotte and Ginny. Both of them so young and happy. She looked away. Unable to bear it.

Nick wasn't home. She didn't know where he was. Didn't care, either. Doubted she would care about anything ever again. If he came home now she'd have to tell him, and she didn't think she had the strength for that.

She hadn't turned on the lights or closed the curtains. She sat in the pale grey half-light, time crawling by as she tried to process what had happened.

She should have stayed at the morgue. If she'd known that was it, the very last time she'd see Ginny, she would have begged to be allowed to stay. At the time, the woman laid out in front of her looked so unlike her friend, she hadn't wanted to. Now, she wished more than anything that she could be there with Ginny. Instead of being here with this unbearable, unending emptiness.

She reached out for the wine bottle and filled the glass. Put the bottle down and stared at the glass, wondering what she was doing. Oblivion. It was the only sensible option, the only thing to aim for in the face of this pain.

Two people dead within a few days of each other. One she'd hated, one she'd loved. She remembered the last time she'd seen Kieran. The awful things he'd whispered in her ear as he pressed his body against her, ignoring her when she told him to stop. Her hands curled into fists, manicured fingernails digging into the palms of her hands.

Ginny never knew. The one secret Charlotte kept from her. Too ashamed of what she'd done. Ginny hadn't known about it and yet ... Two people dead.

The last time they'd been out, on Sunday night, there'd been something off with Ginny. Like she'd wanted to tell Charlotte something but was holding off. Charlotte should have pushed it. She was certain now that whatever Ginny knew, it was important. It had to be. She refused to believe this was an accident.

A sudden noise outside made her jump. The crash of something being knocked over in the garden, followed by a high-pitched, drawn out squeal. Through the glass walls of the conservatory she saw a fox running across the lawn. Something dangled from its mouth. A rat, squealing for its life. Charlotte watched the fox streak across the lawn and disappear through the narrow gap in the hedge. The squeals lingered, faded slowly, disappeared. Until there was nothing left except the bottle and the glass and the pale light of the full moon.

* * *

Abby woke with a start. At first, the presence of someone else in the bed startled her. Then she remembered. He was lying on his side, facing her. Hands clasped under his head. Asleep, he looked younger, more beautiful too. She reached out and stroked his face gently, not wanting to disturb him.

She'd been dreaming. Walking in the East Sussex countryside with her brother. Trudging across wide, open countryside. Trying to catch up with two people in front of them. Something about the dream was annoying her.

She got out of bed and walked over to the window. The apartment was high up and she liked to sleep with the curtains open. From her bed, she could see the sky through the huge windows. It always felt like a luxury, to be able to lie in bed and watch the stars.

A full moon lit up the sky, turning the world silver and grey. There was something liberating, standing naked like this, bathing her body in the moon's pale light. From here, she could see across the river to Greenwich. The lights of south-east London twinkled at her across the dark expanse of river that split the city in two.

Ellen was over there somewhere. Asleep in her own bed, alone.

Or not alone. Abby thought Ellen had said something about Pat sleeping with her these days, but she couldn't recall whether he slept there all night, came in during the night or what.

She tried to imagine what it would be like, having to deal with something like that on top of losing your husband. It couldn't be easy. Abby knew about grief. It had almost destroyed her once. To lose your husband, and to have to manage your own grief alongside that of your children's, Abby didn't know how you did that. And then on top of all that, your son is almost killed.

No wonder Ellen was the way she was.

Andy was with her in the dream. That should have made her happy. Instead, there was something else, something that made her anxious. The two people in front of them. A man and a woman, walking fast. Abby and Andy running after them, trying to catch them because they had something Abby needed to see. If only she could remember what it was. She knew it was important. But when she tried to remember she heard her brother's voice instead, shouting as he'd done in the dream. And remembering that made her sad so she stopped trying to remember.

Behind her, Sam stirred in the bed, mumbled something and was still again. Abby turned and walked back to him. She was lucky. She was alive and she had this. She climbed under the duvet, curled tight into Sam's body, closed her eyes and let sleep claim her once more.

THURSDAY

ONE

Pat didn't want to go to school. If her parents were here, Ellen might have relented, let him spend the day with them instead. But that wasn't an option. She couldn't take the day off. Not in the middle of a murder investigation. Besides, there was nothing wrong with him. Larry had stressed the importance of consistency and normality.

'He'll test you,' Larry had said. 'See how far he can push things. That's normal. What's important is that you don't give into it. I know he's had an awful experience, but he's getting better. That's why I'm here. He needs to realise that the normal boundaries and rules he's lived by until now remain in place. If you give in to every little request, it won't help either of you.'

Ellen knew Larry was right. Even so, she still felt like the worst mother in the world for sending her child to school when he didn't want to go. Feeling utterly crap, she dropped the children off and walked through the park to Nick Gleeson's flagship restaurant in the heart of Greenwich.

The last time she'd passed Nick Gleeson's restaurant, the empty shop beside Totally Tapas had been a building site. Now, she could see Gleeson's new vision taking shape. She peered through the dirty glass for a better look.

The décor inside was retro. A wooden bar ran along one side of the long room. Wooden tables and chairs filled the rest of the space. Old-style lanterns hung from the ceiling; a huge pizza oven took up the entire back wall. A sheet of A4 paper had been glued to the window. *Tipico Totale: a new concept in dining. Opening soon!* Ellen wondered what was new about wood-fired pizza and over-priced pasta.

Totally Tapas, next door, was already open for business. She noted a group of journalists and paparazzi across the road. As she approached the restaurant, someone took her photo, the sudden flash of light disorienting her. She twisted her head to avoid the glare. When she looked again, one of the pack had broken away from the others and was running across the road.

'Ellen!'

Martine Reynolds.

'I've got nothing to say to you,' Ellen said, pushing past the journalist.

'Just one question,' Martine said. 'Are you linking the two murders?'

'There's been a second murder?' Ellen said. 'You obviously know something I don't.'

'Virginia Rau,' Martine said. 'We're working an angle that she was killed because she knew who killed Kieran Burton. Would you like to comment on that?'

'No, I wouldn't.'

Ellen got inside the restaurant and closed the door, pressing her body against it in case Martine tried to follow her inside.

'Those damn journalists.'

A tall, striking woman with bobbed red hair came running over with a smile. 'I'm so sorry they bothered you. Do you want to book a table?'

Ellen had been to this restaurant many times before but never this early in the morning. Despite the time, several tables were occupied and she thought it seemed like a nice place to come for breakfast.

'Actually, I'm looking for Nick Gleeson,' Ellen said. She pulled out her warrant card and showed it to the woman.

'Ah. Nick is due in any minute.' She held out her hand. 'I'm Loretta Lewis, Nick's assistant. Why don't I show you to a table and you can sample some of our coffee and pastries while you wait?'

Ellen allowed herself to be led over to a small table at the back of the restaurant. She sat down and waited as Loretta ordered coffee and 'a selection of pastries' from a handsome waiter with chocolate brown eyes and a strong Spanish accent.

'All our table staff are native Spanish speakers,' Loretta explained after she'd dispatched the Antonio Banderas lookalike. 'Although not all are from Spain, of course. A significant number of staff across our restaurants come from Latin American countries. Authenticity is important in this business. Which is why I'm spending a lot of time in Italy right now, recruiting staff for our new venture. Anyway, that's not why you're here. It's about Kieran, isn't it?'

'I'm just following up some leads,' Ellen said. 'Were you here on Tuesday night?'

'Tuesday?' Loretta frowned. 'Of course. I'm here every night.' Her eyes widened. 'Oh. That's the night the poor woman was killed. You think that's got something to do with what happened to Kieran? That's terrible.'

'Did you know her?' Ellen asked.

'No,' Loretta said. 'Sorry, it's just awful, that's all.'

'Can you tell me who else was working on Tuesday night?' Ellen asked.

'I can print out a list of all the staff who were here if you'd like that?' Loretta said.

'That would be good,' Ellen said. 'Thanks.'

'Oh look,' Loretta said. 'Here's Javier with our food.' She beamed at the waiter and he smiled back. The sort of smile that could make a fool out of you, Ellen thought.

'Isn't he gorgeous?' Loretta whispered as Javier melted away once more. 'Gay, of course. Why is it, do you think, that so many drop-dead gorgeous men are gay? Oh sorry. Ignore me. I was in a relationship until recently and I think I've become a bit unhinged since it ended. Keep finding myself lusting after all sorts of unsuitable men. Gay waiters, for example. Coffee?'

The coffee was good and the pastries were to die for. Ellen tucked in while she carried on with her questions.

'You were telling me about Tuesday,' she said.

'Not much to tell,' Loretta said. 'We were working but that's hardly unusual these days. With so much going on, I seem to be always working. Nick was here until about one in the morning. I was too. The restaurant shut at eleven. Tuesdays tend to be quiet.'

According to the witness, Virginia Rau had been hit just after nine o'clock. Ellen wondered how easy it would have been for Gleeson to slip out, drive up to the heath and back again without anyone noticing he was gone.

'Is Nick usually out here in the restaurant?' she asked. 'Or does he stay in the kitchen?'

'Neither.' Loretta shook her head. 'Most of the time he's locked away in his office. It's back there. Beside the kitchen.'

'And after the restaurant closed?' Ellen asked.

'I went home,' Loretta said. 'You'd have to ask Nick what he did.'

'You're saying he didn't go home?'

'I'm saying what Nick does when he leaves work is Nick's

business. Not mine. Not anymore.'

Ellen took a sip of coffee as she considered this information.

'What about his wife?' she asked.

'They can't stand each other,' Loretta said. 'It's been like that for years. It's not Nick's fault. At least, that's what I used to think. She's a bit of a nightmare, to be honest. I always thought, you know, that the problems they had were all down to her.'

'And now?'

'Well, let's just say I'm not so sure about anything anymore,' Loretta said. 'Look, I know what you're probably thinking. He's a married man and I should have known better, but I thought he was going to leave her. I mean, it's obvious to anyone the marriage is over.'

'Why are they still together?' Ellen asked.

'He always said she'd make it too difficult if they got divorced,' Loretta said. 'Plus, if they separated, he'd have to give her half of what he had. He wouldn't do that. Money's too important to him.'

'So he'd rather stay in an unhappy relationship?' Ellen said.

'He'd rather do anything than give away a single penny of what he's worked so hard for,' Loretta said. 'Until recently, he had the best of both worlds, didn't he? He had his money and he had me on the side, making everything okay and waiting patiently like some stupid, bloody fool for him to come to his senses and leave her.'

The anger in her voice was real. Ellen wondered how far Loretta might go if pushed.

'I must sound like a nutter,' Loretta said. 'And you're probably wondering if I'm the sort of nutter who might kill someone. Can't say I blame you. But if I was going to kill anyone, it would be Nick. Besides, I have an alibi for every night for the past five nights. When Nick finished with me I moved in with an old friend from uni. Couldn't bear being on my own. I've been going to hers every night straight after work. She'll vouch for me if you need her to.'

Ellen took the friend's name and telephone number even though she knew Loretta was right. It didn't make sense for her to kill Kieran or Ginny. She'd said it herself: the person she'd most want to hurt was still alive.

'What happened?' Ellen asked.

'He said he wanted to give his marriage another chance,' Loretta said. 'I don't believe him, though. He met someone else.'

'What makes you say that?'

'I know him,' Loretta said. 'Better than he thinks. I've caught him on his mobile more times than I can count, whispering to someone with that stupid, goofy look on his face. And he's started taking lunch breaks. Long ones.' She shook her head. 'When you're this busy, you don't take long lunches unless you've got someone very special to share them with.'

'Any idea who she is?' Ellen asked.

'Not a clue,' Loretta said. 'He's being all secretive about it.'

'I can understand that,' Ellen said.

Loretta shook her head. 'No. It's weird. When I was, you

know, when we were together, everyone knew about us. Even Freya. She'd had her suspicions for a while and eventually she came right out and asked Nick. He told her the truth. Afterwards, she came to see me. She wanted to make sure, I think, that I was serious about her father. Once she realised I was, she seemed fine with it. Told me things between her parents were difficult and her father deserved any happiness he could find. This is different. No one has a clue who she is.'

Before Ellen could ask anything else, Nick Gleeson came through the front door into the restaurant. He clocked Ellen with Loretta and walked over, his face carefully arranged into a smile that had all the warmth of an iceberg.

'Detective Kelly,' he said. 'I hope Loretta has been taking good care of you? Ah, good. You've had the pastries. Have you tried these? Sunos de Teruel? Little pastry cheesecakes. They're delicious.'

'Loretta's been most helpful,' Ellen said. 'In fact, I think she's given me all the information I wanted. No need to take up any of your time. I know how busy you are.'

The smile slid off his face, replaced by a frown.

'But surely ...?'

'Surely nothing,' Ellen said. She stood up. 'Thanks for the coffee. And you're right. The pastries are delicious. Goodbye.'

Outside, it was raining again. Still buzzed up, Ellen barely noticed. Getting the better of Nick Gleeson brightened her mood. She couldn't remember when she'd last felt this good about life. She paused in the doorway to call Abby and tell her she was on her way in. When she'd finished, she put her phone away and stepped onto the road. At the same time, a red car pulled away from the kerb right in front of her. The driver didn't appear to notice her and Ellen had to jump back to avoid being hit. The car swept past her through a puddle, causing water to splash up and drench the bottom half of Ellen's tights.

She shook her fist at the car but her protest was pointless. The car sped down the road, disappearing in a mist of exhaust fumes and rain. Through the rain she saw a bus approaching. She crossed the road and legged it to the bus stop. It was only once she was sitting down inside the bus that her mind turned back to the red car. There hadn't been time to notice much about the driver, but she'd seen enough to recognise his face.

Looking out the rain-streaked window, Ellen wondered what had happened to make Nick Gleeson leave the restaurant in such a hurry. And where had he been going?

TWO

Thursday morning, Abby was back at the university looking for Cosima. Yesterday's interview at the station had revealed nothing new. Cosima was so closed, Abby had really struggled to break through and make any sort of connection. It was Ellen's idea to try again, this time at the university.

'You're not much older than her,' Ellen said. 'You've got more chance of getting through to her than I have. If you speak to her on her own territory, you may have more luck.'

There was a bounce in Abby's step this morning. Things with Sam were still great and work seemed to be taking a definite turn for the better. Her relationship with Ellen had improved beyond anything she could ever have hoped for. When she thought back to how they used to be, it was impossible to think they could ever have reached a point where they were … what? Colleagues who got on with each other? No. It was more than that. Ellen was her friend. A good friend, at that. As it had many times in the past, Abby's mind flashed back to that terrible moment when Ellen had walked in on her and their ex-boss, Ed Baxter. Maybe some day she'd be able to tell Ellen how that period of madness was all a reaction to her brother's death. Maybe.

A quick phone call to Professor Holmes and Abby learned that Cosima would shortly be finishing a lecture in the Psychology Department. The door was closed and she stood outside, listening to the vaguely soporific voice of the male lecturer rumbling through the wooden door.

She didn't have long to wait before the door opened and a flood of students poured out, all noise and colour and energy. Abby searched the animated faces for Cosima and was on the verge of giving up when she saw the girl trailing along behind the herd, obviously and painfully alone.

'Cosima.'

A flash of animation, Abby couldn't work out if it was interest or anger or fear, and the girl's face reverted to its usual expressionless façade.

'Hello.'

'A quick word?' Abby said.

She looked around, searching for something to say that might resonate with Cosima.

'It brings me back to my own student days,' she said. 'Feels like another lifetime ago now.'

She waited for Cosima to ask her where she'd studied or what she'd studied or anything at all.

'I miss it,' Abby said. 'Although you don't really appreciate it at the time. You know, how lucky you are to be able to be a fulltime student with no worries or responsibilities. I never realised how good I had it until I'd finished and real life caught up with me.'

'You didn't realise?' Cosima frowned. 'How could you take all this for granted?' She waved her hand around, at the high-ceilinged corridor, the throng of students brushing past them, the whole world of academic privilege.

'I was young,' Abby said. 'And stupid, I guess. I really only worked out how lucky I was after my brother died.'

'What happened?'

'He was hit by a car,' Abby said.

That did the trick. Cosima's face flushed red, her eyes bright with emotion. Real and raw.

'The driver was drunk,' Abby said.

'Oh.' Cosima frowned and looked away. 'I'm sorry. That's terrible.'

Abby asked if there was somewhere quiet they could go and Cosima suggested the student canteen.

'It's never busy this time in the morning,' she explained, as she led Abby into the large, modern annex.

The room wasn't quiet, echoing with the clatter of student babble and cutlery clinking against china. But there were plenty of free tables. They found one near the back of the canteen. Cosima sat opposite Abby, arms folded across her chest, waiting.

'I'm really sorry about what happened to your cousin,' Abby said.

'My mother's cousin,' Cosima corrected her. 'It's horrible.' Her shoulders slumped and she looked tired.

'Can I get you anything?' Abby asked. 'Tea or coffee, maybe?'

'I just want to get this over with,' Cosima said. 'I suppose you want to know where I was when it happened?'

'Actually,' Abby said, 'I wanted to ask about your father and Ginny. I understand they didn't always see eye to eye?'

'So? Lots of people don't get on. It doesn't mean they go around killing each other. Anyway, he was interviewed yesterday, wasn't he? I won't be able to tell you anything new.'

'She accused him of killing your mother,' Abby said. 'That's a bit more than *not getting on*, isn't it?'

Cosima closed her eyes and took several deep breaths, like she was working hard to keep her emotions under control.

'Ginny had a lot of problems,' she said, opening her eyes.

'What sort of problems?'

'Oh God. Look, she was one of those frustrated women who wanted children but couldn't have them. It messed her up.'

'How do you know this?' Abby asked.

'It's not exactly a secret,' Cosima said. 'Ask anyone who knew her. She fell out with my mother when Mum got pregnant. Ginny was jealous. Couldn't cope with it.'

'Yet she was friends with Charlotte Gleeson,' Abby said. 'And she must have been pregnant around the same time as your mother.'

Cosima shrugged. 'Maybe there were problems with that too. I don't know.'

Neither did Abby. But she intended to find out.

'When was the last time you saw her?' Abby asked.

'A few weeks ago,' Cosima said. 'Something like that. It was difficult. I would have liked to meet up with her more than we did but Daddy couldn't stand her.'

'She was the only link with your mother,' Abby said. 'It must have been important to you to keep that connection alive.'

'Doesn't matter now, does it?' Cosima said. 'She's dead. Maybe if I hadn't tried so hard to *keep the connection alive*, it wouldn't be so difficult.'

'What wouldn't be?' Abby asked.

'Losing her,' Cosima said. 'Now she's gone, there's no one left, is there?'

THREE

The rain woke her. A crescendo of water, loud and persistent, bouncing off the roof and the large glass windows in the sitting room. For a brief, blissful moment, she didn't remember. And then it hit her. The shock of it almost as bad as the first time.

Her body ached from the awkward way she'd slept on the sofa. A crick in her neck hurt each time she moved her head. Her back too felt stiff and unyielding, and a shock of blinding white pain shot up her bruised arm when she shifted in the seat and knocked her elbow against the arm of the chair.

On the coffee table, her phone started ringing. She saw Freya's number and took the call.

'Hi.'

'Freya. What do you want?'

'I'm calling to see if you're okay,' Freya said. 'I heard about Ginny.'

The rain was like a drumbeat thudding through the house, through her body. She wondered how she'd ever find the energy to do anything ever again. Maybe she never would. Maybe she'd sit here gradually growing weaker, fading until – eventually, thankfully – there was nothing left.

'Mum?'

'Sorry,' Charlotte said. 'It's good of you to call. Thank you.'

'Have they said anything?' Freya asked. 'The police. Have they told you what happened?'

'Hit and run,' Charlotte said. 'I don't know any more than that. Why? What have you heard?'

'Nothing,' Freya said. 'But I can't help wondering if there's any connection with what happened to Kieran.'

There was an open bottle of wine on the table. An empty glass beside it. Charlotte poured some wine into the glass, lifted it to her mouth. The smell of it hit her nostrils, sent her stomach into a spasm of revulsion even before she'd got it down her throat.

A second spasm and she knew she wouldn't be able to keep it down. Throwing the phone onto the sofa, she ran from the room, hand over her mouth. She skidded across the polished, parquet floor and into the downstairs cloakroom. Made it just in time. On her knees, she leaned into the toilet, puking up every last bit of everything that was inside her stomach.

When it was over, she stayed where she was, sweat-drenched

and shaking, nose full of the acid, bitter smell of her own puke. She sat back, leaned against the cool, white tiled wall, tears running down her face, soaking the collar of her YSL shirt.

She lost track of time. Lost track of everything until the distant sound of a mobile phone finally penetrated the grey emptiness. It wasn't her phone; the ringtone was different. Not Nick's either ... his phone had some stupid theme tune from a 1980s action movie. The phone rang, stopped, and then a few minutes later started again. It kept doing this, over and over, until she couldn't bear it any longer.

She pulled herself off the floor and followed the sound, through the hall and down the stairs to the basement kitchen.

* * *

'Ellen.' Ger walked into the open-plan office Ellen shared with the rest of her team. 'You got a moment?'

'Sure.' Ellen swivelled her chair around and waited for Ger to sit down.

'Malcolm's sorting the warrant that will give us access to Kieran's finances,' Ger said. 'It'll go to the Mag's court later. We should have access to his accounts by the end of the day.'

'That's great,' Ellen said. 'I've just been speaking to the lab. Chasing them about that hair sample we found on Kieran's clothes. They promised to have something for us within the next two days.'

Ger nodded. 'So we're slowly making some progress.'

The door opened and Abby walked in, accompanied by Alastair.

'Virginia Rau was hit by a red car,' Alastair said. 'Red paint marks on the victim's clothes. Not enough from the paint to give us anything on the make or model, I'm afraid.'

A memory flickered at the back of Ellen's mind but the conversation was already moving on and she had to concentrate on that instead.

'Are we sure the two deaths are connected?' Abby asked, taking a seat the other side of Ger while Alastair remained standing.

'Not sure,' Ger said. 'But we're working on the assumption that they might be. Both victims were involved with the Gleeson family. And now they're both dead.'

No one spoke for a moment. Ellen didn't know about anyone else but she was imagining the two victims' final moments. The shock and the fear and, worst of all, the terrible knowledge that everything they were was about to end.

'According to Cosima,' Abby said. 'Her mother and Ginny had a falling out over children. Ginny wanted children but couldn't have them. Cosima said Ginny was pretty messed up about it.'

'I wonder if that's what Cooper meant when he said she wasn't right in the head,' Ellen said.

'Possibly,' Ger said. 'Ellen, can you add Charlotte to your list? Drop past the house at some point, pretend you're checking she's okay. See what you can find out about Ginny and ask her again about her husband's mistress. She must have some idea who it is.

Abby, I want you to spend time with Freya. Tell her it's for her own good. Stay with her even if she doesn't want you there. Don't let her out of your sight. Get friendly with her, ask about her relationship with Burton and his relationship with her parents. Is there any way Burton could have got close to her father without her realising it? What might he have found out? Try to crack through that shell and see what you get, okay?'

'What about the wine bar?' Ellen asked. 'Freya said she was there the night Virginia Rau was killed. I was going to drop in and check out her alibi.'

'Abby can call in on her way to Freya's,' Ger said. 'That makes most sense. Time is precious and we don't want to waste it. Okay?'

It wasn't okay. Ellen was used to doing things her own way. Her previous boss, Ed Baxter, wasn't perfect but at least he'd given her free rein to run a case the way she wanted. Ger was much more hands-on. Something Ellen didn't like one single bit.

Around her, people were getting back to work. Abby was standing at her desk, putting things into her bag before driving across to Hither Green. Ellen pushed her chair back, about to stand up, when she remembered.

'Nick Gleeson,' she said.

Everyone stopped what they were doing and looked at her. Ger, already at the door, paused and turned around.

'What about him?' Ger asked.

'He drives a red car,' Ellen said. 'I saw him in it this morning when I was at the restaurant.'

'You're sure about that?' Ger said.

Ellen remembered how fast the car had been driving. She'd seen his face for less than a second. It had all happened so quickly. The bottoms of her tights were still damp. It might have been quick but she remembered enough.

'I'm sure,' she said.

'Good,' Ger said. 'Well done, Ellen. Get onto it straightaway. Check out that car first thing.'

Ger smiled and Ellen found herself smiling back, knowing it was stupid to feel pleased at being praised but enjoying the feeling.

FOUR

Pete paced around the hallway, checking his mobile every few seconds, waiting for a text that never came. It was almost two o'clock. Cosima's lectures ended at midday and she'd promised she would come straight home afterwards. She wasn't home yet and wasn't answering his texts or phone calls. Pete wasn't happy.

He opened the front door and walked outside, stood at the gate and peered down the road, looking for her car. Plenty of vehicles but hers wasn't one of them. He went back inside, stood in the hallway trying to control the thoughts shouting inside his head. Trying to work out what he should do.

Clive, his sometimes-bodyguard, came out of the kitchen and asked Pete if he was all right.

'Fine,' Pete said.

'You look a bit worried, that's all,' Clive said.

'I said I'm fine,' Pete said, waving the idiot away. Clive was a typical muscle man. All meat and no brain. No complexity to him. Truth was, Pete was scared. Didn't want to admit what was frightening him because as soon as he said it, it would become something real that he had to consider. He went into the sitting room and stood in front of the portrait of Annalise. She'd been only a few years older than Cosima when he'd commissioned that piece. Perfect. Before that bastard McNulty got to her.

Flashlight splashes of memory. His mother's face, laughing down at him as he lay in bed, too scared to move. The stink of alcohol and cigarettes on her breath. Her fingers digging into his arm as she dragged him from the bed into the sitting room where the man was waiting for them both.

Annalise, smiling shyly that first time. Her hands shaking as she untied the laces of her white nightdress. The one he'd bought specially. The same one he'd given to Cosima the morning of her twenty-first birthday.

A series of photos laid out on his desk. Annalise on her knees in front of McNulty. Doing things a woman like that should never be forced to do. Standing naked in a hotel bedroom, exposing herself like the cheap tart she'd become.

It still hurt. He'd loved her beyond reason. Had promised her the earth when they'd first met. And he'd given her more than she could ever have dreamed of. Taken her from the shitty estate and brought her here, to this place. The perfect home for the perfect woman.

Her face smiled down at him from above the fireplace, the purest, sweetest smile. He'd have done anything in the world to protect her, keep her safe and create a world for her where that perfection could survive. He'd done everything he possibly could, but it wasn't enough. She'd become the one thing he hadn't wanted. A cheap slut, every bit as bad as his own mother. And when he knew what she was really like, he'd had no choice.

He'd been so sure about her. From the first moment he laid eyes on her, he knew. She was the one. In the beginning, she'd loved him and obeyed him and been everything he'd wanted her to be for a short, perfect period of time.

And then Daniel McNulty took all that away from him.

When Pete first heard the rumours, he'd refused to believe them. Told himself it was nothing more than idle gossip from people who were jealous of him and what he had. Turned out he was a bloody fool.

When it was all over, he'd come in here the following morning with a ladder and started to take down the painting. Midway through, he found himself crying onto the face of his dead wife. He didn't understand it at first. She wasn't worth his tears. Then he realised. The Annalise in the painting wasn't the same woman as the person he'd had to get rid of. The Annalise in the painting didn't deserve to be punished. She could stay where she was. She was blameless. Nothing like the Annalise who'd let herself be ruined beyond redemption by a man with no manners and no prospects. That Annalise deserved to die. This one most certainly did not.

'Daddy?'

Pete's heart stumbled over itself. She was here. She smiled and he tried to smile back, doing his best to ignore the doubt gnawing at the edges of his mind. Not letting himself think about why she'd put a password on her mobile phone recently. Almost as if she didn't want him to see what was on it. And now, there was something tentative, guarded about the way she was looking at him that brought him right back to that other time.

Like mother, like daughter.

No. He wouldn't do that to himself. It wasn't fair on either of them. She crossed the room, walking with her mother's walk, looking at him with her mother's eyes.

'Where have you been?'

'I had a meeting with my course tutor,' she said. 'I forgot to switch my phone on after my last lecture so I didn't know you were trying to get in touch with me. I'm sorry.'

She was close enough now for him to touch her. He reached up, ran his finger along her cheek, the softness of her skin triggering a slew of memories. And something else too. He knew he shouldn't keep touching her when that happened but it was impossible not to.

He kept his finger on her face and closed his eyes, breathing in the flowery scent of the perfume he bought especially for her. It was the easiest thing in the world to imagine she was Annalise, ready to step into his arms and let him do whatever he wanted, always ready to show him how grateful she was for all he'd done.

He took a step closer, heard the sharp intake of breath and opened his eyes, confused. Annalise was staring at him, something in her face he didn't recognise and didn't like.

'Daddy?'

Not Annalise. Of course not. He smiled and patted her face, meaning to reassure her but smacking a little harder than he'd meant to, leaving a faint trace of red on her perfect skin. She remained where she was, not moving or showing any sign that he'd hurt her. Behaving like a perfect lady, just the way he'd taught her to. He lifted his hand and smacked her again, harder this time. The red mark darkened. Still she didn't move.

He traced the mark with the tip of his finger, trailed his finger around the curve her jaw, around her chin and down, not stopping until he reached the base of her neck. He could feel a pulse beating above her collar bone, and hear her breath coming in short, sharp gasps. He spread his palm open so that it wrapped around her neck.

'You'd tell me,' he whispered, 'wouldn't you?'

'Tell you what?'

'If there was anything I needed to worry about.'

'Of course,' she said.

He let her go then, turned away from her and went to the mahogany drinks cabinet. He pulled out the bottle of single malt and poured two fingerfuls into one of the cut crystal glasses. It was only when he tried to drink from the glass and the whiskey missed his mouth and dribbled down his chin, soaking into the soft silk of his cravat, that he realised he was shaking from head to toe.

FIVE

He should have password-protected it. Then Charlotte would never have seen the message. But she had seen it. And now she knew. She was in the kitchen, holding the phone. It wasn't his usual phone. That was a sleek, slim iPhone. Model blah, blah, blah. She didn't care about things like that, but he did. Upgraded his phone every time a new version was released. Like a little boy with his gadgets. Was there really a time she'd thought that was cute?

She read the message again. Tried to think who could have sent it. Loretta? Charlotte was pretty sure that had fizzled out a while ago. The last time she'd been at the restaurant you could feel the tension between them. Icy cold. At the time, Charlotte was pleased. Loretta was a bitch who hadn't thought twice about screwing her married boss. All smiles and charm to Charlotte's face when all the time Charlotte *knew*. Pathetic woman that she was, she'd played along with it. Returned Loretta's smiles, made meaningless small-talk and never once let on that all she could think about was her husband's assistant lying on her back with her legs open while Nick moved up and down on top of her.

She'd played along because she was a coward. Too scared to make a fuss in case it led to an ultimatum. If she said nothing, pretended everything was fine, Nick would stay. And even though she couldn't stand the sight of him, nothing else was an option. No dirty 'D' word was going to end her marriage, thank you very much.

Now, standing in the kitchen with the cheap plastic phone in her hand, reading a text exchange between her husband and some nameless, faceless woman, Charlotte wondered how she could ever have been so stupid.

Outside, the growl of crunching gravel as a car drove down the driveway. Charlotte put the phone down and ran across to the window. Saw her own little Merc pulling up outside the house. The engine stopped and her husband's large frame uncurled out of the car.

She couldn't face him. She needed to clear her head, work out what she thought it all meant and what she wanted to do about it. She already knew one thing. If he had any hand in what had happened to Ginny, she would make him pay.

What was he doing with her car? She tried to remember if he'd told her he was taking it. She couldn't remember but didn't care. He could have the bloody thing if it made him happy.

Her head was light, spinning as if she'd drank a glass of wine too quickly. Her stomach and chest were tight. She closed her eyes, forced herself to breathe slowly – in, out, in, out – the way the shrink had showed her. Far away, a key turned in the front door followed by her husband's voice, calling her name. She slipped the phone in her trouser pocket and left through the back door.

* * *

'Charlotte?'

No answer. Didn't mean anything. Half the time she was so out of it she didn't hear him coming home. Or pretended not to. He'd lost count of the times he'd let himself believe he had the place to himself only to walk into the kitchen or the sitting room and find her waiting for him. A glass of wine always in her hand and a look of martyred misery on her face. That fucking face. Like he was the one with the drink problem and the utter fucking lack of any bit of love or compassion or maternal instinct. The woman he'd married was a monster. A drink-addicted, self-deluding monster who lived in a world of make-believe. The shallowest, emptiest, most self-pitying person he'd ever had the misfortune to know.

He ran upstairs, checked the bedroom and bathroom. Down-stairs again, calling her name the whole time, dreading the moment he would open a door and find her waiting for him like an apparition from a horror movie. Ghostly and martyred and drunk.

But she wasn't here. The stupid cow really had managed to pull herself together and get out somewhere. Which was a huge relief. No moany questioning, no asking what he was looking for and could she help and why didn't he sit down and she'd make him a cup of his favourite coffee while he listened to her moan on and on and fucking on about losing the only friend she'd ever had. Never once pausing to question why it was she'd never managed to find anyone else willing or able to put up with her.

Being married to her was like a slow death. He'd had enough. Until recently, he'd been willing to stick with it. He hated her but, on the surface at least, their marriage worked. And it suited the image he wanted to present to the world. The happily married, successful businessman. Decent and hardworking and loyal. But everything was different now. It was time to move on and get rid of the stupid cow once and for all.

He'd rushed home to get the pay-as-you-go phone. Seeing Ellen Kelly cosying up with Loretta had freaked him out. He'd had to get away. Went for a long drive then stopped to make a call. And realised he only had the iPhone, and he couldn't use that. They'd both agreed. Too easy to trace the calls back to him.

In the hall, he searched the pockets of the jacket hanging on the coat-rack, certain that's where he'd left the phone. When he didn't find it, he tried to think where else it could be. He'd gone for a few drinks with the team last night, when the restaurant closed. He'd been wearing this jacket and definitely had the phone in the pub. The text had come just after he'd bought a round. He remembered excusing himself and going outside. He'd been about to call back when Loretta sidled out to him, started with her usual insinuations and incriminations. In the end, he'd sent a quick text and gone back inside, leaving Loretta alone in the rain.

A moment of cold panic. He pictured the phone falling out of his pocket as he walked into the pub. Imagined Loretta seeing it, picking it up and scrolling through his texts. He shook his head, telling himself he was being stupid. He'd put the phone into his pocket. The inside breast pocket of the jacket. He hadn't taken the jacket off. No way it could have fallen out.

He took out his usual phone, the silver grey iPhone that he loved, and dialled the number he knew off by heart. With the iPhone pressed against his ear, he heard the other phone start to ring, held his breath as he waited to hear the corresponding ring from somewhere inside the house.

But nothing happened.

* * *

The day was grey and overcast. She'd left the house too quickly, forgotten to grab a jacket. The unseasonably cold wind raced across the open heath, cutting through her fat-free frame. The phone in her trouser pocket started to ring. She pulled it out, half-hoping it would be her – the bitch he was two-timing her with. When she saw Nick's number on the display she smiled. He was panicking, calling the phone, hoping to hear it ring so he'd know where it was. She carried on walking, holding the phone in her hand while it rang. She pictured her husband, standing alone in the big, empty house, dialling the number over and over again, desperate to find the phone before anyone else did.

As she reached the edge of the heath and crossed Charlton Way into Greenwich Park, the clouds cleared and the sun came out. The air around her grew warmer and the wind died down. She lifted her face to the sun, closed her eyes and let the warmth wash over her. In her hand, the cheap phone continued to ring.

SIX

A DVLA check confirmed a red Mercedes sports car was registered to the Gleesons' address. Charlotte Gleeson was named as the owner.

'Strange,' Ellen said, re-reading the information. 'It was definitely him driving the car. Not her.'

'Maybe he borrowed his wife's car,' Alastair said.

'Maybe,' Ellen said. 'Either way, I need to get over there. Ask him some questions.'

She put on her jacket, ready to go, when Malcolm burst into the room.

'Got Burton's bank details,' he said, red-faced and out of breath. 'Two bank accounts. A joint one he shared with Freya and a separate one in his own name. Nothing special in the first account. Most of the money is paid in by her. They use that account to pay their rent, bills, *et cetera*.'

'The other account?' Ellen asked.

Malcolm's face lit up.

'Nothing in there for months on end,' he said. 'Twenty-five quid that he hasn't touched for years. Then four weeks ago, a cash deposit of seven and a half grand.'

Seven and a half thousand. Enough to kill someone? Ellen had worked cases where victims had been murdered for substantially smaller sums than that.

'Any idea who made the deposit?' she asked.

'According to the paying-in slip, it was Burton himself,' Malcolm said.

'Good work, Malcolm,' Ellen said. 'Now we need to cross-check that sum of money. Check out the Gleesons first – home and business accounts. You're looking for a cash withdrawal of between five and ten thousand. Check the last three months ... speak to Raj about Cooper, too, although I don't think we'll find anything. Even if the money came from him, he'll have found a way to make it impossible to trace.'

She suspected the same would go for Nick Gleeson. Running a business like his, ten grand was little more than petty cash. But they had to look into it nonetheless. It would be a boring, time-consuming task and she didn't envy Malcolm one bit.

She zipped up her jacket and turned to Alastair.

'I'm going across to Gleeson's place now. Want to come?'

He grinned. 'I'd love to.'

'Good,' Ellen said. 'Call downstairs and arrange for two uniforms to meet us in the car park.'

'Anyone in particular?' Alastair asked.

'Yes.' Ellen remembered the blonde officer from the day the body was found. 'See if PC McKeown is free. If not, then I don't care. Let's go.'

* * *

The atmosphere in the flat was almost as bad as the smell. Abby had suggested opening the windows, but Freya refused to consider it. She sat huddled beside the electric heater, barely speaking while Abby had moved around the flat, tidying things and washing up the pile of dirty plates and cups in the kitchen.

When she'd done as much as she could, Abby asked Freya if she'd like to go for a walk.

Freya shook her head.

'You need to get out,' Abby said. 'Look, it's not raining for once. Let's make the most of the sun.'

Freya sighed. 'If I say yes, will you stop being so bloody perky?'

'I can't promise that,' Abby said. 'But the café in the park does a good hot chocolate. I'll treat you?'

Reluctantly, Freya heaved herself into a shapeless woollen coat that was far too big for her and clumped after Abby down the stairs and out of the house.

Despite the sun, Freya wrapped the coat around her and

buried her face in the collar as they walked up Ennersdale Road towards Mountsfield Park.

'It still has his smell,' she said. 'I wonder how long before that goes too?'

Abby remembered thinking the same thing after her brother Andy died. Lying on his bed with her face buried in his pillow. Inhaling deeply, holding her breath for as long as she possibly could, desperate to keep this last remaining piece of him. She felt a pang of empathy for Freya and wondered if it was grief that had soured Freya's personality or if she'd always been this way.

'Tell me about Kieran,' Abby said. 'How did you meet him?'

Freya smiled. It softened her face and made her suddenly pretty. For the first time, Abby saw a flicker of what might have attracted Kieran to her.

'We were at a rally,' Freya said. 'Protesting against the plans to close Lewisham Hospital. The atmosphere was amazing. So many people from the local community gathered to support our local NHS services. I got talking to Kieran. Nothing serious, just a bit of banter as we marched. Afterwards, a group of us were going to the pub. I asked if he wanted to come with us and that's how it started. He came home with me that evening and barely left since.'

'How long ago was that?' Abby asked.

'Two and a half years,' Freya said. 'The best, happiest time of my life.'

They'd reached the park and walked in silence across to the

café at the top. Abby bought the hot chocolates and joined Freya at a table outside when the drinks were ready. The smell of sweet, warm chocolate circled around her, making the world seem a better place than it really was.

'What about you?' Freya asked. 'You seeing anyone?'

Abby took a sip of coffee and looked across the park as she considered her answer. The urge to speak about Sam, to tell everyone she met everything she knew about him, was new and unexpected. When she finally answered, she spoke slowly, taking care not to gush.

'Sort of,' she said. 'But it's early days yet. We hardly know each other.'

'It's easy for women like you,' Freya said.

'What is?' Abby asked.

Mountsfield Park was glorious when the sun was shining. She pictured herself walking along here with Sam. Hand in hand, taking in the stunning views that stretched all the way across London as far as the London Eye.

'Relationships,' Freya said. 'Men are so shallow. They rarely look beneath the surface, don't take the time to think about the sort of person a woman really is. And women are fooled by it. They end up like my mother, constantly striving to be perfect. And constantly failing.

'Someone who looks like you, I bet you've no shortage of blokes wanting to go out with you. Not one of them caring what sort of a person you are. Or worse, pretending you're something you're not, so you'll fit their ideal of what a perfect little girlfriend should be. Look at you! Perfect hair, perfect body, perfect skin, perfect clothes. But it's all surface, isn't it? Underneath, you could be the biggest cow in the world or thick as a plank and nine guys out of ten won't care one jot. They'll still want to go out with you just because of the way you look.'

The venom in Freya's voice took Abby by surprise. Again, she considered her words carefully before she spoke.

'I agree with you,' she said. 'It is shallow. But that's life. I guess you can choose to rail against it or go with the flow. Maybe I'm not brave enough to rail against it, I don't know.'

'I could be pretty if I wanted to,' Freya said. 'I could lose some weight, get my hair cut and buy some new clothes. But why would I bother? I don't want to be with someone who cares about stuff like that. This is me!' She slammed a fist against her chest, so hard it must have hurt. 'That's why Kieran was different. He saw through all that superficial bollocks. And I loved him for it.'

Except he didn't, Abby thought. He had fooled this poor girl into thinking he cared when all the time he was taking her for a ride.

'I'm not stupid,' Freya said.

For a moment, Abby thought Freya must have guessed what she was thinking.

'I know what people said about us,' Freya continued. 'I could see it in their faces. How did a plain Jane like me manage to get a guy like him? My mother was the worst. She couldn't stand it. Hated that Kieran had chosen me not her. According to her worldview, no good-looking guy would ever look twice at someone like me. I'm sure she's told you she didn't approve of Kieran. It's not true. She flirted with him. All the time. She disapproved, all right. But her disapproval was all based on the fact that he'd chosen me, not her.'

'But your mum is married,' Abby said. 'And she's *your mum*.'

'That's never stopped her,' Freya said. She drained her cup, slammed it on the table and stood up. 'I'm cold. I want to go home. I've had enough of all this sunshine and fake girly-chat. You think I don't know what you're doing? Pretending to be my friend when all the time you're wondering if I killed him.'

Freya pulled Kieran's jacket around her body and walked off. Abby got up and followed her, wondering what she'd said or done to make Freya shut down so suddenly. As she hurried after her, Abby ran back over the conversation. It was when she'd mentioned Charlotte that Freya had shut down.

That's never stopped her.

What did Freya mean exactly? Abby caught up with her, put her hand on her shoulder.

'Sorry,' Abby said. 'I didn't mean to upset you.'

'It's okay,' Freya said. 'I just don't want to speak about my mother.'

'That's fine,' Abby said. 'If you don't want to speak about her, you don't have to. I won't ask you about her again.'

'Promise?'

Abby smiled, the lie coming easily as Ger's words ran through her head. *Try to crack through that shell and see what you get.*

'I promise,' she said.

She linked her arm in Freya's and, together, the two women walked side by side across the park, leaving the views of the city behind them as they walked back into the quiet suburbia of Hither Green.

SEVEN

The red car was parked outside the house when Ellen, Alastair and the two PCs arrived. According to the DVLA, Nick Gleeson drove a navy-blue BMW 730. The same car she'd seen in the driveway the first time she'd visited this house. There was no BMW here today. She rang the doorbell. It was answered a moment later by Nick Gleeson.

'Mind if we come inside?' Ellen stepped past him into the vast hallway before he had a chance to answer. 'We'd like to ask you some more questions. You and your wife.'

'My wife's not here,' Nick said. 'And before you ask, I don't know where she is.'

'Isn't that her car parked in the driveway?' Ellen asked.

He hesitated, like he wasn't sure what answer to give.

'My car's in for a service,' he said. 'I've borrowed Charlotte's Merc for a few days.'

'How many days?'

'Sorry?'

'How many days have you had your wife's car?' Ellen asked. 'It's a simple enough question.'

'Since Wednesday morning,' Nick said. 'Why?'

'We'll need details of the people who have your car,' Ellen said. 'So we can check that out. Can you give me that information now?'

'Well, yes,' Nick said. 'But I don't understand. I'm sorry, Officer ...'

'Detective,' Ellen interrupted. 'It's Detective Inspector Kelly, Mr Gleeson. Try to remember that.'

He scowled at her. 'Sorry, *Detective Inspector*. I'm happy to provide you with any information you need. Of course I am. Can you tell me why you need it?'

Ellen was saved from answering by the appearance of Alastair, who'd joined them in the hall.

'Ma'am? Something to show you.'

Ellen followed him outside, where he pointed at the red car.

'Scratches on the front left-hand side,' he said. 'Damage to the paintwork and some dints in the metal, too.'

Gleeson was standing in the doorway, watching them.

'Mr Gleeson,' Ellen said, 'we're going to have to take you to the station. We've got some further questions for you and we'll need your answers on record.'

He started to protest but Ellen walked away. She left Alastair and the two officers to deal with him, while she went to examine the damage to the red sports car. It was too early to make any assumptions but a jubilant voice was bouncing around inside her head, telling her that once they examined the paintwork on the car it was going to be a match for the paint discovered on Virginia Rau's body.

* * *

Charlotte stood outside Freya's house, wondering whether or not to press the doorbell. She'd walked all the way across from Greenwich. Her feet ached and her legs were shaky-tired. She was out of breath, hot and sweaty.

She didn't know why she'd come here. A vague, unformed hope that maybe she could rebuild some sort of relationship with her daughter. She knew she hadn't been the best mother and she'd change that if she could. If Freya would let her. With Ginny gone, Freya was the only thing she had left. Things between them might not be perfect but Freya was her daughter and that had to mean something.

Music thumped loudly from one of the houses across the street. Charlotte wished they'd turn it down. The noise was giving her a headache. She wondered how the other neighbours could bear it. Although more than likely, it wasn't the worst thing you had to put up with in a neighbourhood like this.

She pressed the doorbell, waited, pressed it again. No answer.

Frustrated, she went onto the street and looked up at Freya's flat. Nothing.

'Mum?'

Charlotte swung around, saw Freya walking towards her down the hill. The pretty detective alongside her. Panicked, Charlotte tried to decide what to do. Stay or go? She trawled through her memories, trying to find something that would link Freya and the detective. Something besides Kieran and Ginny. Nothing came to her but she couldn't stop herself wondering: what the hell was Abby doing here? Out walking with Freya as if they were the best of friends.

'What's wrong?' Freya stopped in front of Charlotte. She wasn't smiling but she didn't look too displeased to see her, either. Which Charlotte took as a good sign.

'I'm sorry, darling,' Charlotte said. 'Is this a bad time?'

'Depends why you're here,' Freya said.

Her hair was greasy and messy, like she hadn't washed it or brushed it in days. Charlotte ran her fingers through her own hair, thought of the care she'd taken getting ready this morning and wondered why Freya couldn't have done the same. She knew her daughter was grieving but so was Charlotte, after all.

'Sorry,' she said again, thinking how stupid and judgemental she was being. Grief affected everyone in different ways. She'd spent time on her appearance this morning because the ritual of getting ready soothed her. She was sure Freya had her own rituals, which – no doubt – Charlotte wouldn't have understood or cared for.

'What for?' Freya asked.

'I should have called first,' Charlotte said. 'But I wanted to see you, darling. Make sure you're okay. Can I come in?'

Freya shrugged, stepped back inside and started up the stairs. When the detective moved to follow her in, Charlotte shook her head.

'Can't you give us some time alone?' she asked.

The detective looked at Freya, who must have indicated it was okay because the detective nodded her head and said that was fine.

'You need food.' She spoke to Freya as if Charlotte was invisible. 'I'll go to the shop. Call if you need me.'

After she left, Charlotte turned to Freya, her expression deliberately quizzical. Unsurprisingly, Freya chose to ignore the look and headed up the stairs, leaving Charlotte no choice but to follow her.

From the state of her daughter, Charlotte had expected to find the flat in a similar state. Instead, the place was spotlessly clean. A vase with fresh lilies stood on the table by the window. The thick, sweet smell of the flowers filled the small room.

'Abby tidied up,' Freya said, watching Charlotte look around the flat.

'Beautiful flowers,' Charlotte said, still trying to work out this new relationship. It crossed her mind – not for the first time – that maybe Freya was a lesbian. The clothes and the hair practically shouted as much. But not Abby, surely. And even if there was something between them, wasn't there some sort of code of ethics that the police were obliged to follow? Charlotte sighed, wishing she understood.

'Kieran used to buy me flowers every week,' Freya said. 'I bought them yesterday in his memory. He would have loved these. See the colour? I've never seen lilies this shade before.'

She was right. The petals were a rich, indigo blue. Very unusual. Charlotte tried to imagine Kieran arriving home each week with a bunch of flowers for Freya, the two of them embracing after he'd handed them over. The whole scenario was so laughably improbable she felt a sharp pang of sympathy for her poor daughter.

'Shall I make us some tea?' she asked.

'Okay,' Freya said. 'I'll help if you'd like?'

'That would be lovely,' Charlotte said. 'Thank you.'

In the galley kitchen she spotted a bottle of red wine, unopened, on the kitchen worktop. With supreme self-control she looked away and set about making two cups of tea.

EIGHT

It was the same detectives again. The icy blonde, DSI Cox, and the brunette who'd come to his house. They asked him if he wanted a solicitor and he said no, it wasn't necessary. Now, he was starting to think that was a mistake. He had assumed this was about Kieran. Turned out they were more interested in where he'd been on Tuesday night. Didn't take long for him to work out it was Ginny's death they wanted to know about.

'Are you all right, Mr Gleeson?'

Cox was looking at him, frowning. For one horrible moment he thought maybe he'd said something he shouldn't have.

'Fine,' he said. 'Sorry. I'm trying to gather my thoughts, that's all. I mean, can you imagine what this is like? Only a week ago, my life was perfectly normal.' A lie but not a serious one. 'And then suddenly two people close to my family are killed. My daughter's boyfriend and my wife's best friend. It's like someone's got it in for me.'

'For you?' Cox asked.

Cow.

'For us,' he said. 'Of course I don't mean just myself. Freya, Charlotte and I. Makes me wonder what will happen next.'

He shuddered, part-dramatic, part-real. Freya and Charlotte had already lost the people they cared most about. What if the same thing happened to him?

'I'm scared,' he said.

'Of what?' The dark one this time. Kelly.

'I'm scared,' he repeated, speaking slowly, the way he might if he was explaining a complex idea to a small child, 'because I don't know why any of this has happened. I'm used to being in control. All of this ... mess, I can't control what will happen next. I hate that.'

Was it his imagination or did he see a softening around Kelly's eyes?

'Which is why you need our help,' she said.

'So let's try again,' Cox said. 'Where were you on Tuesday night? You sure as hell weren't home. Your wife's already confirmed that.'

'I worked late,' Nick said. 'I'm working late every night at the moment. It's a busy time for me, as I'm sure you can understand.' He gave what he knew was his best smile but neither responded.

'You had a visit from Pete Cooper shortly after eight,' Cox said.

Nick nodded but it wasn't enough for Cox. She pointed at the CD-recorder and asked him the same question again.

'Business,' he said. 'Pete wanted to talk about the new restaurant, that's all.'

'There's a CCTV camera near the entrance to the restaurant,' Cox said. 'We've got Mr Cooper entering the restaurant at six minutes past eight and leaving again just before ten. Is that right?'

Nick nodded again, then remembered the CD-recorder and said, 'Yes, that sounds about right.'

Kelly frowned and he wondered how he'd slipped up.

'Do you always have business meetings so late in the evening?' she asked.

Nick nearly laughed with relief. They didn't have a clue.

'Sometimes,' he said. 'Especially when they take place in the restaurant and Pete can get a free meal out of it.'

'Your assistant says you were still at the office when she left at a quarter past one,' Kelly said. 'We have CCTV footage of you leaving the restaurant shortly after that. Twenty-four minutes past one to be precise. Where did you go?'

'My apartment,' he said. 'Look, if I can be frank?' When he got no response from either of them, he carried on regardless. He'd already hinted at what it was like for him. Time to give them the whole picture.

'Charlotte is a very troubled woman,' he said. 'She's an

alcoholic. What some people term a high-functioning alcoholic. Although if you live with it, you quickly see there's very little functioning that actually goes on.' He smiled, the same smile he'd practiced each time he used that line. Again, neither detective smiled back. They really were a pair of heartless cows.

'She drinks all the time,' he continued. 'And she can be abusive. Aggressive, even. Truth be told, our marriage ended years ago.'

'So you're seeing someone else,' Kelly said. 'Is that what you're trying to tell us?'

He felt unaccountably disappointed. He'd have expected a jibe like that from the blonde but not Kelly, who – he suspected – understood him better than she let on. He shook his head, doing his best to look sad, like a man beaten down by the trials he had to endure.

'There's no one else,' he said. 'I rent the apartment because there are times I can't bear to go home, knowing what's waiting for me. That sounds callous, I know. But it's the truth, DI Kelly.'

As she returned his stare, he waited for another flash of warmth. Nothing. Didn't mean she wasn't feeling it. As a detective, he imagined she'd become accustomed to concealing what she thought.

'I feel sorry for her,' he said, the over-used half-truth coming easily. He leaned forward, looked directly into Cox's startling blue eyes. 'You've met my wife, Superintendent. You must have noticed how unstable she is. She's an unpredictable alcoholic. I've tried to leave her several times in the past but each time I have, well, let's just say it didn't end well. I'm worried what might happen if I tried again.'

He saw something like scorn on Cox's face and sat back, repelled by her lack of empathy. How could she know what it was like for him? He wished he could tell her the truth. She thought he was some pathetic creature stuck in a dead-end marriage. He thought of last night and all the other nights over the last months. The new happiness that gave his life the meaning he'd been craving for so long. He wanted to shout it out, watch the look on Cox's face change from contempt to respect. But what if she didn't get it? What if, instead of respecting him, it made her despise him even more? He imagined a different reaction. Supercilious scorn mixed with contempt. She wouldn't understand. Neither of them would. How could they? You only had to look at them to see that passion was a foreign language to women like them.

'Is that it?' he said instead. 'Am I free to go?'

'Nearly finished,' Cox said.

He knew they'd already been to the apartment block. Clarence, the bloke who worked the front desk, had told him they'd come calling. Lucky for Nick he'd had the forethought to give Clarence a tidy handout, collateral in case the police asked any tricky questions. No problems there.

He waited, thinking they must be near the end now. A few more pointless questions and then – surely – they'd wrap things up.

'Any idea when your car will be ready?' Cox asked.

'Tomorrow,' Nick said. 'With a bit of luck. Been using the same BMW dealer for the last eight years. Great bloke. I'd trust him with my life.'

He cringed the moment he said it but they didn't seem to mind.

'Let's hope it doesn't come to that,' Cox murmured.

'There was just one more thing,' Kelly said, as Nick uncrossed his legs and prepared to stand up.

He sighed. 'Yeah?'

'We checked your phone records,' she said. 'Three weeks before he died, you received five separate text messages from Kieran Burton. Why was that?'

For a long, drawn out moment, he couldn't think of a single thing to say. Stupidly – so stupid he could have slapped himself right now – he hadn't thought they'd check his phone records. How could he not have thought of that?

'It was nothing,' he said. 'I'd been trying for a while to persuade Kieran to propose. I'm a father, Detective. Freya's my little girl. If you have children yourself, you'll understand why I was so keen for him to make an honest woman of her.'

'You did that by text?' Kelly asked.

'No,' Nick blustered. 'Of course not. We'd had a chat about it and then, a few days later, he sent me a text. Said he'd thought about it and he was going to do it.'

Kelly barely seemed to be listening. She was consulting the

information on a piece of paper in front of her. Nick tried to read it but the writing was too small.

'On Monday the second of April,' Kelly said, 'the first time he texted you, in fact, Kieran sent you a text message with an image embedded. Seems a strange thing to do. What was the photo of?'

His mind sped back to that terrible moment. He thought he'd managed the situation. And now here they were, bringing the whole mess out into the open again. It wasn't fair.

'The photo,' Kelly repeated like a broken bloody record. 'What was it?'

'A ring.' He said the first thing that popped into his head. 'He was looking at an engagement ring and wanted my opinion.'

'I assume you kept the photo?' Cox said.

'I don't think so,' Nick said. He'd deleted the image almost immediately, making sure no one would ever see it.

'Mr Gleeson?' One of them was speaking. The room was spinning and it was difficult to hear over the other noises pulsating through his head.

'I deleted it,' he said. 'I didn't think anyone would want to see it.'

His voice sounded so normal, so natural. Like there was nothing wrong.

'Not even your wife?' Kelly said.

'I already told you,' he said. 'We're barely on speaking terms.'

'Never mind,' the blonde said. 'I'm sure we can find the image. We've got access to Kieran's online storage, I think DI Kelly?'

Kelly nodded, never taking her eyes off Nick. 'Oh yes,' she said. 'We certainly have.'

She smirked when she said this and he knew the bitch didn't believe him. Which wasn't fair but he knew what the police were like. In their eyes, everyone was a potential criminal, even innocent members of the public. He felt a righteous anger on behalf of all those who'd suffered unfairly at the hands of biased police officers.

They thought he'd killed Kieran. Ginny too, probably.

'It was Charlotte,' he said. 'She's who you should be looking at. Not me.'

Silence. Two faces looking at him. Two pairs of blue eyes. Icy pale and a blue that was so deep it was almost navy. He blinked, startled by the sudden beauty he saw in Kelly's unbeautiful face.

'Would you care to elaborate?' Cox said eventually.

He hesitated, not sure he was doing the right thing. He hadn't wanted this. Any whiff of a scandal was bad for business. He'd thought – stupidly, he could see that now – that somehow he could deflect police attention away from his family. Now, he knew he didn't have a choice. It was him or Charlotte.

He made his decision. Straightened his back, flicked back his hair and looked from Cox to Kelly and back to Cox again.

'She's done this before,' he began.

NINE

They sat in facing armchairs, either side of the fireplace, drinking their tea. A plate of chocolate digestives lay on the coffee table between them. Charlotte watched without comment as Freya stuffed biscuit after biscuit into her mouth. Different ways of grieving, she reminded herself.

'How have you been holding up?' she asked.

'Okay,' Freya mumbled through a mouthful of biscuit. 'Some moments it hits me and I feel I can't bear it another second. Then it passes and I'm fine again. Well, not fine, but you know ...'

Charlotte nodded. A bit like how she felt. The constant, underlying pain of it that sharpened at unexpected moments into something that stuck in your throat until you thought you were suffocating from lack of air.

'I don't know where we go from here,' she said. 'I don't feel as if I know anything anymore. I'm not sure it helps having that police woman here, either. Why is she hanging around you, anyway? Is there something you're not telling me?'

'She's just doing her job,' Freya said. 'That's all. Listen, Mum. There's something I haven't told you. It's about Ginny.'

Charlotte didn't let herself breathe.

'She came to see me,' Freya said. 'On Tuesday afternoon.'

'Why?' She had no clue how she'd got the word out.

'She wanted to talk to me,' Freya said. 'About you.'

No, please God, no. Not this. Not now.

'She wanted me to make more of an effort.'

'What?' Relief mixed with confusion. What on earth was Freya talking about?

'Well, not just me,' Freya said. 'Both of us, actually. You and me. She said it made you sad that we weren't closer and that one day you'd be gone and I'd regret not having a better relationship with you.'

'She really said that?'

Freya's features blurred as tears filled Charlotte's eyes. Dear Ginny. The best friend she'd ever had. Charlotte had no idea. They rarely spoke about Freya. It wasn't their way. Truth was, Charlotte didn't really speak about Freya with anyone. It was too difficult. Her daughter was such a source of shame. Shame at herself and Nick for being such terrible parents. Shame at her daughter for turning out the way she had. And all the time, the shame hiding something else. A deep sadness that she'd messed things up so profoundly.

Somehow, Ginny had understood.

'She really cared about you,' Freya said. 'I know she and I didn't always see eye to eye, but I wanted you to know. She was a good friend to you.'

'Thank you,' Charlotte whispered. 'That means a lot.'

'Do you think she knew?' Freya asked.

The fear again. The giddy, sea-sick feeling that it all came back to that single mistake. 'Knew what?'

'Who killed Kieran,' Freya said. 'What do you think I meant?'

A knife in her hand. The sudden spurt of warm blood on her wrist. Elation replacing rage. Before the fear and panic kicked in.

'Of course,' she said. 'Sorry, darling. I'm all over the place at the moment. Do I think she knew? Maybe. No, definitely. Of course she did. Why else would someone …? I mean, it's not just coincidence, is it?'

'People get hit by cars all the time,' Freya said. 'Probably some drunk driver who shouldn't have been behind the wheel of a car in the first place. Makes me sick to think about it.'

Charlotte wondered if Freya was having a dig, but decided it was her own guilty conscience that made her think that.

She thought of what had happened earlier, tried to sort through the jumble of thoughts swirling around her brain. She hadn't known whether or not to raise it with Freya, but they were getting on so well. And if she couldn't talk to Freya, who else could she possibly talk to?

'Freya, darling,' she said. 'I need to ask you something.'

'What?' Freya's voice was cold, the earlier friendliness all gone. Not a good sign but Charlotte persevered, thinking if only Freya would hear her out, maybe together they could make some sense of it.

'It's about your father,' she said. 'Well, your father and Kieran, actually.'

It was coming out all wrong. She should have thought more about the best way to approach it. She could tell by the way Freya was looking at her that she was already jumping to conclusions.

'I'm not trying to imply anything,' Charlotte said quickly. 'Just hear me out, please.'

'What do you mean, you're not trying to imply anything?' Freya snapped. 'That's why you're here, isn't it? Jesus, Mother, I really believed that for once in your life you'd come to see me with no hidden agenda. You want me to start suspecting my own father of killing my boyfriend? Forget it. Whatever you want to tell me, I don't want to hear it.'

'Please,' Charlotte begged. 'It's really important.'

But Freya was already standing up and coming towards her. Grabbed Charlotte's sore arm and pulled her up.

'I want you to leave,' Freya said. 'Go now. Before I push you down the bloody stairs. Go!'

Charlotte pulled her arm free. It hurt where Freya's fingers had dug into flesh already bruised. The pain helped her focus.

The fog in her head cleared and everything suddenly made sense. Nick had found out what she'd done. Naturally enough, he was angry about it. It was one thing for him to sleep around but quite another for his wife to do the same thing. Or maybe his anger was on behalf of his daughter. Yes, that made more sense. And because of that, Kieran was dead. And so was Ginny.

'I know what happened,' Charlotte said. 'You mightn't be ready to hear it yet, but you will one day.'

'Go,' Freya said.

Charlotte wanted to wrap her arms around her daughter and hold her, tell her everything would be okay. But she'd never done that when Freya was a little girl; it was too late to do it now.

'I'm so sorry,' she whispered.

'I don't care,' Freya said. 'Oh Christ. If you won't leave, then I will.'

'Freya …'

But her daughter was walking away, out of the sitting room, out of the flat altogether. Charlotte heard the clump of footsteps on the stairs and the sound of the front door closing as Freya slammed it shut. Charlotte went across to the window and looked out. Just in time to see her daughter's back as she ran down Ennersdale Road and disappeared out of sight.

* * *

Ger organised a warrant to search the Gleesons' house.

'I don't fancy our chances of finding anything,' she said,

handing the warrant to Ellen. 'By the time Forensics got there on Saturday morning, the place had already been cleaned up.'

'So why bother?' Ellen asked.

'I want to scare them,' Ger said. 'I'm sick of being messed around by Nick Gleeson and his wife.'

'I've just spoken to Abby,' Ellen said. 'Charlotte left Freya's place an hour ago. Got a taxi home. I'll get over there before she has a chance to go out again.'

'Malcolm's getting the medical records for Charlotte's mother,' Ger said. 'We should have that information in the next hour. Do you think Nick was telling the truth?'

She's done this before.

'I think he's clever enough to know we'd find out if he was lying,' Ellen said. 'Even so, I'm not sure how it helps.'

'It means she's got history,' Ger said.

Ellen nodded. She wanted to get across to Blackheath. She wanted to ask Charlotte what had driven her, twenty-eight years earlier, to pick up a knife and use it to stab her own mother in the chest.

TEN

Charlotte's world was falling apart, leaving her exposed and vulnerable. She was in a maze made of fragile glass and all around her the glass was shattering. Outside the maze, there was nothing but danger. She'd made a mess of everything. Her marriage, her daughter, the only friendship she'd ever had. She'd lied to her best friend. And because of that, Ginny was dead.

There was no one she could turn to. Image after image tossed through her head, jumbled together in a giddy mess that made her ill. She closed her eyes, but that only made things worse. Kieran's face was there, up close the way she remembered it. His breath hot and heavy, hands pulling up her skirt, voice in her ear, whispering, telling her this was what she wanted.

In her head, Nick was there too. Standing in the doorway

watching them. Moving across the room, his eyes never leaving her face. Kieran grunting as he pushed himself inside her. Nick smiling.

No!

That's not how it happened. Nick didn't know. No one knew. Three months ago and not a single person had found out.

It's what you want.

And her voice, breathy and desperate. *Yes, oh God, yes.*

Afterwards, she hated him. Told herself he'd taken advantage. Should never have tried it on when she was that drunk. Hated herself more for letting it happen. For giving in to the desperation and loneliness.

She heard a car pull into the driveway. Through the window, she could see two identical navy-blue cars parking outside the front door. DI Ellen Kelly climbed out from the passenger seat of the first car. The other doors opened and three uniformed officers got out too.

When the doorbell rang, she went into the hall. She examined her face in the ornate gilt mirror she'd bought at an auction in Greenwich ten years earlier. She looked gaunt and old. Her skin was dry and wrinkled from too many hours on the sunbed. Her hair was like sheaves of straw sticking out of her head at odd angles. She turned from her reflection and trudged to the front door. Slowly, slowly, her hand moved up to the latch, unlocked it and pulled open the door.

The sudden flash of bright sunshine was like a fast-forward

button pressed down for too long. Noises and voices and Ellen Kelly shoving a piece of paper in her face. Police pushing past her into the house. The clump of footsteps on the parquet flooring. Her own voice, lost in the noise, asking what they were doing, even though she already knew. They thought she'd killed Kieran. Ginny too.

Ellen Kelly was beside her, hand on Charlotte's shoulder, guiding her into the sitting room. She didn't like it. Pushed the hand away and shouted that they'd got it all wrong.

'It was Nick, not me!'

Upstairs, something smashed as it hit the ground. She ran past the detective and up the stairs. A policeman was in her bedroom. Drawers hung open, her clothes were strewn about the place. And on the floor, a smashed photo frame. She knelt down and picked through the shattered pieces of glass, retrieving the photo underneath. The policeman shouted at her, told her not to touch anything, but she ignored him. Got the photo and smoothed it out. Her younger face looked up at her. Unlined and miserable. In her arms, a small child swaddled in a pale pink blanket. Her finger traced the baby's head. At the back of her mind, the flicker of a memory. A smell. The soft, powdery smell she got when she pressed her face against the child's head and breathed in.

A drop of water fell on the photo. And another. She brushed them away, lifted the photo and pressed it against her chest. So many useless tears. Crying over the memory of something that had never been real. She'd hated everything about those early years of motherhood. Hadn't realised until this week – when it was too late to change things – how much she loved her daughter. How could you go through life not knowing something as straightforward and obvious as that?

'Ma'am!'

The policeman was shouting.

'I think you need to see this.'

Charlotte looked up. He was holding something. She must have moved or spoken because he shouted at her to stay where she was. When she realised what he was holding, she thought he was threatening her. A scream caught in her throat and she scrabbled backwards across the carpet, even though he was screaming at her not to move.

Ellen Kelly was in the room now, moving towards the policeman.

'Bag it,' Ellen said.

She turned to Charlotte. 'I need you to come with me.'

Charlotte shook her head. The policeman was still holding the knife. A wide-blade chef's knife with a thick handle. Like the ones Nick used. In the kitchen downstairs he had a full set. Kept them on a display unit along the wall. In the mornings, when the sun rose behind the house and flooded the kitchen, the knives gleamed like bright shining teeth.

Not like this knife, which was dirty with dark stains along the blade and the handle. Nick would never leave a knife like that. She wanted to tell them this. It seemed important, somehow. But when she tried to speak, the words that came out didn't make any sense. She saw Ellen Kelly frowning as she tried to understand.

Charlotte shook her head, giving up. There was no point. This time, when Ellen put her hand on Charlotte's shoulder, she didn't bother to push it away. Like a child, she let herself be led down the stairs, along the hallway and into the bright sunshine. Out of habit, she tilted her head as she passed the huge mirror. An old woman with dry blonde hair and empty eyes stared at her. Charlotte searched the face, looking for anything familiar. She couldn't find a single thing she recognised. The woman in the mirror was a stranger.

ELEVEN

Loretta was waiting for Nick when he got back to the restaurant. She practically ran at him as he came in the door, pushing past Javier who also looked like he was about to approach. Nick shook his head at both of them, indicating this wasn't a good time.

His head was all over the place. Twice on the way over here he'd picked up his phone to call Pete. Both times, he'd stopped himself just in time. Better to say nothing for now. Until he worked out what he was going to do.

Javier got the hint and withdrew into the kitchen. Not Loretta, though. She could be a tenacious bitch when she wanted.

'We need to speak,' she said.

'It'll have to wait till later,' Nick said. 'Spent another bloody morning being questioned by the police. Harassment, if you ask me.'

'Did they ask about Kieran?' Loretta asked. Her voice sounded innocent but he knew by the sly expression on her face exactly what she was getting at.

'It wasn't Kieran they were interested in,' he muttered. 'Not this time.'

She smiled and he wanted to slap her. Couldn't believe there was a time he'd found that smile attractive. She was no better than Kieran, worse maybe – a conniving, money-grabbing bitch, out to get everything she could.

'We can talk about it out here,' Loretta raised her voice and looked around the restaurant. Several customers and all of the staff were looking on, curious and probably relishing the prospect of a row.

'My office,' Nick said. 'Now.'

Inside the office, she sat down and crossed her legs demurely. He remembered a night about two years ago. The two of them more than a bit tipsy at the end of a long day. Loretta sitting where she was now, holding a glass of champagne and smiling at him as she uncrossed her legs and slowly pulled her skirt up over her creamy thighs.

'You owe me,' she said.

The image disappeared, replaced by another memory. Kieran in the very same chair, making similar demands. Nick was tired, exhausted with the effort of trying to keep control over all of it. With Kieran out of the way, he'd thought the problem was sorted. How wrong he'd been. Looking at Loretta's face – full of greedy knowledge that he knew she was going to use to hurt him – he felt like it might never end.

'I don't think so,' he said. 'We made an agreement and you got what you wanted. I'm not made of money, Loretta.'

'I think you could spare me a little more,' she said. 'My friend's getting tired of having me under her feet, Nick. And I really don't want to go back to renting. I need my own place. In Greenwich, naturally. If you could see your way to helping me out, well, I'd really be ever so grateful.'

What was it with people? Every way he turned someone wanted a piece of him. Charlotte – desperate to suck him back into their sham of a life, playing the happy couple in their lonely, over-priced, overlarge house; Kieran – with his increasing demands and hints at what he'd do if Nick didn't comply; Cooper – and his pain-in-the-arse obsessiveness, demanding to know every last detail of how the restaurants were run and how he managed the finances; and now this.

'A house?' His hands clenched into tight fists. Before he could stop himself he was across the room and grabbing the collar of her pale pink blouse and shaking her. 'You want me to buy you a fucking house? You must be out of your mind. I've already paid you to keep quiet and that's what you're going to do. If you open your mouth to the police or anyone else, you'll be sorry.'

He dragged her up, lifted his fist to her face, pressed it against the soft skin, pushed until she yelped. All the smugness was gone from her face now, only fear left. His father's face flashed in front of him, could almost hear the old man's voice, asking what he thought he was doing.

His hands dropped off her and he turned away, disgusted.

'You'll pay for that,' she said. Her voice was shaky and there was no real conviction there.

'Get out.'

He heard her unsteady footsteps move away and the sound of the office door opening and closing. He stayed where he was, body shaking so bad he didn't trust it to stay upright without the support of the table he was leaning against.

When he eventually left the office and went outside, there was no sign of her. Javier said she'd told everyone she wasn't feeling well and had gone home for the rest of the day. Nick knew he should have been pleased she was gone. Instead, he was unable to shake off the terrible sadness that sat on his shoulders like a weight, wrapped itself around his body and pressed so hard on his chest he found it difficult to breathe.

TWELVE

'I haven't done anything wrong. It was Nick, not me.'

Charlotte's voice was high-pitched and hysterical; she looked a mess. Her lawyer had insisted they interview her tonight. Which was why Abby was sitting here at nearly ten pm. Instead of being with Sam, as she'd planned.

At seven, Ger had told Ellen to go home. Ellen wasn't too happy about it and, truth be told, neither was Abby. Under normal circumstances she'd have jumped at the chance to show Ger what she was capable of. Since Sam, nothing was normal. The determined focus she'd always directed at her career had deserted her. Instead, when she should be one hundred percent focussing on the case and nothing else, she found her mind drifting. She tried to drag it back, but a moment later she was off again. Thinking about Sam and the time they'd spent together so far and the sheer, bizarre madness of never having realised it was possible to feel this way about another person.

All her adult life, she'd been so certain – so one hundred per-cent convinced – that romance and love and all that nonsense was something for others to worry about. And then this. Just when everything she'd worked so hard for was starting to fall into place. Turned out she was just another stupid woman in a line of stupid women since time began, ready to drop everything when the right man came along.

Panic gripped her. Sharp and sudden, leaving her breathless. What was she thinking? That she could give all this up? For what? To be stuck at home with a gaggle of children while Sam pursued a glittering career in the City? No way. They hadn't discussed it yet but she had to make it crystal clear to him that there was no chance in hell she would give up her job. Not for any man. Not even one as funny and clever and downright bloody gorgeous as he was. The job was all that mattered. She needed to show DSI Ger Cox that she was the best detective on the team. And if that meant nipping things in the bud with Sam before she went too far and lost herself to him, then so be it.

'You're saying your husband killed Kieran Burton?'

Ger's voiced dragged Abby back to the interview room. Ger beside her, Charlotte and her solicitor sitting opposite, on the other side of the table. A new-style CD-recorder screwed onto the table's surface, recording every word.

'Yes,' Charlotte said. 'No. I don't know. He's ... I mean, why would he? That's what I didn't understand. He didn't like Kieran but neither did anyone else. He bloody hated Ginny and that was mutual, let me tell you. But why kill Kieran? It's not as if he's the sort of overprotective father who would care one way or the other who Freya was seeing. And that was the only reason I could think of. That he did it to protect her. But she doesn't need protecting. Didn't need protecting. She loved Kieran and Nick always said it was her choice, not ours.

'I hated it, you know. The way he didn't seem to care. All that education, all the time and money and *effort* we'd put into giving her the best of everything and she threw it back in our faces by turning up one day with that horrible, horrible man.'

Charlotte stuttered to a halt, eyes darting between Ger and Abby. Like she'd suddenly realised she'd said too much.

'Is that what happened?' Ger asked. 'Your husband refused to act so you decided to take matters into your own hands?'

'That's ridiculous,' Charlotte said. 'It was Nick.'

Abby remembered the last time she'd seen Charlotte. Earlier in the day, when Charlotte had turned up at Freya's house. By the time Abby came back from the shops, Freya was gone and Charlotte was getting a taxi to take her home. Abby found Freya sitting at the bar in The Meridian, drinking coffee. She was in a foul mood but refused to tell Abby what her mother had done to upset her so.

'You told Freya this?' she asked.

'She didn't believe me.' The hysteria was gone and Charlotte was whispering now. Abby had to strain her ears to catch the words. 'She never believes me. In Freya's eyes, Nick can do no wrong. No matter what I tell her, it won't change that.'

'We need to speak about the knife we found in your room,' Ger said. 'Can you tell us how it got there?'

Charlotte looked at her solicitor, as if asking whether or not it was okay to answer the question. He nodded. His name was Jeremy Lawlor, one of the regular duty solicitors working out of Lewisham station. Abby had worked with him several times before and she liked him. He was a competent solicitor and Charlotte could do a lot worse.

'Nick put it there,' Charlotte said. 'He's trying to make it look like I killed Kieran.'

Ger pretended to refer to the notes on the table in front of her. Abby knew she was pretending because she knew Ger was more than familiar with what was written there.

'Would you like to tell us what happened the night you stabbed your mother?' Ger asked.

According to Nick Gleeson, Charlotte had tried to kill her mother with a knife. It happened a few weeks before Nick and Charlotte were due to marry. Abby wondered if she'd want to marry Sam if she found out he'd done something like that. She certainly hoped not.

'That was an accident,' Charlotte said.

'According to the police records,' Ger said. 'your mother

claimed she'd stabbed herself. Although how anyone would stab themselves in the chest *by accident* is beyond me, quite frankly.'

Charlotte shook her head. She looked exhausted. Abby wondered how much longer before she cracked.

'She was drunk,' Charlotte said. 'She was trying to open some letters and the knife slipped. If you know about it, then you'll know that I wasn't even there when it happened. I was at Ginny's. The first I knew about it was when my mother called, asking me to come home. Check your records if you don't believe me.'

'Your husband says that's not what really happened,' Ger said.

Charlotte raked her hands through her hair and groaned dramatically.

'He's a liar. He killed Kieran and now he's trying to get you to think it was me. I found his secret phone and he's scared. He should have password-protected it. I don't know why he didn't. His iPhone has a password. The only reason this one doesn't, of course, is because he keeps it hidden. I read the text. Maybe you think I shouldn't have, but what would you have done? He's my husband and he's got this phone I didn't even know about. And someone has just killed Kieran and Ginny and …'

'Charlotte.' Ger's voice was sharp and Charlotte's words skidded to a halt as her mouth dropped open. 'Start from the beginning. What are you talking about?'

'He has another phone,' Charlotte said. 'A secret one. I found it in the kitchen. I didn't even know it was his at first.'

'When was this?' Ger said.

Charlotte frowned. 'Yesterday? No, not yesterday. This morning. Sorry, it seems much longer than that but I'm sure it was just this morning. I looked at the call log and the messages. He's only ever used it to call one number.'

'Who?' Abby said.

'I don't know. There was no name beside it, just the number. The call log showed twenty or thirty calls between Nick's phone and that number. No one else. Just that one number.'

'You mentioned a text,' Ger said.

'Just one,' Charlotte said. 'I don't know if he'd deleted the rest or what. It was sent on Tuesday. The same day Ginny was killed. It said *I'm scared.* That's all.'

'And you've no idea who sent it or what it means?' Ger asked.

'None,' Charlotte said. 'But Nick sent a reply. *Don't worry,* his text said. *I'll sort it. I promise.*'

Abby released the breath she'd been holding. Charlotte's words hovered in the air between them, dissolving slowly until the only sound in the room was the in-out, in-out of four people breathing and the gentle hum of the CD-recorder storing it all.

'What was she so scared of?' Charlotte asked. 'And what was Nick promising to sort?'

'How do you know it's a she?' Abby said.

'Why else would he have a separate phone?' Charlotte asked.

'Do you still have it?' Ger asked.

Charlotte shook her head and Abby's spirits deflated. They'd been so close and now it looked as if Charlotte was making the whole thing up.

'I don't have it,' Charlotte said. 'You do. You lot made me empty my bag when I came in here. The phone was in there.'

A knock on the door and Alastair came in, whispered something in Ger's ear and left again. Ger paused the CD-recorder, told Charlotte and her solicitor they'd be back in a bit and stood up, motioning for Abby to follow.

'It's Nick Gleeson,' Alastair said when they were outside. 'We still haven't tracked him down but I've checked with the BMW garage. His story checks out. He didn't leave the car in for a service until Wednesday morning, which means he wasn't driving his wife's car on Tuesday night. Or not as far as we know.'

'Good work,' Ger said. 'Thanks. I need you to do something else for me too. Charlotte Gleeson's belongings have been bagged up. Can you go through them and look for a mobile phone? When you find it, bring it to me. Abby, see if Charlotte and her brief want a drink. We'll break until we've taken a look at the phone. Then we'll decide what to do next.'

* * *

Mother refilled her wine glass and stared at Charlotte over the rim of her half-moon glasses. The glasses were a recent addition. Mother had fought it for years. Denied there was anything wrong with her eyesight, even when it was obvious to everyone else she was blind as a bat. Somehow, she'd managed to make the glasses Charlotte's fault as well. The stress of motherhood had aged her prematurely.

'I should have expected it.'

Her voice was hard. One bottle down and her mood had gone from hating herself to hating her daughter. So predictable.

'I should have expected it.'

Charlotte knew she should go. She didn't have to listen to this. Nick hated the way she let her mother talk to her. She wasn't ever able to explain why she put up with it. Except to say she'd never known anything else. She was sitting on the chair opposite Mother, who lay splayed on a matching day-bed. Beside her, on a small round walnut table, was today's post, unopened. The silver paper knife on top of the envelopes, waiting to be used.

Mother was smoking a cigarette lodged into a long, thin cigarette-holder. She sucked on the cigarette and blew a cloud of smoke in Charlotte's direction. The tip of the cigarette-holder was stained red from her mother's smudged lipstick. It reminded Charlotte of blood.

'I mean, what do you even know about him, Charlotte? Who are his people? Have you met them?'

'His parents are dead,' Charlotte said. 'I've told you already, Mother.'

Her mother laughed.

'An orphan. My daughter's marrying a poor little orphan boy. Of course, I should have known you'd open your legs to the first man to look twice at you. Oh Lord, don't tell me. That's why it's happening so quickly, isn't it? You're pregnant. I might have guessed. Stupid little slut. That's what happens when you let men fuck you, darling. You end up with a bloody brat you never wanted in the first place.'

Charlotte wanted to say it wasn't true. But she knew if she tried to speak, she'd cry instead. She'd been so excited coming here to tell Mother the news. Wasn't it what they'd both wanted? Nick was more than she could ever have wished for. Mother was so wrong about him. He already had his own restaurant and that was just the beginning. Nick was going places and taking Charlotte with him.

Mother was screaming, face flushed red from anger and alcohol, leaning forward on the day-bed, shoving her face close to Charlotte's, screaming at her for being so fucking stupid and letting a man have his way with her before he'd even walked her down the aisle. Calling her a slut and a whore and a stupid bitch and …

Later, upstairs in her room, Charlotte picked up the telephone. Her hand was shaking and the phone kept slipping from her blood-stained fingers. It took several tries before she was able to dial the correct number. Eventually, she got it right and the phone at the other end started to ring. It rang and rang and she was about to hang up when it was answered. A sweet, familiar voice asked who was calling.

Charlotte started to speak, found she was crying instead. Big, shaking sobs coursing through her body.

'Lottie? Is that you, honey?'

'Oh Ginny.'

'What is it?' Ginny asked. 'What's happened?'

'Can you come over?' she whispered. 'Something's happened. I really need to see you.'

'Is it your mother?' Ginny asked.

When Charlotte didn't answer, Ginny said it didn't matter.

Whatever it was, she'd be right over.

'Come quickly,' Charlotte begged. 'I can't bear it a moment longer.'

She put the phone down, lay on her bed, closed her eyes and waited. Everything was going to be okay. Ginny was on her way. She would know what to do. She always did.

* * *

Cold ate its way into her bones. So cold she couldn't feel the tips of her fingers. So cold her teeth chattered uncontrollably, a tip-tapping sound that echoed through her head and out again, banging off the walls of the cell and ricocheting around her. Spinning around and around like the images eating away inside her head. She couldn't shut her mind down. Couldn't stop it going into overdrive. Her head hurt, throbbed from a combination of hangover, lack of sleep and pure, unadulterated fear.

Her mother's face, shock and pain as she reeled away from her. The dark stain spreading across the front of her pale blue silk blouse. Ginny's car. Blood on the leather seats. Mother's eyes rolling back, eyelids fluttering.

Say it was me.

Ginny nodding, agreeing with Mother. Telling Charlotte it was for the best. Mother's hand on Charlotte's arm. Fingers gripping tight.

They can never know.

Because Mother couldn't bear the shame of it. Would rather everyone thought she'd done it herself. Less questions, that way.

Less chance of anyone prying underneath the veneer and revealing the truth of what she was really like.

A spasm shot through her, pain that obliterated everything else. She cried out, clasped her arms around her body in a pathetic, futile attempt to stop it happening again. She lay down on the lumpy bed, curled into a ball and waited for the worst of it to pass.

Later – seconds, minutes, hours? – she opened her eyes. The cold was still with her. And the images. But the pain had passed. In its absence, the fear was stronger. The growing realisation that this was real. Not some crazy nightmare. She was lying on her side, facing the wall, her body curled up so tight the muscles in her neck, arms and legs ached. She rolled onto her back, stared up at the grey-white ceiling and unfolded her limbs. Pin-pricks of needles stabbed into toes and fingers as the circulation returned.

She sat up.

She was locked inside a cell inside the police station. Keeping her in overnight, they'd told her. She'd panicked then, really lost it. Screaming and lashing out at that useless solicitor. None of it made any difference. It had taken two men to drag her in here and hold her down while the nurse injected her with something that was meant to make her feel better.

She'd slept for a while after that. When she'd woken again, the last traces of the sanity-sustaining wine had left her system and she found herself alone with the early stages of DTs kicking in.

Fear crawled across her stomach, crept up her throat, erupted from her in one great scream. She threw herself from the bed and flung herself against the door, fists banging on the unyielding metal. Screaming and banging until she had nothing left. Exhausted, she slumped to the ground, tears of rage and grief and fear rolling down her cheeks, pooling in the deep hollows behind her collarbone.

They thought she'd killed Kieran.

She shut her eyes, tried to concentrate on the butterfly-fragile memories of that night. Cocktails, sushi, more cocktails. The compulsion to tell Ginny what had happened. Something else as well. The sudden, drunken urge to fuck him.

She'd hated him.

So why, the night of her party, had she wanted him so badly? What was wrong with her?

Maybe she should have told the truth. She tried to picture how that would play out. The look of shock, followed by sympathy on the two detectives' faces. She imagined them later, in their team briefing or whatever they called it, telling the rest of the detectives what she'd done. Laughing when they heard about it. Worse than the laughter, she imagined what they'd say.

Sad old slut.

Randy lush.

Pathetic, middle-aged bitch.

She could never tell them.

She should tell them.

Maybe she could make them promise not to tell Freya or Nick.

Her stomach twisted and spasmed. Thin trickles of bitter vomit burned the back of her throat. She spat it out onto the floor, too tired and sick to make it as far as the toilet in the corner.

Kieran had done it on purpose. He'd deliberately got her drunk and then, when she was too twisted to know what she was doing, he'd … what?

Her mind skittered back again to that afternoon. Kieran calling over on the pretence that he was looking for Freya. A combination of loneliness and good manners made her invite him in. They'd sat in the kitchen drinking wine and making small-talk. He'd been solicitous and interested, asking about her, pretending he was interested when all the time … She remembered thinking maybe she'd got him wrong. Maybe he wasn't half as bad as she'd made him out to be.

And midway through the third bottle of wine, he'd made his move and she did nothing to stop him. Worse, she'd wanted it. She remembered lying on the white-and-black tiled floor, groaning when he touched her somewhere she hadn't been touched for so long, wrapping her legs around him and begging him not to stop.

She'd thought he was interested. Thought maybe he had some kinky thing about older women.

Stupid, stupid, stupid.

He hadn't called around looking for Freya. Let's face it, Charlotte's house was the last place in the world Kieran was likely to find his girlfriend hanging out.

No.

He knew she would be home alone. Knew how lonely she was. Knew she'd be happy – sad, pathetic creature – for an excuse to have a drink with someone. He'd orchestrated the whole thing. Flattered her, got her drunk and seduced her. All so he could use it whenever he needed to.

Stupid, stupid, stupid.

He told Nick. She was certain of it. Because of that, Nick killed him. And now he was trying to make it look as if Charlotte had done it. Getting his revenge on both of them for what they'd done. Kieran and Nick, both using her to get what they wanted. She'd had enough. Now it was her turn to use them.

FRIDAY

ONE

Ellen got into work early and made a start on the extensive store of photos from Kieran's phone. WPC McKeown had already gone through them once and hadn't found anything. Ellen wanted to check herself, afraid McKeown might have missed something important.

Image after moody image, mainly black-and-white and almost all different scenes of the city. Not one of Freya and not one that gave Ellen any clue as to who might have killed him. The most recent batch were taken along the river, mostly down on the Peninsula. In some of these, Kieran had captured people as well as inanimate objects. The camera used to take the photos was obviously good quality but the photos themselves lacked anything special.

'Found anything?'

Abby came and stood behind her, looking at Ellen's computer screen.

'Nothing interesting so far.' Ellen stood up and stretched. 'Certainly no pictures of the ring he was supposedly buying.'

'Briefing's about to start,' Abby said. 'You coming?'

Ellen checked the time. She'd been trawling through the images for an hour already. No wonder her neck and shoulders hurt so much.

'Okay,' she said. 'Let's go.'

In the incident room, Ellen sat at the back, listening as Ger summarised the developments in the case so far.

'We won't have any results back from Forensics until after the weekend,' Ger said. 'But I'm hopeful the blood found on the knife will be a match. We already know the blade matches the type Pritchard believes caused the wounds. Malcolm, anything else?'

'The knife was wrapped in a lady's blouse,' Malcolm said. 'No traces of blood on it. Which means it was wrapped around the knife some time after the attack.'

'It doesn't make sense,' Ellen said. 'Why would Charlotte kill Kieran then hide the knife in her own bedroom?'

'Maybe she was planning to get rid of it,' Abby said. 'Only she never got around to it.'

'Kieran was killed outside,' Ellen said. 'It would have been easier to dump the knife before coming back to the house. And what about the jacket? The one with the orange logo. Why didn't we find that at the house?'

'We don't know the jacket belonged to the killer,' Alastair said. 'Could have been someone else walking down there. Someone with no connection to the killer or the victim.'

Ellen didn't buy that. She knew St Joseph's Vale. Knew how dark and unappealing it would have been at that time of night. Knew too how improbable it was that someone could have been passing the lane around the same time a person was being stabbed to death and not noticed a thing out of place.

'She swears she doesn't know how the knife got there,' Abby said.

Ellen sensed Abby's pride at being able to give a first-hand account of last night's interview. Strangely, she didn't resent Abby for it. Maybe she was finally discovering some balance in her life.

'So how does she explain it?' Ellen asked.

'She blames her husband,' Abby said. 'But so far she hasn't given us a decent reason why her husband would want to kill Burton.'

Several ideas were jostling for attention in Ellen's head. She tried to sort her way through them, work out which was most important and which she could put aside until later.

'Maybe Charlotte was telling the truth,' Alastair said. 'About someone being in the house. What if the killer sneaked in to plant the knife and Charlotte startled them by coming home earlier than expected?'

'Someone who knew Charlotte had a motive of her own for wanting Burton dead,' Ellen said, the chaos in her head clearing as she got her thoughts in order.

'We need to speak to Charlotte again,' Ger said. 'Ellen and Abby, can you lead on that? Maybe a night in the cells will have made her more co-operative.'

Ellen stood up. 'We'll go now.'

She waited for Abby and the two women left the room.

* * *

It was the same lawyer who'd been with her yesterday. Charlotte wanted to protest, ask for someone else, but she didn't know if she was allowed to do that. Besides, she didn't have the energy to make a fuss. She asked timidly if Jeremy Lawlor had been able to track down Nick. The last, lingering flicker of hope died inside her as the lawyer shook his head and gave her a smile so thick with sympathy she had to clench her hands tight behind her back to stop her hitting him.

'The police want to interview you again this morning,' Jeremy said. 'They'll be ready for us in a few minutes. Before that, are you sure there's nothing else you'd like to tell me, Charlotte?'

He had a kind voice and a kind face but it wasn't kindness she needed right now. It was one of Nick's ruthless associates, the sort of high-paid legal sleaze he schmoozed on the golf course and drank expensive wines with late at night. Not this tuppeny-ha'penny Legal Aid do-gooder.

'I've already told you,' she said. 'I didn't kill Kieran and I have no idea how that knife ended up in my bedroom or why there was blood on my trainers. Okay?'

'You're sure about that?' Jeremy said. 'This is your last chance to let me help you.'

He meant well, she could see that. And maybe he was right. This *was* her chance.

'This is all Nick's doing,' she whispered.

'You really believe that?'

She heard the weary resignation in his voice and felt a brief, triumphant thrill, knowing she was about to knock that right out of him.

'Oh yes,' she said, voice strong now she'd made the decision. 'He's doing it to get back at me.'

'And why would he want to do that?' Jeremy asked.

She waited until he was looking right at her before she replied.

'Something terrible happened,' she began.

TWO

The atmosphere in the small interview room was different this morning. Abby felt it the moment she stepped inside. There was an energy, a sense of anticipation that things were moving forward. A sense that, finally, Charlotte was ready to talk.

Abby and Ellen sat on one side of the table, opposite Charlotte and her lawyer. Ellen set up the CD-recorder, gave the necessary information – time, date, the names of those present in the room – and began the interview.

'My client has some information she'd like to share with you,' Jeremy said.

'First, a question,' Ellen said. 'Mrs Gleeson, did you kill Kieran Burton?'

'No,' Charlotte said. Her voice was clear and calm, no trace of last night's nerves and uncertainty. 'I didn't kill him. On my daughter's life. But I know who did.'

Abby leaned towards Charlotte, sensing they were getting closer to the truth.

'It was Nick,' Charlotte said. 'You see, he … this is difficult, I'm sorry. Something happened and Nick found out about it. I think. Well, I'm certain actually. He killed Kieran and made it look as if I'd done it. That way he was getting his revenge on both of us.'

'Why would he do that?' Ellen asked.

'Kieran raped me,' Charlotte said. 'In my kitchen, if you must know. He called over one afternoon, said he was looking for Freya. Naturally, she wasn't with me but I invited him in. I offered him a glass of wine, we got chatting … I'm sorry. This isn't easy.'

'It's okay,' Ellen said. 'Take your time.'

She's lying. The certainty lodged its way into Abby's head and stayed there, even though she hated herself for thinking it.

'I was drunk,' Charlotte said. 'No excuse, I know. And I'm not using it as an excuse, just telling you how it was. I didn't like Kieran. Hated him, in fact.'

'Why did you invite him in?' Abby asked.

Charlotte shrugged. 'Loneliness? Good manners? I don't know. Some combination of both, maybe. He was so different at first. Up until then, he'd always seemed so … combative, I guess. We didn't approve, of course, and he knew that. Truth be told, I think he quite liked the fact we disapproved. I sometimes suspected he acted in a particular way just to get at us. To make us like him even less, if you know what I mean?'

'But not that afternoon,' Ellen said.

'No.' She said it like a sigh. The sigh of a woman so disappointed by life she had nothing left to lose. Charlotte Gleeson was a lesson in how not to waste a life, Abby thought.

'He was charming,' Charlotte said. 'I remember thinking I'd misjudged him terribly. I actually felt bad about it. I may have even told him something to that effect. It was only later, we'd had quite a bit to drink by then, that I realised he was flirting with me. I thought it was the drink, at first. I didn't take it seriously. But then he … well, maybe I should have tried harder not to let him.'

She paused, as if she wanted Ellen or Abby to reassure her. When they said nothing, she continued speaking.

'I barely knew what was happening,' she said. 'Before I could stop it, he was on top of me, pawing me like an animal. I was begging him to stop but he wouldn't. And I tried, I mean I really did try to fight him off but he was so strong. And afterwards, when he'd finished, he acted like it was what we'd both wanted. I was crying and telling him to go but he wouldn't. Kept telling me how much I'd enjoyed it.'

Abby felt sick. The sordid picture of Kieran Burton forcing himself on his girlfriend's mother repulsed her. The fact she couldn't find it in herself to feel any sympathy for Charlotte only made it worse.

A single tear rolled down Charlotte's orange cheek, reminding Abby of the last trace of water in a dried-out riverbed. Charlotte caught Abby looking at her and stared back, her face twisted into an expression of pained self-pity. Mixed with something else, less obvious at first but the longer Abby looked, the more certain she became. The other emotion she saw behind Charlotte Gleeson's dark blue eyes was cunning.

* * *

'Do you believe her, Abby?' Ger asked.

'I don't know,' Abby said. 'I mean, it's a serious allegation. I think maybe they slept together but it was consensual. But why would he sleep with his girlfriend's mother? That's sick.'

The two women were in Ger's office, discussing Charlotte's statement.

'People do all sorts of sick and strange things,' Ger said. 'And for all we know she's telling the truth. Either way, with Kieran not here to give his side of the story, Charlotte's version is the only one we have and now she's said it, I doubt she'll retract it.'

'Isn't it wrong to assume that she's making it up?' Abby said. 'I mean, if it's true and we don't believe her, what does that say about us?'

Ger smiled. 'A good question. The way I see it is this. If something did happen, even if it was consensual, she was probably drunk. So you've got to ask yourself: if she did agree to have sex with him, would she have done so if she was sober? If you think the answer to that question is no, then I guess you might want to wonder what sort of man would take advantage of a woman that drunk?'

'Unless she's making the whole thing up and nothing happened at all,' Abby said.

'There is that, of course,' Ger said.

'Okay. I need you to talk to Freya. Find out what she knew about her mother and Kieran. She's already told us Charlotte flirted with him. Maybe she knows more than she's letting on. If she thinks something happened between them, there's our motive.'

On the way down to the car park, Abby's mind kept returning to the image of Kieran Burton forcing himself on Charlotte. By the time she got into the pool car and was driving across to Greenwich, she felt as if a dark cloud had settled over her, turning everything grey and draining her world of colour and light.

THREE

Ellen drove to Greenwich. A wasted journey. Nick wasn't at work and none of his staff seemed to know where he was. There was no sign of Loretta, either. She called both of them but her calls were diverted to voicemail. She left short messages on each phone. Frustrated, she decided to go and see Mark. The PM report on Virginia Rau wasn't back yet and she hoped he might have an update for her.

At the morgue, the door to Mark's office was closed. Ellen knocked and went straight in. He was sitting at his desk, tapping something on his computer keyboard. When he saw Ellen, a smile lit up his face. He was wearing glasses and they suited him. Sometimes, he looked too boyish, like someone had plastered a child's face onto an adult head. The glasses sorted that out.

'Ellen!' He stood and embraced her in a warm hug. 'What a lovely surprise. How are you? And don't give me the usual pat answer. I mean how are you really?'

'I'm good,' Ellen said. '*Really.*'

'How's Pat?'

'He's okay,' Ellen said. She thought about this for a moment, then nodded. 'Yes. He is.'

And then, maybe because she hadn't told anyone else, maybe because she felt more comfortable with Mark than most people she knew, she told him more. She spoke about the therapy sessions and how they really seemed to be working. How he was doing well at school. Best of all, she said, he'd recently started sleeping in his own bed again.

'I think he's going to be fine,' she said.

She was smiling. So was Mark. He reached out and squeezed her hand. 'Of course he'll be okay, Ellen. He's got you, hasn't he?'

'Poor boy,' she said, withdrawing her hand. 'Sorry, Mark. I didn't mean to go on for so long. I know you're busy. We both are. I dropped by on the off-chance you might have finished the PM on Virginia Rau?'

Before Mark could answer, Ellen's phone started ringing. Apologising, she answered it.

'It's Loretta,' the caller said. 'Nick's assistant. I got your message and I'm wondering if you're free to meet? There's something I need to tell you.'

'Of course,' Ellen said. 'I'm in Lewisham right now. I can drive straight over to Greenwich if you'd like?'

'No,' Loretta said quickly. 'Not the restaurant. Could we meet in Starbucks? In an hour?'

They agreed a time and a place and Ellen hung up. 'Sorry Mark. I'm going to have to leave. Something's come up.'

He smiled but it seemed forced, or perhaps that was her imagination.

'We should do a drink sometime,' he said. 'Maybe when this case is over and you have a bit more time. What do you say?'

'That sounds great,' Ellen said.

'I have done the PM on the Rau woman,' Mark said. 'Was just about to call you, actually. She died from injuries sustained when the car hit her. No doubt about that. I've sent off for a tox test but we won't have the results of that for at least a week. Judging by the stomach contents, she'd had a decent dinner about an hour before she died. I did find one thing unusual. It might not mean anything but I thought you should know. She had a hyster-ectomy. Which is strange for a woman her age, wouldn't you say?

'The operation was carried out a long time ago. Twenty-three years, in fact. I checked her medical records. It's quite tragic really. Her partner beat her up, left her in a bad way.'

Ellen thought of the pretty, bubbly woman she'd bumped into on Ennersdale Road. Thought of her own children and what her life would be like if she'd never had them. She shivered.

'There's something else too,' Mark said. 'The poor woman was pregnant at the time. Seven months. So she didn't just lose her womb. She lost her unborn child as well.'

As he spoke, Ellen saw Virginia Rau's face, not as she'd been that day outside Freya's house, but the way she looked in the photos on the whiteboard in the incident room. Photos taken from the crime scene. A woman's broken, battered body lying on the side of a road in Blackheath, dark eyes wide open and staring, mouth open in a silent scream.

* * *

'Cup of tea?' Freya asked.

'No thanks.' Abby shook her head. 'Too warm for tea today.'

Freya peered at the sun streaming through the window, looking at it as if she'd just noticed it for the first time.

'It's a bit of a change, all right,' she said. 'Might try and get out for a walk later. It's getting to me, you know? Sitting here all day, waiting for you lot to tell me you've found who killed him.'

'We're doing the best we can,' Abby said. She gestured at one of the armchairs. 'Do you mind if I sit down?'

'Yeah, sure.' Freya plonked herself in the other chair and waited.

'Well?' she said once Abby was sitting as well. 'Why are you here?'

She looked pale and tired and her hair hung in greasy strings around her face. The smell of BO lingered around the flat and Abby wondered if she should suggest running a bath. Maybe she would in a little bit. She had to get this out of the way first.

'Well,' she said, 'I wanted to see how you were doing. And I had a question for you too.'

'Yeah?'

Abby nodded. 'Something's been bugging me. A while ago, you told me that your mum made a pass at Kieran when she was drunk one time. Do you remember that?'

'Of course.' Freya frowned. 'I was mortified. So was Kieran. Why do you want to know about that now?'

'When did it happen?' Abby asked.

Freya's jaw tensed.

'Why do you want to know?' she asked. 'Please, Abby. Tell me what's made you suddenly interested in that.'

'It's probably nothing,' Abby said. 'I'm just doing my job, that's all. You mentioned it and I never followed it up at the time so that's what I'm doing now.'

Freya shook her head. 'What has she told you?'

'Why do you think she's told us anything?' Abby said.

'Of course she has,' Freya said. 'I know you've been questioning her. Who do you think she called when she couldn't get through to my father last night? So what has she said? Whatever she's told you, it's a lie. She's a drunk who cannot be trusted. Do you understand that?'

'Yes,' Abby said. 'I do understand that, I promise you.'

'You think something happened between them,' Freya said. 'Don't you? That's why you're here. She's told you some lie and you believe it because you look at her and then you look at me and you're just like everyone else. You think, well, why wouldn't he?'

'What do you mean, just like everyone else?' Abby asked.

Freya shook her head. 'It doesn't matter.'

'Freya?'

'One of the guys who works at the bar,' Freya said. 'Tom. I thought he was a mate. Turns out he's another lying piece of shit. He tried to convince me that Kieran and my mother … he said Kieran told him something had happened between them. But it was a lie, right? I asked Kieran about it and he got so upset. I mean, he can't stand my mother. Couldn't. Couldn't stand her. They hated each other.'

Her voice wobbled and she started to cry. Abby, hating herself for being the cause of the tears, went over and tried to comfort her but Freya pushed her away. Abby thought she'd probably do the same in Freya's position.

She waited, standing awkwardly beside Freya, waiting for the worst of the crying to pass.

'Can I get you anything?' she asked.

'You can go,' Freya said. 'Please. I want to be on my own.'

She buried her face in her hands and continued crying.

Abby touched the girl's shoulder, as gently as she possibly could, and stayed where she was. Freya might want to be alone but Abby wasn't leaving any time soon.

FOUR

Ellen was the first to arrive at Starbucks in Blackheath. She didn't have long to wait. She had just ordered a double espresso when Loretta burst through the coffee shop door.

'Get you a drink?' Ellen asked.

'Green tea,' Loretta said. 'Thanks.'

Once they both had their drinks, Ellen and Loretta found a seat at the back of the coffee shop and sat down.

'Thanks for seeing me at such short notice,' Loretta said.

'Not a problem,' Ellen said. 'Are you okay?'

Loretta nodded and attempted a smile. It didn't even reach the end of her lips, never mind any other part of her face. Her green eyes looked at Ellen then slid away, back to the cup she was twisting nervously between her hands.

'Maybe we should have done this someplace else,' she said. 'We used to come here, Nick and I, when we first started ... well, you know, seeing each other. God, that feels like another lifetime ago now.'

'He used to take you to Starbucks?' Ellen said. 'Classy.'

Loretta smiled again. More genuine this time.

'It was the one place we could be sure of not bumping into anyone who knew us. Charlotte would rather die than be seen inside a Starbucks.'

'How long were you together?' Ellen asked.

'A few years,' Loretta said. 'On and off. I really thought he'd leave her, you know. Sorry. I've already told you that, haven't I?'

'It's okay,' Ellen said. 'I understand. He treated you badly and you're still hurting.'

She wanted to shake the woman, tell her to stop feeling sorry for herself and get on with her life. What had she expected, having an affair with a married man? Didn't Loretta know they never, ever left their wives? But Ellen didn't say anything because she needed this foolish woman to believe she was on her side.

'The problem is,' Loretta said, 'I think I still believed we might get back together.'

'The last time we met.' Ellen forced her voice to sound soft and sympathetic. 'You didn't sound like someone who believed that.'

'I must have been having one of my better days,' Loretta said. 'I mean, there are days when I know that won't happen and I feel fine about it. But there are other days, like this one I guess, when

I still hold out hope. Even though I know it won't happen. Not now that little bitch has got her claws into him.'

'I thought you didn't know who she was,' Ellen said.

Loretta blinked. 'I don't. I just meant whoever she is.'

'Loretta,' Ellen said, 'if you know who she is, it's important that you tell me. It may be relevant to our case.'

'Sorry,' Loretta said. 'What am I thinking? You're so busy and here I am, waffling like some lovesick teenager. You must think I'm pathetic.'

'Not at all,' Ellen lied. 'But I do have a lot on right now. It would be helpful if you could tell me why you wanted to see me.'

'I wasn't straight with you the other day,' Loretta said. 'I didn't lie exactly, but I did leave something out.'

'What?'

'I didn't think it was important,' Loretta said. 'And I didn't want to get Nick into trouble. I still care for him, you see. But the more I thought about it, the more I realised I have to put aside my personal feelings and do the right thing.'

It was just as well Loretta was finally getting to the point. If Ellen had to listen to anymore self-pitying waffle, she wouldn't be accountable for her actions.

'Kieran came to see Nick,' Loretta said. 'He didn't have an appointment or anything. Just walked into the restaurant like he owned the place, demanding to speak to Nick. I asked him to take a seat while I went to tell Nick he had a visitor. Except when I told Nick he went ballistic.'

'Ballistic?' Ellen said. 'How do you mean?'

'He completely lost his rag,' Loretta said. 'Started shouting at me and saying didn't I realise what a busy time it was for him and there was no way he had time for visitors who didn't have appointments. The problem was, he was making such a racket I think the people in the restaurant must have overheard him because the next moment, while he was in the middle of all his shouting, the office door opened and Kieran was there.'

Ellen drank her espresso down in a single swallow, forcing herself to pause before she spoke in case her voice betrayed the excitement she felt.

'What happened then?' she asked.

'Nick went white,' Loretta said. 'You know they talk about people going pale? I swear to you that's exactly what happened. The colour literally drained from his face and he just stared at Kieran like, well, like he was frightened of him.'

'Why would he be frightened?' Ellen asked.

'I don't know,' Loretta said. 'All I know is Nick asked me to leave. I didn't want to but Nick insisted. Kieran was inside the office with Nick for about ten minutes. No more than that. Obviously, I couldn't hear what they were saying but I can tell you this. When the door opened, Kieran came out and his face was like thunder. He stormed through the restaurant and out the door without a word. And when I went to see if Nick was okay, he roared at me to shut the door and leave him in peace. I've never seen him so angry.'

The different pieces of the puzzle were starting to slot into place. Bits and pieces of truth hidden amongst the lies everyone was telling. Something had happened between Kieran and Charlotte. Kieran had used this to get at Nick. Blackmail, or something else?

'When was this?' she asked.

Loretta's eyes widened. 'Friday night. Why, the same night Kieran was killed. Oh my word, I hadn't thought of that.'

The pathetic attempt at amateur dramatics was too much for Ellen.

'I'm taking you to the station,' she said. 'Now. I need you to make a formal statement.'

Loretta started to protest but Ellen held a hand up, stopping her mid-sentence.

'If you don't,' Ellen said, 'I'll have you arrested for concealing important information and perverting the course of justice. And while we're there, you can tell me anything you know about the *little bitch* Nick is seeing. Now then.' She flashed a smile every bit as false as the ones Loretta had been giving her all morning. 'That's your choice. What's it to be?'

FIVE

Abby watched Nick Gleeson come out of the apartment build-ing and run to his car, his hand over his head, protecting him-self from the rain. When he switched on his engine, she did the same and followed him as he drove along the path that led away from the water. She passed several people jogging, oblivious to the weather, and remembered that Kieran Burton used to like running. She wondered if he'd ever run out this way and, if he had, whether that had any relevance to their case. Probably not.

She'd driven over here on a whim. After leaving Freya, she'd called the office and got Alastair, who told her Ellen had no luck finding Nick Gleeson at either of the restaurants. Abby asked Alastair to give her the address of the riverside apartment where Nick Gleeson went when he didn't go home. She'd experienced a sharp sense of satisfaction when she saw his blue BMW parked by the river.

At Surrey Quays, Nick continued on the A200, heading towards the river. For a moment, Abby wondered if he knew – somehow – that she was following him and was playing a trick by driving directly to her home in Canary Wharf. Her sense of unease increased as they approached the Rotherhithe Tunnel and she realised he was definitely heading north of the river.

Out of the tunnel, he swung right. Now, they were only a short walk from Abby's apartment. But instead of slowing down, Gleeson drove faster, following the north curve of the Docklands development, driving past New Billingsgate Market and further east.

Until now, the buildings around her had been the familiar mix of brash new glass-and-concrete modernism interspersed every now and then with tired-looking, post-war concrete high-rises. Another right turn and everything changed. They were on a street lined with Victorian terraced cottages. At the end of the road, Abby could see the river. She had seen pictures of roads like this from an earlier era. Black-and-white images of children playing outside. Behind them, the street made tiny by the looming dark outline of a huge container ferry pulled into the dock.

There were no ships today, hadn't been any for a long time. These were no longer working docks and the children in that old black-and-white photo were mostly dead by now. Those families, Abby knew, all moved out of this area during the sixties and seventies, relocating to modern, soulless housing estates on the outer fringes of East London where city met countryside and London became Essex.

Ahead of her, Nick slowed down, parked his car in the only free space on the street. Abby drove past, pulling her hair over the side of her face so he wouldn't see her if he looked. There was a pub at the end of the street. A well-maintained, modern affair – more gastropub than local boozer. Through her rear-view mirror, Abby watched Nick climb out of his car and run into the pub.

She turned into a narrow street lined with imposing warehouse buildings that had been converted into luxury apartments. She squeezed the car into a space outside one of them, ignoring the yellow lines. From here, she had a clear view of the pub and would be able to see Nick Gleeson as soon as he left.

She switched off the engine, sat back and waited.

SIX

Charlotte had been released on bail. The solicitor, Jeremy, said she shouldn't read anything into this.

'They can only hold you for 24 hours without charging you,' he said. 'So it's good in one sense because it means they don't have enough to charge you. And they haven't applied for an extension to keep you in longer. But it doesn't mean they won't want to see you again. You understand that, don't you?'

She should have gone straight home but the station was close to Ennersdale Road and she was lonely. And more than a little bit scared. If she went home, Nick might be there and that would mean confronting him. She didn't have the strength for that. So she chose another sort of confrontation instead.

When Freya answered the door, Charlotte burst into tears. She moved forward, hoping for some affection, but Freya stepped out of her reach.

'Oh darling, I've had the most terrible time. I've been kept in a police cell all night. It was truly terrifying. Of course, they've had to let me go because they can't find a shred of evidence against me, but I was so scared. And I know maybe I shouldn't have come here but I didn't know what else to do or where else to go. Please don't turn me away, Freya. I've never needed anyone as much as I need you right now.'

'Get a grip,' Freya said. 'And tell me what's happened.'

The prospect of sitting up there in that gloomy room with her daughter's judgemental eyes drilling into her was such a horrible one that Charlotte wondered – with a rare flash of insight – why on earth she'd thought this was a good idea.

'Couldn't we go to the pub?' she asked meekly. 'The rain has stopped and it's quite nice out now. I promise I'll behave, darling. It's just, well, I could really do with something to settle my nerves. And food. My gosh, I can't remember the last time I ate. I know the little place where you work serves wonderful food, doesn't it? Let's go there and I'll treat us both to some lunch. How does that sound?'

She smiled brightly and willed Freya to say yes. She expected Freya to put up a fight, but instead her daughter nodded her head and said, 'Okay. Let me go upstairs and grab my bag. Wait here.'

At the wine bar, Charlotte made herself order a small glass

of wine and a large plate of chips, resisting the more attractive option of a large glass and a small plate. She watched with a distaste she did her best to hide as Freya ordered a mineral water, a club sandwich and a large portion of chips. Orders placed, the waitress went to get their drinks while mother and daughter stared at each other across the table. Freya was so cold, so difficult to read. The opposite of Charlotte, who could never hide how she felt.

'We're so different,' she murmured. 'Maybe I'd have been a better mother if we'd been more alike.'

'If you'd been a better mother,' Freya said, 'maybe I wouldn't have tried so hard to make sure I turned out nothing like you.'

That hurt, and Charlotte was about to say so when Kieran's face flashed in front of her. What right did she have to ask for mercy?

She remembered Freya's sixth birthday. Charlotte had bought her a dress, a beautiful crushed silk knee-length green dress. Green was Freya's colour and Charlotte chose the dress for that reason. Freya refused to wear it. Told Charlotte she didn't like it and insisted – *insisted* – on wearing her old, torn jeans, which were dirty and disgusting and made Freya look like a boy.

They'd planned a big birthday party. Hired a magician and every child in Freya's class had been invited. Nick had taken the day off work and was doing his best to play happy families, even though it was obvious the tension between mother and daughter was rubbing off on him.

Charlotte sneaked a few glasses of wine early on, the only way she knew to stop herself exploding with the tension that made her feel like she was a pressure cooker on the boil. Because if she didn't put a lid on the anger, she knew she might not be able to stop herself slapping Freya's lumpy, grumpy, ungrateful face. And if she did that, it would give Nick the perfect excuse he'd been looking for to finish things between them.

'What is it?'

Freya's voice dragged Charlotte back from that awful day, but the memories stayed even as she smiled at Freya and attempted some sort of conversation. She'd fallen asleep. Woken to find Freya standing by the bed, pulling her arm and crying.

'I'm sorry, Mummy. I'm so sorry, I didn't mean it. Please, Mummy. Wake up. Don't be dead, please Mummy?'

And behind Freya, staring at her with a look of such loathing, her husband.

'Are you okay?'

The lack of concern in Freya's voice was a reminder of how far removed she was from that little girl from that long ago afternoon. Charlotte's eyes filled with tears as she reached across the table and took her daughter's hand.

'I'm sorry,' she said.

Freya pulled her hand away.

'What for?'

She seemed colder than normal today. It occurred to her that maybe Freya had found out what she'd told the police but she dismissed the thought almost immediately. She was pretty sure they had rules about that sort of thing. Didn't they?

'For not being very good at anything,' she said. 'And for all the sadness you're experiencing right now. I know how much you cared for Kieran. This business is terrible.'

'I loved him,' Freya said. 'Not that my feelings ever mattered to you, did they?'

The waitress appeared with their drinks, easing the need for either of them to find something else to say. Charlotte lifted her glass and drank down the cool wine.

'Why did the police keep you in?' Freya asked.

Charlotte took another sip of wine, taking care not to drink too much too quickly.

'They found some things at the house,' she said. 'A knife, in fact. The police think it was the knife used to, well, you know ...'

Freya stared at her. Charlotte didn't like the expression on her face.

'Can you say that again?' Freya asked.

'You heard me the first time,' Charlotte said. 'The police found a knife at our home. It had blood on it, if you must know.'

'Kieran's blood?' Freya's voice was little more than a whisper and Charlotte realised – too late – the effect this information would have on her daughter.

'I'm sorry,' Charlotte said, hating herself for apologising – again – for something that wasn't her fault. She knew how pathetic she must sound but didn't know what else to say or do.

Freya's face was white apart from two little spots of pink on both her cheeks. When she was a little girl, those pink spots were a precursor to a crying fit. Charlotte hadn't seen her daughter cry for a long time. Not even the day they'd got the news about Kieran. Her daughter was a cold fish, no doubt about it. She wondered if Freya had always been that way but honestly couldn't remember. She certainly hadn't been the most loving of children. Acted most of the time as if she hated Charlotte. But then, Charlotte hadn't exactly been a model parent either. Her mother's voice, high-pitched and angry, started up inside Charlotte's head. She lifted her glass, took a decent swig this time and tried not to think about the past.

SEVEN

Ellen switched off the CD-recorder and told Loretta she was free to go.

'What happens now?' Loretta asked.

'I speak to my boss,' Ellen said. 'And we make a decision whether or not to charge you for obstruction.'

'But I told you what you wanted to know,' Loretta said.

Ellen leaned forward across the table, pushing her face close to Loretta's.

'You should have told me straightaway,' she said. 'Instead of lying and keeping secrets. Two people are dead. And you're so caught up in some silly game of revenge that you haven't been able to get your head out of your backside for long enough to be able to see what really matters. I'm not surprised Nick doesn't want anything to do with you. In fact, the only thing I find surprising is that he was ever attracted to you in the first place. He must have been pretty desperate.'

It was cruel, and the sudden look of pain on Loretta's face made Ellen regret the words as soon as she'd said them. Too late to take them back now, though.

Back at her desk, Ellen opened the file containing the photos from Kieran's phone. Thanks to Loretta, she knew what she was looking for now. She wanted to find the evidence first, before she went to Ger. She spent half an hour scrolling through the images until she found it.

'Boss!'

Irritated at the interruption, she looked up to see Alastair bouncing into the room. In all the years Ellen had worked with him, she'd only ever seen him animated on a handful of occasions. This was another one.

He was breathing fast, his face flushed. 'I've got something, Ma'am.'

'Make it quick,' Ellen said. 'I've got something too.'

'I've just been speaking with Clarence Granville,' Alastair said. 'He's the security guard at the block of apartments where Gleeson has his flat. I spoke to Clarence the other day and he swore blind he'd never seen Gleeson with anyone. He was lying. He's just called. Says Gleeson paid him to keep his mouth shut but he's not felt good about it. Says his conscience has been at him, making it difficult to sleep.'

'Did he give you her name?'

'No,' Alastair said. 'But he's given a pretty good description. And this is going to sound weird but the description he gave, she sounds just like …'

'This?' Ellen pointed to the photo on her screen. 'These were uploaded from Kieran's mobile,' she said. 'This one was taken just over five weeks before Kieran was killed.'

Unlike a lot of the moody scene shots, this photo was in colour. A pale blue sky with a white sun casting a silver light on the river. An apartment block stood near the water's edge. Two people standing in the open doorway.

Ellen held her breath, waiting for Alastair to see it too.

'Clarence was right,' he said.

'He sure was,' Ellen said. 'I had Nick's PA in earlier. The jilted girlfriend. Turns out she's been doing a bit of stalking on the side. Following her ex to see what he's been getting up to. Kieran must have seen them coming out of the apartment and taken this photo. Which he then used to blackmail Nick. I bet there's more too.' She clicked onto the next image. The same scene. Nothing changed except the couple in the doorway. In the first image, they looked like they were speaking to each other. In this photo, they were holding hands as they walked away from the apartment block.

Ellen zoomed in, so that the woman's face filled the screen. At the same time, Alastair's phone rang. He took the call, listened, thanked the caller and hung up. 'No prizes for guessing who sent that text message to Nick Gleeson's other mobile phone,' he said.

Ellen looked at the woman's face on the computer screen and smiled.

'I think I already know.'

* * *

Charlotte paid the taxi driver, got out and walked across the gravel to the front door. She felt nervous, scared of what she'd find inside the house. When she'd left yesterday, this was her home. Now, walking into the hallway and breathing in the musty smell of neglect, she felt like a stranger in this place.

'Nick?'

His car hadn't been in the driveway but she called his name anyway. Wanting to make sure she was alone. She strained her ears, listening for any sounds that would indicate he was here.

She went upstairs. Moved like someone wading through mounds of cotton wool, her senses muffled to everything she saw and heard and felt. The police had left the place in chaos but she barely noticed the pulled-out drawers, the clothes scattered on the beds and floors, the open bathroom cabinet or the squeezed-empty bottles of shampoo and other products. She didn't care about any of that.

Downstairs, more of the same. Her tidy kitchen was like the aftermath of a hysterical children's party. In the fridge, she found a bottle of wine, pulled it out and drank straight from the bottle.

She leaned against the island in the centre of the kitchen and waited to feel something. When nothing happened, she took another slug before replacing the cork and putting the bottle back in the fridge. For once, she wasn't seeking oblivion. Quite the opposite. She wanted to feel something.

Another row with Freya. Again. What had she expected? Ever since Freya had been able to express an opinion, she'd always taken Nick's side. Usually, Charlotte didn't mind. Not really. She'd been a useless mother and didn't blame the girl for hating her. Didn't blame her for the way her face closed down when Charlotte tried to tell her what was going on. Didn't even blame her when Freya threw the glass of water in Charlotte's face and screamed that she hated her and wished she was dead. Right before storming out of the pub leaving a wet Charlotte to pick up the bill.

They'd failed. Her and Nick. All that love, all that naive belief in the future had come to nothing. And by the time either of them noticed, it was too late to get it back. She'd been a fool. Let herself fall for every bit of the bullshit they'd spun each other. Telling each other they loved each other and that was all that mattered. As if it was possible to move beyond a childhood ruined by a mad mother and an absent father. Their life together had been built on nothing stronger than a youthful naivety that drifted out of reach like a cloud of dandelion feathers carried away on a warm summer breeze.

Nick saw it first. He'd been able to look the truth clearly in the face and see that there was no hope for their marriage. She'd clung on, every bit as determined, desperate and pathetic as the mother she'd sworn she would never become.

She knew now the sort of man she'd married. Knew, deep down inside her hollowed-out self, that he hated her. She knew what he was like and what he was capable of.

His ruthlessness was one of the things she'd once loved about him. The way he would stop at nothing to get what he wanted. Never caring who he hurt along the way. Once, she'd been the focus of that single-minded determination. She had been the thing he wanted.

The business first, Charlotte second. She hadn't minded. Told herself that his desire to succeed was driven by a need to provide and prove he was the sort of man who could give her all the things he said she deserved. Even though a tiny part of her had always known that it was really all about him and nothing to do with anyone else.

The Greenwich restaurant was his first proper success. Turning a faded Greek restaurant from failure to success in just six months. He'd had to make changes, of course. And no one could possibly blame Nick when Robert, the chef, couldn't get another job after Nick sacked him. It certainly wasn't Nick's fault that Robert chose to top himself instead of facing up to things, leaving his wife and three children with no one to support them.

Back then, home was the tiny flat over the restaurant. Charlotte was pregnant when the restaurant started making a profit. She was proud of her husband for how far he'd gone in such a short space of time. Already proving her mother wrong.

Turned out her mother was right. Nick was a bad choice of husband. A murderer. He had killed Kieran and was trying to make it look as if she'd done it. This was his opportunity to get rid of her. For good. With Charlotte locked up for murder, Nick was free – finally – from his failed marriage and his needy, boozy embarrassment of a wife.

I'll sort it. I promise.

Who was he making that promise to?

I'm scared.

Loretta? Charlotte couldn't imagine anything scaring that bitch.

Don't worry. I'll sort it. I promise.

And that's exactly what he was doing.

She closed her eyes, pictured Nick, the man she'd once loved so much. Imagined him waiting for Kieran at the bottom of St Joseph's Vale, holding the knife, stepping back into the shadows as Kieran got closer, waiting until he passed then lunging …

Later, sneaking into the house and hiding the knife in her wardrobe. Hearing her come home, moving to the staircase and putting his hand out, pushing hard into her back and shoving her forward, listening to the sound of her body as she hit the floor. Following her down the stairs, stepping over her and walking out. Not even stopping to check if she was still alive.

Something stirred inside her, grew stronger the more she thought about his betrayal. It rose up her stomach, wrapped its way around her heart and drove through her veins. Ice cold and scorching hot.

Rage.

She didn't deserve this.

She'd been a crap mother and a crap wife but he hadn't been perfect, either. Whatever she'd done, she didn't deserve this. He was the one who would go to prison for what he'd done. Not her.

The cotton wool was gone. She felt alive, alert to everything. The clatter of her feet on the varnished wooden floor as she walked through the house, the soft whoosh of traffic driving on the heath outside, the slight tremor in her hands as she locked the front door behind her.

And through it all, the rage burned inside her.

EIGHT

Abby's legs were stiff from sitting in the same position for too long. Nick Gleeson had been inside the pub for almost an hour and a half. She got out of the car, thinking if she walked past she might be able to see him inside.

She stretched, enjoying the sensation across the taut muscles of her calves and thighs. She shook her legs several times and walked away from the car, keeping close to the edge of the path. The last thing she wanted was for Gleeson to come out and see her standing there.

A cold wind blew in from the river. Abby shivered and wrapped her jacket tighter around her body. She was underdressed. Always underdressed these days. Some misplaced sense of optimism that led her to believe that the weather wasn't really as miserable as everyone said it was.

She liked the look of the pub and made a mental note to check it out on the internet later. If the reviews were good, it was the sort of place she might like to take Sam one night. If he was still in her life when this case was over.

It was painted yellow and had big glass windows which Abby imagined let in lots of light. At the first window she dared to sneak a look inside. Friday lunchtime and the pub was full. Docklands office-workers enjoying an extended liquid lunch. The start of their weekend. Strange to think she lived so close but had never even heard of this place. That was London for you, always somewhere new to discover no matter how well you thought you knew the city.

She scanned the crowd, looking for Nick Gleeson's blonde head. Saw one man who looked like him but when he turned to speak to someone she realised it wasn't him. This man was younger, less handsome. She'd nearly given up when she saw him at the bar. He was alone. She waited, expecting to see someone joining him. He handed his credit card to the barman and entered his PIN number into the electronic payment unit. When he was finished, he took his card back, buttoned up the jacket of his grey suit and started walking towards the door.

Abby ran back to her car and climbed in. She crouched down, keeping her head just high enough to be able to see Gleeson. He came outside, lit a cigarette and started walking, not in the direction of his car but the other way, towards her.

She ducked beneath the steering wheel and waited for a rap

on the window that never came. She risked peeking up, half-expecting to see his face peering in at her. She couldn't see him at first. Panicked, afraid she'd lost him, she lifted her head a little more and scanned the street. Saw him a few feet away, leaning against the side of the pub, smoking. He took a few more drags then flicked the cigarette to the ground and stubbed it out with the toe of his shoe.

A moment later, a woman walked out of the pub. Abby recognised her immediately and had to put a hand over her mouth to block her yelp of surprise.

Nick pushed himself away from the wall, walked up to the woman, put his hands on either side of her face, and kissed her. It was the sort of kiss couples gave each other in the early stages of their relationship. The sort of kiss Sam and Abby shared at the end of their first date. The sort of kiss no man ever gave a woman unless he was really serious about her. Or trying to prove that he was.

When they drew apart, Nick Gleeson wrapped his arm around the woman's slender shoulders and they walked away from Abby, looking every inch like the perfect couple walking into the sunset at the end of a dreary Hollywood romcom.

* * *

'*That's* the secret girlfriend?'

Ger stared at the image on Ellen's laptop as if she expected the face in the picture to morph into someone else.

'Looks like it,' Ellen said.

'The pictures were taken outside the block where Gleeson has his apartment,' Alastair said. 'I'm sure someone mentioned that Kieran used to go running around there. He must have seen them coming out, taken the photos and then used them to blackmail Gleeson.'

'Which would explain what they rowed about the day Kieran was killed,' Ellen said. 'I just can't believe he'd be so stupid. What was he thinking? She's the same age as his own daughter.'

Ger snorted. 'He's a man. They're all stupid when they let their dicks rule what they do.'

Ellen caught the look of mild outrage on Alastair's face and was about to say something to annoy him further when her phone started to ring.

'Ellen.' Abby sounded breathless and excited.

'What is it?' Ellen said.

'You won't believe this,' Abby said. 'Gleeson's just had lunch in a pub by the river. The Gun in Coldharbour. Do you know it? Beautiful location right on the curve of the river.'

'Abby.'

'Sorry,' Abby said. 'He's with a woman. They came out of the pub and started kissing. I mean, really proper kissing. But you will never in a million years guess who she is.'

Ellen glanced at the frozen image on the screen in front of her. A pair of hands, a man's and a woman's, holding onto each other the way couples did.

'Cosima Cooper,' Ellen said.

Abby started to speak, asking how the hell Ellen could possibly have known about Nick and Cosima before she did. Ellen wasn't listening. She was remembering what Raj had told her about Pete Cooper and how protective he was of his only child. She remembered, too, Loretta's face in the interview room when she finally revealed who Nick's girlfriend was.

'I have a horrible feeling Cooper's about to find out what's going on,' she said. 'We need to get to Gleeson before that happens.'

NINE

'I hate having to be so secretive all the time,' Nick said.

'And so do I,' Cosima said. 'But we don't have any choice.'

'We have to tell him sometime,' Nick said. His voice came out harsher than he'd meant it to, and he regretted it immediately.

She turned her face away.

'Sorry,' he said.

Still she refused to look at him. He wondered, sometimes, why he did this. She could be such hard work.

'Cosima,' he said. 'I really am sorry.'

She looked at him then and when he saw the tears in her eyes. He could have kicked himself for being such an insensitive bastard.

'I'm sorry too,' she said. 'It's just so difficult, Nick. Ever since my mother left us, he's never been the same. I can't explain it to you without making him sound mad. And he's not. He's just a lonely old man who is confused and scared of losing the only person he has left.'

'You can't stay with him forever,' Nick said. 'It's not healthy for either of you.'

It was pointless. They'd had this conversation so many times and it always ended the same way. Stalemate. Of course she was scared of hurting her father. Nick understood that and respected her for it. Her father loved her. And who could blame him? She loved Pete, too, of course. In her own way. Hadn't Nick himself been the same once? Continuing to love his old man even when it was evident to anyone with half an eye that the man he'd spent his entire life looking up to was nothing more than a pathetic dreamer.

He tried to think how he'd feel if Freya went out with a friend of his. He doubted he'd be happy about it. Not at first. But if the man loved his daughter, really loved her the way he loved Cosima, then Nick thought he'd get used to it in due course. Let's face it, anyone would be an improvement on the last bastard.

'I just want everything out in the open,' he said. 'I can't bear this secrecy any longer.'

'Well you'll have to,' Cosima said. 'I need more time.'

Her stubbornness irritated him. In his darker moments, it made him doubt she was serious about him. Even though he knew she was. She made it crystal clear how she felt about him, how much she wanted him. All the time.

He didn't think he'd get through the afternoon without having her. If he could, he would take her right now. Drag her down the alley beside the pub, push her against the wall, pull her skirt up over that fucking perfect arse and …

Her phone rang. The sound cut through the fantasy, made him jump. She looked at the caller's name on-screen and diverted the call without answering it.

'It's him,' she said.

The image of Cosima with her skirt up disappeared in a flash.

Nick looked around. Terrified for a single, mad moment that Pete was here somewhere. Watching. He shook his head. He was being paranoid. He pressed against her again, breathing in her soft, flowery smell.

'Not here.' Gently she moved his hands away. 'I have work to do. My exams are coming up. Let me get through those and then we'll talk about how to tell my father.'

'You promise?'

It was a stupid question. He knew she'd never do it and he knew he'd stay with her anyway. He'd never met a woman like her. Never even dreamed he could be this happy. She held all the cards and he was helpless to do anything about it and, most of the time, he didn't care because having her in his life was the best thing that had ever happened to him.

Maybe she was right. Maybe telling Pete wasn't such a good idea. He could be a nasty bastard when he wanted to be. More than once, Nick had watched him in action, thinking he wouldn't want to be at the receiving end of that.

Still … Pete had to be told. Nick loved her, wanted her like no other woman he'd ever known. She was his everything. He adored her and would do anything for her. If that meant standing up to her bully father and declaring his love openly, then so be it. She was worth it.

* * *

Charlotte walked to the restaurant. Usually she would jump in a taxi but she needed to clear her head. Without the help of a drink, walking was the best way to do that. It was a cold, grey day and she walked fast. When she was young, she used to walk everywhere. Walking was her escape. Leaving behind the stultifying, suffocating, sadistic atmosphere of home and out into the open countryside.

Growing up, home was an elegant Georgian detached house in its own grounds outside the village of Berwick St James, a small hamlet near Salisbury in Wiltshire. The village nestled in beautiful countryside. All around her, Charlotte was surrounded by rolling green fields and wide skies.

Her mother approved of walking, it was exercise, after all, and therefore a way of maintaining the extreme skinniness her mother deemed so important. She wasn't allowed to get dirty when she walked, which was difficult given that she walked through fields and woods. But she kept a pair of boots in the scullery by the back door and her mother never saw these, the kitchen and scullery being areas of the house that didn't interest her whatsoever.

Mrs Evans, the woman who came to cook for them, knew about the boots and told Charlotte it was okay to keep them there. Said the boots could be 'our little secret'. Over the years, as Charlotte's feet got bigger, the boots got bigger too. It was always a surprise to her how a new pair would be there waiting for her, just when she needed them. It was only years later, when Mrs Evans was long gone, that Charlotte realised the kind woman must have been buying the boots herself.

The boots weren't the only secret. There were the picnics that Mrs Evans used to make for Charlotte to take with her. She would pack the food small so that Charlotte was able to fit it into the shoulder bag she carried with her everywhere.

The shoulder bag was for pens and paper. As a girl, Charlotte wanted to be a writer. A dream she carried with her for years, along with the bag. Until the day her mother found out about it and that was the end of the dream.

She walked fast, her body remembering the rhythm of all those country walks from long ago. Across the heath, over Charlton Road and into the park. Curving down the western edge, past the tennis courts and down the steep hill towards King William Walk. All around her, people – men, women, children – were walking, running, playing, laughing, talking. She felt separate from it all. Like a spirit, drifting unnoticed through the mess and vitality of other people's lives.

The restaurant was in the heart of Greenwich village, on the corner of Nevada Street and Crooms Hill. Charlotte remembered the pride she'd felt when Nick bought it. At the end of the first night, after all the customers had gone home, she'd stayed late with Nick and his staff, watching them celebrate with glass after glass of Moët. She was pregnant and stuck to mineral water. She'd never been so happy in her entire life. If only she'd known then that that was the happiest she would ever be. That one month later, her daughter would come along and everything would change.

Inside, the restaurant was quiet. Too late for lunch, too early for dinner. Only a few tables occupied. People dragging boozy lunches through the afternoon and into the evening. A group of office-workers, rowdy and happy. In the corner, a middle-aged couple, heads close together whispering to each other. They looked happy and Charlotte thought they were probably having an affair. Not married, that was for sure.

Nick's office was at the back of the restaurant. She walked straight there, pushed open the door without knocking and went inside.

'Charlotte.'

Loretta was sitting at Nick's desk, working on his laptop. She looked surprised to see Charlotte, and slightly shifty too, as if Charlotte had caught her doing something she shouldn't. Like sleeping with Charlotte's husband.

'Where is he?' Charlotte asked.

Loretta shook her head. 'I don't know. He went out for lunch. Didn't tell me where he was going. I'd expected him to be back by now but …' She shrugged.

The adrenaline that had carried Charlotte out of the house and across the heath evaporated. Suddenly, she felt drained, exhausted; unsure how much longer she could remain standing. She grabbed the side of the door, holding tight for support. Loretta's face, staring up at her, went in and out of focus.

Through the mist, Charlotte saw Loretta stand up and walk towards her. Felt Loretta's hand on her arm and let the other woman lead her to a chair.

'Sit down,' Loretta said. 'You look awful. Let me get you a drink.'

Charlotte shook her head, or tried to at least.

'Tea,' Loretta said. 'And something to eat. Tea and toast. You look as if you need it.'

Charlotte was vaguely aware of Loretta going to the door and calling for things. Then Loretta was pulling up a chair and sitting beside her, holding Charlotte's hand.

'Are you okay?'

Charlotte pulled her hand away. 'What sort of question is that? My daughter's boyfriend and my best friend have been murdered. The police think I killed them. Of course I'm not okay.'

'Sorry,' Loretta said. 'Ah, here's our tea. Good.'

A fabulously handsome man with dark skin and sparkling eyes came into the room carrying a tray. He smiled at Charlotte as he put the tray down on the table in front of her.

'Mrs Gleeson,' he said. 'Good to see you. Enjoy the tostada.'

He spoke with a Spanish accent and she remembered meeting him once before. She'd had too much to drink and couldn't remember his name. Remembered he had a boyfriend, though. Michael. Funny she could remember the boyfriend's name but not the waiter's.

'Sugar?' Loretta asked.

Charlotte nodded. She never took sugar with her tea or coffee but right now she needed it. She didn't speak until she'd drank a full cup of tea and eaten two slices of buttery toast with homemade raspberry jam.

The sugar and carbohydrate acted like an amphetamine. With each mouthful she could feel the energy returning, warming her, clearing the mist and sharpening her mind.

She chewed the final piece of toast, swallowed and looked at Loretta. The woman was attractive enough, Charlotte supposed, although she had the sort of looks that wouldn't last. Fair, freckled skin that would wrinkle early and take on that papery texture you so often saw with woman of that colouring.

'Did you love him?' Charlotte asked.

The horrified look on Loretta's face was gratifying.

'Sorry?'

'Oh for goodness sake,' Charlotte said. 'Is that all you can say? Sorry for what? For sleeping with him? For taking me for an idiot? What exactly are you sorry for, Loretta?'

'I'm not sleeping with your husband,' Loretta said.

'Not now,' Charlotte said.

Loretta shook her head. 'No. We ... okay, I'll be honest with you. I did sleep with him. But it was only a handful of times, Charlotte. And it never meant anything.'

'Sleeping with another woman's husband never meant anything?' Charlotte said. 'Charming.'

She couldn't believe the way she was speaking. So confident and knowing. More like Ginny than poor, pathetic Charlotte. She imagined Ginny watching her, smiling her approval. Normally, she'd rather die than have a conversation like this. Now, she thought she might die if she didn't face up to it.

'It wasn't serious,' Loretta said. 'Well, I mean, I wasn't serious. I knew Nick was married and I felt awful about it. I told him it couldn't continue. I said, if you're that unhappy, you need to talk to Charlotte, you need to try to tell her how you feel. I suggested couples counselling.'

Loretta smiled. Managed to make the smile bright, sympathetic and utterly false. Quite an achievement, Charlotte thought.

'I don't suppose he spoke to you,' Loretta continued. 'Did he?'

A chemical reaction was taking place in Charlotte's body. Adrenaline combining with years of being lied to, mixed with everything that had happened over the last few weeks. Turning it all into a blinding surge of raging energy that wanted to lash out and hurt someone.

'You slept with my husband,' she said. 'That is a terrible thing to do. You slept with him and then continued to act as if you were my friend every time we met.'

An image in her head. A snapshot. Kieran's face over hers. She was no better than Loretta. Worse, maybe. She blinked and the image disappeared.

'I *am* your friend,' Loretta said. 'It's Nick, he's the one who's acted badly here. You should be having this conversation with him, not me. I mean, I'm not the person you're married to. And I'm certainly not the only woman he's slept with, let me tell you.'

'He's not here,' Charlotte said, 'but you are, so I'm having the conversation with you. Tell me about Nick and Kieran.'

The sudden change of topic seemed to confuse Loretta.

'What do you mean?' she asked.

'Just tell me,' Charlotte said.

'Well, there is something,' Loretta said. 'But I'm not covering up for him, Charlotte. I've already told the police.'

'Told them what?'

'Kieran was here,' Loretta said. 'The day he was killed. He came in just after lunch.'

'And?' Charlotte said.

'And they rowed,' Loretta said.

'What about?' She braced herself. This was it. The moment she would find out the truth.

'Well,' Loretta said, 'I'm not sure, really. I mean, the door was closed and I'm not one to eavesdrop.'

Charlotte almost laughed. Loretta's desk was right outside

Nick's office. Even with the door closed, it wouldn't have been that hard to hear something if you put your mind to it.

'The row was about Pete Cooper,' Loretta said. 'I couldn't get everything. Well, I wasn't trying to, of course. But I heard Cooper's name several times. Kieran was threatening to tell Cooper something.'

'Tell him what?' Charlotte asked.

'How would I know?' Loretta said. 'I heard Kieran saying, Cooper will kill you if he finds out. I assumed it was to do with the business. I mean, what else could it be about?'

Loretta smiled and Charlotte realised Loretta was implying the row was about something else. Charlotte tried to think what else it could be but her mind drew a blank.

'Was it to do with Freya?' she asked.

The smile disappeared and Charlotte felt that Loretta was disappointed in her for something.

'You really haven't a clue, do you?' Loretta said. 'Poor Charlotte. Your relationship with Nick, it's really none of my business. If you think he's seeing someone else, why don't you ask him straight out instead of coming here and throwing accusations around the place?'

'That's not what I was doing,' Charlotte said. 'I'm trying to find out who killed my daughter's boyfriend.'

'I'd have thought that was obvious,' Loretta said. 'Wouldn't you?'

Charlotte left without saying goodbye.

I'd have thought that was obvious. Was Loretta talking about Pete or Nick?

Charlotte thought of all the stories she'd heard about Pete Cooper, the things Ginny had told her. Charlotte had begged Nick not to go into business with a man like that but Nick had refused to listen. Now, it seemed they were all about to pay.

TEN

Nick watched Cosima's taxi drive away. He wished he could run after it and climb into the back of the car beside her. Just the two of them. Start a new life without any of the complications of the real world. Each time they parted, he experienced a sharp sense of loss, as if this might be the last time he would ever see her.

His phone started to ring. Pete. Nick's breath caught in his throat. First Pete called Cosima, now him. A coincidence, surely. It couldn't be anything else. Pete didn't know. No one did. The only person who'd found out about them was dead. And good riddance, too.

Nick felt bad for Freya, of course. She was his daughter, after all. But over time, he was sure Freya would come to see that she was better off without that useless lump. She might even find herself someone half decent the next time around.

He got into the car and his phone rang again. Thinking it was Pete, he answered without checking the caller display. Then wished he hadn't.

'Where are you?'

Loretta.

Another problem that needed sorting. He should have got rid of her the moment they stopped seeing each other. He'd been too soft. Let her stay on even though he knew it was the wrong decision. As soon as the new restaurant was up and running, he'd deal with it.

'Had a meeting,' he said. 'Not that it's any of your business. Is there a problem?'

'You tell me,' she said. 'Your dear little wife's been here. Asking all sorts of questions about you and your dead son-in-law.'

'He wasn't my son-in-law,' Nick said. 'They weren't married.'

Loretta made some smart comment about common-law relationships but he wasn't listening. Too busy trying to work out what Charlotte was up to.

'Was she drunk?' he asked, interrupting Loretta who was still banging on about something or other.

'Not that I noticed,' Loretta said. 'But it can be hard to tell with alcoholics sometimes, can't it?'

Bitch. He remembered the times she'd comforted him when things with Charlotte got particularly bad. Which, let's face it, was most of the time.

'What did you tell her?' he said.

'What do you mean?' There was an edge of almost joy in her voice and his spirits sank lower as he realised Loretta had probably loved telling Charlotte about his row with Kieran.

But Loretta didn't know everything. It was important to remember that. For all her blustering, Loretta didn't know enough to cause him any real harm – couldn't know because if she did, she wouldn't have been able to stop herself from doing something about it.

'She knows about you and me,' Loretta said. 'Strangely enough, she already knew it was over between us. Of course, I told her why you ended it. That you'd found someone else stupid enough to believe your bullshit. She was very interested, I must say. Although she clearly has no idea who your new girlfriend is. I dropped some hints, but she didn't get it. She's not very bright, is she?'

He hung up and called Charlotte. She didn't pick up. He thought about leaving a message but changed his mind. This needed to be dealt with in person. He needed to find out what Loretta had told her. He threw the phone onto the passenger seat, switched on the engine and pulled away from the kerb.

* * *

Gleeson left Coldharbour and drove south, following signs for the Blackwall Tunnel. As she queued up for the tunnel, three cars behind him, Abby put her phone into the hands-free unit, called

Ellen and explained what she was doing.

'We're on our way back to Greenwich,' Abby said. 'Traffic's atrocious. We've been at a standstill for forty-five minutes. I think there's been a breakdown in the tunnel.'

'You shouldn't be on your own,' Ellen said. 'He could be dangerous.'

Like you've never done anything dangerous, Abby thought, although she had the sense not to say it out loud.

'What do you want me to do?' Abby said. 'I assume he's going to the restaurant.'

The traffic started to move slowly. Three cars ahead, she could see Gleeson's car disappearing into the mouth of the tunnel.

'Stay with him as far as the restaurant,' Ellen said. 'I'll meet you there. How much longer do you think you'll be?'

'Give us another half an hour,' Abby said. 'Forty minutes tops.'

'Okay,' Ellen said. 'See you there. We'll go in together and ask him a few questions about his relationship with Pete Cooper's daughter. I imagine that will be an interesting conversation.'

Abby was at the mouth of the tunnel now, daylight disappearing as she entered the darkness. On the phone, Ellen was still speaking.

'If he doesn't go to the restaurant …'

Inside the tunnel now, under the river. Ellen's voice cut out as the mobile signal was lost.

Ellen's problem, Abby reflected, was that she was a control freak. In Ellen's world, it was perfectly okay to break the rules if you were Ellen Kelly and you felt it was the best thing to do. But that never translated to the rest of the team. Ellen was the first to put herself in danger – and she had done it time and again – if she thought it would solve a case. But woe betide anyone else who dared do the same.

Out of the tunnel, Abby was blinded by the sudden brightness of an unfamiliar sun creeping out behind a layer of thick clouds. The city, slick from the recent rain, glowed and glimmered. Drops of water sparkled in the sunshine like a vast carpet of fairy lights across the city, making it brighter and fresher and more beautiful than Abby had ever seen it.

Instead of turning off for Greenwich, Gleeson continued south in the direction of Blackheath and Lewisham. Abby drove after him. No point calling Ellen. Not until she knew where they were going.

She couldn't explain it, but this moment felt important. For the first time in her career, the possibility that she might solve a murder investigation was within her reach. She wasn't going to miss out on that. Not for Ellen Kelly, not for anyone.

ELEVEN

Ellen dialled Abby's number and waited. When the call went to voicemail she hung up, frustrated. She had a bad feeling about this. She wanted to warn Abby not to do anything stupid. Like following Nick Gleeson to the restaurant and confronting him on her own. Ellen had told her to wait, but she wasn't sure that message had got through. And now the bloody woman wasn't answering her phone.

She told Alastair he was coming with her. They took a pool car. With the help of the blue light, the siren and some dodgy driving, they made it across to Greenwich in nine-and-a-half minutes. Around the corner from the restaurant, Ellen found a parking bay reserved for deliveries in and out of the market. She took the space, switched off the engine and turned to Alastair.

'Okay?' she asked.

He swallowed several times and nodded his head.

'Fine.'

He didn't sound fine and he didn't look fine, but as long as he didn't throw up inside the car, Ellen wasn't too bothered.

She knew from previous visits that Gleeson had his own reserved parking bay right outside the restaurant. Today, the space was empty. There was no sign of Abby, either. Ellen hoped she was still stuck in traffic and not somewhere she shouldn't be.

She called Abby's phone again, but it went to voicemail again.

'Let's go inside,' she said to Alastair. 'Hopefully Abby will be here any second now.'

The sun had come out, stripping layers off the city. Wet streets dazzled in the rare sunshine. Ellen pushed open the restaurant door and stepped inside.

'He's not here.'

Ellen saw Loretta standing in front of her, looking jubilant.

'What do you mean?' Ellen asked.

'I assume you're looking for Nick?' Loretta said. 'He hasn't come back from lunch and I doubt he will at this point.'

'He's stuck in traffic,' Ellen said. 'But he's on his way. Mind if we wait?'

Loretta smirked. 'Seems everyone wants to see him this afternoon. I wonder what he could possibly have done to become popular so suddenly?'

'Who else has been looking for him?' Ellen asked.

'Pete and Charlotte were both here earlier,' Loretta said. 'Oh they didn't come together, of course. Although that would be amusing, I suppose. No, Charlotte was here first and then Pete a few minutes after that.'

'What did you tell them?' Ellen asked.

'Well, poor Charlotte didn't seem to know what she wanted,' Loretta said. 'I tried to help her but, truth be told, she really wasn't interested. Pete, on the other hand, was very interested. I emailed him earlier, you see. I thought it was only fair he knew what was going on. Naturally, he wanted to speak to Nick. I told him the apartment was his best chance.'

'You gave him the address?'

'Of course,' Loretta said. 'He asked, so I told him. Oh, I am sorry. I haven't done anything wrong, have I?'

* * *

Nick parked in front of the house and ran inside. The journey from Docklands had taken a torturous two hours. Luckily, it hadn't affected Cosima. She'd sent him a text over an hour ago, saying she had arrived at the apartment. He went to switch off the alarm but it wasn't on. He called Charlotte's name but there was no answer. The silly cow had forgotten to turn it on again.

Often, too many times to count, he'd come home to find Charlotte crashed out on one of the beds upstairs. Today, the one time he wanted her to be here, he couldn't find her. He went upstairs, searched each bedroom but there was no sign of her anywhere.

He heard a noise downstairs. A creaking, like the sound the back door made when you opened it.

'Charlotte?' He stood at the top of the stairs, listening.

Nothing. Of course she wasn't here. He was alone. He'd been alone for the longest time. Even with Loretta, there'd been no real connection between them. She hadn't filled the aching emptiness he'd learned to live with. He'd grown to believe nothing could ever fill that emptiness. And then he met Cosima and everything changed.

All changed, changed utterly

A terrible beauty is born

As a young man, he'd loved poetry. Hadn't picked up a book of any sort in years, of course, because he'd been so busy with work. Maybe once the divorce was sorted out, after he'd escaped the mess of his current life and started again, maybe then he would go back to reading. Cosima loved poetry. One of their first conversations had been about their favourite poems, both of them surprised to find someone at that God-awful party who shared the same passion. Funny how things worked out. Just when he'd given up on that side of things, he turned up at Cooper's networking event and pow!

There was a library downstairs, a small, book-lined room off the dining room. He didn't use the room as much as he probably should. Mostly, he used it to impress visitors. Any business meetings that took place in the house were conducted in the library. Nick felt the book-lined shelves played an important part in creating the image of himself he wanted to present to the world.

The books were stored alphabetically and by genre. Fiction on the right, poetry along the wall on the left and the longer middle wall filled with business manuals and other uninspiring nonsense he'd once thought was so important. He went to the poetry section, found the book he wanted, took it out and flicked through it until he reached the poem he was looking for.

It was his father who'd introduced him to the poetry of William Butler Yeats. The old man had preferred the poems about Ireland and the war, but Nick had always been drawn to the love poems. He'd recited this poem to her early in their relationship. He'd wanted her to understand that he was in it for the long haul. That there was substance to his feelings for her. Substance to him.

He was no good with words. Never had been, never would be. Numbers were his thing. That's why his restaurants were so successful. Yes, he was an adequate chef but not one of the best. He didn't care enough. The only thing he'd cared about was success. Making something of himself. Doing it for his father who had sacrificed so much for his only child.

And because he knew this about himself, he chose another man's words to tell her how he really felt. Like all the love poems, this one was written for Maud Gonne, the woman Yeats had loved so single-mindedly and unrequitedly. *When you are old and grey and full of sleep, and nodding by the fire.*

It was about loving the real person, more than the superficial attraction all men felt for a pretty woman. Yeats is telling his beloved he will love her long after all that outer beauty is stripped away. Because what he really loves is her soul.

That's what Pete needed to understand. That this was more than a middle-aged infatuation with a younger woman. He loved Cosima like no one else ever could or would. They were destined to be together. Soulmates. Nick smiled. He liked that expression. Felt it properly described the depth of their relationship.

He needed a pen. Wanted to write something special at the front of the book. He went across the hall to his study. *To C, Soulmates forever.* That's what he'd write. Nothing fancy because he didn't do fancy. Besides, there were enough fancy words in the rest of the book.

He kept a gold Cross fountain pen on his desk. Didn't use it often, preferring the ease and lack of mess you got with a ball-point. But he kept the pen on his desk because it looked good. He had an identical one in his office in Greenwich.

The pen was a present from Charlotte. Given to him years ago, when there had still been some hope for the relationship. Before he'd realised quite how bad she really was. Even if there was no Cosima, he knew he couldn't do this anymore. The destructive nature of their so-called relationship disgusted him. She disgusted him. Worst of all, he disgusted himself for staying with her all this time. For not being man enough to end it once and for all.

He closed his eyes, breathed in and out three times, then wrote the note in the front of the book, taking care not to leave ink marks on the page. He'd just written the last word when the man behind him coughed.

TWELVE

At Heath Lane, Nick turned left towards his house. Abby drove past, found a parking space in Pagoda Gardens, locked her car and ran back to the Gleesons' house.

Nick's car was parked outside the front of the house. Empty. The entrance gates were open. Abby walked up the drive, trying to walk quietly on the gravel.

At the front door, she paused. She was scared, but she couldn't let that cloud her judgement. She should call Ellen. Tell her where she was and wait for back-up. It was the sensible thing to do. But being sensible hadn't ever worked in Ellen's favour. If Abby put in the call, she might as well go home. All she'd be doing was giving Ellen yet another opportunity to steal the limelight.

No.

No way.

She was close. That's what made the difference between a good detective and a great one. Feel the fear but do it anyway. Or something.

* * *

He dropped the pen. He heard the clatter of it hitting the ground as he swung around. He already knew who was there. And why. All the lies he'd told himself drifted in and out of his consciousness, as insignificant and useless as bits of broken wood floating on the ebb and flow of a vast sea.

He'd let himself believe it would be all right. That there was nothing wrong with what they were doing and if he just got a chance to explain, to make Pete see how much she mattered to him, that Pete would be fine with it all.

It was a foolish belief to have held onto all this time. As he turned and looked into Pete Cooper's eyes, Nick knew. This was it. Fear loosened his insides, dried his mouth. He wanted to speak, to say something – anything – which would delay things. But Pete was too quick. Came at him with a fist into the stomach. Nick lurched back. Another fist to the side of his face knocked him to the ground. From far away, he heard himself screaming, begging Pete not to hurt him, to give him a chance to explain. Pete was screaming too, calling him a pervert and a dirty bastard. Kicking and punching, fists and feet in his stomach, back and head.

Nick curled into a ball, arms over his head trying to protect himself, but Pete kept coming, wasn't going to stop until he'd done what he came here to do. Through the pain, a line from a different poem was there. He couldn't focus on the detail, but the sense of it was with him. Something about bodies broken like thorns. And he knew that's what Pete would do to him. Break him like a thorn. Keep breaking him until there was nothing left.

* * *

Abby moved around the outside of the house, sliding up to each window and looking into the rooms. Nothing seemed out of place. As she edged closer to the back, she heard a man's voice. Shouting. No, not shouting. Screaming.

The thick walls made it impossible to hear what he was screaming about. Or whether there was more than one person doing the screaming. She made herself move forward, creeping closer and closer to the source of the sound.

Abruptly, the screaming stopped. The silence felt worse, somehow. It made the unsteady in-out, in-out of her own breathing and the rapid thumping of her heart seem too loud.

A large Victorian-style conservatory jutted out from the back of the house. When she reached the glass, Abby stopped. Someone was moving around in there. She could hear a scraping sound, as if something heavy was being dragged across the floor.

Taking a deep breath, Abby poked her head forward, just far enough to peek into the conservatory.

It was furnished to look like a colonial drawing room. All wicker furniture, green plants and a low-hanging, old-style ceiling fan. A long, low table ran along one glass wall, covered in family photos. Nick and Charlotte. A few of Freya. Even one of Freya with Kieran. Surprising given the way her parents had felt about Freya's boyfriend. The photo was familiar. A copy of one she'd seen somewhere else. Freya and Kieran standing on a hill somewhere. Freya's arms wrapped around his neck, wind whipping the hair around her smiling face. Kieran looking like he'd rather be anywhere else.

Something about the photo …

The door swung open. Two men, their backs to her, dragged something across the conservatory floor. Abby pulled her head back quickly. One of the men was Pete Cooper. Even from the back she recognised his tall, broad body. But what was he dragging? Who was the other man? And where the hell was Nick Gleeson? She calculated the time that had passed between Gleeson arriving home and now. Long enough for something bad to have happened.

She pulled out her phone to call Ellen. At the same moment, it started ringing. The sound of it, shrill and unexpected, made her jump. The phone fell from her hand, landing on the soft ground, as it carried on ringing.

It was too loud. Her fingers were shaking and she tried to press the button to switch it off. Again, the phone slipped from her grasp. Again, it hit the ground. This time it stopped ringing.

Giving a silent prayer of thanks, she picked it up a second time. Put it in her pocket and turned to go, but her path was blocked by Pete Cooper. She screamed and staggered back, turned to run in the opposite direction but that way was blocked too.

The man had his fist out. As Abby turned, he slammed it into the side of her face. The force of it lifted her body off the ground and sent her flying back, right into Pete Cooper's waiting arms.

THIRTEEN

Nick was a weak man. Charlotte realised that in the first few years of their marriage. It didn't take long to understand that all the charm was superficial, nothing underneath except a greedy, selfish, weak person out for all he could get. His single-minded focus on the business wasn't fuelled by anything as admirable as ambition. It was nothing more than a pathetic need to prove himself.

She walked into the park and up the steepest part of the hill to the top. At some point the sun had come out, making the world a brighter place, matching the sudden clear understanding inside her head.

She didn't love her husband. She'd clung on to the marriage because of her own pathetic need to prove her mother wrong. In a way, she was no better than Nick. Both leading lives they didn't want in order to prove things to parents no longer here to care what they did. How had they become so stupid and unaware?

Her stomach churned and tightened, the pain of it making her double over, arms clutched around her middle. She wanted to find the nearest bar and drink until all this went away. There would be a murder trial. It would be all over the press. Nick's precious reputation that he cared so much about would be destroyed. No coming back from murder. Just look at OJ. And he hadn't even been convicted.

Her stomach contracted, forcing bile up her throat. The spasms were part shock, part DTs. Drying out. That part of her life was over. The drinking, the self-delusion, the stupid, pointless, pathetic self-pity.

Something new was about to start.

She needed to know the truth. For Ginny, for Freya, for herself. She needed to know what Kieran had discovered that was so important Pete and Nick had to kill him. She took her phone out, called Nick's mobile, but he didn't answer. She hung up without leaving a message.

He'd have to come home at some point. And when he did, she would be waiting for him. She'd get him to tell her what really happened. Charlotte put her phone away and started walking.

* * *

No answer. Ellen ended the call without leaving a message and slammed the palm of her hand against the steering wheel. She was parked by the river outside Nick Gleeson's apartment. There was no sign of his car but that didn't mean anything. He could have parked it anywhere. She'd taken her phone out to call Abby one last time but – again – there was no answer.

'She'll be okay,' Alastair said. 'She's too clever to let anything happen to her.'

'Sometimes clever isn't enough,' Ellen said.

She unstrapped her seatbelt and climbed out.

'Come on,' she said. 'Let's go.'

Inside the building, a tall, black man dressed in a navy-blue uniform stepped forward to greet them.

'Clarence Granville,' he said. 'You must be Detective Inspector Kelly. I understand you want to get into one of the apartments?'

The reception area was light, airy and welcoming. White tiled floor, white walls and lots of green plants. Ellen had noticed a CCTV camera over the door as she came in. She pointed to this now and asked Clarence Granville if it had been turned on while he was on his lunch break.

'Sure was,' Granville said. 'But I haven't had a chance to look at it yet. Do you want to do that now?'

'No time,' Ellen said. 'We need to get into the apartment. Can you take us straight there?'

'Sure thing,' Granville said. 'Mr Gleeson's not in any trouble, I hope? He's a decent bloke. Always polite and friendly.

Remembers I've got a little girl and asks how she's doing. He doesn't live here, but you probably already know that.'

'You've seen his girlfriend?' Ellen asked.

'She's a real stunner,' Granville said. 'A bit on the cold side, though. A lot of them are like that. Don't notice the little people.'

'Little' was the last word you'd choose to describe Clarence Granville. Six five, at least, with rich mahogany skin, tight-cropped hair and at least fifteen stone of pure muscle. He was a difficult man not to notice.

Granville took a set of keys from the counter behind the reception desk. 'This way.' He headed for the lift but Ellen stopped him and shook her head.

'We'll take the stairs,' she said.

If Cooper was up there, he would hear the lift. She didn't want to give him any warning.

On her way to the stairwell, Ellen pulled out her phone and tried Abby's number once more. The line connected, Abby's phone rang. Once. Twice. A sudden click and then Abby's voice. The relief as Ellen started to speak was replaced with panic when she realised she'd reached Abby's voicemail, not Abby herself. Frustrated, she hung up and redialled. This time, the phone rang and rang.

It was still ringing as Ellen followed Granville up through the building. She held it to her ear, willing Abby to answer and tell her that she was okay. But Abby didn't answer. Instead, after an eternity, the ringing stopped and the line went dead, leaving a silence so complete it stayed with Ellen long after she'd put the phone away, reached the top of the building and stood at the end of a long corridor, looking at the door to Nick Gleeson's apartment, wondering what was on the other side.

FOURTEEN

'Wake up.'

A man's voice, too loud and too close. Nick knew the voice. Couldn't remember the man's name but he knew the voice. He was tired. Wanted the man to go away, leave him alone and let him sleep.

He groaned, trying to shut out the sound. The crack of an open palm against his cheek flung his head sideways. Pain shot up his face and exploded inside his head.

A hand grabbed his hair. Pulled until it felt like his head was being ripped off his neck. The pressure on his stretched throat made it impossible to breathe. Panicked, his body bucked and jerked and twisted, trying to pull away from the unbearable pressure.

'Wake up!'

Another slap on his other cheek.

He tried to open his eyes. His left eye, swollen, remained closed. Through his right eye, he saw a man's face. Too close to make out the features. A brown eye. The stubbly start of a black beard. A name floated through his head and disappeared before he could hold on to it. He knew that face.

Couldn't move. Arms tied behind his back. Legs bound together. A sharp pain across his wrists and ankles. Something wrong with his body. Pain everywhere.

Scatter shots of memory pow-powed through his head. Fragments he couldn't piece together. His car. A pub. Cosima.

A car crash!

Cosima. He tried to call her name. Something came out of his mouth but it didn't sound right. A dribble of spit ran from the corner of his mouth and trickled down his chin.

Not a car crash.

He'd put her in a taxi.

Relief that she was okay was replaced by another grip of fear. Old and grey. A poem. He'd come home to get the book.

'You're awake. Good.'

The lower part of his torso loosened, sick with terror as it came rushing back to him.

'It's not what you think.'

His voice sounded different. Muffled, like there were wads of cotton wool in his mouth. Or maybe the problem was with his ears. But when Pete spoke, his voice sounded the same as ever. Cold and dangerous.

'Don't fucking tell me what I think.'

Nick nodded, tried to say no, of course, he'd never try to tell Pete what to think. He wasn't stupid and he respected Pete and was glad they were in business together and he'd never do anything to damage that relationship because he wasn't that stupid.

But he couldn't say any of that because Pete's fist, from nowhere, plunged deep into Nick's stomach. Vomit rose up his throat, burst from his mouth, splattering his face and chest. Another spasm and more watery vomit. He tried to keep his head down so it only went on himself and not on Pete, but Pete had his hair again, was forcing his head up, making Nick look at him.

'You dirty pig.'

Pete drew his fist back. This time, Nick saw it coming, tried to cower away but he was pinned to the chair, unable to move. The fist flew through the air, smashed into Nick's face. A loud crack as the bones in his nose shattered. Pain like he'd never known, blocked out everything else.

He heard himself crying, heard his voice through the pain and the cotton wool, begging. Somewhere nearby he could hear Pete but the words were jumbled up, impossible to make any sense from them.

The darkness was reaching for him. He tried to resist, scared there would be no way back from there. But the pull was too strong. Behind Pete, he saw a woman lying face-down on the floor. Shiny black hair covering her face.

No! She shouldn't be part of this. He wanted to call her name, tell her he was here and it would be okay, that he would save her. But the darkness took him before he could tell her anything.

* * *

Four apartments on each floor. Nick Gleeson's was the last one on the top floor. The silence up here was complete. And unnatural. Thick walls and doors that blocked out all sound from behind them. Even their footsteps got muffled and lost in the double-pile carpet. Ellen's own breathing echoed through her head like puffs of breath from the ghosts crowding around her.

Billy Dunston. Dai Davies. Brian Fletcher. Adam Telford. And Vinny.

As she waited for Granville to open the door, Ellen thought she heard something – a low, moaning sound, so distant she could have imagined it. She didn't want to go in there. Her head was full of them. The dead people. Strangled, shot, stabbed. Kieran Burton and Virginia Rau. The smell of burning flesh. The sudden, shocking way a face disappeared from a man's body when you held a gun to the side of his head and pulled the trigger.

The door was open now. She could see inside the apartment. When she stepped past Granville into the room, the moaning grew louder. The ghosts rushed forward to greet her.

'Boss?' Alastair's voice made her jump.

The ghosts faded back.

It was a characterless space with pale walls and paler furniture. The only thing going for it was the view. There was no one here and no sign that anything bad had happened, apart from a sick sensation in the pit of Ellen's stomach and, over by the window, a small table lying upside-down. Four skinny legs sticking up, reminding Ellen of her daughter's handstands.

At first, she thought the moaning was coming from the table. A feeling that intensified when she put her hand on one of the upturned legs and the sound stopped. It started again as soon as she took her hand away.

The window was in two parts. The main part – a large glass section that seemed to be some sort of sliding door – was closed. The smaller top section was open. A cool breeze drifted through the open section, tickled her neck and sent a trail of goosebumps scattering across her skin. She touched the table again. The moaning stopped. Again.

She had a freaked-out moment where she thought the ghosts had won. Another moan carried to her along the breeze. Her hand was still on the table leg and she realised the sound had come from outside the window.

Except all she could see was the sweeping curve of the river and the Isle of Dogs on the far bank. Beyond that, the city stretched out to infinity. She scanned the river, wondering if maybe the sound could be coming from the engine of a boat or something. Even though she knew that only a living thing could make that sort of sound.

She watched a white sailing boat drift west along the river while she listened out for the next sound. Nothing. She relaxed, about to turn away from the view when a face appeared outside the window.

Ellen screamed and jumped back.

'What's wrong?' Alastair was beside her, his hand on her shoulder, steady and sure.

'The window,' Ellen said. 'There's someone out there.'

'Impossible,' Alastair said. 'We're six floors off the ground.'

'There!' Ellen shook his hand off her shoulder and pointed. But there was no one there. The face was gone as suddenly as it had appeared.

Down on the river, the little white boat was moving faster. Being carried along on the same wind that was blowing through the window, curling its way around Ellen's body, cutting through her and past her as the ghosts crowded in.

FIFTEEN

Nick's car was outside the house. Good. Charlotte pushed open the front door and shouted his name. No answer, but she could hear him moving around in the conservatory. She pictured him in there; his furtive movements as he tried to sneak out the back without having to see her. Wouldn't be the first time he'd done it, but he was a fool if he thought that would work today.

The conservatory door was open. She knew before she reached it that something was wrong. She should have turned and run back but she didn't falter. Not once. She knew something was wrong and she kept going because she had no choice. Nick was in there and he was the only one who could tell her why Ginny had to die.

'Nick!'

He didn't answer. He couldn't answer. Unconscious and tied to a chair, he was sitting directly across from her when she banged through the open door. His head was hanging to one side. Eyes closed. Face swollen and bruised. Unrecognisable but she knew it was him because the hair was his and he was wearing that grey Paul Smith she hated because he looked so good in it and by God did he know it.

She was still moving, her body propelling her across to where he sat. She'd reached the centre of the room when a deeper, more primal instinct kicked in and she halted. This place was dangerous. She had to go. Now.

'Nick?'

Nothing. He was dead.

Her stomach heaved but she didn't vomit. The conservatory swayed; she put her hand on a chair, steadying herself. Nick moaned once then was silent.

Go.

She swung around. A man blocked her way. Short and wide. She tried to duck past him but he grabbed her arm, shoved her back. She screamed and he slapped her across the face. Hard.

She had no idea who he was. But she knew the other man, walking towards her from the corner of the room where he must have been the whole time. A sudden, childish rage rose above the fear. She'd told Nick, warned him about going into business with Pete Cooper. He hadn't listened. Of course he hadn't.

This was his fault. In that moment, she hated him more than

she'd ever thought it was possible to hate anyone. Hated him more than her own mother. And that was saying something.

The hate and rage made her reckless. Cooper was in front of her, pushing his face in close to hers, so close she could feel his breath and smell the stinking, clogging perfume of that horrible cologne he always wore.

'Hello Charlotte.'

He smiled.

She pulled her head back and spat. The globule of liquid flew from her mouth and landed splat in the middle of Pete Cooper's face. The anger disappeared as instantly as it had come, leaving in its place a terror that intensified as she watched the silvery, phlegmy water trickle down Cooper's cheek and catch in the dark bristles of stubble shadowed across his jaw.

* * *

Cold. A deeper, more intense cold than she'd ever known. She didn't know where she was. A dark place. Difficult to tell if her eyes were open or closed. She tried to move but her arms and legs weren't working. Frozen. An ice princess. There was a film about that. Disney. Songs in it. Lucy's niece had the DVD.

Sam. The name came to her but she didn't know what it meant. Too cold to care. Too cold for anything. Sam's voice. Telling her to wake up. Someone else there too. Her brother, Andy. His hands reaching out to take her.

'Don't worry,' Andy said. 'It's nearly over.'

She wanted to ask him what he meant. Difficult to talk because of the cold and the thick piece of fabric cutting across her mouth and pressing down on her tongue. But she heard her voice say his name.

'Andy.'

She tried to say something else, but the effort of that word had taken the last bit of energy she had. Ice princess. Floating across the ice desert. Antarctica. White ice and deep, dark, endless seas. This was her world.

'Abby.'

Sam again. Only a voice. Why couldn't she see him? A sudden panic jolted her awake. Sam. Through the rough fabric that filled her mouth, she screamed his name. Screamed it over and over. Rolled her body from side to side, banging against the sides of whatever this place was.

She was crying. Snot filled her nose, making it difficult to breathe. She was choking, her throat closing from lack of air, her lungs about to burst.

She could hear her voice, screaming his name. Somewhere, down in the dark place where her mind was still working, she realised the voice was only inside her head. No one else could hear her. No one ever would. Her mouth was gagged and her nose was blocked and she was suffocating and freezing and very soon it would all be over.

Sam would never know that his name was the last and only one she'd held onto.

SIXTEEN

Even wrapped in a blanket, white-faced and scared-looking, Cosima Cooper was beautiful. No wonder Nick Gleeson was willing to risk so much for her.

'You have to find them.'

It was the first thing she'd said after Granville had unlocked the sliding door and they'd pulled her in from the balcony.

'Did you father lock you out there?' Ellen asked.

Her voice came out harsher than she'd intended. She was still recovering from the shock of seeing the woman's face appearing as if from nowhere. And the immediate, terrifying thought that the face at the window was her dead sister, Eilish.

'I was trying to study,' Cosima said. 'There was a knock on the door and I thought it was Nick. He does that sometimes, comes over to surprise me. I ran to answer it and when I saw my father standing there, I knew he'd found out about us ...'

'So he put you on the balcony,' Ellen said. 'Why?'

She was a parent herself and knew how she'd feel if one of her children ended up going out with a friend of hers. Even so, Cooper's reaction seemed extreme.

'He's jealous,' Cosima said, her voice flat and without emotion.

Everything Ellen had thought until now shifted and changed. Pete Cooper and his own daughter?

'I'm so sorry,' Ellen said. 'I had no idea.'

'No.' Cosima shook her head. 'It's not what you think.'

'So tell me,' Ellen said. 'What is it then? What am I missing, Cosima?'

'I'll explain,' Cosima said. 'But first you need to find Nick. My father will kill him. You have to find them before it's too late.'

Ellen thought of Abby's phone, going straight to voicemail. Beside her, Alastair sighed and she knew he was thinking the same thing as she was.

They were already too late.

* * *

He jerked awake suddenly, woken by the screaming. His good eye opened and he looked around, disoriented. No memory of where he was or why Charlotte was screaming.

The crack of a slap and the screaming stopped.

'No!' Pete's voice.

'Sorry.'

Memories rose and fell inside his head like dust. Settled into something that made a sort of sense. And with understanding came the fear.

'I told you before,' Pete said, his voice rising the way it did when he was angry or impatient. 'You don't hit women. Never, you hear?'

'Charlie?'

She was nearby. He could hear her crying quietly, a sound as familiar as his own breathing. Her crying had never touched him when he was the cause of the tears but now, when it was someone else's fault, he felt a sharp, unexpected stab of pity for her.

'Over here.'

Pete crossed the room in front of Nick, disappeared out of view again. Nick tried to swivel his head around to see what Pete was doing but a shaft of pain up his neck stopped him. A moment later, Pete was back, dragging a snivelling Charlotte with him.

Pete pushed Charlotte onto the sofa opposite Nick and sat beside her. Kept his hand wrapped around her upper arm. Charlotte stared at Nick, blue eyes wide and terrified. Her face was deathly white with the exception of a deep red mark across her right cheek where Pete's bastard sidekick, Clive, had whacked her. She looked sober. Might be better if she was drunk. Clive was a nasty brute who Nick tried to avoid whenever he could.

'Nick, what's happening?'

Pete shook her arm and told her to shut up. When she cowered away from him, self-loathing washed through Nick.

'I'm sorry.' He was speaking to both of them, wanted them to understand there was no need for any of this. 'Pete, it's not what you think. I swear to you. And none of it has anything to do with Charlotte. She doesn't even know, for God's sake. Let her go at least. Please?'

'Seems you and me are the last to find out, love,' Pete said, speaking to Charlotte.

'Is this to do with Kieran?' Charlotte asked.

Pete chuckled. 'You poor cow. You haven't a clue, have you?'

'What are you talking about?' Charlotte said. 'I've had enough of not knowing. I don't care that Kieran's dead but he was living with our daughter and she's broken-hearted and I care about that.'

Pete slammed his fist on the arm of the sofa, making Charlotte jump.

'This isn't about that scumbag,' he said. 'It's about him!'

He pointed at Nick.

'She's been my life's work, you know. Everything I've done, it's been so I can keep her safe, protect her from men who only want one thing. Men who don't care that she's the purest, most perfect human being who ever lived. After her mother died, I made Cosima a promise. She was only a kid then, didn't understand it. Not at first. It took time and dedication and self-sacrifice. Words that mean nothing to a self-serving piece of shit like you. Did you stop for one minute to even think about what you were doing? Did it never occur to you that she was special? Did it fuck.

You're like every other prick, aren't you? Took one look at her and all you could think about was getting into her knickers.'

'Nick?' Charlotte's voice wobbled. She sounded lost, like a little girl. It reminded him of Freya and the pain of what he was about to lose hit him afresh.

'It's not like that, Pete. Swear to you. I love her. I really, really love her and I'd never do a single thing to hurt her. I wanted to tell you but she wouldn't let me.'

'Shut up!'

Pete stood and suddenly he was towering over Nick, specks of spittle landing on Nick's face as Pete shouted at him.

'It's too fucking late, you lying pig. You've ruined everything. How can I look at her again, knowing what she's been up to with you?'

Nick's stomach flipped. It had been there all along, staring him in the face. Except he'd been so stupid, so naively besotted with her that it had never occurred to him for a single moment.

'You bastard,' he said. 'Your own daughter. Jesus fucking wept.'

'No.' Pete leaned down, shoved his face into Nick's. 'You accusing me of being some dirty pervert, Nick? You think I'd do that to my own kid? You're even worse than I thought, you know that? Christ, how could she? How *could* she?'

Pete slapped him hard across the face. Slapped him again and might have kept slapping if Clive hadn't shouted at him to stop.

'Not here,' Clive said. 'We don't want to do it here, Pete, remember?'

Charlotte started to say something but Pete lunged across the room, grabbed her, put his finger on her lips and spoke softly to her.

'Hush, hush, sweet Charlotte. You need to stay quiet now. It'll be easier that way.'

Charlotte pulled her head back and started to speak. Shut up pretty quickly when Pete pulled a gun from inside his coat and pressed it against her face.

A flash of light on metal as Clive moved closer. A wide-bladed hunting knife in his right hand. Nick pressed his body against the chair, as if that could protect him. He started crying, begging for his life, telling Pete over and over that he'd got it all wrong.

'I love her,' he screamed. 'And she loves me.'

Clive lifted the knife. Nick screamed louder. Saw the knife flash through the air, pass down in front of him without touching. Realised, when his mind started working again, that Clive was untying the rope around his ankles. Not killing him. Not yet.

Clive reached around, cut the ropes on Nick's wrists and pulled him up. Pressed the knife against Nick's throat and laughed.

'Think I'd be stupid enough to do it here?'

Clive pulled Nick through the conservatory towards the front door. More than once, Nick stumbled and the knife pricked his skin, causing trickles of blood to roll down his neck and soak into the collar of his shirt.

Outside, the boot of Nick's car was open and Charlotte was climbing into it. Pete kept the gun on her until she was completely inside. Then he slammed down the lid, locked it and turned to Nick.

'Your turn now,' he said.

Pete's Jaguar 4x4 was parked, boot already open. Waiting. Nick shook his head, tried to pull away from Clive's iron grip, but he had no strength left. He was dragged closer and closer to the open boot, like Jonah being swept along the water into the mouth of the whale. He dug his heels into the ground, trailing gravel and muck as he went.

'I won't get in there,' he said.

Pete slammed the gun against the side of Nick's face. Nick slumped against the car. Saw Pete moving towards him. Tried to kick out but couldn't get his legs working. Felt his feet lifting as Pete grabbed his ankles. Felt Clive move behind him and shove him forward, face first into the waiting, unwelcoming darkness.

SEVENTEEN

Ellen drove. Blue light flashing the whole way. Siren screaming as she swerved in and out of the heavy traffic, swearing at drivers who didn't pull over quickly enough to let them pass. At Blackheath she passed a grey Jaguar 4x4 pulling out of Heath Lane. She raced past it and turned into the first house at the top of the lane.

Cosima was in the back of the car. She'd begged to come with them and Ellen had relented because she didn't want to wait until a back-up team arrived to take care of her. Plus, she thought the girl might be a useful bargaining tool when she confronted Cooper.

No cars in the driveway but that didn't mean there was no one home. She jumped from the car and ran up the steps to the front porch. When she touched the door it swung open. The fear she'd been trying so hard to control flamed up inside her. Images of Abby lying dead or injured filled her brain. She tried to push them down, make her mind go blank, but the fear wouldn't let her.

She shouted at Alastair to stay with Cosima while she searched the house. She moved around the side of the hall, keeping close to the wall, head moving left and right, eyes darting around the room, catching the dark corners, checking for any sign of an ambush. Two doors on either side. Ellen started with the two on the left.

The first room was the living room. Two pristine, floral-patterned sofas sat facing each other either side of the giant-sized fireplace. Ellen and Abby had sat side by side on one of them. Abby had been wearing a pair of dark blue Diesel jeans and a crisp white shirt. Hair tied back in a tidy ponytail. Looking young and beautiful and invincible.

And dead. The image changed. Abby's head thrown back. A bullet-hole through her chest. A dark stain spreading across her white shirt and out across the back of the white sofa. No! Ellen wouldn't believe it and if she didn't believe it, then it couldn't happen. They would find her.

The next room she checked was a library. A pretentious, wood-panelled room with dark shelves and rows of boring-looking business books sitting – incongruously – alongside a collection of poetry anthologies. Something not right in here. She couldn't put her finger on it at first. The room was perfectly tidy. Then her brain registered the anomaly. Over in the corner, a book lay face-down and open. From where she stood, Ellen could read the title. A collection of poems by the Irish poet, WB Yeats.

Do you like poetry, Detective?

There was such perfect order in the room that the book, lying as if it had been thrown, told another story. Ellen listened to the silence of the house, hoping to hear Abby's voice calling out, telling Ellen she was still alive.

She checked the rest of the house, even though she knew it was pointless. There was no one here. The back door had been forced open, which proved Cooper had been here. There were splatters of blood in the conservatory and a turned-over chair. But Pete Cooper, Nick and Abby were gone. Whatever Cooper was planning to do, it wasn't going to happen here in Gleeson's house.

* * *

Sam was back. Calling for her. Abby remembered being cold and scared, but that was a long time ago. Now, all she wanted was for it to be over. To be with Andy, back home in East Sussex. A family again. The way they were meant to be.

'It doesn't hurt,' Andy was telling her. His dear, lost voice whispering to her. For so long, this was all she'd wanted. To be with him again just one more time so she could capture every bit of him, savour him, and maybe then – if she had that one final chance – she would be better able to remember him.

'It doesn't hurt.'

He was wrong. It never stopped hurting.

* * *

In the kitchen, Alastair was on the phone, arranging for a trace on Gleeson's car. Cosima sat at the table, watching him. Ellen was on her mobile, calling for back-up. They needed to search the house and surrounding area, not stopping until they found Abby.

A utility room led off the main kitchen. A washing machine, tumble dryer and a large chest freezer took up most of the space. The only other items in the room were several black plastic refuse bags stacked against the wall near the freezer.

'And Cooper's car,' she called to Alastair.

Ellen lifted one of the bags, testing the weight of it. Heavy but nowhere near human body heavy. Even so, something about it piqued her attention. As she bent to look inside, she heard Alastair repeating back something he'd just been told.

'A grey Jaguar, XE model. Registration PN32 ONW.'

In Ellen's brain, the synapses sizzled and connected. A flash of memory. Abby overexcited, hyper after her date with Sam the lawyer. Walking to Cooper's front door, passing his shiny new car.

'Shit.'

She dropped the bag and ran back into the kitchen.

'Cooper's car! We just missed them. They turned left onto Elliot Vale. She replayed the moment, trying desperately to see which way Cooper had gone after he'd turned out of Heath Lane. But she'd been so focussed on getting to Abby, she hadn't paid any attention to it.

'We just missed them,' she repeated. She grabbed Alastair's arm. 'We may not be too late. Tell Malcolm to get all units on this. Cooper can't have gone far.'

Their first flicker of hope. She clung onto it. Abby was still alive. They would find her. Every cell in her body was focussed on finding Pete Cooper's car. All thought of the black plastic bags and the freezer completely forgotten.

EIGHTEEN

The terror was all-consuming, paralysing. Curled up inside the black boot, her body jerked from side to side as the car twisted and turned its way towards her certain death. At first, her mind shut down, unable to process what was going on. Which was infinitely better than what happened after that. When the overload of images rushed in to fill every corner of the dark space inside her head. Nick and Cosima. Kieran's hands pushing up the inside of her legs. Cosima's perfect face and huge dark eyes that hid all her secrets. A hand holding a knife, plunging into Kieran's body over and over and over. The same hand on the steering wheel of a car. Ginny caught in the headlights, eyes wide open, scared. The screech of brakes blocking out her friend's screams as the car roared towards her.

She needed to pee. Only realised how desperate she was when her bladder muscles relaxed and a stream of piss soaked its way through her pants and Jaeger trousers. Filling the small space with its bitter stench.

The warm water cooled, turned to ice that stuck to her clothes and seeped into her bones, making her shiver until her teeth chattered. Freezing cold, she wrapped her arms tight around her body and tried not to think about what would happen when the car stopped.

* * *

WPC Laura McKeown was pulling into the driveway of the big house on Heath Lane as Ellen Kelly came running out.

'Here comes trouble,' Gary murmured, unbuckling his seat belt and climbing out. 'Get ready, Laura.'

Laura got out too, not bothering to answer. Gary Locke was an idiot. She smiled at Ellen but got no smile in response, just a series of short-fire instructions to search the house and call Ellen as soon as they found anything. Or anyone. And then Ellen was gone, jumping into the car with Alastair Dillon and speeding off, leaving a cloud of dust in the air after her.

'Who's the bird in the back?' Gary asked.

'Cosima Cooper,' Laura said, recognising the girl from the photos on the board in the incident room.

Gary pulled a pack of cigarettes from his jacket pocket and lit up.

'We're meant to be searching the house,' Laura said.

'No rush, is there?' Gary said. 'You go on in. I'll just have my nicotine hit and I'll be right in.'

'You'd better,' she said.

In fact, she didn't care less if he stayed out here smoking. She would rather be on her own, anyway. Saved her ears from having to listen to his endless, pointless stream of chat.

Ellen had left the front door open and Laura walked inside, stood in the massive hallway, wondering where to begin. It would take time to search this place properly. Especially if she was doing it alone.

She looked over her shoulder, saw Gary standing in the same spot, smoking his cigarette and looking like he was in no hurry to start working. Sod him. If she found anything, Laura would make damn sure he didn't try to pretend he'd had any hand in helping her.

Unsure what exactly she was looking for, Laura moved slowly through the rooms. She had her phone with her, making notes into the voice-recorder so she could use them later to write up her report.

She worked her way through the ground floor, noting a book on the floor in the library, an upturned chair and splashes of something that looked like blood in the conservatory. Down-stairs, in the basement kitchen – bigger than the entire size of Laura's small flat in Ladywell – there were more signs that some-thing bad had happened here. Rust-coloured splashes across the white marble worktop that looked like blood; a broken glass on the ground, shards of glass crunching under her feet as she walked towards the utility room at the back.

'Washing machine, dryer,' she recorded. 'Cupboard full of cleaning materials. Large chest freezer in the far corner. Black plastic refuse bags stacked in a row near the freezer.'

She paused her recording to examine the bags. They hadn't been tied up and she saw a ready-meal carton sticking out from one of them.

She pressed the Pause button on her recording App and continued speaking.

'First bag has food inside it. Boxes of ready meals. Frozen. Defrosting, actually. Like someone's just taken them ...'

Laura's throat dried up. The hand holding her phone dropped to her side. Her other hand reached out, wrapped around the handle of the freezer door, pulled it up and open. She leaned forward, looked inside the freezer.

Later, when she played back the recording on her phone, Laura could hear her own breathing, harsh and uneven as she stepped closer to the freezer. She could hear her footsteps echoing on the concrete floor, the sudden catch of breath in her throat when she leaned forward to look inside. And finally, the last sound before the recording ended when her phone fell from her hand, the ear-shattering sound of her own voice, screaming for that useless lump Gary Locke to call for back-up.

NINETEEN

'He has a house near Eastbourne,' Cosima said. 'At Birling Gap. You know, along the coast from Beachy Head?'

Beachy Head. Where Annalise Cooper's body had been found.

'No one knows about it,' Cosima said. 'It's where he goes to do all his dirty work. He thinks I don't know it's what he uses it for. But I know far more than he realises.'

She spoke in the same monotone voice she'd been using ever since they'd found her on the balcony. Ellen guessed the girl was in a state of shock.

'Do you know the address?' Ellen asked.

'Not a clue,' Cosima said. 'But I can take you there. I've been there with him a few times.'

'I can't ask you to do that,' Ellen said. 'You need to see a doctor.'

'I don't need a doctor,' the girl said. 'I need to come with you. Please.'

'I'm not sure.' Ellen knew her protest was half-hearted at best, but her concern for Abby outweighed other considerations.

'You have no choice,' Cosima said. 'I'm the only person who knows where he is.'

* * *

'Out!'

The voice was insistent. A hand on his arm, shaking him, pulling him awake. His good eye opened. Blinding light. A white line of it cutting through the dark night.

The shadow of a man behind the light. He cowered back, away from the torch, begging for his life. Words tumbled from his mouth, pathetic, pleading, useless. Pete had a gun and was pointing it at him. Pete's other hand was on Nick's arm, dragging him out of the boot.

Every movement sent spasms of pain through his body. Arms, head, face, back and stomach. Everything was pain. Shadows moved behind the torch, seemed to crowd around him, suffocating him.

He had no idea where he was.

Pete pulled him and he shuffled forward. A huge expanse of star-speckled sky stretched out in every direction. He looked around for houses, a road, any sign that they weren't alone out here. Listened for the sound of traffic or people, but all he could hear was the whistling of the wind and the crashing, crunching, roaring sound that he remembered from childhood trips to the seaside in the south of Ireland.

'No.'

Charlotte's voice rose above the wind and the waves. She sounded scared. He swung his head around. Saw two shapes coming towards him through the shadows. The beam of Pete's torch brought them into focus. Charlotte and the bodyguard, Clive. A dark stain had spread across the front of Charlotte's trousers and down the insides of both legs. When he realised what it was, a sudden sadness swooped down on him. She'd been so lovely once.

'No.'

Clive was holding an open bottle of wine. He grabbed her head and pushed it back, forced the bottle into her mouth, tilting it up so the wine poured in. She struggled and gagged, arms flailing uselessly as the wine went into her mouth and dribbled down her chin.

Nick's legs wobbled. He would have fallen if Pete wasn't holding him so tightly.

'You always said the booze would be the death of her,' Pete said. 'Pity the poor cow had to bring you with her too.'

Pete continued talking. *Tragic accident. Drunk driving. Not the first time. Way over the legal limit.* Words swimming at him through the sickening sounds Charlotte was making. Sobbing and gagging and retching.

'Lucky for you this needs to look like an accident,' Pete said, pulling him closer to the sound of the sea. 'Otherwise I'd cut your fucking dick off first.'

Nick strained his eyes, looking for the white horses, but all he saw was sky and stars. Suddenly he understood. The sea wasn't in front of him. It was down there somewhere. At the bottom of these cliffs. He tried to resist but the gun against his cheek gave him no choice. Like a small child, he let himself be pulled towards his death.

Pete stopped. They couldn't go any further. Another step and they'd be over the edge.

* * *

'He's in love with me,' Cosima said.

Her flat voice fell into rhythm with the movements of the car as they drove south out of London, towards the coast.

'His mother was a prostitute. Did you know that? She messed him up good and proper and now he's doing the same to me, even though in his head he believes he's saving me. He thinks sex is dirty. The way he sees it, sex destroyed his mother and then his wife. So even though he's in love with me, he'll never touch me. Not that way. He wants to. I can see it in his face. It's like a hunger. And when he looks at me like that, it scares me because I know what he's capable of.

'I suppose you'd say I'm a coward. I've always been too scared to leave. I knew he'd find me, no matter where I went. And if he did, I don't want to think about what he might do to me.'

She stopped speaking and they continued the journey in silence.

It was dark now, the only light from the pale new moon and the thousands of stars that twinkled across the night sky. Ellen had read somewhere that the stars we could see on Earth were already dead. It took so long for the light to reach us from their part of the universe to ours, the stars were dead by the time we could see them. She'd felt sad when she'd first read that and felt sad now, remembering it.

* * *

Too much wine hit her stomach too quickly. Her body rebelled, spasming and retching as it tried to get rid of the poison. But more kept coming. Pouring into her mouth and throat until she was drowning in it. Until she couldn't take it a second longer. She fought against it, lashed out, hitting nothing. The man's hand steady on her head, the bottle hitting her teeth, hurting her.

Suddenly, he let her go. She fell forward, retching and coughing.

'Over here. With him.'

She saw a gun. And she saw Nick, his face white in the silvery half-light of the new moon. Tears were running down her face but she wasn't crying. Nothing left to cry for. The tears were just another reaction to the wine.

The gun clicked.

Pete wanted it to look like this was her fault. Easy enough to believe. Drunk woman gets behind the wheel of her car. A terrible accident. He was going to make them jump and then he'd send the car after them. Everyone would think she'd driven the car over the cliff, killing herself and her husband.

'I'm not mad,' she said. Noticed the slur in her voice but kept speaking. 'Besides, won't they be able to tell? If we jump, it will be obvious we weren't in the car.'

'Doesn't work that way,' Pete said. 'The sort of injuries you get from a fall like that, it will be difficult for anyone to guess how it happened.'

She could make a run for it. But he would shoot her. Better that than everyone thinking this was her doing.

'You don't have a choice,' Pete said, as if he knew what she was thinking. 'You jump and we make it look like a tragic accident. Or I shoot you. But I swear to you, Charlotte, if I have to do that, I will go straight back to London and shoot your daughter too.'

'How do I know you won't shoot her, anyway?' she asked.

He smiled and the fear was back, blocking out everything else, making any choices impossible.

'You'll have to trust me.'

He waved the gun towards the edge.

'Move,' he said.

She put one foot out and her body froze, refused to do what she told it to. Clive pushed her. She stumbled forward, towards the edge.

* * *

'No record of Pete Cooper owning any house on the south coast,' Alastair said, coming off the phone from Malcolm. 'We've organised for two local units to meet us at Birling Gap. One from Eastbourne and an armed response from Brighton. Helicopter as well.'

'East Sussex has their own helicopter unit?' Ellen asked.

'Beachy Head,' Alastair said. 'Suicides. They need the helicopter to find the bodies apparently.'

Ellen was familiar with the coast between Eastbourne and Brighton. Stunning white cliffs that rose high above the sea. Miles and miles of wild, unspoiled countryside. The perfect place to kill someone and dispose of their body. She pressed her foot down on the accelerator and willed the car to get them there before it was too late.

* * *

'For God's sake, please. You don't have to do this.'

Pete swung the torch so the light was shining in Nick's face. Wet with tears, white with terror. He looked pathetic. Maybe it was the wine, but Charlotte wasn't feeling anything. Or maybe she'd already given up.

Nick's crying triggered a memory. And with it, a flash of emotion that cut through the deadness. The last time she'd seen him cry. It was right after Freya was born. Standing over the bed where Charlotte lay, body and mind shut down from the shock and the pain and the awfulness of what she'd gone through. Freya in his arms, wrapped in a pale pink blanket, screaming her rage at the brutal way she'd been taken from her mother's body. Each scream like a knife through Charlotte's heart.

He didn't notice. Too wrapped up in his own happiness. Tears of joy pouring down his face as he looked down at his child. Their child. A little fist shot up from the blanket. Nick lifted Charlotte's hand so that the child could wrap its tiny fingers around one of hers. Held on so tight that Charlotte, weak and exhausted, couldn't pull away from the strength of that tiny grip.

She felt a surge of love – unexpected and unfamiliar. Their child. A lifetime of waiting to feel this way and now, just when it was nearly over, she understood what it meant to be a mother.

'Hold her.' Pete shone the torch in Charlotte's face, blinding her. Clive grabbed her arm, twisted it behind her back.

The torch went off.

The world went black.

Nearby, very close, she could hear Pete and Nick struggling. Someone grunted. Nick screamed, still begging for his life. Another scream. Louder and longer, gradually fading, until there was nothing.

She kicked back, hit Clive's shin, making him shout out. The grip on her arm loosened. The torch came on. A beam of light cut through the darkness, swung through the air. Coming for her.

She kicked again. Harder. Clive let her go. She started running.

The light from the torch followed her through the night, latched onto her and refused to let go. She dodged left, right, left again, but the torch found her every time. A loud bang rocked the air. Instinctively, she ducked. Kept running. The whistle of air as the bullet sped past her ear. Too close.

She kept running even though she knew she wouldn't make it. Images of her daughter kept her going. Freya at every stage of her life. An endless spool of lost moments she should have cherished.

Another gunshot. Something slammed into her shoulder, sent her flying forward. She hit the ground face first. Tried to get up. Too weak, no energy left. She crawled on, dragging herself across the damp ground, crying. Tears for a lifetime of regrets.

The whole world lit up, bright and white. A roaring monster hovered over her. Death. Through the dark tunnel to the welcoming light. Death coming for her. Roaring its rage, turning the world into a hurricane, making the air swirl around her, blades of grass and dirt flying around her face, catching in her mouth and nose and eyes.

Through her stomach, she felt the ground vibrating; the tremors of the earth ending. A steady thump-thump that seemed to get stronger. A foot in front of her face. A man's voice, telling her it was okay, she was okay, it was all over now and she was safe.

She wanted to ask if he was God or the Devil, but she had no breath left to speak. She let her body slump forward, her face on the wet grass, her eyes closing. God or the Devil. No need to ask. She already knew the answer.

* * *

Everything happened at once. The deafening roar of the helicopter, the air whipping around his face and body, making it difficult to know which way he should turn. Bright lights, voices, someone screaming. He still had the gun. He lifted it, ready to shoot his way out of it if he had to. A man's voice through a megaphone, telling him to drop the gun. Panic made it difficult to think straight. He swung around, saw Clive standing with his arms over his head, staring at the helicopter. And then, like a miracle, through the noise and the lights and the spinning air, there she was.

Cosima!

Running towards him, tears pouring down her face. Someone coming after her. Ellen Kelly. Pete lifted the gun and aimed. Kelly stopped, put her hands in the air. Cosima was still hurtling towards him. He grabbed her with his free arm, tried to pull her close and tell her it was all right, everything was going to be all right. She was here now and he forgave her. He wanted to tell her this but she wouldn't let him. She was screaming at him and beating her fists against his chest, asking what he'd done, what the hell had he done?

He shook her and shouted at her to stop. Everything he'd done, all of it, was for her. He didn't understand why she couldn't see that. If he could get her to shut up, just for a second, then maybe she'd listen to him and she would understand. But she kept screaming and hitting him and he didn't want to hurt her, because he loved her and he'd never harm a single hair on her head but he had to get her to shut up because he couldn't bear it. He lifted the gun before he knew what he was doing. And he wasn't going to hurt her, not for a second, but even with the gun pushed into her cheek she carried on screaming and accusing him of things, such terrible things. And then Kelly was running towards them and she was screaming too and suddenly the world exploded and after that there was no screaming.

There was nothing at all.

MONDAY

ONE

Nick Gleeson's body was found at the bottom of Beachy Head early on Monday morning. Ger called the team together to tell them the news.

'We can start to shut things down now,' Ger said. 'We'll need to notify the family, of course. Once that's done, it's over. Well done, everyone.'

The end of a case brought something special. Weeks of hard work, long hours and the slow sapping of hope replaced by a giddy, infectious euphoria and the self-satisfied belief that it had all been worthwhile. This time, Ellen wasn't feeling it. Partly because of Abby, of course, but something else too. The sense of things left unfinished.

Pete Cooper was dead. Shot by his own daughter, who'd fought him and managed to turn his gun on him at the last moment. Whether the gun had gone off by accident or on purpose, they would never know. The CPS had decided to believe Ellen, who swore Cosima had shot her father in self-defence. There would be no case against her.

Cooper's bodyguard, Clive Merchants, was in custody, charged with accessory to murder and attempted murder. Nick Gleeson had been named as the killer of Kieran Burton and Virginia Rau. Cosima confirmed that Kieran had been blackmailing Nick, although she swore she knew nothing about her lover's involvement in any killings.

The hair sample found on Kieran Burton's jumper had come from Freya. But, as Ger pointed out, Freya was his girlfriend so that was hardly a surprise.

'Two people dead,' Ellen said. 'And no one charged for their murder. Maybe that's the problem. It feels unfinished, somehow.'

'Nick Gleeson got his punishment,' Ger said. 'He was killed too. Some would say that's worse than any punishment he would have got if he'd stayed alive and gone through the courts.'

'Some might say it's a fairer punishment,' Ellen said.

She locked eyes with Ger, waited for the usual lecture on vigilantism and the death penalty not being an answer to anything. Ger's expression darkened, like something about Ellen bothered her. And then, abruptly, she looked away.

'It's been a difficult few weeks,' she said. 'But it's all been worth it. The Dacre Arms at four o'clock. And that's an order, guys.'

She scanned the room, making eye contact with everyone. Except Ellen.

For a moment, Ellen was back at primary school, standing on the edge of a group of girls planning a game they were about to play. All ignoring Ellen, who was doing her level best not to show just how desperately she wanted someone – anyone – to ask her to join in.

* * *

The doctor said Abby could go home tomorrow. It was good news, she supposed. Except she didn't know where home was anymore. Sam wanted her to stay with him for a few days but she wasn't sure she wanted that, either. She didn't know what she wanted.

'You need time,' Sam said. 'And we've got plenty of that. As much as you need.'

He patted her hand, reminding her of Ellen, who'd done a lot of that earlier. Patting Abby's hand and asking all sorts of questions about Sam and generally acting in a most un-Ellen-like fashion. When Abby first woke in the hospital, she'd found Ellen sitting by her bed looking suspiciously as if she'd been crying.

She'd almost died. Hypothermia and lack of air working together to finish her off. She wouldn't be here now if it wasn't for Laura McKeown.

She couldn't think about it. She lay back on the pillow and closed her eyes. Wished she hadn't. She was back inside that dark place. Confusion, terror, grief surged through her as everything else shut down. She tried to breathe but nothing happened. Tried to speak, to cry out for help, but something in her throat made that impossible too.

'Abby!'

Hands on her shoulders, shaking her, pulling her up. Arms wrapped around her, warm and tight, and a voice saying her name and telling her she was okay. Everything was going to be okay.

But she pushed him away. The memories were unlocking, reordering themselves inside her head. The fragments coming together, creating a cohesive picture of what had happened that afternoon. And as it all clicked into place, she realised a piece was still missing.

'Your phone,' she said. 'Give me your phone.'

Sam frowned. 'You're not supposed to use them in here. There are signs everywhere.'

'Give me the phone!'

It was in the pocket of his jacket. She'd seen him put it in when he'd first come in. Too impatient to wait, she reached forward, grabbed the phone from his pocket and dialled Ellen's number.

* * *

Ellen's phone started to ring. A number she didn't recognise but she answered it anyway.

'Ellen? It's me,' Abby said. 'I've just remembered something.'

As Abby explained why she was calling, the playground memory disappeared. By the time she hung up, Ellen was smiling. She had been right all along. The case wasn't solved. Not yet. She might be an outsider, but there was a reason for it. It wasn't – as she used to believe – because she wasn't good enough. The opposite was true. The reason she found it so difficult to fit in was because there weren't many people as bloody good at being a detective as she was. And that, she told herself, was their problem, not hers.

* * *

Freya was on her way out when Ellen and Alastair arrived at Ennersdale Road. She opened the front door and stood there in the doorway, blocking their way.

'I've got nothing to say to you lot anymore,' Freya said. 'Unless you're here to tell me you've arrested my mother.'

'This is about your father, actually,' Ellen said.

Freya's eyes filled with tears.

'Please tell me he's alive?' she said. 'I keep thinking … he can't be dead. If he was dead, I'd feel something, wouldn't I? But I haven't felt anything. Not a single thing. I think he's scared. That's why he hasn't made contact with me. He didn't kill Kieran, you know. I've told you that but no one will listen. All of this is her fault. Not his. How can I get you to see that?'

Ellen took a step forward. 'Freya.'

Freya must have picked up something in Ellen's voice. She

shook her head, put her hands over her ears.

'Shut up. Shut up, shut up, shut up! He isn't dead! I know he's not dead and if you're here to tell me he is, I won't listen.'

Ellen reached out and touched the girl's shoulder. Freya jumped as if she'd been electrocuted.

'We found a body,' Ellen said.

Freya's hands fell to her sides and she slumped against the doorframe. Her breath was coming in short, sharp bursts. Ellen worried she was about to start hyperventilating.

'I don't know why you're so keen to protect him,' Ellen said, speaking loudly so the girl would hear her. 'It's not like he really even cared about you, is it?'

'He loved me.'

'No.' Ellen shook her head. 'The only person your father loved was Cosima. He would have done anything for her, wouldn't he?'

'I told you!' Freya shoved her face close to Ellen's. 'Shut up.'

'I don't blame you for wanting to set him up,' Ellen said, forcing herself not to take a step back, away from Freya's angry red face. 'I mean, if my father behaved like that, I'd want him to pay for it.'

'It was never about him,' Freya screamed. 'Why couldn't you see that?'

'Who was it about then?' Ellen said. 'If you don't tell me, people will never know the truth. He'll be remembered as the man who killed Kieran Burton and Virginia Rau and had an affair with his business partner's daughter. All his hard work, everything he's done for you – no one will remember any of that.'

'No!' Freya lunged, hands like claws as she went for Ellen's face. Alastair jumped forward, grabbed Freya in a headlock.

'You bitch.' Freya struggled hard but Alastair held her tight. 'You lying fucking bitch. I made it so easy for you and you still messed it up. You have your story now and you're sticking to it. Even though you know it's bullshit. Dad and Cosima? Who came up with that story? It's all there, staring you in the face. You're just too stupid to see it.'

Freya's head jerked back. At first, Ellen thought she was scared. By the time she realised what was happening, it was too late. The back of Freya's head connected with Alastair's face. A loud crack and Alastair cried out, let go of Freya and staggered back, hands on his face. Freya pushed past him and started running.

TWO

Freya raced down the hill, feet pounding on the pavement, the impact vibrating up her ankles and shins. Running from Ellen Kelly and her lies. She ran fast, but it wasn't fast enough. Behind her she could hear Ellen Kelly, shouting at her to stop, and Kelly's footsteps. Getting closer.

Too fat to run fast.

Too fat and stupid and ugly to keep her man.

His face. Sneering at her like she was a piece of shit. Like she was nothing and all the things she'd done for him counted for nothing. All the work and money and support, all the twisted perverted things he got her to do when they were in bed together; none of it meant anything to him.

Stupid, fat, ugly.

She thought it was about bringing them closer together.

When all the time, he was using her.

And sleeping with her mother.

He laughed when he told her.

Right before he announced he was leaving her.

Her lungs were about to explode. She had to keep going. As soon as she stopped, it would all be over.

She reached the bottom of the hill. Barely running now, barely moving at all. Heard Ellen Kelly before she felt her. The detective dived into her and she fell forward, Kelly's arms around her middle. Kelly's body on top of hers as she hit the ground.

She tried to fight Kelly off her, but she had no strength left. There was nowhere to go.

It was over.

* * *

'How did you know?' Freya asked.

It was the first thing she'd said since Ellen had tackled her and knocked her to the ground. After that, all the fight seemed to go from the girl. She let Ellen caution her, handcuff her and stood silently beside her while they waited for the squad car that Alastair promised was on its way.

'Does it matter?' Ellen asked.

She wasn't about to tell Freya about the CCTV footage. How Abby had suddenly remembered the jacket Freya was wearing in the photo on the mantelpiece in her apartment.

'You were never meant to think my dad had anything to do with it,' Freya said. 'I *told* you she rowed with Kieran. I *told* you they hated each other. But you ignored it all like it was nothing. How could you think Dad would do something like that? How could you not see?'

'Is that what it was all about?' Ellen asked. 'You killed him so that we'd think your mother had done it?'

'She had sex with him,' Freya said. 'Even saying it makes me want to throw up. My own *mother*. But that's not why I did it. I *killed* him because he was going to leave me. After everything I'd done for him. Three years of that fucking Masters. Three years working in that wine bar, listening to all those boring people with their boring lives and boring shitting stories. Three years and then he turns around and tells me he's had enough. And you know what? I could have got him to change his mind. I'd done it before but this time … *this time* he was ready for me.'

Her voice dropped to a whisper and Ellen had to lean in to catch what she said next.

'He said he was going to her party. Said he wanted to see if she was up for a second round. I asked him what he was talking about and he told me. And he said he wanted to do it again. That I could watch if I wanted.'

Ellen had to stop herself putting her arms around Freya's shoulders and comforting her. The poor, deluded woman.

'She turned him against me,' Freya said. 'I'd worked so hard at keeping him. I wanted to prove everyone wrong. All those stupid people who thought he wouldn't stay with me. I know that's what people thought. A guy like him, he's not going to stay with someone like you. Someone as fat and ugly and useless as you are.'

Ellen wondered about the damage it would take to make someone think about themselves in those terms. She thought of her own family, her birth mother Noreen and her adopted parents. She thought of the damage passed down from one generation to the next, how important it was to do everything you could to break that cycle when it was your turn to be a parent.

'If I'd let him go,' Freya said, 'it would be like telling everyone they were right all along. I couldn't do that.'

Ellen heard sirens. The sound coming from Lewisham, getting closer.

'And Ginny?'

Freya sighed. 'She saw me getting the knife from the kitchen. She was going to tell you lot about it. I couldn't let her do that. I had a spare set of keys for my mum's car. For the times she'd had too much to drink and she'd have to call me to drive her home. God, the number of times I had to do that. You wouldn't believe it.'

A black squad car pulled up in front of them. Ellen took Freya's arm, led her towards the car.

'It's time to go.'

'None of it was my fault,' Freya said. 'I think you know that, don't you?'

'You didn't have to kill them,' Ellen said. 'You can't blame anyone else for that.'

An officer got out of the car and opened the back door. Ellen put her hand on top of Freya's head and pushed her inside.

'Families,' Alastair said, as they watched the car drive away. 'Larkin had it right, hey?'

Ellen ran through the names of everyone they knew in common. Came up with a blank.

'Larkin?'

'You know,' Alastair said. '*This Be The Verse*? They f... ach, never mind.'

Ellen left it at that. He could be a funny old fish sometimes. She looked at his face. The bleeding had stopped but his nose was a right mess.

'Come on.' She linked her arm in his and walked him in the direction of the wine bar. 'Let's get that cleaned up.'

'And then a pint?' Alastair said. 'I'd say we've got something to celebrate.'

'Not for me,' Ellen said.

'Aw, come on,' Alastair said. 'What's so important you can't have a quick drink first?'

'Sorry,' Ellen said. 'It really can't wait. There's something I need to do.'

EPILOGUE

It was a perfect early summer's day. Three days after she'd arrested Freya and Ellen was taking a day off. Family time. Greenwich was alive with colour. Thick green leaves on the tall trees in the park; red and yellow and pink roses in the flower beds that ran along the edge of the pirate playground; and the shimmering, silvery sparkle from the river winding its way out of the city on its journey towards the North Sea.

Ellen, the children, Sean and Terry stood at the top of the park, eating ice creams and looking at the city, spread out from the banks of the river, north, east, west, as far as they could see. Her favourite place in the world, with her favourite people in the world. Ellen knew how lucky she was.

'Can we go on the donkeys?'

Eilish tugged at Ellen's arm, her little face scrunched up, pleading.

'Aren't you too old?' Ellen asked.

'Please?' Eilish said. 'I love the donkeys.'

'Come on, then.' Sean grabbed Eilish and swung her in the air, making her giggle.

The donkeys were kept by the Blackheath entrance to the park. Eilish ran ahead with Sean and Terry, while Ellen and Pat followed more slowly.

'Do you mind if I don't go on?' Pat asked.

'Of course not,' Ellen said. 'Why would I?'

'Cos it's the sort of thing you love and you take loads of photos and get that *look* on your face.'

'What look?'

He wrinkled his nose.

'You know, like the donkeys are so cute and we're so cute. Ugh.'

Ellen laughed and gave his arm a gentle punch.

'Ugh yourself, mister. If you're not careful, I'll pull out all those photos of you as a little kid later tonight and make you look at every one of them. I just need to post this letter first.'

She ran over to the postbox on the edge of the heath. A notice on the front gave the collection times. The next collection was at four pm today. Two hours from now. Still time to change her mind, if she wanted to. No. She shoved the envelope into the box, quickly.

'Who are you writing to?' Pat asked.

'Someone I used to know a long time ago,' Ellen said.

She linked his arm in hers and pointed at Eilish, sitting on top of a donkey that was being led slowly along a narrow path between the donkeys and an ice-cream van. The sound of her daughter's laughter travelled across the heath, filling every dark corner of Ellen's soul.

This was all that mattered. This moment, right here, right now, with her son beside her and her daughter's laughter all around her and her brother and his partner and the bright sunshine with its promise of summer and better times to come.

Dear Noreen,

My name is Ellen. A long time ago, I was your daughter. We lived together in a small flat in Peckham. You, me, my twin brother Sean and our baby sister Eilish. There's a lot I don't remember from that time but the things I do remember are probably the most important. I remember your smile. I remember Sean and I sitting on a lumpy sofa, one either side of you, while you read to us. I remember us being in a cafe with you, both of us giggling as we took it in turns to take mouthfuls of creamy hot chocolate from the spoon you were holding. I remember you singing to us in the evenings. You used to sit between our beds and sing to get us off to sleep. Do you remember that too? You were warm and kind and funny and we loved you very much. I think you loved us too.

I don't remember our father. I don't know if he lived with us or if he lived somewhere else. I wonder what he was like and if he made you happy. For some reason, I don't think he did make you happy, but I don't know why I think this.

I remember the night Eilish died. It was the last time I ever saw you. I was crying. I held onto your legs and begged you not to go. The policeman said you had to come with him, but I thought I could make you understand that was the wrong thing to do. I was scared because I'd never been away from you before. Not even for a day. You were crying too but you wiped your tears and you bent down, right down until your face was level with mine. You told me to be a good girl and you told me not to worry. You promised me you would be back soon.

For the longest time, I believed that promise. All through my growing up and way beyond that. Even more so after I married and had children of my own. I would look at them and think: how could any parent make a promise like that and not keep it?

I don't know the answer to that. There are so many things I don't have answers to. I've realised it doesn't matter. The fact is, there are some things I don't know and never will know. I can choose to spend my life letting that eat away at me, picking at it like a scab that will never heal. Or I can let it go. I'm choosing now to let it go. I'm choosing to let you go.

You'll see my address isn't on this letter. That's not because I don't want you to find me. It's because if I put down an address, I would be watching the post everyday, obsessing over whether or not you were going to write back to me. I would spend my time and energy on that, instead of on the things that matter: my own family, my own life.

I don't know how Eilish died, or why. I don't know if you killed her *on purpose or if it was an accident or even if you didn't kill her at all and the whole terrible business was some tragic miscarriage of justice. I don't know why you promised you would come back for me and you never did.*

All I know is that you were my mother once. And during that short time when we were together, I loved you.

Nothing else matters.

Ellen.

* * *

A wooden cross marked the grave. This would be replaced eventually with the permanent headstone Charlotte had ordered. White marble with gold inlay. Ginny's name inscribed across it in an ornate, curling font. No age or date of birth. She wouldn't have wanted that.

Being here felt awkward. She'd thought it might help. Hoped she would feel closer to Ginny here, where her body rested. But it made no difference. Nothing did. The empty numbness surrounded her like a fog. Cold and impenetrable, it seeped through her skin and into her bones, leaving no room for anything else.

'I'm sorry,' she whispered.

It wasn't enough, but she had nothing else to offer. She might as well have driven the car herself. Her fault. All of it. She stood a while longer, waiting. Nearby, a man and woman were tending a grave, pulling weeds from around it, the woman crying the whole time.

Her legs quickly grew tired and the back of her throat tickled. She put her hand on the cross, felt the shakes vibrate up her arm and knew it was time to go. She'd spotted a pub down the road. Ten minutes away. She'd timed it on the way here.

As she hurried through the paths of dead people, the voices swirled around her, weaving in and out of the fog around her. It always happened this way. The throat first, then the shakes, followed by the voices that grew louder until she got rid of them the only way she knew how. The only voice she never heard was the one she'd come here to find today.

She wanted to remember it, but already it was fading. The music, the way Ginny's voice rose and fell when she was happy or sad, Charlotte was finding it difficult to hold onto that.

It was me. I pushed you.

Charlotte shook her head, couldn't bear her daughter's voice. Not here in this place.

I wish I'd killed you.

Freya's voice but Mother's face. Charlotte walked faster. Through the gates and onto the busy road. Ankles twisting as she wobbled down the hill, heels too high.

Stupid little girl!

Mother screaming. Charlotte's fault. Always.

Stupid slag. The sneer in Freya's voice matched Mother's and they both started laughing.

Charlotte started singing. Anything to block out the noise. Sang the first song that came to her. An old, familiar song. Sang out loud, her voice rising over the others. Mother and Freya joining in until it was impossible to know which voice was which.

'Sugar and spice and all things nice
Kisses sweeter than wine,
Sugar and spice and all things nice
You know that little girl is mine."

She was at the pub, throwing open the door and walking inside. It was dark and quiet and smelled of stale beer and greasy food and the underlying odour of unwashed bodies. Behind her, the door swung closed. The voices disappeared, leaving her all alone.

She walked across to the bar, her heels sinking into the soggy carpet, gave the barman her best smile and ordered her first drink.